The Red True Story Book

The Red True Story Book

Andrew Lang and
H. Rider Haggard

MINT EDITIONS

The Red True Story Book was first published in 1895.

This edition published by Mint Editions 2021.

ISBN 9781513281742 | E-ISBN 9781513286761

Published by Mint Editions®

 MINT
EDITIONS

minteditionbooks.com

Publishing Director: Jennifer Newens
Design & Production: Rachel Lopez Metzger
Project Manager: Micaela Clark
Typesetting: Westchester Publishing Services

Contents

Introduction

*T*he *Red True Story Book* needs no long Introduction. The Editor, in presenting *The Blue True Story Book*, apologised for offering tales so much less thrilling and romantic than the legends of the Fairies, but he added that even real facts were, sometimes, curious and interesting. Next year he promises something quite as true as History, and quite as entertaining as Fairies!

For this book, Mr. Rider Haggard has kindly prepared a narrative of "Wilson's Last Fight," by aid of conversations with Mr. Burnham, the gallant American scout. But Mr. Haggard found, while writing his chapter, that Mr. Burnham had already told the story in an "Interview" published by the *Westminster Gazette*. The courtesy of the proprietor of that journal, and of Mr. Burnham, has permitted Mr. Haggard to incorporate the already printed narrative with his own matter.

"The Life and Death of Joan the Maid" is by the Editor, who has used M. Quicherat's *Procès* (five volumes, published for the Historical Society of France), with M. Quicherat's other researches. He has also used M. Wallon's Biography, the works of Father Ayroles, S.J., the *Jeanne d'Arc à Domremy* of M. Siméon Luce, the works of M. Sepet, of Michelet, of Henri Martin, and, generally, all printed documents to which he has had access. Of unprinted contemporary matter perhaps none is known to exist, except the Venetian Correspondence, now being prepared for publication by Father Ayroles.

"How the Bass was held for King James" is by the Editor, mainly from Blackadder's *Life*.

"The Crowning of Ines de Castro" is by Mrs. Lang, from Schäfer. "Orthon," from Froissart, "Gustavus Vasa," "Monsieur de Bayard's Duel" (Brantôme), are by the same lady; also "Gaston de Foix," from Froissart, and "The White Man," from Mile. Aïssé's Letters.

Mrs. McCunn has told the story of the Prince's Scottish Campaign, from the contemporary histories of the Rising of 1745, contemporary tracts, *The Lyon in Mourning*, Chambers, Scott, Maxwell of Kirkconnel, and other sources.

The short Sagas are translated from the Icelandic by the Rev. W. C. Green, translator of *Egil Skalagrim's Saga*.

Mr. S. R. Crockett, Author of *The Raiders*, told the tales of "The Bull of Earlstoun" and "Grisell Baillie."

Miss May Kendall and Mrs. Bovill are responsible for the seafarings and shipwrecks; the Australian adventures are by Mrs. Bovill.

Miss Minnie Wright compiled "The Conquest of Peru," from Prescott's celebrated History.

Miss Agnes Repplier, that famed essayist of America, wrote the tale of Molly Pitcher.

"The Adventures of General Marbot" are from the translation of his Autobiography by Mr. Butler.

With this information the Editor leaves the book to children, assuring them that the stories are *true*, except perhaps that queer tale of "Orthon"; and some of the Sagas also may have been a little altered from the real facts before the Icelanders became familiar with writing.

WILSON'S LAST FIGHT

They were men whose fathers were men'

To MAKE IT CLEAR HOW Major Wilson and his companions came to die on the banks of the Shangani on December 4, 1893, it will be necessary, very briefly, to sketch the events which led to the war between the English settlers in Mashonaland in South Africa and the Matabele tribe, an offshoot of the Zulu race.

In October 1889, at the instance of Mr. Cecil Rhodes and others interested, the Chartered Company of British South Africa was incorporated, with the sanction of Her Majesty's Government.

In 1890 Mashonaland was occupied, a vast and fertile territory nominally under the rule of Lobengula, king of the Matabele, which had been ceded by him to the representatives of the Company in return for certain valuable considerations. It is, however, an easier task for savage kings to sign concessions than to ensure that such concessions will be respected by their subjects, especially when those "Subjects" are warriors by nature, tradition, and practice, as in the present case, and organised into regiments, kept from year to year in perfect efficiency and readiness for attack. Whatever may have been Lobengula's private wishes and opinions, it soon became evident that the gathering of the white men upon their borders, and in a country which they claimed by right of conquest if they did not occupy it, was most distasteful to the more warlike sections of the Matabele.

Mashonaland takes its name from the Mashona tribes who inhabit it, a peaceful and, speaking by comparison, an industrious race, whom, ever since they first settled in the neighbourhood, it had been the custom of the subjects of Lobengula and of his predecessor, Mosilikatze, "the lion," to attack with every cruelty conceivable, raiding their cattle, slaughtering their men, and sweeping their maidens and young children into captivity. Terrified, half exterminated indeed, as they were by these constant and unprovoked onslaughts, the Mashonas welcomed with delight the occupation of their country by white men, and thankfully placed themselves under the protection of the Chartered Company.

The Matabele regiments, however, took a different view of the question, for now their favourite sport was gone: they could no longer practise rapine and murder, at least in this direction, whenever the spirit moved them. Presently the force of habit overcame their fear of the white men and their respect for treaties, and towards the end of 1891 the chief Lomaghondi, who lived under the protection of the Company, was killed by them. Thereon Dr. Jameson, the Administrator of Mashonaland, remonstrated with Lobengula, who expressed regret, saying that the incident had happened by mistake.

This repudiation notwithstanding, an impi, or armed body of savages, again crossed the border in 1892, and raided in the Victoria district. Encouraged by the success of these proceedings, in July 1893 Lobengula sent a picked company to harry in the neighbourhood of Victoria itself, writing to Dr. Jameson that he made no excuse for so doing, claiming as he did the right to raid when, where, and whom he chose. The "indunas," or captains, in command of this force were instructed not to kill white men, but to fall particularly upon those tribes who were in their employ. On July 9, 1893, and the following days came the climax, for then the impi began to slaughter every Mashona whom they could find. Many of these unfortunates were butchered in the presence of their masters, who were bidden to "stand upon one side as the time of the white men had not yet come."

Seeing that it was necessary to take action, Dr. Jameson summoned the head indunas of the impi, and ordered them to cross the border within an hour or to suffer the consequences of their disobedience. The majority obeyed, and those who defied him were attacked by Captain Lendy and a small force while in the act of raiding a kraal, some of them being killed and the rest driven away.

From this moment war became inevitable, for the question lay between the breaking of the power of Lobengula and the evacuation of Mashonaland. Into the details of that war it is not proposed to enter; they are outside the scope of this narrative. It is enough to say that it was one of the most brilliant and successful ever carried out by Englishmen. The odds against the little force of a thousand or twelve hundred white men who invaded Matabeleland were almost overwhelming, and when it is remembered that the Imperial troops did not succeed in their contest against Cetywayo, the Zulu king, until nearly as many soldiers were massed in the country as there were able-bodied Zulus left to oppose them, the brilliancy of the achievement of these colonists led by a civilian, Dr. Jameson, can be estimated. The Matabele were beaten in two pitched battles: that of the Shangani on October 25, and that of the

Imbembezi on November 1. They fought bravely, even with desperation, but their valour was broken by the skill and the cool courage of the white man. Those terrible engines of war, the Maxim guns and the Hotchkiss shells, contributed largely to our success on these occasions. The Matabele, brave as they were, could not face the incessant fire of the Maxims, and as to the Hotchkiss they developed a curious superstition. Seeing that men fell dead in all directions after the explosion of a shell, they came to believe that as it burst out of each missile numbers of tiny and invisible imps ran forth carrying death and destruction to the white men's foes, and thus it happened that to their minds moral terrors were added to the physical dangers of warfare. So strong was this belief among them, indeed, that whenever a shell struck they would turn and fire at it in the hope that thus they might destroy the "live devils" who dwelt within it.

After these battles Lobengula, having first set fire to it, fled from his chief place, Buluwayo, which was occupied by the white men within a month of the commencement of the campaign.

In reply to a letter sent to him by Dr. Jameson, demanding his surrender and guaranteeing his safety, Lobengula wrote that he "would come in."

The promised period of two days' grace having gone by, however, and there being no sign of his appearance, a force was despatched from Buluwayo to follow and capture him. This force, which was under the leadership of Major Patrick W. Forbes, consisted of ninety men of the Salisbury Column, with Captains Heany and Spreckley and a mule Maxim gun under Lieutenant Biscoe, R.N.; sixty men of the Victoria Column commanded by Major Wilson, with a horse Maxim under Captain Lendy; sixty men of the Tuli Column, and ninety men of the Bechuanaland Border Police, commanded by Captain Raaf, C.M.G., accompanied by two horse Maxims and a mule seven-pounder, commanded by Captain Tancred.

The column, which started on or about November 14, took with it food for three days only, carried by natives, and a hundred rounds of ammunition per man. After several days' journeying northward the patrol reached the Bubye River, where dissensions arose between Captain Raaf and Major Forbes, the former being of opinion, rightly enough as the issue showed, that the mission was too dangerous to be pursued by a small body of men without supplies of food, and having no reserve of ammunition and no means of carrying the wounded. The upshot was that Major Forbes decided to return, but was prevented from doing so by a letter received from Dr. Jameson, stating that he was sending forward a reinforcement of dismounted men under Captain Napier with food, ammunition, and wagons, also sixteen mounted men under Captain Borrow. The force then proceeded to a deserted Mission Station known as Shiloh. On November 25 the column, three hundred strong and carrying with it three-quarter rations for twelve days, took up the King's wagon spoor about one mile from Shiloh, and followed it through much discomfort, caused by the constant rain and the lack of roads, till, on December S, a point was reached on the Shangani River, N.N.W. of Shiloh and distant from it about eighty miles.

On November 29, however, Major Forbes, finding that he could make small progress with the wagons, sent them away, and proceeded with the best mounted men and two Maxims only, so that the actual force which reached the Shangani on the 3rd consisted of about one hundred and sixty men and a couple of machine guns.

At this time the information in possession of the leaders of the column was to the effect that the King was just in front of them across the river, accompanied only by a few of his followers. Under these circumstances Major Forbes instructed Major Wilson and eighteen men to go forward and reconnoitre along Lobengula's spoor; the understanding seeming to have been that the party was to return by sundown, but that if it did not return it was, if necessary, to be supported by the whole column. With this patrol went Mr. Burnham, the American scout, one of the three surviving white men who were eye-witnesses of that eventful night's work, which ended so tragically at dawn.

What followed is best told as he narrated it by word of mouth to the compiler of this true story, and to a reporter of the "Westminster Gazette," the editor of which paper has courteously given permission for the reproduction of the interview. Indeed, it would be difficult to tell it so well in words other than Mr. Burnham's own.

"In the afternoon of December 8," says Mr. Burnham, "I was scouting ahead of the column with Colenbrander, when in a strip of bush we lit on two Matabele boys driving some cattle, one of whom we caught and brought in. He was a plucky boy, and when threatened he just looked us sullenly in the face. He turned out to be a sort of grandson or grand-nephew of Lobengula himself. He said the King's camp was just ahead, and the King himself near, with very few men, and these sick, and that he wanted to give himself up. He represented that the King had been back to this place that very day to get help because his wagons were stuck in a bog. The column pushed on through the strip of bush, and there, near by, was the King's camp—quite deserted. We searched the huts, and in one lay a Maholi slave-boy, fast asleep. (The Maholis are the slaves of the Matabele.) We pulled him out, and were questioning him, when the other boy, the sulky Matabele, caught his eye, and gave him a ferocious look, shouting across to him to take care what he told.

"The slave-boy agreed with the others that the King had only left this camp the day before; but as it was getting dark, Major Forbes decided to reconnoitre before going on with the column. I learnt of the decision to send forward Major Wilson and fifteen men on the best horses when I got my orders to accompany them, and, along with Bayne, to do their scouting. My horse was exhausted with the work he had done already; I told Major Forbes, and he at once gave me his. It was a young horse, rather skittish, but strong and fairly fresh by comparison.

"Ingram, my fellow-scout, remained with the column, and so got some hours' rest; thanks to which he was able not only to do his part of tracking for the twenty men afterwards sent on to us through the bush at night, but also, when he and I got through after the smash, to do the long and dangerous ride down country to Buluwayo with the despatches—a ride on which he was accompanied by Lynch.

"So we set off along the wagon track, while the main body of the column went into laager.

"Close to the river the track turned and led down stream along the west bank. Two miles down was a drift" (they call a fordable dip a drift in South Africa), "and here the track crossed the Shangani. We splashed through, and the first thing we scouts knew on the other side was that we were riding into the middle of a lot of Matabele among some scherms, or temporary shelters. There were men, and some women and children. The men were armed. We put a bold face on it, and gave out the usual announcement that we did not want to kill anybody, but must have the King. The natives seemed surprised and undecided; presently, as Major Wilson and the rest of the patrol joined us, one of them volunteered to come along with us and guide us to the King. He was only just ahead, the man said. How many men were with him? we asked. The man put up his little finger—dividing it up, so. Five fingers mean an impi; part of the little finger, like that, should mean fifty to one hundred men. Wilson said to me, 'Go on ahead, taking that man beside your saddle; cover him, fire if necessary, but don't you let him slip.'

"So we started off again at a trot, for the light was failing, the man running beside my horse, and I keeping a sharp eye on him. The track led through some thick bush. We passed several scherms. Five miles from the river we came to a long narrow vlei (a vlei is a shallow valley, generally with water in it), which lay across our path. It was now getting quite dark. Coming out of the bush on the near edge of the vlei, before going down into it, I saw fires lit, and scherms and figures showing dark against the fires right along the opposite edge of the vlei. We skirted the vlei to our left, got round the end of it, and at once rode through a lot of scherms containing hundreds of people. As we went, Captain Napier shouted the message about the King wherever there was a big group of people. We passed scherm after scherm, and still more Matabele, more fires, and on we rode. Instead of the natives having been scattering from the King, they had been gathering. But it was too late to turn. We were hard upon our prize, and it was understood among the Wilson patrol that they were going to bring the King in if man could do it. The natives were astonished: they thought the whole column was on them: men jumped up, and ran hither and thither, rifle in hand. We went on without stopping, and as we passed more and more men came running after us. Some of them were crowding on the rearmost men, so Wilson told off three fellows to 'keep those niggers back.' They turned, and kept the people in check. At last, nearly at the other end of the vlei, having passed five sets of scherms, we came upon what seemed to be the King's wagons, standing in a kind of enclosure, with a saddled white horse tethered by it. Just before this, in the crowd and hurry, my man slipped away, and I had to report to Wilson that I had lost him. Of course it would not have done to fire. One shot would have been the match in the powder magazine. We had ridden into the middle of the Matabele nation.

"At this enclosure we halted and sang out again, making a special appeal to the King and those about him. No answer came. All was silence. A few drops of rain fell. Then it lightened, and by the flashes we could just see men getting ready to fire on us, and Napier shouted to Wilson, 'Major, they are about to attack.' I at the same-time saw them closing in on us rapidly from the right. The next thing to this fifth scherm was some thick bush; the order was given to get into that, and in a moment we were out of sight there. One minute after hearing us shout, the natives with the wagons must have been unable to see a sign of us. Just then it came on to rain heavily; the sky, already cloudy, got black as ink; the night fell so dark that you could not see your hand before you.

"We could not stay the night where we were, for we were so close that they would hear our horses" bits. So it was decided to work down into the vlei, creep along close to the other edge of it to the end we first came round, farthest from the King's camp, and there spend the night. This, like all the other moves, was taken after consultation with the officers, several of whom were experienced Kaffir campaigners. It was rough going; we were unable to see our way, now splashing through the little dongas that ran down into the belly of the vlei, now working round them, through bush and soft bottoms. At the far end, in a clump of thick bush, we dismounted, and Wilson sent off Captain Napier, with a man of his called Robinson, and the Victoria scout, Bayne, to go back along the wagon-track to the column, report how things stood, and bring the column on, with the Maxims, as sharp as possible. Wilson told Captain Napier to tell Forbes if the bush bothered the Maxim carriages to abandon them and put the guns on horses, but to bring the Maxims without fail. We all understood—and we thought the message was this—that if we were caught there at dawn without the Maxims we were done for. On the other hand was the chance of capturing the King and ending the campaign at a stroke.

"The spot we had selected to stop in until the arrival of Forbes was a clump of heavy bush not far from the King's spoor—and yet so far from the Kaffir camps that they could not hear us if we kept quiet. We dismounted, and on counting it was found that three of the men were missing. They were Hofmeyer, Bradburn and Colquhoun. Somewhere in winding through the bush from the King's wagons to our present position these men were lost. Not a difficult thing, for we only spoke in whispers, and, save for the occasional click of a horse's hoof, we could pass within ten feet of each other and not be aware of it.

"Wilson came to me and said, 'Burnham, can you follow back along the vlei where we've just come?' I doubted it very much as it was black and raining; I had no coat, having been sent after the patrol immediately I came in from firing the King's huts, and although it was December, or midsummer south of the line, the rain chilled my fingers. Wilson said, 'Come, I must have those men back.' I told him I should need some one to lead my horse so as to feel the tracks made in the ground by our horses. He replied, 'I will go with you. I want to see how you American fellows work.'

"Wilson was no bad hand at tracking himself, and I was put on my mettle at once. We began, and I was flurried at first, and did not seem to get on to it somehow; but in a few minutes I picked up the spoor and hung to it.

"So we started off together, Wilson and I, in the dark. It was hard work, for one could see nothing; one had to feel for the traces with one's fingers. Creeping along, at last we stood close to the wagons, where the patrol had first retreated into the bush.

"'If we only had the force here now,' said Wilson, 'we would soon finish.'

"But there was still no sign of the three men, so there was nothing for it but to shout. Retreating into the vlei in front of the King's camp, we stood calling and cooeying for them, long and low at first, then louder. Of course there was a great stir along the lines of the native scherms, for they did not know what to make of it. We heard afterwards that the natives were greatly alarmed as the white men seemed to be everywhere at once, and the indunas went about quieting the men, and saying 'Do you think the white men are on you, children? Don't you know a wolf's howl when you hear it?'

"After calling for a bit, we heard an answering call away down the vlei, and the darkness favouring us, the lost men soon came up and we arrived at the clump of bushes where the patrol was stationed. We all lay down in the mud to rest, for we were tired out. It had left off raining, but it was a miserable night, and the hungry horses had been under saddle, some of them twenty hours, and were quite done.

"So we waited for the column.

"During the night we could hear natives moving across into the bush which lay between us and the river. We heard the branches as they pushed through. After a while Wilson asked me if I could go a little way around our position and find out what the Kaffirs were doing. I always think he heard something, but he did not say so. I slipped out and on our right heard the swirl of boughs and the splash of feet. Circling round for a little time I came on more Kaffirs. I got so close to them I could touch them as they passed, but it was impossible to say how many there were, it was so dark. This I reported to Wilson. Raising his head on his hand he asked me a few questions, and made the remark that if the column failed to come up before daylight, 'we are in a hard hole,' and told me to go out on the King's spoor and watch for Forbes, so that by no possibility should he pass us in the darkness. It was now, I should judge, 1 A.M. on the 4th of December.

"I went, and for a long, long time I heard only the dropping of the rain from the leaves and now and then a dog barking in the scherms, but at last, just as it got grey in the east, I heard a noise, and placing my ear close to the ground, made it out to be the tramp of horses. I ran back to Wilson and said 'The column is here.'

"We all led our horses out to the King's spoor. I saw the form of a man tracking. It was Ingram. I gave him a low whistle; he came up, and behind him rode—not the column, not the Maxims, but just twenty men under Captain Borrow. It was a terrible moment—'*If* we were caught there at dawn'—and already it was getting lighter every minute.

"One of us asked 'Where is the column?' to which the reply was, 'You see all there are of us.' We answered, 'Then you are only so many more men to die.'

"Wilson went aside with Borrow, and there was earnest talk for a few moments. Presently all the officers' horses" heads were together; and Captain Judd said in my hearing, 'Well, this is the end.' And Kurten said quite quietly, 'We shall never get out of this.'

"Then Wilson put it to the officers whether we should try and break through the impis which were now forming up between us and the river, or whether we would go for the King and sell our lives in trying to get hold of him. The final decision was for this latter.

"So we set off and walked along the vlei back to the King's wagons. It was quite light now and they saw us from the scherms all the way, but they just looked at us and we at them, and so we went along. We walked because the horses hadn't a canter in them, and there was no hurry anyway.

"At the wagons we halted and shouted out again about not wanting to kill anyone. There was a pause, and then came shouts and a volley. Afterwards it was said that somebody answered, 'If you don't want to kill, we do.' My horse jumped away to the right at the volley, and took me almost into the arms of some natives who came running from that side. A big induna blazed at me, missed me, and then fumbled at his belt for another cartridge. It was not a proper bandolier he had on, and I saw him trying to pluck out the cartridge instead of easing it up from below with his finger. As I got my horse steady and threw my rifle down to cover him, he suddenly let the cartridge be and lifted an assegai. Waiting to make sure of my aim, just as his arm was poised I fired and hit him in the chest; he dropped. All happened in a moment. Then we retreated. Seeing two horses down, Wilson shouted to somebody to cut off the saddle pockets which carried extra ammunition. Ingram picked up one of the dismounted men behind him, Captain Fitzgerald the other. The most ammunition anyone had, by the way, was a hundred and ten rounds. There was some very stiff fighting for a few minutes, the natives having the best of the position; indeed they might have wiped us out but for their stupid habit of firing on the run, as they charged. Wilson ordered us to retire down the vlei; some hundred yards further on we came to an ant-heap and took our second position on that, and held it for some time. Wilson jumped on the top of the ant-heap and shouted—'Every man pick his nigger.' There was no random firing, I would be covering a man when he dropped to somebody's rifle, and I had to choose another.

"Now *we* had the best of the position. The Matabele came on furiously down the open. Soon we were firing at two hundred yards and less; and the turned-up shields began to lie pretty thick over the ground. It got too hot for them; they broke and took cover in the bush. We fired about twenty rounds per man at this ant-heap. Then the position was flanked by heavy reinforcements from among the timbers; several more horses were knocked out and we had to quit. We retreated in close order into the bush on the opposite side of the vlei—the other side from the scherms. We went slowly on account of the disabled men and horses.

"There was a lull, and Wilson rode up to me and asked if I thought I could rush through to the main column. A scout on a good horse might succeed, of course, where the patrol as a whole would not stand a chance. It was a forlorn hope, but I thought it was only a question of here or there, and I said I'd try, asking for a man to be sent with me. A man called Gooding said he was willing to come, and I picked Ingram also because we had been through many adventures together, and I thought we might as well see this last one through together.

"So we started, and we had not gone five hundred yards when we came upon the horn of an impi closing in from the river. We saw the leading men, and they saw us and fired. As they did so I swerved my horse sharp to the left, and shouting to the others, 'Now for it!' we thrust the horses through the bush at their best pace. A bullet whizzed past my eye, and leaves, cut by the firing, pattered down on us; but as usual the natives fired too high.

"So we rode along, seeing men, and being fired at continually, but outstripping the enemy. The peculiar chant of an advancing impi, like a long, monotonous baying or growling, was loud in our ears, together with the noise they make drumming on their hide shields with the assegai—you must hear an army making those sounds to realise them. As soon as we got where the bush was thinner, we shook off the niggers who were pressing us, and, coming to a bit of hard ground, we turned on our tracks and hid in some thick bush. We did this more than once and stood quiet, listening to the noise they made beating about for us on all sides. Of course we knew that scores of them must have run gradually back upon the river to cut us off, so we doubled and waited, getting so near again to the patrol that once during the firing which we heard thickening back there, the spent bullets pattered around us. Those waiting moments were bad. We heard firing soon from the other side of the river too, and didn't know but that the column was being wiped out as well as the patrol.

"At last, after no end of doubling and hiding and riding in a triple loop, and making use of every device known to a scout for destroying a spoor—it took us about three hours and a half to cover as many miles— we reached the river, and found it a yellow flood two hundred yards broad. In the way African rivers have, the stream, four feet across last night, had risen from the rain. We did not think our horses could swim it, utterly tired as they now were; but we were just playing the game through, so we decided to try. With their heads and ours barely above the water, swimming and drifting, we got across and crawled out on the other side. Then for the first time, I remember, the idea struck me that we might come through it after all, and with that the desire of life came passionately back upon me.

We topped the bank, and there, five hundred yards in front to the left, stood several hundred Matabele! They stared at us in utter surprise, wondering, I suppose, if we were the advance guard of some entirely new reinforcement. In desperation we walked our horses quietly along in front of them, paying no attention to them. We had gone some distance like this, and nobody followed behind, till at last one man took a shot at us; and with that a lot more of them began to blaze away. Almost at the same moment Ingram caught sight of horses only four or five hundred yards distant; so the column still existed—and there it was. We took the last gallop out of our horses then, and—well, in a few minutes I was falling out of the saddle, and saying to Forbes: 'It's all over; we are the last of that party!' Forbes only said, 'Well, tell nobody else till we are through with our own fight,' and next minute we were just firing away along with the others, helping to beat off the attack on the column."

Here Mr. Burnham's narrative ends.

WHAT HAPPENED TO WILSON AND his gallant companions, and the exact manner of their end after Burnham and his two comrades left them, is known only through the reports of natives who took part in the fight. This, however, is certain: since the immortal company of Greeks died at Thermopylæ, few, if any, such stands have been made in the face of inevitable death. They knew what the issue must be; for them there was no possibility of escape; the sun shone upon them for the last time, and for the last time the air of heaven blew upon their brows. Around them, thousand upon thousand, were massed their relentless foes, the bush echoed with war-cries, and from behind every tree and stone a ceaseless fire was poured upon their circle. But these four-and-thirty men never wavered, never showed a sign of fear. Taking shelter behind the boles of trees, or the bodies of their dead horses, they answered the fire shot for shot, coolly, with perfect aim, without haste or hurry.

The bush around told this tale of them in after days, for the bark of every tree was scored with bullets, showing that wherever an enemy had exposed his head there a ball had been sent to seek him. Also there was another testimony—that of the bones of the dead Matabele, the majority of whom had clearly fallen shot through the brain. The natives themselves state that for every white man who died upon that day, there perished at least ten of their own people, picked off, be it remembered, singly as they chanced to expose themselves. Nor did the enemy waste life needlessly, for their general ordered up the King's elephant hunters, trained shots, every one of them, to compete with the white man's fire.

For two long hours or more that fight went on. Now and again a man was killed, and now and again a man was wounded, but the wounded still continued to load the rifles that they could not fire, handing them to those of their companions who were as yet unhurt. At some period during the fray, so say the Matabele, the white men began to "sing." What is meant by the singing we can never know, but probably they cheered aloud after repelling a rush of the enemy. At length their fire grew faint and infrequent, till by degrees it flickered away, for men were lacking to handle the rifles. One was left, however, who stood alone and erect in the ring of the dead, no longer attempting to defend himself, either because he was weak with wounds, or because his ammunition was exhausted. There he stood silent and solitary, presenting one of the most pathetic yet splendid sights told of in the generation that he adorned. There was no more firing now, but the natives stole out of their cover and came up to the man quietly, peering at him half afraid. Then one of them lifted his assegai and drove it through his breast. Still he did not fall; so the soldier drew out the spear and, retreating a few yards, he hurled it at him, transfixing him. Now, very slowly, making no sound, the white man sank forward upon his face, and so lay still.

There seems to be little doubt but that this man was none other than Major Allan Wilson, the commander of the patrol. Native reports of his stature and appearance suggest this, but there is a stronger piece of evidence. The Matabele told Mr. Burnham who repeated it to the present writer, that this man wore a hat of a certain shape and size, fastened up at the side in a peculiar fashion; a hat similar to that which Mr. Burnham wore himself. Now, these hats were of American make, and Major Wilson was the only man in that party who possessed one of them, for Mr. Burnham himself had looped it up for him in the American style, if indeed he had not presented it to him.

The tragedy seemed to be finished, but it was not so, for as the natives stood and stared at the fallen white men, from among the dead a man rose up, to all appearance unharmed, holding in each hand a revolver, or a "little Maxim" as they described it. Having gained his feet he walked slowly and apparently aimlessly away towards an ant-heap that stood at some distance. At the sight the natives began to fire again, scores, and even hundreds, of shots being aimed at him, but, as it chanced, none of them struck him. Seeing that he remained untouched amidst this hail of lead, they cried out that he was "tagati," or magic-guarded, but the indunas ordered them to continue their fire. They did so, and a bullet passing through his hips, the Englishman fell down paralysed. Then finding that he could not turn they ran round him and stabbed him, and he died firing with either hand back over his shoulders at the slaughterers behind him.

So perished the last of the Wilson patrol. He seems to have been Alexander Hay Robertson—at least Mr. Burnham believes that it was he, and for this reason. Robertson, he says, was the only man of the party who had grey hair, and at a little distance from the other skeletons was found a skull to which grey hair still adhered.

It is the custom among savages of the Zulu and kindred races, for reasons of superstition, to rip open and mutilate the bodies of enemies killed in war, but on this occasion the Matabele general, having surveyed the dead, issued an order: "Let them be," he said; "they were men who died like men, men whose fathers were men."

No finer epitaph could be composed in memory of Wilson and his comrades. In truth the fame of this death of theirs has spread far and wide throughout the native races of Southern Africa, and Englishmen everywhere reap the benefit of its glory. They also who lie low, they reap the benefit of it, for their story is immortal, and it will be told hundreds of years hence when it matters no more to them whether they died by shot and steel on the banks of the Shangani, or elsewhere in age and sickness. At least through the fatal storm of war they have attained to peace and honour, and there within the circle of the ruins of Zimbabwe they sleep their sleep, envied of some and revered by all. Surely it is no small thing to have attained to such a death, and England may be proud of her sons who won it.

THE LIFE AND DEATH OF JOAN THE MAID

I

The Fairies' Tree

FOUR HUNDRED AND SEVENTY YEARS ago, the children of Domremy, a little village near the Meuse, on the borders of France and Lorraine, used to meet and dance and sing beneath a beautiful beech-tree, "lovely as a lily." They called it "The Fairy Tree," or "The Good Ladies' Lodge," meaning the fairies by the words "Good Ladies." Among these children was one named Jeanne (born 1412), the daughter of an honest farmer, Jacques d'Arc. Jeanne sang more than she danced, and though she carried garlands like the other boys and girls, and hung them on the boughs of the Fairies" Tree, she liked better to take the flowers into the parish church, and lay them on the altars of St. Margaret and St. Catherine. It was said among the villagers that Jeanne's godmother had once seen the fairies dancing; but though some of the older people believed in the Good Ladies, it does not seem that Jeanne and the other children had faith in them or thought much about them. They only went to the tree and to a neighbouring fairy well to eat cakes and laugh and play. Yet these fairies were destined to be fatal to Jeanne d'Arc, JOAN THE MAIDEN, and her innocent childish sports were to bring her to the stake and the death by fire. For she was that famed Jeanne la Pucelle, the bravest, kindest, best, and wisest of women, whose tale is the saddest, the most wonderful, and the most glorious page in the history of the world. It is a page which no good Englishman and no true Frenchman can read without sorrow and bitter shame, for the English burned Joan with the help of bad Frenchmen, and the French of her party did not pay a *sou*, or write a line, or strike a stroke to save her. But the Scottish, at least, have no share in the disgrace. The Scottish archers fought on Joan's side; the only portrait of herself that Joan ever saw belonged to a Scottish man-at-arms; their historians praised her as she deserved; and a Scottish priest from Fife stood by her to the end.[1]

---

1. This unnamed monk of Dunfermline describes Joan as "a maid worthy to be remembered, who caused the recovery of the kingdom of France from the hands of the tyrant Henry, King of England. This maid I saw and knew, and was with her in her conquests and sieges, ever present with her in her life and at her end." The monk proposed to write

To understand Joan's history it is necessary to say, first, how we come to know so much about one who died so many years ago, and, next, to learn how her country chanced to be so wretched before Joan came to deliver it and to give her life for France.

We know so much about her, not from poets and writers of books who lived in her day, but because she was tried by French priests (1431), and all her answers on everything that she ever did in all her life were written down in Latin. These answers fill most of a large volume. Then, twenty years later (1550–1556), when the English had been driven out of France, the French king collected learned doctors, who examined witnesses from all parts of the country, men and women who had known Joan as a child, and in the wars, and in prison, and they heard her case again, and destroyed the former unjust judgment. The answers of these witnesses fill two volumes, and thus we have all the Maid's history, written during her life, or not long after her death, and sworn to on oath. We might expect that the evidence of her friends, after they had time to understand her, and perhaps were tempted to overpraise her, would show us a picture different from that given in the trial by her mortal enemies. But though the earlier account, put forth by her foes, reads like a description by the Scribes and Pharisees of the trial of Our Lord, yet the character of Joan was so noble that the versions by her friends and her enemies practically agree in her honour. Her advocates cannot make us admire her more than we must admire her in the answers which she gave to her accusers. The records of these two trials, then, with letters and poems and histories written at the time, or very little later, give us all our information about Joan of Arc.

Next, as to "the great pitifulness that was in France" before Joan of Arc came to deliver her country, the causes of the misery are long to tell and not easy to remember. To put it shortly, in Joan's childhood France was under a mad king, Charles VI, and was torn to pieces by two factions, the party of Burgundy and the party of Armagnac. The English took advantage of these disputes, and overran the land. France was not so much one country, divided by parties, as a loose knot of states, small and great, with different interests, obeying greedy and selfish chiefs rather than the king. Joan cared only for her country,

Joan's history; unhappily his manuscript ends in the middle of a sentence. The French historians, as was natural, say next to nothing of their Scottish allies. See Quicherat, *Procès*, v. 339; and *The Book of Pluscarden*, edited by Mr. Felix Skene.

ANDREW LANG AND H. RIDER HAGGARD

not for a part of it. She fought not for Orleans, or Anjou, or Britanny, or Lorraine, but for France. In fact, she made France a nation again. Before she appeared everywhere was murder, revenge, robbery, burning of towns, slaughter of peaceful people, wretchedness, and despair. It was to redeem France from this ruin that Joan came, just when, in 1429, the English were besieging Orleans. Had they taken the strong city of Orleans, they could have overrun all southern and central France, and would have driven the natural king of France, Charles the Dauphin, into exile. From this ruin Joan saved her country; but if you wish to know more exactly how matters stood, and who the people were with whom Joan had to do, you must read what follows. If not, you can "skip" to Chapter III.

II

A Page of History

As you know, Edward III had made an unjust claim to the French crown, and, with the Black Prince, had supported it by the victories of Creçy and Poictiers. But Edward died, and the Black Prince died, and his son, Richard II, was the friend of France, and married a French princess. Richard, too, was done to death, but Henry IV, who succeeded him, had so much work on his hands in England that he left France alone. Yet France was wretched, because when the wise Charles V died in 1380, he left two children, Charles the Dauphin, and his brother, Louis of Orleans. They were only little boys, and the Dauphin became weak-minded; moreover, they were both in the hands of their uncles. The best of these relations, Philip, Duke of Burgundy, died in 1404. His son, John the Fearless, Duke of Burgundy, was the enemy of his own cousin, Louis of Orleans, brother of the Dauphin Charles, who was now king, under the title of Charles VI John the Fearless had Louis of Orleans murdered, yet Paris, the capital of France, was on the side of the murderer. He was opposed by the Count of Armagnac. Now, the two parties of Armagnac and Burgundy divided France; the Armagnacs professing to be on the side of Charles the Dauphin. They robbed, burned, and murdered on all sides. Meanwhile, in England, Henry V had succeeded to his father, and the weakness of France gave him a chance to assert his unjust claim to its throne. He defeated the French at Agincourt in 1415, he carried the Duke of Orleans a prisoner to London, he took Rouen, and overran Normandy. The French now attempted to make peace among themselves. The Duke of Burgundy had the mad Charles VI in his power. The Dauphin was with the opposite faction of Armagnac. But, if the Dauphin and the Duke of Burgundy became friends, the Armagnacs would lose all their importance. The power would be with the Duke of Burgundy. The Armagnacs, therefore, treacherously murdered the duke, in the name of the Dauphin, at a meeting on the Bridge of Montereau (1419). The son of the duke, Philip the Good, now became Duke of Burgundy, and was determined to revenge his murdered father. He therefore made friends with Henry V and the English. The English being now so strong in the Burgundian alliance, their terms were accepted in the Peace of Troyes (1420). The Dauphin was to be shut out from succeeding to the French crown, and was called a Pretender. Henry V married the Dauphin's sister Catherine, and when the mad Charles VI died, Henry and Catherine were to be King and Queen of England and France. Meantime, Henry V was to punish the Dauphin and the Armagnacs. But Henry V died first, and, soon after, the mad Charles died. Who, then, was to be King of France? The Armagnacs held for the Dauphin, the rightful heir. The English, of course, and the Burgundians, were for Henry VI, a baby of ten months old. He, like other princes, had uncles, one of them, the Duke of Gloucester, managed affairs in England; another, the Duke of Bedford, the Regent, was to keep down France. The English possessed Paris and the North; the Dauphin retained the Centre of France, and much of the South, holding his court at Bourges. It is needless to say that the uncles of the baby Henry VI, the Dukes of Gloucester and Bedford, were soon on bad terms, and their disputes made matters easier for the Dauphin. He lost two great battles, however, Crevant and Verneuil, where his Scottish allies were cut to pieces. The hearts of good Frenchmen were with him, but he was indolent, selfish, good-humoured, and governed by a fat, foolish favourite, La Tremouille. The Duke of Bedford now succeeded in patching up the quarrels among the English, and then it was determined (but not by Bedford's advice) to cross the Loire, to invade Southern France, to crush the Dauphin, and to conquer the whole country. But, before he could do all this, Bedford had to take the strong city of Orleans, on the Loire. And against the walls of Orleans the tide of English victory was broken, for there the flag of England went down before the peasant girl who had danced below the Fairy Tree of Domremy, before Joan the Maiden.

III

The Childhood of Joan the Maiden

THE ENGLISH WERE BESIEGING ORLEANS; Joan the Maid drove them from its walls. How did it happen that a girl of seventeen, who could neither read nor write, became the greatest general on the side of France? How did a woman defeat the hardy English soldiers who were used to chase the French before them like sheep?

We must say that France could only be saved by a miracle, and by a miracle she was saved. This is a mystery; we cannot understand it. Joan the Maiden was not as other men and women are. But, as a little girl, she was a child among children, though better, kinder, stronger than the rest, and, poor herself, she was always good and helpful to those who were poorer still.

Joan's parents were not indigent; they had lands and cattle, and a little money laid by in case of need. Her father was, at one time, *doyen*, or head-man, of Domremy. Their house was hard by the church, and was in the part of the hamlet where the people were better off, and had more freedom and privileges than many of their neighbours. They were devoted to the Royal House of France, which protected them from the tyranny of lords and earls further east. As they lived in a village under the patronage of St. Remigius, they were much interested in Reims, his town, where the kings of France were crowned, and were anointed with Holy Oil, which was believed to have been brought in a sacred bottle by an angel.

In the Middle Ages, the king was not regarded as really king till this holy oil had been poured on his head. Thus we shall see, later, how anxious Joan was that Charles VII, then the Dauphin, should be crowned and anointed in Reims, though it was still in the possession of the English. It is also necessary to remember that Joan had once an elder sister named Catherine, whom she loved dearly. Catherine died, and perhaps affection for her made Joan more fond of bringing flowers to the altar of her namesake, St. Catherine, and of praying often to that saint.

Joan was brought up by her parents, as she told her judges, to be industrious, to sew and spin. She did not fear to match herself at spinning and sewing, she said, against any woman in Rouen. When very young she sometimes went to the fields to watch the cattle, like the goose-girl in the fairy tale. As she grew older, she worked in the house, she did not any longer watch sheep and cattle. But the times were dangerous, and, when there was an alarm of soldiers or robbers in the neighbourhood, she sometimes helped to drive the flock into a fortified island, or peninsula, for which her father was responsible, in the river near her home. She learned her creed, she said, from her mother. Twenty years after her death, her neighbours, who remembered her, described her as she was when a child. Jean Morin said that she was a good industrious girl, but that she would often be praying in church when her father and mother did not know it. Beatrix Estellin, an old widow of eighty, said Joan was a good girl. When Domremy was burned, Joan would go to church at Greux, "and there was not a better girl in the two towns." A priest, who had known her, called her "a good, simple, well-behaved girl." Jean Waterin, when he was a boy, had seen Joan in the fields; "and when they were all playing together, she would go apart, and pray to God, as he thought, and he and the others used to laugh at her. She was good and simple, and often in churches and holy places. And when she heard the church bell ring, she would kneel down in the fields." She used to bribe the sexton to ring the bells (a duty which he rather neglected) with presents of knitted wool.

All those who had seen Joan told the same tale: she was always kind, simple, industrious, pious, and yet merry and fond of playing with the others round the Fairy Tree. They say that the singing birds came to her, and nestled in her breast.[2]

Thus, as far as anyone could tell, Joan was a child like other children, but more serious and more religious. One of her friends, a girl called Mengette, whose cottage was next to that of Joan's father, said: "Joan was so pious that we other children told her she was too good."

In peaceful times Joan would have lived and married and died and been forgotten. But the times were evil. The two parties of Burgundy and Armagnac divided town from town and village from village. It was as in the days of the Douglas Wars in Scotland, when the very children took sides for Queen Mary and King James, and fought each other in the streets. Domremy was for the Armagnacs—that is, against the

---

2. M. Quicherat thinks that this is a mere fairy tale, but the author has sometimes seen wild birds (a lark, kingfisher, robin, and finch) come to men, who certainly had none of the charm of Joan of Arc. A thoughtful child, sitting alone, and very still, might find birds alight on her in a friendly way, as has happened to the author. If she fed them, so much the better.

English and for the Dauphin, the son of the mad Charles VI But at Maxey, on the Meuse, a village near Domremy, the people were all for Burgundy and the English. The boys of Domremy would go out and fight the Maxey boys with fists and sticks and stones. Joan did not remember having taken part in those battles, but she had often seen her brothers and the Domremy boys come home all bruised and bleeding.

The Raid of Domremy

ONCE JOAN SAW MORE OF war than these schoolboy bickers. It was in 1425, when she was a girl of thirteen. There was a kind of robber chief on the English side, a man named Henri d'Orly, from Savoy, who dwelt in the castle of Doulevant. There he and his band of armed men lived and drank and plundered far and near. One day there galloped into Domremy a squadron of spearmen, who rode through the fields driving together the cattle of the villagers, among them the cows of Joan's father. The country people could make no resistance; they were glad enough if their houses were not burned. So off rode Henri d'Orly's men, driving the cattle with their spear-points along the track to the castle of Doulevant. But cows are not fast travellers, and when the robbers had reached a little village called Dommartin le France they rested, and went to the tavern to make merry. But by this time a lady, Madame d'Ogévillier, had sent in all haste to the Count de Vaudemont to tell him how the villagers of Domremy had been ruined. So he called his squire, Barthélemy de Clefmont, and bade him summon his spears and mount and ride. It reminds us of the old Scottish ballad, where Jamie Telfer of the Fair Dodhead has seen all his cattle driven out of his stalls by the English; and he runs to Branxholme and warns the water, and they with Harden pursue the English, defeat them, and recover Telfer's kye, with a great spoil out of England. Just so Barthélemy de Clefmont, with seven or eight lances, galloped down the path to Dommartin le France. There they found the cattle, and d'Orly's men fled like cowards. So Barthélemy with his comrades was returning very joyously, when Henri d'Orly rode up with a troop of horse and followed hard after Barthélemy. He was wounded by a lance, but he cut his way through d'Orly's men, and also brought the cattle back safely—a very gallant deed of arms. We may fancy the delight of the villagers when "the kye cam' hame." It may have been now that an event happened, of which Joan does not tell us herself, but which was reported by the king's seneschal, in June 1429, when Joan had just begun her wonderful career. The children of the village, says the seneschal, were running races and leaping in wild joy about the fields; possibly their gladness was caused by the unexpected rescue of their cattle. Joan ran so much more fleetly than the rest, and leaped so far, that the children believed she actually *flew*, and they told her so! Tired and breathless, "out of herself," says the seneschal, she paused, and in that moment she heard a Voice, but saw no man; the Voice bade her go home, because her mother had need of her. And when she came home the Voice said many things to her about the great deeds which God bade her do for France. We shall later hear Joan's own account of how her visions and Voices first came to her.[3]

Three years later there was an alarm, and the Domremy people fled to Neufchâteau, Joan going with her parents. Afterwards her enemies tried to prove that she had been a servant at an inn in Neufchâteau, had lived roughly with grooms and soldiers, and had learned to ride. But this was absolutely untrue. An ordinary child would have thought little of war and of the sorrows of her country in the flowery fields of Domremy and Vaucouleurs; but Joan always thought of the miseries of *France la belle*, fair France, and prayed for her country and her king. A great road, on the lines of an old Roman way, passed near Domremy, so Joan would hear all the miserable news from travellers. Probably she showed what was in her mind, for her father dreamed that she "had gone off with soldiers," and this dream struck him so much, that he told his sons that he, or they, must drown Joan if she so disgraced herself. For many girls of bad character, lazy and rude, followed the soldiers, as they always have done, and always will. Joan's father thought that his dream meant that Joan would be like these women. It would be interesting to know whether he was in the habit of dreaming true dreams. For Joan, his child, dreamed when wide awake, dreamed dreams immortal, which brought her to her glory and her doom.

The Calling of Joan the Maid

WHEN JOAN WAS BETWEEN TWELVE and thirteen, a wonderful thing befell her. We have already heard one account of it, written when Joan was in the first flower of her triumph, by the seneschal of the King of France. A Voice spoke to her and prophesied of what she was to do. But

---

3. See M. Siméon Luce, *Jeanne d'Arc in Domremy*.

about all these marvellous things it is more safe to attend to what Joan always said herself. She told the same story both to friends and foes; to the learned men who, by her king's desire, examined her at Poictiers, before she went to war (April 1429); and to her deadly foes at Rouen. No man can read her answers to them and doubt that she spoke what she believed. And she died for this belief. Unluckily the book that was kept of what she said at Poictiers is lost. Before her enemies at Rouen there were many things which she did not think it right to say. On one point, after for long refusing to speak, she told her foes a kind of parable, which we must not take as part of her real story.

When Joan was between twelve and thirteen (1424), so she swore, "a *Voice came to her from God for her guidance*, but when first it came, she was in great fear. And it came, that Voice, about noonday, in the summer season, she being in her father's garden. And Joan had not fasted the day before that, but was fasting when the Voice came.[4] And she heard the Voice on her right side, towards the church, and rarely did she hear it but she also saw a great light." These are her very words. They asked her if she heard these Voices there, in the hall of judgment, and she answered, "If I were in a wood, I should well hear these Voices coming to me." The Voices at first only told her "to be a good girl, and go to church." She thought it was a holy Voice, and that it came from God; and the third time she heard it she knew it was the voice of an angel. The Voice told her of "the great pity there was in France," and that one day she must go into France and help the country. She had visions with the Voices; visions first of St. Michael, and then of St. Catherine and St. Margaret.[5] She hated telling her hypocritical judges anything about these heavenly visions, but it seems that she really believed in their appearance, believed that she had embraced the knees of St. Margaret and St. Catherine, and she did reverence to them when they came to her. "I saw them with my bodily eyes, as I see you," she said to her judges, "and when they departed from me I wept, and well I wished that they had taken me with them."

---

4. Here we follow Father Ayroles's correction of Quicherat's reading of the manuscripts.
5. The Voice and vision of St. Michael alarmed her at first. In 1425 the French had defeated the English by sea, under Mount St. Michael, the only fortress in Normandy which never yielded to England. Consequently St. Michael was in high esteem as the patron of France, and, of all saints, he was most likely to be in Joan's mind. (See Siméon Luce, *Jeanne d'Arc à Domremy*.) On the other hand, Father Ayroles correctly argues that Joan first heard the Voices the year before the victory near Mount St. Michael.

What are we to think about these visions and these Voices which were with Joan to her death?

Some have thought that she was mad; others that she only told the story to win a hearing and make herself important; or, again, that a trick was played on her to win her aid. The last idea is impossible. The French Court did not want her. The second, as everyone will admit who reads Joan's answers, and follows her step by step from childhood to victory, to captivity, to death, is also impossible. She was as truthful as she was brave and wise. But was she partially insane? It is certain that mad people do hear voices which are not real, and believe that they come to them from without. But these mad voices say mad things. Now, Joan's Voices never said anything but what was wise beyond her own wisdom, and right and true. She governed almost all her actions by their advice. When she disobeyed "her counsel," as she called it, the result was evil, and once, as we shall see, was ruinous. Again, Joan was not only healthy, but wonderfully strong, ready, and nimble. In all her converse with princes and priests and warriors, she spoke and acted like one born in their own rank. In mind, as in body, she was a marvel, none such has ever been known. It is impossible, then, to say that she was mad.

In the whole history of the world, as far as we know it, there is only one example like that of Joan of Arc. Mad folk hear voices; starved nuns, living always with their thoughts bent on heaven, women of feeble body, accustomed to faints and to fits, have heard voices and seen visions. Some of them have been very good women; none have been strong, good riders, skilled in arms, able to march all day long with little food, and to draw the arrow from their own wound and mount horse and charge again, like Joan of Arc. Only one great man, strong, brave, wise, and healthy, has been attended by a Voice, which taught him what to do, or rather what *not* to do. That man was Socrates, the most hardy soldier, the most unwearied in the march, and the wisest man of Greece. Socrates was put to death for this Voice of his, on the charge of "bringing in new gods." Joan of Arc died for her Voices, because her enemies argued that she was no saint, but a witch! These two, the old philosopher and the untaught peasant girl of nineteen, stand alone in the endless generations of men, alone in goodness, wisdom, courage, strength, combined with a mysterious and fatal gift. More than this it is now forbidden to us to know. But, when we remember that such a being as Joan of Arc has only appeared once since time began, and *that* once just when France seemed lost beyond all hope, we need not wonder at those who say that France was saved by no common good fortune and happy chance, but by the will of Heaven.[6]

In one respect, Joan's conduct after these Voices and visions began, was perhaps, as regarded herself, unfortunate. She did not speak of them to her parents, nor tell about them to the priest when she confessed. Her enemies were thus able to say, later, that they could not have been holy visions or Voices, otherwise she would not have concealed them from her father, her mother, and the priest, to whom she was bound to tell everything, and from whom she should have sought advice. Thus, long afterwards, St. Theresa had visions, and, in obedience to her priest, she at first distrusted these, as perhaps a delusion of evil, or a temptation of spiritual pride. Joan, however, was afraid that her father would interfere with her mission, and prevent her from going to the king. She believed that she must not be "disobedient to the heavenly vision."

How Joan the Maid Went to Vaucouleurs

IT WAS IN 1424 THAT the Voices first came to Joan the Maid. The years went on, bringing more and more sorrow to France. In 1428 only a very few small towns in the east still held out for the Dauphin, and these were surrounded on every side by enemies. Meanwhile the Voices came more frequently, urging Joan to go into France, and help her country. She asked how she, a girl, who could not ride or use sword and lance, could be of any help? Rather would she stay at home and spin beside her dear mother. At the same time she was encouraged by one of the vague old prophecies which were as common in France as in Scotland. A legend ran "that France was to be saved by a Maiden from the Oak Wood," and there was an Oak Wood, *le bois chènu*, near Domremy. Some such prophecy had an influence on Joan, and probably helped people to believe in her. The Voices, moreover, instantly and often commanded her to go to Vaucouleurs, a neighbouring town which was loyal, and there meet Robert de Baudricourt, who was captain of the French garrison. Now, Robert de Baudricourt was not what is called a romantic person. Though little over thirty, he had already married, one

---

6. M. Quicherat distinguishes three strange kinds of power in Joan. These are the power of seeing at a distance, the power of learning the secret thoughts of men, and the power of foretelling future events. Of each class "one example at least rests on evidence so solid, that it cannot be rejected without rejecting the whole basis of the history." He merely states facts, which he makes no attempt to explain. *Aperçus Nouveaux*, p. 61.

after the other, two rich widows. He was a gallant soldier, but a plain practical man, very careful of his own interest, and cunning enough to hold his own among his many enemies, English, Burgundian, and Lorrainers. It was to him that Joan must go, a country girl to a great noble, and tell him that she, and she alone, could save France! Joan knew what manner of man Robert de Baudricourt was, for her father had been obliged to visit him, and speak for the people of Domremy when they were oppressed. She could hardly hope that he would listen to her, and it was with a heavy heart that she found a good reason for leaving home to visit Vaucouleurs. Joan had a cousin, a niece of her mother's, who was married to one Durand Lassois, at Burey en Vaux, a village near Vaucouleurs. This cousin invited Joan to visit her for a week. At the end of that time she spoke to her cousin's husband. There was an old saying, as we saw, that France would be rescued by a Maid, and she, as she told Lassois, was that Maid. Lassois listened, and, whatever he may have thought of her chances, he led her to Robert de Baudricourt.

Joan came, on May 18, 1423, in her simple red dress, and walked straight up to the captain among his men. She knew him, she said, by what her Voices had told her, but she may also have heard him described by her father. She told him that the Dauphin must keep quiet, and risk no battle, for before the middle of Lent next year (1429) God would send him succour. She added that the kingdom belonged, not to the Dauphin, but to her Master, who willed that the Dauphin should be crowned, and she herself would lead him to Reims, to be anointed with the holy oil.

"And who is your Master?" said Robert.

"The King of Heaven!"

Robert, very naturally, thought that Joan was crazed, and shrugged his shoulders. He bluntly told Lassois to box her ears, and take her back to her father. So she had to go home; but here new troubles awaited her. The enemy came down on Domremy and burned it; Joan and her family fled to Neufchâteau, where they stayed for a few days. It was perhaps about this time that a young man declared that Joan had promised to marry him, and he actually brought her before a court of justice, to make her fulfil her promise.

Joan was beautiful, well-shaped, dark-haired, and charming in her manner.

We have a letter which two young knights, André and Guy de Laval, wrote to their mother in the following year. "The Maid was armed from neck to heel," they say, "but unhelmeted; she carried a lance in her hand.

Afterwards, when we lighted down from our horses at Selles, I went to her lodging to see her, and she called for wine for me, saying she would soon make me drink wine in Paris" (then held by the English), "and, indeed, she seems a thing wholly divine, both to look on her and to hear her sweet voice."

It is no wonder that the young man of Domremy wanted to marry Joan; but she had given no promise, and he lost his foolish law-suit. She and her parents soon went back to Domremy.[7]

How Joan the Maid Went again to Vaucouleurs

IN DOMREMY THEY FOUND THAT the enemy had ruined everything. Their cattle were safe, for they had been driven to Neufchâteau, but when Joan looked from her father's garden to the church, she saw nothing but a heap of smoking ruins. She had to go to say her prayers now at the church of Greux. These things only made her feel more deeply the sorrows of her country. The time was drawing near when she had prophesied that the Dauphin was to receive help from heaven— namely, in the Lent of 1429. On that year the season was held more than commonly sacred, for Good Friday and the Annunciation fell on the same day. So, early in January, 1429, Joan the Maid turned her back on Domremy, which she was never to see again. Her cousin Lassois came and asked leave for Joan to visit him again; she said good-bye to her father and mother, and to her friend Mengette, but to her dearest friend Hauvette she did not even say good-bye, for she could not bear it. She went to her cousin's house at Burey, and there she stayed for six weeks, hearing bad news of the siege of Orleans by the English. Meanwhile, Robert de Baudricourt, in Vaucouleurs, was not easy in his mind, for he was likely to lose the protection of René of Anjou, the Duc de Bar, who was on the point of joining the English. Thus Robert may have been more inclined to listen to Joan than when he bade her cousin box her ears and take her back to her father. A squire named Jean de Nouillompont met Joan one day.

"Well, my lass," said he, "is our king to be driven from France, and are we all to become English?"

"I have come here," said Joan, "to bid Robert de Baudricourt lead me to the king, but he will not listen to me. And yet to the king I

---

7. The date of this affair and that of the flight to Neufchâteau are uncertain.

must go, even if I walk my legs down to the knees; for none in all the world—king, nor duke, nor the King of Scotland's daughter—can save France, but myself only. *Certes*, I would rather stay and spin with my poor mother, for to fight is not my calling; but I must go and I must fight, for so my Lord will have it."

"And who is your Lord?" said Jean de Nouillompont.

"He is God," said the Maiden.

"Then, so help me God, I shall take you to the king," said Jean, putting her hands in his. "When do we start?"

"To-day is better than to-morrow," said the Maid.

Joan was now staying in Vaucouleurs with Catherine le Royer. One day, as she and Catherine were sitting at their spinning-wheels, who should come in but Robert de Baudricourt with the *curé* of the town. Robert had fancied that perhaps Joan was a witch! He told the priest to perform some rite of the Church over her, so that if she were a witch she would be obliged to run away. But when the words were spoken, Joan threw herself at the knees of the priest, saying, "Sir, this is ill done of you, for you have heard my confession and know that I am not a witch."

Robert was now half disposed to send her to the king and let her take her chance. But days dragged on, and when Joan was not working she would be on her knees in the crypt or underground chapel of the Chapel Royal in Vaucouleurs. Twenty-seven years later a chorister boy told how he often saw her praying there for France. Now people began to hear of Joan, and the Duke of Lorraine asked her to visit him at Nancy, where she bade him lead a better life. He is said to have given her a horse and some money. On February 12 the story goes that she went to Robert de Baudricourt.

"You delay too long," she said. "On this very day, at Orleans, the gentle Dauphin has lost a battle."

This was, in fact, the Battle of Herrings, so called because the English defeated and cut off a French and Scottish force which attacked them as they were bringing herrings into camp for provisions in Lent. If this tale is true, Joan cannot have known of the battle by any common means; but though it is vouched for by the king's secretary, Joan has told us nothing about it.[8]

---

8. It occurs in the *Chronique de la Pucelle*, by Cousinot de Montreuil, at that time the king's secretary, and elsewhere.

Now the people of Vaucouleurs bought clothes for Joan to wear on her journey to the Dauphin. They were such clothes as men wear—doublet, hose, surcoat, boots, and spurs—and Robert de Baudricourt gave Joan a sword.

In the end this man's dress, which henceforth she always wore, proved the ruin of Joan. Her enemies, the English and false French, made it one of their chief charges against her that she dressed, as they chose to say, immodestly. It is not very clear how she came to wear men's garments. Jean de Nouillompont, her first friend, asked her if she would go to the king (a ten days' journey on horseback) dressed as she was, in her red frock. She answered "that she would gladly have a man's dress," which he says that he provided. Her reason was that she would have to be living alone among men-at-arms, and she thought that it was more modest to wear armour like the rest. Also her favourite saint, St. Margaret, had done this once when in danger. St. Marina had worn a monk's clothes when obliged to live in a monastery. The same thing is told of St. Eugenia.[9] Besides, in all the romances of chivalry, and the favourite poems of knights and ladies, we find fair maidens fighting in arms like men, or travelling dressed as pages, and nobody ever thought the worse of them. Therefore this foolish charge of the English against Joan the Maid was a mere piece of cruel hypocrisy.

How Joan the Maid Rode to Chinon

ON FEBRUARY 23, 1429, THE GATE of the little castle of Vaucouleurs, "the Gate of France," which is still standing, was thrown open. Seven travellers rode out, among them two squires, Jean de Nouillompont and Bertrand de Poulengy, with their attendants, and Joan the Maid. "Go, and let what will come of it come!" said Robert de Baudricourt. He did not expect much to come of it. It was a long journey—they were eleven days on the road—and a dangerous. But Joan laughed at danger. "God will clear my path to the king, for to this end I was born." Often they rode by night, stopping at monasteries when they could. Sometimes they slept out under the sky. Though she was so young and so beautiful, with the happiness of her long desire in her eyes, and the glory of her future shining on her, these two young gentlemen never dreamed of

---

9. Theod. de Leliis, *Procès*, ii. 42.

paying their court to her and making love, as in romances they do, for they regarded her "as if she had been an angel." "They were in awe of her," they said, long afterwards, long after the angels had taken Joan to be with their company in heaven. And all the knights who had seen her said the same. Dunois and d'Aulon and the beautiful Duc d'Alençon, "*le beau Duc*" as Joan called him, they all said that she was "a thing enskied and sainted." So on they rode, six men and a maid, through a country full of English and Burgundian soldiery. There were four rivers to cross, Marne, Aube, Seine, and Yonne, and the rivers were "great and mickle o' spate," running red with the rains from bank to bank, so that they could not ford the streams, but must go by unfriendly towns, where alone there were bridges. Joan would have liked to stay and go to church in every town, but this might not be. However, she heard mass thrice at the church of her favourite saint, Catherine de Fierbois, between Loches and Chinon, in a friendly country. And a strange thing happened later in that church.

From Fierbois Joan made some clerk write to the king that she was coming to help him, and that she would know him among all his men. Probably it was here that she wrote to beg her parents' pardon, and they forgave her, she says. Meanwhile news reached the people then besieged in Orleans that a marvellous Maiden was riding to their rescue. On March 6 Joan arrived in Chinon, where for two or three days the king's advisers would not let him see her. At last they yielded, and she went straight up to him, and when he denied that he was the king, she told him that she knew well who he was.

"There is the king," said Charles, pointing to a richly dressed noble.

"No, fair sire. You are he!"

Still, it was not easy to believe. Joan stayed at Chinon in the house of a noble lady. The young Duc d'Alençon was on her side from the first, bewitched by her noble horsemanship, which she had never learned. Great people came to see her, but, when she was alone, she wept and prayed. The king sent messengers to inquire about her at Domremy, but time was going on, and Orleans was not relieved.

How Joan the Maid Showed a Sign to the King

JOAN WAS WEARY OF BEING asked questions. One day she went to Charles and said, "Gentle Dauphin, why do you delay to believe me? I tell you that God has taken pity on you and your people, at the prayer of St. Louis and St. Charlemagne. And I will tell you, by your leave, something which will show you that you should believe me."

Then she told him secretly something which, as he said, none could know but God and himself. A few months later, in July, a man about the court wrote a letter, in which he declares that none knows what Joan told the king, but he was plainly as glad as if something had been revealed to him by the Holy Spirit. We have three witnesses of this, one of them is the famous Dunois, to whom the king himself told what happened.

What did Joan say to the king, and what was the sign? About this her enemies later examined her ten times. She told them from the very first that she would never let them know; that, if they made her speak, what she spoke would not be the truth. At last she told them a kind of parable about an angel and a crown, which neither was nor was meant to be taken as true. It was the king's secret, and Joan kept it.

We learn the secret in this way. There was a man named Pierre Sala in the service of Louis XI and Charles VIII of France. In his youth, Pierre Sala used to hunt with M. de Boisy, who, in his youth, had been gentleman of the bedchamber to Charles VII, Joan's king. To de Boisy Charles VII told the secret, and de Boisy told it to Pierre Sala. At this time of his misfortunes (1429), when his treasurer had only four crowns in his coffers, Charles went into his oratory to pray alone, and he made his prayer to God secretly, not aloud, but in his mind.

Now, what Joan told the king was the secret prayer which he had made in his own heart when alone. And, ten years later, when Joan was long dead, an impostor went about saying that *she* was the Maid, who had come to life again. She was brought to Charles, who said, "Maiden, my Maid, you are welcome back again if you can tell me the secret that is between you and me." But the false Maid, falling on her knees, confessed all her treason.

This is the story of the sign given to the king, which is not the least strange of the things done by Joan the Maid. But there is a thing stranger yet, though not so rare.

The king to whom Joan brought this wonderful message, the king whom she loved so loyally, and for whom she died, spoiled all her plans. He, with his political advisers, prevented her from driving the English quite out of France. These favourites, men like the fat La Tremouille, found their profit in dawdling and delaying, as politicians generally do. Thus, in our own time, they hung off and on, till our soldiers were too late to rescue Gordon from the Arabs. Thus, in Joan's time, she had literally to goad them into action, to drag them on by constant prayers and tears. They were lazy, comfortable, cowardly, disbelieving; in their hearts they hated the Maid, who put them to so much trouble. As for Charles, to whom the Maid was so loyal, had he been a man like the Black Prince, or even like Prince Charlie, Joan would have led him into Paris before summer was ended. "I shall only last one year and little more," she often said to the king. The Duc d'Alençon heard her,[10] and much of that precious year was wasted. Charles, to tell the truth, never really believed in her; he never quite trusted her; he never led a charge by her side; and, in the end, he shamefully deserted her, and left the Maid to her doom.

How Joan the Maid was Examined at Poictiers

WEEKS HAD PASSED, AND JOAN had never yet seen a blow struck in war. She used to exercise herself in horsemanship, and knightly sports of tilting, and it is wonderful that a peasant girl became, at once, one of the best riders among the chivalry of France. The young Duc d'Alençon, lately come from captivity in England, saw how gallantly she rode, and gave her a horse. He and his wife were her friends from the first, when the politicians and advisers were against her. But, indeed, whatever the Maid attempted, she did better than others, at once, without teaching or practice. It was now determined that Joan should be taken to Poictiers, and examined before all the learned men, bishops, doctors, and higher clergy who still were on the side of France. There was good reason for this delay. It was plain to all, friends and foes, that the wonderful Maid was not like other men and women, with her Voices, her visions, her prophecies, and her powers. All agreed that she had some strange help given to her; but who gave it? This aid must come, people thought then, either from heaven or hell—either from God and his saints, or from the devil and his angels. Now, if any doubt could be thrown on the source whence Joan's aid came, the English might argue (as of course they did), that she was a witch and a heretic. If she was a heretic and a witch, then her king was involved in her wickedness, and so he might be legally shut out from his kingdom. It was necessary, therefore, that Joan should be examined by learned men. They must find out whether she had

---

10. *Procès*, iii. 99.

always been good, and a true believer, and whether her Voices always agreed in everything with the teachings of the Church. Otherwise her angels must be devils in disguise. For these reasons Joan was carried to Poictiers. During three long weeks the learned men asked her questions, and, no doubt, they wearied her terribly. But they said it was wonderful how wisely this girl, who "did not know A from B," replied to their puzzling inquiries. She told the story of her visions, of the command laid upon her to rescue Orleans. Said Guillaume Aymeri, "You ask for men-at-arms, and you say that God will have the English to leave France and go home. If that is true, no men-at-arms are needed; God's pleasure can drive the English out of the land."

"In God's name," said the Maid, "the men-at-arms will fight, and God will give the victory." Then came the learned Seguin; "a right sour man was he," said those who knew him.

Seguin was a Limousin, and the Limousins spoke in a queer accent at which the other French were always laughing.

"In what language do your Voices speak?" asked he.

"In a better language than *yours*," said Joan, and the bishops smiled at the country quip.

"We may not believe in you," said Seguin, "unless you show us a sign."

"I did not come to Poictiers to work miracles," said Joan; "take me to Orleans, and I shall show you the signs that I am sent to do." And show them she did.

Joan never pretended to work miracles. Though, in that age, people easily believed in miracles, it is curious that none worth mentioning were invented about Joan in her own time. She knew things in some strange way sometimes, but the real miracle was her extraordinary wisdom, genius, courage, and power of enduring hardship.

At last, after examining witnesses from Domremy, and the Queen of Sicily and other great ladies to whom Joan was entrusted, the clergy found nothing in her but "goodness, humility, frank maidenhood, piety, honesty, and simplicity." As for her wearing a man's dress, the Archbishop of Embrun said to the king, "It is more becoming to do these things in man's gear, since they have to be done amongst men."

The king therefore made up his mind at last. Jean and Pierre, Joan's brothers, were to ride with her to Orleans; her old friends, her first friends, Jean de Nouillompont and Bertrand de Poulengy, had never left her. She was given a squire, Jean d'Aulon, a very good man, and a page, Louis de Coutes, and a chaplain. The king gave Joan armour and horses, and offered her a sword. But her Voices told her that, behind the altar of St. Catherine de Fierbois, where she heard mass on her way to Chinon, there was an old sword, with five crosses on the blade, buried in the earth. That sword she was to wear. A man whom Joan did not know, and had never seen, was sent from Tours, and found the sword in the place which she described. The sword was cleaned of rust, and the king gave her two sheaths, one of velvet, one of cloth of gold, but Joan had a leather sheath made for use in war. She also commanded a banner to be made, with the Lilies of France on a white field. There was also a picture of God, holding the round world, and two angels at the sides, with the sacred words, JHESU MARIA. On another flag was the Annunciation, the Virgin holding a lily, and the angel coming to her. In battle, when she led a charge, Joan always carried her standard, that she might not be able to use her sword. She wished to kill nobody, and said "she loved her banner forty times more than her sword." Joan afterwards broke St. Catherine's sword, when slapping a girl (who richly deserved to be slapped) with the flat of the blade. Her enemies, at her trial, wished to prove that her flag was a kind of magical talisman, but Joan had no belief in anything of that kind. What she believed in was God, her Voices, and her just cause. When once it was settled that she was to lead an army to relieve Orleans, she showed her faith by writing a letter addressed to the King of England; Bedford, the Regent; and the English generals at Orleans. This letter was sent from Blois, late in April. It began JHESU MARIA. Joan had no ill-will against the English. She bade them leave France, "and if you are reasonable, you yet may ride in the Maid's company, where the French will do the fairest feat of arms that ever yet was done for Christentie." Probably she had in her mind some Crusade. But, before France and England can march together, "do ye justice to the King of Heaven and the Blood Royal of France. Yield to the Maid the keys of all the good towns which ye have taken and assailed in France." If they did not yield to the Maid and the king, she will come on them to their sorrow. "Duke of Bedford, the Maid prays and entreats you not to work your own destruction!"

We may imagine how the English laughed and swore when they received this letter. They threw the heralds of the Maid into prison, and threatened to burn them as heretics. From the very first, the English promised to burn Joan as a witch and a heretic. This fate was always before her eyes. But she went where her Voices called her.

AT LAST THE MEN-AT-ARMS WHO were to accompany Joan were ready. She rode at their head, as André de Laval and Guy de Laval saw her, and described her in a letter to their mother. She was armed in white armour, but unhelmeted, a little axe in her hand, riding a great black charger, that reared at the door of her lodging and would not let her mount.

"'Lead him to the Cross!' cried she, for a Cross stood on the roadside, by the church. There he stood as if he had been stone, and she mounted. Then she turned to the church, and said, in her girlish voice, 'You priests and churchmen, make prayers and processions to God.' Then she cried, 'Forwards, Forwards!' and on she rode, a pretty page carrying her banner, and with her little axe in her hand." And so Joan went to war.[11] She led, she says, ten or twelve thousand soldiers.[12] Among the other generals were Xaintrailles and La Hire. Joan made her soldiers confess themselves; as for La Hire, a brave rough soldier, she forbade him to swear, as he used to do, but, for his weakness, she permitted him to say, *By my bâton!* This army was to defend a great convoy of provisions, of which the people of Orleans stood in sore need. Since November they had been besieged, and now it was late April. The people in Orleans were not yet starving, but food came in slowly, and in small quantities. From the first the citizens had behaved well; a Scottish priest describes their noble conduct. They had burned all the outlying suburbs, beyond the wall, that they might not give shelter to the English. They had plenty of cannon, which carried large rough stone balls, and usually did little harm. But a gun was fired, it is said by a small boy, which killed Salisbury, the English general, as he looked out of an arrow-slit in a fort that the English had taken.

The French general-in-chief was the famous Dunois, then called the Bastard of Orleans. On the English side was the brave Talbot, who fought under arms for sixty years, and died fighting when he was over eighty. There were also Suffolk, Pole, and Glasdale, whom the French called "Classidas." The English had not soldiers enough to surround and take so large a town, of 30,000 people, in ordinary war. But as Dunois

---

11. This description is a few weeks later than the start from Blois.
12. This estimate was probably incorrect; 3,500 was more like the actual number.

said, "two hundred English could then beat a thousand French"—that is, as the French were before the coming of the Maid.

The position of Orleans was this; it may be most easily understood from the map.

Looking *down* the river Loire, Orleans lies on your right hand. It had strong walls in an irregular square; it had towers on the wall, and a bridge of many arches crossing to the left side of the river. At the further end of this bridge were a fort and rampart called Les Tourelles, and this fort had already been taken by the English, so that no French army could cross the bridge to help Orleans. Indeed, the bridge was broken. The rampart and the fort of Les Tourelles were guarded by another strong work, called Les Augustins. All round the outside of the town, on the right bank, the English had built strong redoubts, which they called *bastilles*. "Paris" was the bastille which blocked the road from Paris, "London" and "Rouen" were bastilles on the western side, but on the east, above the town, and on the Orleans bank of the Loire, the English had only one bastille, St. Loup. Now, as Joan's army mustered at Blois, south of Orleans, further down the river, she might march on the *left* side of the river, cross it by boats above Orleans, and enter the town where the English were weakest and had only one fort, St. Loup. Or she might march up the *right* bank, and attack the English where they were strongest, and had many bastilles. The Voices bade the Maid act on the boldest plan, and enter Orleans where the English were strongest, on the right bank of the river. The English would not move, said the Voices. She was certain that they would not even sally out against her. But Dunois in Orleans, and the generals with the Maid, thought this plan very perilous, as, indeed, it was. They therefore deceived her, caused her to think that Orleans was on the *left* bank of the Loire, and led her thither. When she arrived, she saw that they had not played her fair, that the river lay between her and the town, and the strongest force of the enemy.

The most astonishing thing about Joan is that, though she had never yet seen a sword-stroke dealt in anger, she understood the great operations of war better than seasoned generals. It was not only that she, like old Blücher, always cried *Forwards!* Audacity, to fight on every chance, carries men far in battle. Prince Charlie, who was no great general, saw that, and while his flag went forward he never lost a fight. But Joan "was most expert in war," said the Duc d'Alençon, "both with the lance and in massing an army, and arraying battle, and

ANDREW LANG AND H. RIDER HAGGARD

in the management of artillery. For all men marvelled how far-sighted and prudent she was in war, as if she had been a captain of thirty years" standing, and, above all, in the service of the artillery, for in that she was right well skilled."[13]

This girl of seventeen saw that, if a large convoy of provisions was to be thrown into a besieged town, the worst way was to try to ferry the supplies across a river under the enemy's fire. But Dunois and the other generals had brought her to this pass, and the Maid was sore ill-pleased. Now we shall see what happened, as it is reported in the very words of Dunois, the French general in Orleans. Joan had been brought, as we said, to the wrong bank of the Loire; it ran between her and the town where she would be. The wind was blowing in her teeth; boats could not cross with the troops and provisions. There she sat her horse and chafed till Dunois came out and crossed the Loire to meet her. This is what he says about Joan and her conduct.

How Joan the Maid Entered Orleans

THEY WERE ON THE WRONG side of the Loire, opposite St. Loup, where the English held a strong fort.[14] "I did not think, and the other generals did not think," says Dunois, "that the men-at-arms with the Maid were a strong enough force to bring the provisions into the town. Above all, it was difficult to get boats and ferry over the supplies, for both wind and stream were dead against us. Then Joan spoke to me thus:

"'Are you the Bastard of Orleans?'

"'That am I, and glad of your coming.'

"'Is it you who gave counsel that I should come hither by that bank of the stream, and not go straight where Talbot and the English are?'

"'I myself, and others wiser than I, gave that advice, and we think it the better way and the surer.'

"'In God's name, the counsel of our God is wiser and surer than yours. You thought to deceive me, and you have deceived yourselves, for

---

13. *Procès*, iii. 100.

14. *Procès*, iii. pp. 5, 6, 7. They were "near Saint Loup," he says, "on the *right* bank of the Loire above Orleans." But (p. 7) he says that after their conversation he and Joan crossed to the right from the left bank. At all events they were some six miles higher up the river than Orleans.

I bring you a better rescue than ever shall come to soldier or city—that is, the help of the King of Heaven. . .'

"Then instantly, and as it were in one moment, the wind changed that had been dead against us, and had hindered the boats from carrying the provisions into Orleans, and the sails filled."

Dunois now wished Joan to cross by boat and enter the town, but her army could not cross, and she was loth to leave them, lest they fell into sin, for she had made them all confess at Blois. However, the army returned to Blois, to cross by the bridge there, and come upon the Orleans bank, as Joan had intended from the first. Then Joan crossed in the boat, holding in her hand the lily standard. So she and La Hire and Dunois rode into Orleans, where the people crowded round her, blessing her, and trying to kiss her hand. Night had fallen, there were torches flaring in the wind, and, as the people thronged about her, a torch set fire to the fringe of her banner. "Then spurred she her horse, and turned him gracefully and put out the flame, as if she had long followed the wars, which the men-at-arms beheld with wonder, and the folk of Orleans." So they led her with great joy to the Regnart Gate, and the house of Jacques Boucher, treasurer of the Duke of Orleans, and there was she gladly received, with her two brothers and her gentlemen, her old friends, Nouillompont and Poulengy.

Next day, without leave from Joan, La Hire led a sally against the English, fought bravely, but failed, and Joan wished once more to bid the English go in peace. The English, of course, did not obey her summons, and it is said that they answered with wicked words which made her weep. For she wept readily, and blushed when she was moved. In her anger she went to a rampart, and, crying aloud, bade the English begone; but they repeated their insults, and threatened yet again to burn her. Next day (May 1), Dunois went off to bring the troops from Blois, and Joan rode round and inspected the English position. They made no attempt to take her. A superstitious fear of her "witchcraft" had already fallen on them; they had lost heart and soon lost all. On May 4 the army returned from Blois. Joan rode out to meet them, priests marched in procession, singing hymns, but the English never stirred. They were expecting fresh troops under Fastolf. "If you do not let me know when Fastolf comes," cried the Maid merrily to Dunois, "I will have your head cut off." But for some reason, probably because they did not wish her to run risk, they did not tell Joan when the next fight began. She had just lain down to sleep when she leaped up with a noise, wakening her squire. "My Voices tell me," she said, "that I must go against the English, but whether to their forts or against Fastolf I know not."

There was a cry in the street; Joan armed herself; her page came in.

"Wretched boy!" she said. "French blood is flowing, and you never told me!"

In a moment she was in the street, the page handed to her the lily flag from the upper window. Followed by her squire, d'Aulon, she galloped to the Burgundy Gate. They met wounded men. "Never do I see French blood but my hair stands up on my head," said Joan. She rode out of the gate to the English fort of St. Loup, which the Orleans men were attacking. Joan leaped into the fosse, under fire, holding her banner, and cheering on her men. St. Loup was taken by the French, in spite of a gallant defence, and Joan wept for the dead English, fearing that they had died unconfessed. Next day was Ascension Day. Joan, thinking "the better the day the better the deed," was for fighting. There was no battle, but she again summoned the English to withdraw, and again was insulted, and wept.

The French generals now conceived a plan to make a feint, or a sham attack, on the English forts where they were strongest, on the Orleans side of the river. The English on the left side would cross to help their countrymen, and then the French would take the forts beyond the bridge. Thus they would have a free path across the river, and would easily get supplies, and weary out the English. They only told Joan of the first part of their plan, but she saw that they were deceiving her. When the plan was explained she agreed to it, her one wish was to strike swiftly and strongly. However, they did not carry out the plan, they only assailed the forts on the left bank.

The French attacked the English fort of Les Augustins, beyond the river, but suddenly they fled to their bridge of boats; while the English sallied out, yelling their insults at Joan. She turned, she gathered a few men, and charged. The English ran before her like sheep; she planted her banner again in the ditch. The French hurried back to her, a great Englishman, who guarded the breach, was shot; two French knights leaped in, the others followed, and the English took refuge in the redoubt of Les Tourelles, their strong fort at the bridge-head.

The Maid returned to Orleans, and, though it was a Friday, and she always fasted on Fridays, she was so weary that she ate some supper. A bit of bread, her page reports, was all that she usually ate. Now the generals sent to Joan and said that enough had been done. They had food, and could wait for another army from the king. "You have been with your council," she said, "I have been with mine. The wisdom of God is greater than yours. Rise early to-morrow, do better than your best, keep close by me; for to-morrow have I much to do, and more than ever yet I did, and to-morrow shall my blood flow from a wound above my breast."[15]

Joan had always said at Chinon that she would be wounded at Orleans. From a letter by a Flemish ambassador, written three weeks before the event happened, we know that this is true.[16]

Next morning Joan's host had got a fine fish for breakfast. "Keep it till evening, and I will bring you a God-damn" (an Englishman) "to eat his share," said the Maid, "and I will return by the bridge;" which was broken.

The generals did not wish to attack the bridge-tower, but Joan paid them no attention. They were glad enough to follow, lest she took the fort without them.

About half-past six in the morning the fight began. The French and Scottish leaped into the fosse, they set ladders against the walls, they reached the battlements, and were struck down by English swords and axes. Cannon-balls and great stones and arrows rained on them. "Fight on!" cried the Maid; "the place is ours." At one o'clock she set a ladder against the wall with her own hands, but was deeply wounded by an arrow, which pierced clean through between neck and shoulder. Joan wept, but seizing the arrow with her own hands she dragged it out. The men-at-arms wished to say magic spells over the wound to "charm" it, but this the Maid forbade as witchcraft. "Yet," says Dunois, "she did not withdraw from the battle, nor took any medicine for the wound; and the onslaught lasted from morning till eight at night, so that there was no hope of victory. Then I desired that the army should go back to the town, but the Maid came to me and bade me wait a little longer. Next she mounted her horse and rode into a vineyard, and there prayed for the space of seven minutes or eight. Then she returned, took her banner, and stood on the brink of the fosse. The English trembled when they saw her, but our men returned to the charge and met with no resistance. The English fled or were slain, and Glasdale, who had insulted the Maid, was drowned" (by the burning of the drawbridge

---

15. Following Pasquerel, her priest. *Procès*, iii, 109.
16. Quicherat, *Nouveaux Aperçus*, p. 76.

between the redoubt and Les Tourelles. The Maid in vain besought him, with tears, to surrender and be ransomed), "and we returned gladly into Orleans." The people of Orleans had a great share in this victory. Seeing the English hard pressed, they laid long beams across the broken arches of the bridge, and charged by this perilous way. The triumph was even more that of the citizens than of the army. Homer tells us how Achilles, alone and unarmed, stood by the fosse and shouted, and how all the Trojans fled. But here was a greater marvel; and the sight of the wounded girl, bowed beneath the weight of her banner, frighted stouter hearts than those of the men of Troy.

Joan returned, as she had prophesied, by the bridge, but she did not make her supper off the fish: she took a little bread dipped in wine and water, her wound was dressed, and she slept. Next day the English drew up their men in line of battle. The French went out to meet them, and would have begun the attack. Joan said that God would not have them fight.

"If the English attack, we shall defeat them; we are to let them go in peace if they will."

Mass was then said before the French army.

When the rite was done, Joan asked: "Do they face us, or have they turned their backs?"

It was the English backs that the French saw that day: Talbot's men were in full retreat on Meun.

From that hour May 8 is kept a holiday at Orleans in honour of Joan the Maiden. Never was there such a deliverance. In a week the Maid had driven a strong army, full of courage and well led, out of forts like Les Tourelles. The Duc d'Alençon visited it, and said that with a few men-at-arms he would have felt certain of holding it for a week against any strength however great. But Joan not only gave the French her spirit: her extraordinary courage in leading a new charge after so terrible a wound, "six inches deep," says d'Alençon, made the English think that they were fighting a force not of this world. And that is exactly what they were doing.

How Joan the Maid took Jargeau from the English

THE MAID HAD SHOWN HER sign, as she promised; she had rescued Orleans. Her next desire was to lead Charles to Reims, through a country occupied by the English, and to have him anointed there with the holy oil. Till this was done she could only regard him as Dauphin—king, indeed, by blood, but not by consecration.

After all that Joan had accomplished, the king and his advisers might have believed in her. She went to the castle of Loches, where Charles was: he received her kindly, but still he did not seem eager to go to Reims. It was a dangerous adventure, for which he and his favourites like La Tremouille had no taste. It seems that more learned men were asked to give their opinion. Was it safe and wise to obey the Maid? On May 14, only six days after the relief of Orleans, the famous Gerson wrote down his ideas. He believed in the Maid. The king had already trusted her without fear of being laughed at; she and the generals did not rely on the saints alone, but on courage, prudence, and skill. Even if, by ill fortune, she were to fail on a later day, the fault would not be hers, but would be God's punishment of French ingratitude. "Let us not harm, by our unbelief or injustice, the help which God has given us so wonderfully." Unhappily the French, or at least the Court, were unbelieving, ungrateful, unjust to Joan, and so she came to die, leaving her work half done. The Archbishop of Embrun said that Joan should always be consulted in great matters, as her wisdom was of God. And as long as the French took this advice they did well; when they distrusted and neglected the Maid they failed, and were defeated and dishonoured. Councils were now held at Tours, and time was wasted as usual. As usual, Joan was impatient. With Dunois, who tells the story, she went to see Charles at the castle of Loches. Some nobles and clergy were with him; Joan entered, knelt, and embraced his knees.

"Noble Dauphin," she said, "do not hold so many councils, and such weary ones, but come to Reims and receive the crown."

Harcourt asked her if her Voices, or "counsel" (as she called it) gave this advice.

She blushed and said: "I know what you mean, and will tell you gladly."

The king asked her if she wished to speak before so many people.

Yes, she would speak. When they doubted her she prayed, 'and then she heard a Voice saying to her:

"'*Fille Dé, va, va, va, je serai à ton aide, va!*'"[17]

---

17. "Daughter of God, go on, and I will help thee."

ANDREW LANG AND H. RIDER HAGGARD

"And when she heard this Voice she was right glad, and wished that she could always be as she was then; and as she spoke," says Dunois, "she rejoiced strangely, lifting her eyes to heaven." And still she repeated: "I will last for only one year, or little more; use me while you may."

Joan stirred the politicians at last. They would go to Reims, but could they leave behind them English garrisons in Jargeau, where Suffolk commanded, in Meun, where Talbot was, and in other strong places? Already, without Joan, the French had attacked Jargeau, after the rescue of Orleans, and had failed. Joan agreed to assail Jargeau. Her army was led by the "fair duke," d'Alençon. He had but lately come from prison in England, and his young wife was afraid to let him go to war. "Madame," said Joan, "I will bring him back safe, and even better than he is now." We shall see how she saved his life. It was now that Guy and André de Laval saw her, and wrote the description of her black horse and white armour. They followed with her gladly, believing that with her glory was to be won.

Let us tell what followed in the words of the Duc d'Alençon.

"We were about six hundred lances, who wished to go against the town of Jargeau, then held by the English. That night we slept in a wood, and next day came Dunois and Florence d'Illiers and some other captains. When we were all met we were about twelve hundred lances; and now arose a dispute among the captains, some thinking that we should attack the city, others not so, for they said that the English were very strong, and had many men.[18] Seeing this difference, Jeanne bade us have no fear of any numbers, nor doubt about attacking the English, because God was guiding us. She herself would rather be herding sheep than fighting, if she were not certain that God was with us. Thereon we rode to Jargeau, meaning to occupy the outlying houses, and there pass the night; but the English knew of our approach, and drove in our skirmishers. Seeing this, Jeanne took her banner and went to the front, bidding our men be in good heart. And they did so much that they held the suburbs of Jargeau that night. . . Next morning we got ready our artillery, and brought guns up against the town. After some days a council was held, and I, with others, was ill content with La Hire, who was said to have parleyed with Lord Suffolk. La Hire was sent for, and

---

18. Sir Walter Scott reckons that there were five men to each "lance"; perhaps four men is more usually the right number.

came. Then it was decided to storm the town, and the heralds cried, 'To the attack!' and Jeanne said to me, 'Forward, gentle duke.' I thought it was too early, but she said, 'Doubt not; the hour is come when God pleases. Ah, gentle duke, are you afraid? Know you not that I promised your wife to bring you back safe and sound?' as indeed she had said. As the onslaught was given, Jeanne bade me leave the place where I stood, 'or yonder gun,' pointing to one on the walls, 'will slay you.' Then I withdrew, and a little later de Lude was slain in that very place. And I feared greatly, considering the prophecy of the Maid. Then we both went together to the onslaught; and Suffolk cried for a parley, but no man marked him, and we pressed on. Jeanne was climbing a ladder, banner in hand, when her flag was struck by a stone, and she also was struck on her head, but her light helmet saved her. She leaped up again, crying, 'Friends, friends, on, on! Our Lord has condemned the English. They are ours; be of good heart.' In that moment Jargeau was taken, and the English fled to the bridges, we following, and more than eleven hundred of them were slain."

One Englishman at least died well. He stood up on the battlements, and dashed down the ladders till he was shot by a famous marksman of Lorraine.

Suffolk and his brother were taken prisoners. According to one account, written at the time, Suffolk surrendered to the Maid, as "the most valiant woman in the world." And thus the Maid stormed Jargeau.

How the Maid Defeated the English at Pathay,
and of the Strange Guide

THE FRENCH SLEW SOME OF their prisoners at Jargeau. Once Joan saw a man-at-arms strike down a prisoner. She leaped from her horse, and laid the wounded Englishman's head on her breast, consoling him, and bade a priest come and hear his confession. Cruel and cowardly deeds are done in all wars, but when was there ever such a general as the Maid, to comfort the dying?

From Jargeau the Maid rode back to Orleans, where the people could not look on her enough, and made great festival. Many men came in to fight under her flag, among them Richemont, who had been on bad terms with Charles, the uncrowned king. Then Joan took the bridge-fort at Meun, which the English held; next she drove the English at Beaugency into the citadel, and out of the town.

As to what happened next, we have the story of Wavrin, who was fighting on the English side under Fastolf.[19] The garrison of the English in Beaugency, he says, did not know whether to hold out or to yield. Talbot reported all this to Bedford, at Paris, and large forces were sent to relieve Beaugency. Wavrin rode with his captain, Fastolf, to Senville, where Talbot joined them, and a council was held. Fastolf said that the English had lost heart, and that Beaugency should be left to its fate, while the rest held out in strong places and waited for reinforcements. But Talbot cried that, if he had only his own people, he would fight the French, with the help of God and St. George. Next morning Fastolf repeated what he had said, and declared that they would lose all King Henry had won, But Talbot was for fighting. So they marched to a place between Meun and Beaugency, and drew up in order of battle. The French saw them, and occupied a strong position on a little hill. The English then got ready, and invited the French to come down and fight on the plain. But Joan was not so chivalrous as James IV at Flodden.

"Go you to bed to-night, for it is late; to-morrow, so please God and Our Lady, we will see you at close quarters."

The English then rode to Meun, and cannonaded the bridge-fort, which was held by the French. They hoped to take the bridge, cross it, march to Beaugency, and relieve the besieged there. But that very night Beaugency surrendered to the Maid! She then bade her army march on the English, who were retreating to Paris as soon as they heard how Beaugency had yielded. But how was the Maid to find the English? "Ride forward," she cried, "and you shall have a sure guide." They had a guide, and a strange one.

The English were marching towards Paris, near Pathay, when their *éclaireurs* (who beat the country on all sides) came in with the news that the French were following. But the French knew not where the English were, because the deserted and desolate country was overgrown with wood.

Talbot decided to do what the English did at Creçy, where they won so glorious a victory. He lined the hedges in a narrow way with five hundred archers of his best, and he sent a galloper to bring thither the rest of his army. On came the French, not seeing the English in ambush. In a few minutes they would have been shot down, and choked the pass

---

19. In *Procès*, iv. 414.

with dying men and horses. But now was the moment for the strange guide.

A stag was driven from cover by the French, and ran blindly among the ambushed English bowmen. Not knowing that the French were so near, and being archers from Robin Hood's country, who loved a deer, they raised a shout, and probably many an arrow flew at the stag. The French *éclaireurs* heard the cry, they saw the English, and hurried back with the news.

"Forward!" cried the Maid; "if they were hung to the clouds we have them. To-day the gentle king will gain such a victory as never yet did he win."[20]

The French dashed into the pass before Talbot had secured it. Fastolf galloped up, but the English thought that he was in flight; the captain of the advanced guard turned his horse about and made off. Talbot was taken, Fastolf fled, "making more sorrow than ever yet did man." The French won a great victory. They needed their spurs, as the Maid had told them that they would, to follow their flying foes. The English lost some 3,000 men. In the evening Talbot, as a prisoner, was presented to the Duc d'Alençon.

"You did not expect this in the morning?" said the duke.

"Fortune of war!" said Talbot.

So ended the day of Pathay, and the adventure of the Strange Guide.

How the Maid had the King Crowned at Reims

HERE ARE THE EXPLOITS WHICH the Maid and the loyal French did in one week. She took Jargeau on June 11; on June 15 she seized the bridge of Meun; Beaugency yielded to her on June 17; on June 18 she defeated the English army at Pathay. Now sieges were long affairs in those days, as they are even to-day, when cannon are so much more powerful than they were in Joan's time. Her success seemed a miracle to the world.

This miracle, like all miracles, was wrought by faith. Joan believed in herself, in her country, and in God. It was not by visions and by knowing things strangely that she conquered, but by courage, by strength (on one occasion she never put off her armour for six days and six nights), and by inspiring the French with the sight of her valour. Without her

---

20. d'Alençon, *Procès*, iii. 98.

visions, indeed, she would never have gone to war. She often said so. But, being at war, her word was "Help yourselves, and God will help you." Who could be lazy or a coward when a girl set such an example?

The King of France and his favourites could be indolent and cowards. Had Charles VII been such a man as Charles Stuart was in 1745, his foot would have been in the stirrup, and his lance in rest. In three months the English would have been driven into the sea. But the king loitered about the castles of the Loire with his favourite, La Tremouille, and his adviser, the Archbishop of Reims. They wasted the one year of Joan. There were jealousies against the Constable de Richemont of Brittany who had come with all his lances to follow the lily flag. If once Charles were king indeed and the English driven out, La Tremouille would cease to be powerful. This dastard sacrificed the Maid in the end, as he was ready to sacrifice France to his own private advantage.

At last, with difficulty, Charles was brought to visit Reims, and consent to be crowned like his ancestors. Seeing that he was never likely to move, Joan left the town where he was and went off into the country. This retreat brought Charles to his senses. The towns which he passed by yielded to him; Joan went and summoned each. "Now she was with the king in the centre, now with the rearguard, now with the van." The town of Troyes, where there was an English garrison, did not wish to yield. There was a council in the king's army: they said they could not take the place.

"In two days it shall be yours, by force or by good will," said the Maid.

"Six days will do," said the chancellor, "if you are sure you speak truth."

Joan made ready for an attack. She was calling "Forward!" when the town surrendered. Reims, after some doubts, yielded also, on July 16, and all the people, with shouts of "*Noel!*" welcomed the king. On July 17 the king was crowned and anointed with the Holy Oil by that very Archbishop of Reims who always opposed Joan. The Twelve Peers of France were not all present—some were on the English side—but Joan stood by Charles, her banner in her hand. "It bore the brunt, and deserved to share the renown," she said later to her accusers.

When the ceremony was ended, and the Dauphin Charles was a crowned and anointed king, the Maid knelt weeping at his feet.

"Gentle king," she said, "now is accomplished the will of God, who desired that you should come to Reims to be consecrated, and to prove that you are the true king and the kingdom is yours."

Then all the knights wept for joy.

The king bade Joan choose her reward. Already horses, rich armour, jewelled daggers, had been given to her. These, adding to the beauty and glory of her aspect, had made men follow her more gladly, and for that she valued them. She, too, made gifts to noble ladies, and gave much to the poor. She only wanted money to wage the war with, not for herself. Her family was made noble; on their shield, between two lilies, a sword upholds the crown. Her father was at Reims, and saw her in her glory. What reward, then, was Joan to choose? She chose nothing for herself, but that her native village of Domremy should be free from taxes. This news her father carried home from the splendid scene at Reims.

Would that we could leave the Maiden here, with Orleans saved, and her king crowned! Would that she, who wept when her saints left her in her visions, and who longed to follow them, could have been carried by them to their Paradise!

But Joan had another task; she was to be foiled by the cowardice of her king; she was to be captured, possibly by treachery; she was to be tried with the most cruel injustice; she was to die by fire; and was to set, through months of agony, such an example of wisdom, courage, and loyal honour as never was shown by man.

Did Joan look forward to her end, did she know that her days were numbered? On the journey to Reims she met some Domremy people at Chalons, and told them that she "feared nothing but treachery." Perhaps she already suspected the political enemies, the Archbishop of Reims and La Tremouille, who were to spoil her mission.

As they went from Reims after the coronation, Dunois and the archbishop were riding by her rein. The people cheered and cried *Noel*.

"They are a good people," said Joan. "Never saw I any more joyous at the coming of their king. Ah, would that I might be so happy when I end my days as to be buried here!"

Said the archbishop:

"Oh, Jeanne, in what place do you hope to die?"

Then she said:

"Where it pleases God; for I know not that hour, nor that place, more than ye do. But would to God, my maker, that now I might depart, and lay down my arms, and help my father and mother, and keep their sheep with my brothers and my sister, who would rejoice to see me!"[21]

21. Dunois. *Procès*, iii. 14.

Some writers have reported Joan's words as if she meant that she wished the king to let her go home and leave the wars. In their opinion Joan was only acting under heavenly direction till the consecration of Charles. Afterwards, like Hal of the Wynd, she was "fighting for her own hand," they think, and therefore she did not succeed. But from the first Joan threatened to drive the English quite out of France, and she also hoped to bring the Duc d'Orléans home from captivity in England. If her Voices had told her *not* to go on after the coronation, she would probably have said so at her trial, when she mentioned one or two acts of disobedience to her Voices. Again, had she been anxious to go home, Charles VII and his advisers would have been only too glad to let her go. They did not wish her to lead them into dangerous places, and they hated obeying her commands.

Some French authors have, very naturally, wished to believe that the Maid could make no error, and could not fail; they therefore draw a line between what she did up to the day of Reims, and what she did afterwards. They hold that she was divinely led till the coronation, and not later. But it is difficult to agree with them here. As we saw, Gerson told the French that by injustice and ingratitude they might hinder the success of the Maid. His advice was a prophecy.

IV

How the Maid Rode to Paris

WHAT WAS TO BE DONE after the crowning of the king? Bedford, the regent for the child Henry VI, expected to see Joan under the walls of Paris. He was waiting for the troops which the Cardinal of Winchester had collected in England as a crusading army against the Hussite heretics, a kind of Protestants who were giving trouble. Bedford induced Winchester to bring his men to France, but they had not arrived. The Duke of Burgundy, the head of the great French party which opposed Charles, had been invited by the Maid to Reims. Again she wrote to him: "Make a firm, good peace with the King of France," she said; "forgive each other with kind hearts"—for the Duke's father had been murdered by the friends of Charles. "I pray and implore you, with joined hands, fight not against France. Great pity it would be of the great battle and bloodshed if your men come against us."

The Duke of Burgundy, far from listening to Joan's prayer, left Paris and went to raise men for the English. Meanwhile Charles was going from town to town, and all received him gladly. But Joan soon began to see that, instead of marching west from Reims to Paris, the army was being led south-west towards the Loire. There the king would be safe among his dear castles, where he could live indoors, "in wretched little rooms," and take his ease. Thus Bedford was able to throw 5,000 men of Winchester's into Paris, and even dared to come out and hunt for the French king. The French should have struck at Paris at once as Joan desired. The delays were excused, because the Duke of Burgundy had promised to surrender Paris in a fortnight. But this he did merely to gain time. Joan knew this, and said there would be no peace but at the lance-point.

Here we get the best account of what happened from Perceval de Cagny, a knight in the household of the Duc d'Alençon. He wrote his book in 1436, only five years after Joan was burned, and he spoke of what he knew well, as a follower of Joan's friend, "the fair duke." The French and English armies kept watching each other, and there were skirmishes near Senlis. On August 15 the Maid and d'Alençon hoped for a battle. But the English had fortified their position in the night with ditches, palisades, and a "laager" of wagons. Come out they would not, so Joan rode up to their fortification, standard in hand, struck the palisade, and challenged them to sally forth. She even offered to let them march out and draw themselves up in line of battle. La Tremouille thought this a fine opportunity of distinguishing himself. He rode into the skirmish, his horse fell with him, but, by evil luck, he was rescued. We do not hear that La Tremouille risked himself again.[22] The Maid stayed on the field all night, and next day made a retreat, hoping to draw the English out of their fort. But they were too wary, and went back to Paris.

More towns came in to Charles. Beauvais yielded, and the Bishop of Beauvais, Pierre Cauchon, had to fly to the English. He revenged himself by managing Joan's trial and having her burned. Compiègne, an important place north of Paris, yielded, and was handed to Guillaume de Flavy as governor. In rescuing this fatal place later, Joan was taken prisoner. Now the fortnight was over, after which the Duke of Burgundy

---

22. Journal du Siège. *Procès*, iv. 195. As it stands, this authority is thirty years later than the events.

was to surrender Paris. But he did nothing of the kind, and there were more "long weary councils," and a truce was arranged with Burgundy till Christmas. But the Maid was weary of words. She called the Duc d'Alençon and said: "My fair duke, array your men, for, by my staff, I would fain see Paris more closely than I have seen it yet."

On August 23 the Maid and d'Alençon left the king at Compiègne and rode to St. Denis, where were the tombs of the kings of France. "And when the king heard that they were at St. Denis, he came, very sore against his will, as far as Senlis, and it seems that his advisers were contrary to the will of the Maid, of the Duc d'Alençon, and of their company."

The great captains, Dunois, Xaintrailles, d'Alençon, were soldiers, and the king's advisers and favourites were clergymen, like the Archbishop of Reims, or indolent men of peace, like La Tremouille. They declared, after the Maid was captured, that she "took too much on herself," and they were glad of her fall. But she had shown that nobody but herself and her soldiers and captains were of any use to France.

The king was afraid to go near Paris, but Bedford was afraid to stay in the town. He went to Rouen, the strongest English hold in Normandy, leaving the Burgundian army and 2,000 English in Paris.

Every day the Maid and d'Alençon rode from St. Denis and insulted the gates of Paris, and observed the best places for an attack in force. And still Charles dallied and delayed, still the main army did not come up. Meanwhile Paris was strengthened by the English and Burgundians. The people of the city were told that Charles intended to plunder the place and utterly destroy it, "which is difficult to believe," says the Clerk of Parliament, who was in the city at that time.[23] It was "difficult to believe," but the Paris people believed it, and, far from rising for their king and country, they were rather in arms against the Maid. They had no wish to fall in a general massacre, as the English and Burgundians falsely told them would be their fate.

Thus the delay of the king gave the English time to make Paris almost impregnable, and to frighten the people, who, had Charles marched straight from Reims, would have yielded as Reims did.

---

23. This man was Clement de Fauquemberque. When he recorded the relief of Orleans, he drew on the margin of his paper a little fancy sketch of Joan, with long hair, a woman's dress, a sword, and a banner with the monogram of Jesus. This sketch still exists. (*Procès*, iv. 451.)

d'Alençon kept going to Senlis urging Charles to come up with the main army. He went on September 1—the king promised to start next day. d'Alençon returned to the Maid, the king still loitered. At last d'Alençon brought him to St. Denis on September 7, and there was a skirmish that day.

How the Maid was Wounded in Attacking Paris, and how the King Would not Let the Assault Begin Again

IN ALL DESCRIPTIONS OF BATTLES different accounts are given, each man telling what he himself saw, or what he remembers. As to the assault on Paris on September 8, the Maid herself said a few words at her trial. Her Voices had neither commanded her to attack nor to abstain from attacking. Her opinion was that the captains and leaders on her side only meant to skirmish in force, and to do deeds of chivalry. But her own intention was to press onwards, and, by her example, to make the army follow her. It was thus that she took Les Tourelles at Orleans. This account scarcely agrees with what we read in the book of Perceval de Cagny, who was with his lord, the Duc d'Alençon. He says that about eight on the morning of September 8, the day of Our Lady, the army set forth; some were to storm the town; another division was to remain under cover and protect the former if a sally was made by the English. The Maid, the Marshal de Rais, and De Gaucourt led the attack on the Porte St. Honoré.[24] Standard in hand, the Maid leaped into the fosse near the pig market. "The assault was long and fierce, and it was marvel to hear the noise of cannons and culverins from the walls, and to see the clouds of arrows. Few of those in the fosse with the Maid were struck, though many others on horse and foot were wounded with arrows and stone cannon-balls, but by God's grace and the Maid's good fortune, there was none of them but could return to camp unhelped. The assault lasted from noon till dusk, say eight in the evening. After sunset the Maid was struck by a crossbow bolt in the thigh; and, after she was hurt, she cried but the louder that all should attack, and that the place was taken. But as night had now fallen, and she was wounded, and the men-at-arms were weary with the long attack, De Gaucourt and others came and

---

24. This was not far from the present Théâtre Français. The statue of the Maid, on horseback, is near the place where she was wounded.

found her, and, against her will, brought her forth from the fosse. And so ended that onslaught. But right sad she was to leave, and said, 'By my bâton, the place would have been taken.' They put her on horseback, and led her to her quarters, and all the rest of the king's company who that day had come from St. Denis."

So Cagny tells the story. He was, we may believe, with d'Alençon and the party covering the attack. Jean Chartier, who was living at the time, adds that the Maid did not know that the inner moats were full of water. When she reached the water, she had faggots and other things thrown in to fill up a passage. At nightfall she would not retreat, and at last d'Alençon came and forced her to return. The Clerk of Parliament, who, of course, was within the walls, says that the attack lasted till ten or eleven o'clock at night, and that, in Paris, there was a cry that all was lost.

Joan behaved as gallantly as she did at Les Tourelles. Though wounded she was still pressing on, still encouraging her men, but she was not followed. She was not only always eager to attack, but she never lost heart, she never lost grip. An army of men as brave as Joan would have been invincible.

"Next day," says Cagny, "in spite of her wound, she was first in the field. She went to d'Alençon and bade him sound the trumpets for the charge. d'Alençon and the other captains were of the same mind as the Maid, and Montmorency with sixty gentlemen and many lances came in, though he had been on the English side before. So they began to march on Paris, but the king sent messengers, the Duc de Bar, and the Comte de Clermont, and compelled the Maid and the captains to return to St. Denis. Right sorry were they, yet they must obey the king. They hoped to take Paris from the other side, by a bridge which the Duc d'Alençon had made across the Seine. But the king knew the duke's and the Maid's design, and caused the bridge to be broken down, and a council was held, and the king desired to depart and go to the Loire, to the great grief of the Maid. When she saw that they would go, she dedicated her armour, and hung it up before the statue of Our Lady at St. Denis, and so right sadly went away in company with the king. And thus were broken the will of the Maid and the army of the king."

The politicians had triumphed. They had thwarted the Maid, they had made her promise to take Paris of no avail. They had destroyed the confidence of men in the banner that had never gone back. Now they might take their ease, now they might loiter in the gardens of the Loire. The Maid had failed, by their design, and by their cowardice.

The treachery that she, who feared nothing else, had long dreaded, was accomplished now. "The will of the Maid and the army of the king were broken."[25]

How the Maid and her Fair Duke
were Separated from Each Other

THE KING NOW WENT FROM one pleasant tower on the Loire to another, taking the Maid with him. Meanwhile, the English took and plundered some of the cities which had yielded to Charles, and they carried off the Maid's armour from the chapel in Saint Denis, where she had dedicated it, "because *Saint Denis!* is the cry of France." Her Voices had bidden her stay at Saint Denis, but this she was not permitted to do, and now she must hear daily how the loyal towns that she had won were plundered by the English. The French garrisons also began to rob, as they had done before she came. There was "great pity in France" again, and all her work seemed wasted. The Duc d'Alençon went to his own place of Beaumont, but he returned, and offered to lead an army against the English in Normandy, if the Maid might march with him. Then he would have had followers in plenty, for the people had not wholly lost faith. "But La Tremouille, and Gaucourt, and the Archbishop of Reims, who managed the king and the war, would not consent, nor suffer the Maid and the duke to be together, nor ever again might they meet." So says Cagny, and he adds that the Maid loved the fair duke above other men, "and did for him what she would do for no other." She had saved his life at Jargeau, but where was the duke when Joan was a prisoner? We do not know, but we may believe that he, at least, would have helped her if he could. They were separated by the jealousy of cowards, who feared that the duke might win too much renown and become too powerful.

How Marvellously the Maid Took Saint-pierre-le-moustier

EVEN THE BANKS OF LOIRE, where the king loved to be, were not free from the English. They held La Charité and Saint-Pierre-le-Moustier.

---

25. Paris, as the Clerk of Parliament wrote in his note-book, could only be taken by blockade. It was a far larger city than Orleans, and we see how long the English, in the height of courage and confidence, were delayed by Orleans. But the Maid did not know the word "impossible." Properly supported, she could probably have taken Paris by assault; at the least she would not have left it while she lived.

Joan wanted to return to Paris, but the council sent her to take La Charité and Saint-Pierre-le-Moustier. This town she attacked first. Her squire, a gentleman named d'Aulon, was with her, and described what he saw. "When they had besieged the place for some time, an assault was commanded, but, for the great strength of the forts and the numbers of the enemy, the French were forced to give way. At that hour, I who speak was wounded by an arrow in the heel, and could not stand or walk without crutches. But I saw the Maid holding her ground with a handful of men, and, fearing ill might come of it, I mounted a horse and rode to her, asking what she was doing there alone, and why she did not retreat like the others. She took the *salade* from her head, and answered that she was not alone, but had in her company fifty thousand of her people; and that go she would not till she had taken that town.

"But, whatever she said, I saw that she had with her but four men or five, as others also saw, wherefore I bade her retreat. Then she commanded me to have faggots brought, and planks to bridge fosses. And, as she spoke to me, she cried in a loud voice, 'All of you, bring faggots to fill the fosse.' And this was done, whereat I greatly marvelled, and instantly that town was taken by assault with no great resistance. And all that the Maid did seemed to me rather deeds divine than natural, and it was impossible that so young a maid should do such deeds without the will and guidance of Our Lord."

This was the last great feat of arms wrought by the Maid. As at Les Tourelles she won by sheer dint of faith and courage, and so might she have done at Paris, but for the king. At this town the soldiers wished to steal the sacred things in the church, and the goods laid up there. "But the Maid right manfully forbade and hindered them, nor ever would she permit any to plunder." So says Reginald Thierry, who was with her at this siege. Once a Scottish man-at-arms let her know that her dinner was made of a stolen calf, and she was very angry, wishing to strike that Scot. He came from a land where "lifting cattle" was thought rather a creditable action.

How the Maid Waited Wearily at Court

FROM HER LATEST SIEGE THE Maid rode to attack La Charité. But, though the towns helped her as well as they might with money and food, her force was too small, and was too ill provided with everything, for the king did not send supplies. She raised the siege and departed in great displeasure. The king was not unkind, he ennobled her and her family, and permitted the dignity to descend through daughters as well as sons; no one else was ever so honoured. Her brothers called themselves Du Lys, from the lilies of their crest, but Joan kept her name and her old banner. She was trailed after the Court from place to place; for three weeks she stayed with a lady who describes her as very devout and constantly in church. People said to Joan that it was easy for her to be brave, as she knew she would not be slain, but she answered that she had no more assurance of safety than any one of them. Thinking her already a saint, people brought her things to touch.

"Touch them yourselves," she said; "your touch is as good as mine."

She wore a little cheap ring, which her father and mother had given her, inscribed JHESU MARIA, and she believed that with this ring she had touched the body of St. Catherine. But she was humble, and thought herself no saint, though surely there never was a better. She gave great alms, saying that she was sent to help the poor and needy. Such was the Maid in peace.

How the Maid Met an Impostor

THERE WAS A CERTAIN WOMAN named Catherine de la Rochelle, who gave out that she had visions. A beautiful lady, dressed in cloth of gold, came to her by night, and told her who had hidden treasures. These she offered to discover that there might be money for the wars, which Joan needed sorely. A certain preacher, named Brother Richard, wished to make use of this pretender, but Joan said that she must first herself see the fair lady in cloth of gold. So she sat up with Catherine till midnight, and then fell asleep, when the lady appeared, so Catherine said. Joan slept next day, and watched all the following night. Of course the fair lady never came. Joan bade Catherine go back to her family; she needed money for the war, but not money got by false pretences. So she told the king that the whole story was mere folly. This woman afterwards lied against the Maid when she was a prisoner.

How the Maid's Voices Prophesied of her Taking

WINTER MELTED INTO SPRING; THE truce with Burgundy was prolonged, but the Burgundians fought under English colours. The king did nothing, but in Normandy La Hire rode in arms to the gates of Rouen. Paris became doubtfully loyal to the English. The Maid could be idle no longer. Without a word to the king she rode to Lagny, "for there they had fought bravely against the English." These men were Scots, under Sir Hugh Kennedy. In mid-April she was at Melun. There "she heard her Voices almost every day, and many a time they told her that she would presently be taken prisoner." Her year was over, and as the Voices prophesied her wound at Orleans, now they prophesied her captivity. She prayed that she might die as soon as she was taken, without the long sorrow of imprisonment. Then her Voices told her to bear graciously whatever befell her, for so it must be. But they told her not the hour of her captivity. "If she had known the hour she would not then have gone to war. And often she prayed them to tell her of that hour, but they did not answer."

These words are Joan's. She spoke them to her judges at Rouen.

Among all her brave deeds this was the bravest. Whatever the source of her Voices was, she believed in what they said. She rode to fight with far worse than death under shield before her eyes, knowing certainly that her English foes would take her, they who had often threatened to burn her.

How the Maid Took Franquet D'Arras

THERE WAS IN THESE PARTS a robber chief on the Burgundian side named Franquet d'Arras. The Maid had been sent, as she said, to help the poor who were oppressed by these brigands. Hearing that Franquet, with three or four hundred men-at-arms, was near Lagny-sur-Marne, the Maid rode out to seek him with four hundred French and Scots. The fight is described in one way by Monstrelet, in another by Cagny and Joan herself. Monstrelet, being a Burgundian writer, says that Franquet made a gallant resistance till he was overwhelmed by numbers, as the Maid called out the garrison of Lagny. Cagny says that Franquet's force was greater than that of the Maid who took him. However this may be, Franquet was a knight, and so should have been kept prisoner till he paid his ransom. Monstrelet tells us that Joan had his head cut off. She herself told her judges that Franquet confessed to being a traitor, robber, and murderer; that the magistrates of Senlis and Lagny claimed him as a criminal; that she tried to exchange him for a prisoner of her own party, but that her man died, that Franquet had a fair trial, and that then she allowed justice to take its course. She was asked if she paid money to the captor of Franquet.

"I am not treasurer of France, to pay such moneys," she answered haughtily.

Probably Franquet deserved to die, but a trial by his enemies was not likely to be a fair trial.

At Lagny the Maid left a gentler memory. She was very fond of children, and had a girl's love of babies. A boy of three days old was dying or seemed dead, and the girls of Lagny carried it to the statue of Our Lady in their church, and there prayed over it. For three days, ever since its birth, the baby had lain in a trance without sign of life, so that they dared not christen it. "It was black as my doublet," said Joan at her trial, where she wore mourning. Joan knelt with the other girls and prayed; colour came back into the child's face, it gasped thrice, was baptised, then died, and was buried in holy ground. So Joan said at her trial. She claimed no share in this good fortune, and never pretended that she worked miracles.

How the Maid Fought her Last Fight

THE NAME OF JOAN WAS now such a terror to the English that men deserted rather than face her in arms. At this time the truce with Burgundy ended, and the duke openly set out to besiege the strong town of Compiègne, held by de Flavy for France. Joan hurried to Compiègne, whence she made two expeditions which were defeated by treachery. Perhaps she thought of this, perhaps of the future, when in the church of Compiègne she declared one day to a crowd of children whom she loved that she knew she was sold and betrayed. Old men who had heard her told this tale long afterwards.

Burgundy had invested Compiègne, when Joan, with four hundred men, rode into the town secretly at dawn. That day Joan led a sally against the Burgundians. Her Voices told her nothing, good or bad, she says. The Burgundians were encamped at Margny and at Clairoix, the English at Venette, villages on a plain near the walls. Joan crossed the bridge on a grey charger, in a surcoat of crimson silk, rode through the redoubt beyond the bridge, and attacked the Burgundians. Flavy in the town was to prevent the English from attacking her in the rear. He had boats on the river to secure Joan's retreat if necessary.

Joan swept through Margny, driving the Burgundians before her;

the garrison of Clairoix came to their help; the battle was doubtful. Meanwhile the English came up; they could not have reached the Burgundians, to aid them, but some of the Maid's men, seeing the English standards, fled. The English followed them under the walls of Compiègne; the gate of the redoubt was closed to prevent the English from entering with the runaways. Like Hector under Troy, the Maid was shut out from the town which she came to save.

Joan was with her own foremost line when the rear fled. They told her of her danger, she heeded not. For the last time rang out in that girlish voice: *"Allez avant! Forward, they are ours!"*

Her men seized her bridle and turned her horse's head about. The English held the entrance from the causeway; Joan and a few men (her brother was one of them) were driven into a corner of the outer wall. A rush was made at Joan. "Yield I yield! give your faith to me!" each man cried.

"I have given my faith to Another," she said, "and I will keep my oath."

Her enemies confess that on this day Joan did great feats of arms, covering the rear of her force when they had to fly.

Some French historians hold that the gates were closed by treason that the Maid might be taken. We may hope that this was not so; the commander of Compiègne held his town successfully for the king, and was rescued by Joan's friend, the brave Pothon de Xaintrailles.

How the Maid Leaped from the Tower of Beaurevoir

THE SAD STORY THAT IS still to tell shall be shortly told. There is no word nor deed of the Maid's, in captivity as in victory, that is not to her immortal honour. But the sight of the wickedness of men, their cowardice, cruelty, greed, ingratitude, is not a thing to linger over.

The Maid, as a prisoner of the Bastard of Wandomme, himself a man of Jean de Luxembourg, was led to Margny, where the Burgundian and English captains rejoiced over her. They had her at last, the girl who had driven them from fort and field. Luxembourg claimed her and carried her to Beaulieu. Not a French lance was laid in rest to rescue her; not a sou did the king send to ransom her. Where were Dunois and d'Alençon, Xaintrailles and La Hire? The bold Buccleugh, who carried Kinmont Willie out of Carlisle Castle, would not have left the Maid unrescued at Beaulieu. "What is there that a man does *not* dare?" he said to the angry Queen Elizabeth. But Dunois, d'Alençon, Xaintrailles, La Hire, dared all things. Something which we do not know of must have held these heroes back, and, being ignorant, it does not become us to blame them.

Joan was the very spirit of chivalry, but in that age of chivalry she was shamefully deserted. As a prisoner of war she should properly have been held to ransom. But, within two days of her capture, the Vicar-General of the Inquisition in France claimed her as a heretic and a witch. The English knights let the priests and the University of Paris judge and burn the girl whom they seldom dared to face in war. The English were glad enough to use French priests and doctors who would sell themselves to the task of condemning and burning their maiden enemy. She was the enemy of the English, and they did actually believe in witchcraft. The English were hideously cruel and superstitious: we may leave the French to judge Jean de Luxembourg, who sold the girl to England; Charles, who moved not a finger to help her; Bishop Cauchon and the University of Paris, who judged her lawlessly and condemned her to the stake; and the Archbishop of Reims, who said that she had deserved her fall. There is dishonour in plenty; let these false Frenchmen of her time divide their shares among themselves.

From Beaulieu, where she lay from May to August, Luxembourg carried his precious prize to Beaurevoir, near Cambrai, further from the French armies. He need not have been alarmed, not a French sword was drawn to help the Maid. At Beaurevoir, Joan was kindly treated by the ladies of the Castle. These ladies alone upheld the honour of the great name of France. They knelt and wept before Jean de Luxembourg, imploring him not to sell Joan to Burgundy, who sold her again to England. May their names ever be honoured! One of the gentlemen of the place, on the other hand, was rude to Joan, as he confessed thirty years later.

Joan was now kept in a high tower at Beaurevoir, and was allowed to walk on the leads. She knew she was sold to England, she had heard that the people of Compiègne were to be massacred. She would rather die than fall into English hands, "rather give her soul to God, than her body to the English." But she hoped to escape and relieve Compiègne. She, therefore, prayed for counsel to her Saints; might she leap from the top of the tower? Would they not bear her up in their hands? St. Catherine bade her not to leap; God would help her and the people of Compiègne.

Then, for the first time as far as we know, the Maid wilfully disobeyed her Voices. She leaped from the tower. They found her, not wounded, not a limb was broken, but stunned. She knew not what had happened; they told her she had leaped down. For three days she could not eat, "yet was she comforted by St. Catherine, who bade her confess and seek pardon of God, and told her that, without fail, they of Compiègne should be relieved before Martinmas." This prophecy was fulfilled. Joan was more troubled about Compiègne, than about her own coming doom. She was already sold to the English, like a sheep to the slaughter; they bought their French bishop Cauchon, he summoned his shavelings, the doctors of the University and of the Inquisition.

The chivalry of England locked up the Maid in an iron cage at Rouen. The rest was easy to men of whom all, or almost all, were the slaves of superstition, fear, and greed. They were men like ourselves, and no worse, if perhaps no better, but their especial sins and temptations were those to which few of us are inclined. We, like Charles, are very capable of deserting, or at least of delaying to rescue, our bravest and best, like Gordon in Khartoum. But, as we are not afraid of witches, we do not cage and burn girls of nineteen. If we were as ignorant as our ancestors on this point, no doubt we should be as cowardly and cruel.

V

How the Maid was Tried and Condemned,
and how Bravely she Died

ABOUT THE TRIAL AND THE death of the Maid, I have not the heart to write a long story. Some points are to be remembered. The person who conducted the trial, itself illegal, was her deadly enemy, the false Frenchman, the Bishop of Beauvais, Cauchon, whom she and her men had turned out of his bishoprick. It is most unjust and unheard of, that any one should be tried by a judge who is his private enemy. Next, Joan was kept in strong irons day and night, and she, the most modest of maidens, was always guarded by five brutal English soldiers of the lowest rank. Again, she was not allowed to receive the Holy Communion as she desired with tears. Thus weakened by long captivity and ill usage, she, an untaught girl, was questioned repeatedly for three months, by the most cunning and learned doctors in law of the Paris University. Often many spoke at once, to perplex her mind. But Joan always showed a wisdom which confounded them, and which is at least as extraordinary as her skill in war. She would never swear an oath to answer *all* their questions. About herself, and all matters bearing on her own conduct, she would answer. About the king and the secrets of the king, she would not answer. If they forced her to reply about these things, she frankly said, she would not tell them the truth. The whole object of the trial was to prove that she dealt with powers of evil, and that her king had been crowned and aided by the devil. Her examiners, therefore, attacked her day by day, in public and in her dungeon, with questions about these visions which she held sacred, and could only speak of with a blush among her friends. Had she answered (as a lawyer said at the time), "*it seemed to me* I saw a saint," no man could have condemned her. Probably she did not know this, for she was not allowed to have an advocate of her own party, and she, a lonely girl, was opposed to the keenest and most learned lawyers of France. But she maintained that she certainly did see, hear, and touch her Saints, and that they came to her by the will of God. This was called blasphemy and witchcraft. And now came in the fatal Fairies! She was accused of dealing with devils under the Tree of Domremy.

Most was made of her refusal to wear woman's dress. For this she seems to have had two reasons; first, that to give up her old dress would have been to acknowledge that her mission was ended; next, for reasons of modesty, she being alone in prison among ruffianly men. She would wear woman's dress if they would let her take the Holy Communion, but this they refused. To these points she was constant, she would not deny her visions; she would not say one word against her king, "the noblest Christian in the world" she called him, who had deserted her. She would not wear woman's dress in prison. We must remember that, as she was being tried by churchmen, she should have been, as she often prayed to be, in a prison of the church, attended by women. They set a spy on her, a caitiff priest named L'oyseleur, who pretended to be her friend, and who betrayed her. The English soldiers were allowed to bully, threaten, and frighten away every one who gave her any advice. They took her to the torture-chamber, and threatened her with torture, but from this even these priests shrunk, except a few more cruel and cowardly than the rest. Finally, they put her up in public, opposite a pile of wood ready for burning, and then set a priest to preach at her. All through her trial, her Voices bade her "answer boldly," in three months she would give her last answer, in three months "she would be free with great victory, and come into the Kingdom of Paradise." In three months from the first day of her trial she went free through the gate of fire. Boldly she answered, and wisely. She would submit the truth of her visions to the Church, that is, to God, and the Pope. But she would *not* submit them to "the Church," if that meant the clergy round her. At last, in fear of the fire, and the stake before her, and on promise of being taken to a kindlier prison among women, and released from chains, she promised to "abjure," to renounce her visions, and submit to the Church, that is to Cauchon, and her other priestly enemies. Some little note on paper she now signed with a cross, and repeated "with a smile," poor child, a short form of words. By some trick this signature was changed for a long document, in which she was made to confess all her visions false. It is certain that she did not understand her words in this sense.

Cauchon had triumphed. The blame of heresy and witchcraft was cast on Joan, and on her king as an accomplice. But the English were not satisfied; they made an uproar, they threatened Cauchon, for Joan's life was to be spared. She was to be in prison all her days, on bread and water, but, while she lived, they dared scarcely stir against the French. They were soon satisfied.

Joan's prison was not changed. There soon came news that she had put on man's dress again. The judges went to her. She told them (they say), that she put on this dress of her own free will. In confession, later, she told her priest that she had been refused any other dress, and had been brutally treated both by the soldiers and by an English lord. In self-defence, she dressed in the only attire within her reach. In any case, the promises made to her had been broken. The judge asked her if her Voices had been with her again?

"Yes."

"What did they say?"

"God told me by the voices of St. Catherine and St. Margaret of the great sorrow of my treason, when I abjured to save my life; that I was damning myself for my life's sake."

"Do you believe the Voices come from St. Margaret and St. Catherine?"

"Yes, and that they are from God."

She added that she had never meant to deny this, had not understood that she had denied it.

All was over now; she was a "relapsed heretic."

The judges said that they visited Joan again on the morning of her death, and that she withdrew her belief in her Voices; or, at least, left it to the Church to decide whether they were good or bad, while she still maintained that they were *real*. She had expected release, and, for the first time, had been disappointed. At the stake she understood her Voices: they had foretold her martyrdom, "great victory" over herself, and her entry into rest. But the document of the judges is not signed by the clerks, as all such documents must be. One of them, Manchon, who had not been present, was asked to sign it; he refused. Another, Taquel, is said to have been present, but he did not sign. The story is, therefore, worth nothing.

Enough. They burned Joan the Maid. She did not suffer long. Her eyes were fixed on a cross which a priest, Martin L'Advenu, held up before her. She maintained, he says, to her dying moment, the truth of her Voices. With a great cry of JESUS! she gave up her breath, and her pure soul was with God.

Even the English wept, even a secretary of the English king said that they had burned a Saint. One of the three great crimes of the world's history had been committed, and, of the three, this was the most cowardly and cruel. It profited the English not at all. "Though they ceased not to be brave," says Patrick Abercromby, a Scot,[26] "yet they were almost on all occasions defeated, and within the short space of twenty-two years, lost not only all the conquests made by them in little less than a hundred, but also the inheritances which they had enjoyed for above three centuries bypast. It is not my part to follow them, as the French and my countrymen did, from town to town, and from province to province; I take much more pleasure in relating the glories than the disgraces of England."

This disgrace the English must, and do, most sorrowfully confess, and, that it may never be forgotten while the civilised world stands, there lives, among the plays of Shakspeare, whether he wrote or did not write it, that first part of "Henry VI," which may pair with the yet more abominable poem of the Frenchman, Voltaire.

Twenty years after her death, as we saw, Charles VII, in his own interest, induced the Pope and the Inquisition, to try the case of Joan over again. It was as certain that the clergy would find her innocent, now, as that they would find her guilty before. But, happily, they collected the evidence of most of the living people who had known her. Thus we have heard from the Domremy peasants how good she was as a child, from Dunois, d'Alençon, d'Aulon, how she was beautiful,

---

26. In 1715.

courteous, and brave, from Isambart and L'Advenu, how nobly she died, and how she never made one complaint, but forgave all her enemies freely. All these old Latin documents were collected, edited, and printed, in 1849, by Monsieur Jules Quicherat, a long and noble labour. After the publication of this book, there has been, and can be, no doubt about the perfect goodness of Joan of Arc. The English long believed silly stories against her, as a bad woman, stories which were not even mentioned by her judges. The very French, at different times, have mocked at her memory, in ignorance and disbelief. They said she was a tool of politicians, who, on the other hand, never wanted her, or that she was crazy. Men mixed up with her glorious history the adventures of the false Maid, who pretended to be Joan come again, and people doubted as to whether she really died at Rouen. In modern times, some wiseacres have called the strongest and healthiest of women "hysterical," which is their way of accounting for her Voices. But now, thanks mainly to Monsieur Quicherat, and other learned Frenchmen, the world, if it chooses, may know Joan as she was; the stainless Maid, the bravest, gentlest, kindest, and wisest woman who ever lived. Her country people, in her lifetime, called her "the greatest of Saints, after the Blessed Virgin," and, at least, she is the greatest concerning whose deeds and noble sufferings history preserves a record. And her Voices we leave to Him who alone knows all truth.

How the Bass was Held for King James

The Bass Rock is a steep black mass of stone, standing about two miles out to sea, off the coast of Berwickshire. The sheer cliffs, straight as a wall, are some four hundred feet in height. At the top there is a sloping grassy shelf, on which a few sheep are kept, but the chief inhabitants of the rock are innumerable hosts of sea-birds. Far up the rock, two hundred years ago, was a fortress, with twenty cannons and a small garrison. As a boat can only touch at the little island in very fine weather, the fortress was considered by the Government of Charles II an excellent prison for Covenanters. There was a house for the governor, and a chapel where powder was kept, but where no clergyman officiated. As the covenanting prisoners were nearly all ministers, and a few of them prophets, it was thought, no doubt, that they could attend to their own devotions for themselves. They passed a good deal of their time in singing psalms. One prisoner looked into the cell of another late at night, and saw a shining white figure with him, which was taken for an angel by the spectator. Another prisoner, a celebrated preacher, named Peden, once told a merry girl that a "sudden surprising judgment was waiting for her," and instantly a gust of wind blew her off the rock into the sea. The Covenanters, one of whom had shot at the Archbishop of St. Andrews, and hit the Bishop of Orkney, were very harshly treated. "They were obliged to drink the twopenny ale of the governor's brewing, scarcely worth a half-penny the pint," an inconvenience which they probably shared with the garrison. They were sometimes actually compelled to make their own beds, a cruel hardship, when their servants had been dismissed, probably for plotting their escape. They had few pleasures except writing accounts of their sufferings, and books on religion; or studying Greek and Hebrew.

When King James II was driven from his throne, in 1688, by the Prince of Orange, these sufferers found release, they being on the Orange side. But the castle of the Bass did not yield to William till 1690; it was held for King James by Charles Maitland till his ammunition and stores were exhausted. The Whigs, who were now in power, used the Bass for a prison, as their enemies had done, and four Cavalier prisoners were shut up in the cold, smoky, unwholesome jail, just as the Covenanters had been before. These men, Middleton, Halyburton, Roy, and Dunbar, all of them young, had been in arms for King James, and were taken when his Majesty's forces were surprised and defeated by Livingstone at Cromdale Haugh. Middleton was a lieutenant; his friends were junior in rank, and were only ensigns.

These four lads did not devote their leisure to the composition of religious treatises, nor to the learning of Latin and Greek. On the other hand they reckoned it more worthy of their profession to turn the Whig garrison out of the Bass, and to hold it for King James. For three years they held it against all comers, and the Royal flag, driven out of England and Scotland, still floated over this little rock in the North Sea.

This is how the Four took the Bass. They observed that when coals were landed all the garrison except three or four soldiers went down to the rocky platform where there was a crane for raising goods. When they went, they locked three of the four gates on the narrow rocky staircase behind them.

On June 15, 1691, the soldiers went on this duty, leaving, to guard the Cavaliers, La Fosse, the sergeant, Swan, the gunner, and one soldier. These men were overpowered, or won over, by Middleton, Roy, Dunbar, and Halyburton, who then trained a gun on the garrison below, and asked them whether they would retire peacefully, or fight? They preferred to sail away in the coal vessel, and very foolish they must have felt, when they carried to the Whigs in Edinburgh the news that four men had turned them out of an impregnable castle, and held it for King James.

Next night young Crawford of Ardmillan, with his servant and two Irish sailors, seized a long-boat on the beach, sailed over, and joined the brave little garrison of the Bass. Crawford had been lurking in disguise for some time, and the two Irishmen had escaped from prison in Edinburgh, and were not particularly well disposed to the government of William.

When the news reached King James, in France, he sent a ship, laden with provisions and stores of all kinds, and two boats, one of them carrying two light guns. The Whigs established a force on the shore opposite, and their boats cruised about to intercept supplies, but in this they failed, the Cavaliers being too quick and artful to be caught easily.

On August 15, however, the enemy seized the large boat at night. Now Ardmillan and Middleton were absent in search of supplies, and, being without their leader, Roy and Dunbar thought of surrendering. But just as they were about signing articles of surrender, Middleton returned with a large boat and plenty of provisions, and he ran his boat under the guns of his fort, whence he laughed at the enemies of his king. Dunbar, however, who was on shore engaged in the business of the surrender, was held as a prisoner. The Whigs were not much nearer taking the Bass. On September 3 they sent a sergeant and a drummer to offer a free pardon to the Cavaliers. They were allowed to land on the rock, but Middleton merely laughed at the promise of a free pardon, and he kept the sergeant and drummer, whom he afterwards released. A Danish ship, sailing between the Bass and shore, had a gun fired across her bows, and was made prize of; they took out everything that they needed, and then let her go.

The Cavaliers lived a gay life: they had sheep on the Bass, plenty of water, meat, biscuits, beer and wine. Cruising in their boats they captured several ships, supplied themselves with what they wanted, and held the ships themselves to ransom. When food ran short they made raids on the shore, lifted cattle, and, generally, made war support war.

The government of the Prince of Orange was driven beyond its patience, and vowed that the Bass should be taken, if it cost all the revenue of the country. But Middleton had plenty of powder, he had carefully collected more than five hundred balls fired at his fort by the English, and he calmly awaited the arrival of hostile men-of-war. The "Sheerness" (Captain Roope) and the "London Merchant" (Captain Orton) were sent with orders to bombard the Bass and destroy the fort. After two days of heavy firing, these vessels had lost a number of men, their rigging was cut to pieces, and the ships were so damaged that they were glad to slink off to harbour.

A close watch was now set, the "Lion" (Captain Burd), a dogger of six guns, and a long-boat cruised constantly in the neighbourhood. Captain Burd is described as "a facetious and intelligent man," and a brave officer, but his intelligence and courage were no match for Middleton. In August 1693 a French frigate of twelve guns sailed under the Bass and landed supplies. But the Cavaliers were so few that they had to borrow ten French sailors to help in the landing of the provisions. At this moment the "Lion" bore down on the French vessel, which was obliged to cut her cables to avoid being run down. The garrison of the Bass was thus left with ten more mouths to feed, and with only the small supplies that had been landed. They were soon reduced to two ounces of raw rusk dough for each man, every day. Halyburton was caught and condemned to be hanged, and a Mr. Trotter, who had helped the Cavaliers, was actually hanged on shore, within sight of the

Bass. Middleton fired a shot and scattered the crowd, but that did not save poor Trotter.

Middleton had now only a few pounds of meal left. He therefore sent in a flag of truce, and announced that he would surrender, but upon his own terms. Very good terms they were. Envoys were dispatched by the Whigs: Middleton gave them an excellent luncheon out of provisions kept for the purpose, and choice French wines. He had also set coats and caps on the muzzles of guns, above, on the rocks, so that the Whig envoys believed he had plenty of men, and no scarcity of provisions. Their lordships returned, and told the Privy Council that the Bass was in every respect well provisioned and well manned. Middleton's terms were, therefore, gladly accepted.

He got a full pardon for every one then in the garrison, and for every one who had ever been in it (including Halyburton, now under sentence, of death), "and none hereafter shall call them to account." They were to depart with all the honours of war, with swords and baggage, in their own boat. They were to be at liberty to come or go, whenever they pleased, till May 15, 1694; and a ship, properly supplied, was to be ready to carry them to France, if they preferred to join Dundee's gallant officers in the French service. Finally, *all their expenses were to be paid*! The "aliment" formerly granted to them, and unpaid when they seized the Bass, was to be handed over to them. On these terms Middleton took leave of the fortress which he could not have held for a week longer. There have been greater deeds of arms, but there never was one so boyish, so gallant, and so gay.

The Crowning of Ines de Castro

About the year 1340, when Edward III was King of England, a young Spanish lady set out from Castile on the long journey to the Court of Portugal. She was the only daughter of John Manuel, Duke of Villena, a very rich and powerful noble, much dreaded by the King of Castile for his boldness and restlessness. Not many years before he had suddenly left his post as Warden of the French Marches, to fight against the Moors in the province of Murcia, and though the King was very angry at his conduct, he did not dare to punish him, for fear that in some way he himself would suffer. Villena's daughter Constance had passed much of her time at the Castilian Court, where she lived in the state that was expected of a great lady of those days, but when the treaty was made which decided that she was to marry Dom Pedro, Crown Prince of Portugal, her household was increased, and special attendants appointed to do honour to her rank.

Now among the ladies chosen to form part of Constance's court, was a distant cousin of her own, the beautiful and charming Ines de Castro. Like Henry II at the sight of Fair Rosamond, the young Dom Pedro, who was not more than twenty years of age, fell passionately in love with her. He did all in his power to hide his feelings from his bride, the Infanta Constance, but did not succeed, and in a few years she died, it was said of grief at her husband's coldness, after giving birth to the Infant, Dom Fernando (1345). After her death, Dom Pedro's father King Alfonso was anxious that he should marry again, but he refused all the brides proposed for him, and people whispered among themselves that he was already secretly wedded to Ines de Castro. Time went on, and they had four children, but Ines preferred to live quietly in a convent in the country, and never took her place as Dom Pedro's wife. Still, however secluded she might be, large numbers of her fellow Castilians, weary of the yoke of their own King, Pedro the Cruel, flocked into Portugal, and looked to her for protection, which Dom Pedro for her sake always gave them, and chief among these foreign favourites were Ines' two brothers, Fernando and Alvaro Perez de Castro. This state of things was very bitter to the old Portuguese courtiers, who complained to the King that in future the country would only be governed by Spaniards. These rumours grew so loud that in time they even reached the ears of the Queen, and she, with the Archbishop of Braga, gave

Dom Pedro solemn warning that some plot was assuredly forming which would end in his ruin. But Dom Pedro, naturally fearless, had faith in his father's goodwill towards him, and looked on these kindly warnings as mere empty threats, so proceeded gaily on his path. Thus in silence was prepared the bloody deed.

When the courtiers thought all was ready they went in a deputation to Alfonso IV, and pointed out what might be expected in the future if Ines de Castro was allowed to remain the fountainhead for honours and employments to all her countrymen who were attracted to Portugal by the hopes of better pay. They enlarged on the fact that the national laws and customs would be changed, and Portugal become a mere province of Spain; worse than all, that the life of the Infant Dom Fernando was endangered, as upon the death of the King, the Castros would naturally desire to secure the succession to the children of Ines. If Ines were only out of the way, Dom Pedro would forget her, and consent to make a suitable marriage. So things went on, working together for the end of Ines.

At last the King set forth, surrounded by many of his great nobles and high officials, for Coimbra, a small town in which was situated the Convent of Santa Clara, where Ines de Castro quietly dwelt, with her three surviving children. On seeing the sudden arrival of Alfonso with this great company of armed knights, the soul of Ines shrank with a horrible fear. She could not fly, as every avenue was closed, and Dom Pedro was away on the chase, as the nobles very well knew. Pale as an image of death, Ines clasped her children in her arms, and flung herself at the feet of the King. "My lord," she cried, "have I given you cause to wish my death? Your son is the Prince; I can refuse him nothing. Have pity on me, wife as I am. Kill me not without reason. And if you have no compassion left for me, find a place in your heart for your grandchildren, who are of your own blood."

The innocence and beauty of the unfortunate woman, who indeed had harmed no one, moved the King, and he withdrew to think better what should be done. But the envy and hatred of the courtiers would not suffer Ines to triumph, and again they brought forward their evil counsels.

"Do what you will," at length said the King. And they did it.

A nameless pain filled the soul of Dom Pedro when on his return he stood before the bloody corpse of Ines, whom he had loved so well. But soon another feeling took possession of him, which shut out everything else—the desire to revenge himself on her murderers. Hastily calling together the brothers of Ines and some followers who were attached to his person, he took counsel with them, and then collecting all the men-at-arms within his reach, he fell upon the neighbouring provinces and executed a fearful vengeance, both with fire and sword, upon the innocent inhabitants. How long this rage for devastation might have lasted cannot be told, but Dom Pedro was at length brought to a better mind by Gonçalo Pereira, Archbishop of Braga, who, by the help of the Queen, succeeded in establishing peace between father and son.

So a parchment deed was drawn up between the King and the Infant, in which Dom Pedro undertook to pardon all who had been engaged in the murder of Ines, and Alfonso promised to forgive those who had taken his son's side, and borne arms against himself. And for his part Dom Pedro vowed to perform the duties of a faithful vassal, and to banish from his presence all turbulent and restless spirits. So peace was made.

Two years had hardly passed after this event before King Alfonso lay on his death-bed in Lisbon, and then, thinking over what would happen when he was dead, the feeling gradually came over him that in spite of Dom Pedro's solemn oath the murderers of Ines would not be safe from his revenge. Therefore he sent for the three knights, Diogo Lopez Pacheco, Alvaro Gonçalves, and Pedro Coelho, who had counselled him to do the dreadful deed and had themselves struck the blow, and bade them leave their property and all they had, and fly while there was yet time to foreign lands for refuge. The knights saw the wisdom of the advice, and sought shelter in Castile. Then Alfonso prepared himself to die, the murder of Ines lying heavy on his soul in his last days (1357).

King Pedro was thirty-seven years old when he ascended the throne, and his first care was to secure peace to his kingdom. To this end he sent several embassies to the King of Castile, who made a compact with Alfonso "to be the friend of his friends, and the enemy of his enemies." The results of this treaty may be easily guessed at. The King of Portugal engaged to send back to Castile all who had fled to his dominions from the tyranny of Pedro the Cruel, the ally of the Black Prince, and was to receive in return the murderers of Ines, two of whom he put to a horrible death. The third, Pacheco, was more fortunate. A beggar to whom he had been accustomed to give alms discovered his danger, and hastened to warn the knight, who was away from the city on a hunting expedition. By his advice Pacheco changed clothes with the beggar, and made his way through Aragon to the borders of France, where he took refuge with Henry of Trastamara, half-brother of the King of Castile. Here he remained, a poor knight without friends or property, till the year 1367, when on his death-bed the King of Portugal suddenly remembered that when dying the other two knights had sworn that Pacheco was guiltless of the murder of Ines, and ordered his son to recall him from exile and to restore all his possessions. Which Dom Fernando joyfully did.

That, however, happened several years after the time we are speaking of, when Dom Pedro had only just ascended the throne. Having satisfied his feelings of revenge against the murderers of Ines, a nobler desire filled his heart. He resolved that she who had been so ill-spoken of during her life, and had died such a shameful death, should be acknowledged openly as his wife and queen before his Court and his people. So he assembled all the great nobles and officers, and, laying his hand on the sacred books, swore solemnly that seven years before he had taken Ines de Castro to wife, and had lived with her in happiness till her death, but that through dread of his father the marriage had been kept secret; and he commanded the Lord High Chamberlain to prepare a deed recording his oath. And in case there should still be some who did not believe, three days later the Bishop of Guarda and the Keeper of the King's Wardrobe bore witness before the great lords gathered together in Coimbra that they themselves had been present at the secret marriage, which had taken place at Braganza, in the royal apartments, according to the rites of the Church.

This solemn function being over, the last act in the history of Ines was begun. By command of the King her body was taken from the convent of Santa Clara, where it had lain in peace for many years, and was clad in royal garments: a crown was placed on her head and a sceptre in her hand, and she was seated on a throne for the subjects, who during her life had despised her, to kneel and kiss the hem of her robe. One by one the knights and the nobles and the great officers of the Crown did homage to the dead woman, and when all had bowed before what was left of the beautiful Ines they placed her in a splendid coffin, which was borne by knights over the seven leagues that lay between Coimbra and Alcobaça, the royal burying-place of the Portuguese. In this magnificent cloister a tomb had been prepared carved in white marble, and at the head stood a statue of Ines in the pride of her beauty, crowned a queen. Bishops and soldiers, nobles and peasants, lined the road to watch the coffin pass, and thousands with lighted torches followed the dead woman to her resting place, till the whole long road from Coimbra to Alcobaça was lit up with brightness. So, solemnly, Ines de Castro was laid in her grave, and the honours which had been denied her in life were heaped around her tomb.[1]

---

1. Schäfer's *Geschichte von Portugal.*

THE STORY OF ORTHON

(There may be some who doubt whether the following story is in all respects perfectly true. It is taken, however, from a history book, the "Chronicle of Jean Froissart," who wrote about the wars of the Black Prince.)

Great marvel it is to think and consider of a thing that I will tell you, and that was told to me in the house of the Comte de Foix at Orthez, by him who gave me to know concerning the battle of Juberot. And I will tell you of this matter, what it was, for since the Squire told me this tale, whereof you shall presently have knowledge, certes I have thought over it a hundred times, and shall think as long as I live.

"Certain it is," quoth the Squire, "that the day after the fight at Juberot the Comte de Foix knew of it, whereat men marvelled much how this might be. And all day, on the Sunday and the Monday and the Tuesday following, he made in his castle of Orthez such dull and simple cheer that none could drag a word out of him. All these three days he would not leave his chamber, nor speak to knight or squire, howsoever near him they might be. And when it came to Tuesday at evening, he called his brother, Sir Ernault Guillaume, and said to him in a low voice:

"'Our men have fought, whereat I am grieved; for that has befallen them of their journey which I told them before they set out.'

"Sir Ernault, who is a right wise knight and of good counsel, knowing well the manner and ways of his brother the Count, held his peace for a little while. Then the Count, willing to show his heart, and weary of his long sadness, spoke again, and louder than before, saying:

"'By God, Sir Ernault, it is as I tell you, and shortly we shall have news; for never did the land of Béarn lose so much in one day—no, not these hundred years—as it has lost this time in Portugal.'

"Many knights and squires standing round who heard the Count noted these words, and in ten days learned the truth from them who had been in the fight, and who brought tidings, first to the Court, and afterwards to all who would hear them, of what befell at Juberot. Thereby was the Count's grief renewed, and that of all in the country who had lost brothers and fathers, sons and friends, in the fray."

"Marry!" said I to the Squire, who was telling me his tale, "and how could the Count know or guess what befell? Gladly would I learn this."

"By my faith," said the Squire, "he knew it well, as appeared."

"Is he a prophet, or has he messengers who ride at night with the wind? Some art he must have."

Then the Squire began to laugh.

"Truly he must learn by some way of necromancy; we know not here truly how he does it, save by phantasies."

"Ah, good sir, of these fancies prithee tell me, and I will be grateful. If it is a matter to keep silent, silent will I keep it, and never, while I am in this country, will I open my mouth thereon."

"I pray you do not, for I would not that any should know I had spoken. Yet others talk of it quietly when they are among their friends."

Thereon he drew me apart into a corner of the castle chapel, and then began his tale, and spoke thus:

"It may be twenty years since there reigned here a baron named Raymond, lord of Corasse, a town and castle seven leagues from Orthez. Now, the lord of Corasse, at the time of which I speak, held a plea at Avignon before the Pope against a clerk of Catalonia who laid claim to the tithes of his town, the said clerk belonging to a powerful order, and claiming the right of the tithes of Corasse, which, indeed, amounted to a yearly sum of one hundred florins. This right he set forth and proved before all men, for in his judgment, given in the Consistory General, Pope Urban V declared that the clerk had won his case, and that the Chevalier had no ground for his claim. The sentence once delivered, letters were given to the clerk enabling him to take possession, and he rode so hard that in a very short time he reached Béarn, and by virtue of the papal bull appropriated the tithes. The Sieur de Corasse was right wroth with the clerk and his doings, and came to him and said:

"'Master Martin, or Master Pierre, or whatever your name may be, do you think that I am going to give up my rights just because of those letters of yours? I scarce fancy you are bold enough to lay hands on property of mine, for you will risk your life in the doing. Go elsewhere to seek a benefice, for of my rights you shall have none, and this I tell you, once and for all.'

"The mind of the clerk misgave him, for he knew that the Chevalier cared not for men's lives, and he dared not persevere. So he dropped his claims, and betook himself to his own country or to Avignon. And when the moment had come that he was to depart, he entered into the presence of the Sieur de Corasse, and said:

"'Sir, it is by force and not by right that you lay hands on the property of the Church, of which you make such ill-use. In this land you are stronger than I, but know that as soon as I may I will send you a champion whom you will fear more than you fear me.'

"The Sieur de Corasse, who did not heed his words, replied:

"'Go, do as you will; I fear you as little alive as dead. For all your talk, I will never give up my rights.'

"Thus parted the clerk and the Sieur de Corasse, and the clerk returned to his own country, but whether that was Avignon or Catalonia I know not. But he did not forget what he had told the Sieur de Corasse when he bade him farewell; for three months after, when he expected it least, there came to the castle of Corasse, while the Chevalier was quietly sleeping, certain invisible messengers, who began to throw about all that was in the castle, till it seemed as if, truly, nothing would be left standing. The Chevalier heard it all, but he said nought, for he would not be thought a coward, and indeed he had courage enough for any adventure that might befall.

"These sounds of falling weights continued for a long space, then ceased suddenly.

"When the morning came, the servants all assembled, and their lord having arisen from bed they came to him and said, 'Sir, have you also heard that which we have heard this night?' And the Sieur de Corasse hid it in his heart and answered, 'No; what have you heard?' And they told him how that all the furniture was thrown down, and all the kitchen pots had been broken. But he began to laugh, and said it was a dream, and that the wind had caused it. 'Ah no,' sighed his wife; 'I also have heard.'

"When the next night arrived, the noise-makers arrived too, and made more disturbance than before, and gave great knocks at the doors, and likewise at the windows of the Sieur de Corasse. And the Chevalier leaped out of his bed and demanded, 'Who is it that rocks my bed at this hour of the night?'.

"And answer was made him, 'That which I am, I am.'

"Then asked the Chevalier, 'By whom are you sent here?'

"'By the clerk of Catalonia, to whom you have done great wrong, for you have taken from him his rights and his heritage. Hence you will never be suffered to dwell in peace till you have given him what is his due, and he is content.'

"'And you, who are so faithful a messenger,' inquired the Chevalier, 'what is your name?'

"'They call me Orthon.'

"'Orthon,' said the knight, 'the service of a clerk is worth nothing, and if you trust him, he will work you ill. Leave me in peace, I pray you, and take service with me, and I shall be grateful.'

"Now, the knight was pleasing to Orthon, so he answered, 'Is this truly your will?'

"'Yes,' replied the Sieur de Corasse. 'Do no ill unto those that dwell here, and I will cherish you, and we shall be as one.'

"'No,' spoke Orthon. 'I have no power save to wake you and others, and to disturb you when you fain would sleep.'

"'Do as I say,' said the Chevalier; 'we shall agree well, if only you will abandon this wicked clerk. With him there is nothing but pain, and if you serve me—'

"'Since it is your will,' replied Orthon, 'it is mine also.'

"The Sieur de Corasse pleased Orthon so much that he came often to see him in his sleep, and pulled away his pillow or gave great knocks against the window of the room where he lay. And when the Chevalier was awakened he would exclaim, 'Let me sleep, I pray you, Orthon!'

"'Not so,' said Orthon; 'I have news to give you.'

'And what news will you give me? Whence come you?'

"Then said Orthon, 'I come from England, or Germany, or Hungary, or some other country, which I left, yesterday, and such-and-such things have happened.'

"Thus it was that the Sieur de Corasse knew so much when he went into the world; and this trick he kept up for five or six years. But in the end he could not keep silence, and made it known to the Comte de Foix in the way I shall tell you.

"The first year, whenever the Sieur de Corasse came into the presence of the Count at Ortais or elsewhere, he would say to him: 'Monseigneur, such-and-such a thing has happened in England, or in Scotland, or in Germany, or in Flanders, or in Brabant, or in some other country,' and the Comte de Foix marvelled greatly at these things. But one day he pressed the Sieur de Corasse so hard that the knight told him how it was he knew all that passed in the world and who told him. When the Comte de Foix knew the truth of the matter, his heart leapt with joy, and he said: 'Sieur de Corasse, bind him to you in love. I would I had such a messenger. He costs you nothing, and knows all that passes throughout the world.'

"'Monseigneur,' said the Chevalier, 'thus will I do.'

ANDREW LANG AND H. RIDER HAGGARD

"Thus the Sieur de Corasse was served by Orthon, and that for long. I know not if Orthon had more than one master, but certain it is that every week he came, twice or thrice during the night, to tell to the Sieur de Corasse the news of all the countries that he had visited, which the Sieur wrote at once to the Comte de Foix, who was of all men most joyed in news from other lands. One day when the Sieur de Corasse was with the Comte de Foix, the talk fell upon Orthon, and suddenly the Count inquired, 'Sieur de Corasse, have you never seen your messenger?'

"He answered, 'No, by my faith, Monseigneur, and I have never even asked to.'

"'Well,' he replied, 'it is very strange. If he had been as friendly to me as he is to you, I should long ago have begged him to show me who and what he is. And I pray that you will do all you can, so that I may know of what fashion he may be. You tell me that his speech is Gascon, such as yours or mine.'

"'By my faith,' said the Sieur de Corasse, 'it is only the truth. His Gascon is as good as the best; and, since you advise it, I will spare myself no trouble to see what he is like.'

"Two or three nights after came Orthon, and finding the Sieur de Corasse sleeping soundly, he pulled the pillow, so as to wake him. So the Sieur de Corasse awoke with a start and inquired, 'Who is there?'

"He answered, 'I am Orthon.'

"'And whence do you come?'

"'From Prague in Bohemia. The Emperor of Rome is dead.'

"'And when did he die?'

"'The day before yesterday.'

"'And how far is it from Prague to this?'

"'How far?' he answered. 'Why, it is sixty days' journey.'

"'And you have come so quickly?'

"'But, by my faith, I travel more quickly than the wind.'

"'And have you wings?'

"'By my faith, no.'

"'How, then, do you fly so fast?'

"Said Orthon, 'That does not concern you.'

"'No,' he replied; 'but I would gladly see of what form you are.'

"Said Orthon, 'My form does not concern you. Content you with what I tell you and that my news is true.'

"'Now, as I live,' cried the Sieur de Corasse, 'I should love you better if I had but seen you.'

"Said Orthon, 'Since you have such burning desire to see me, the first thing you behold to-morrow morning on getting out of bed will be I.'

"'It is enough,' answered the Sieur de Corasse. 'Go. I take leave of you for this night.'

"When the day dawned, the Sieur de Corasse arose from his bed, but his wife was filled with such dread of meeting Orthon that she feigned to be ill, and protested she would lie abed all day; for she said, 'Suppose I were to see him?'

"'Now,' cried the Sieur de Corasse, 'see what I do,' and he jumped from his bed and sat upon the edge, and looked about for Orthon; but he saw nothing. Then he threw back the windows so that he could note more clearly all that was in the room, but again he saw nought of which he could say, 'That is Orthon.'

"The day passed and night came. Hardly had the Sieur de Corasse climbed up into his bed than Orthon arrived, and began to talk to him, as his custom was.

"'Go to, go to,' said the Sieur de Corasse; 'you are but a bungler. You promised to show yourself to me yesterday, and you never appeared.'

"'Never appeared,' said he. 'But I did, by my faith.'

"'You did not.'

"'And did you see nothing,' said Orthon, 'when you leapt from your bed?'

"The Sieur de Corasse thought for a little; then he answered. 'Yes,' he replied; 'as I was sitting on my bed and thinking of you, I noticed two long straws on the floor twisting about and playing together.'

"'That was I,' said Orthon. 'That was the form I had taken upon me.'

"Said the Sieur de Corasse: 'That is not enough. You must take another form, so that I may see you and know you.'

"'You ask so much that I shall become weary of you and you will lose me,' replied Orthon.

"'You will never become weary of me and I shall never lose you,' answered the Sieur de Corasse; 'if only I see you once, I shall be content.'

"'So be it,' said Orthon; 'to-morrow you shall see me, and take notice that the first thing you see as you leave your room will be I.'

"'It is enough,' spoke the Sieur de Corasse; 'and now go, for I fain would sleep.'

"So Orthon went; and when it was the third hour next morning[1] the Sieur de Corasse rose and dressed as was his custom, and, leaving his chamber, came out into a gallery that looked into the central court of the castle. He glanced down, and the first thing he saw was a sow, larger than any he had ever beheld, but so thin that it seemed nothing but skin and bone. The Sieur de Corasse was troubled at the sight of the pig, and said to his servants: 'Set on the dogs, and let them chase out that sow.'

"The varlets departed and loosened the dogs, and urged them to attack the sow, which uttered a great cry and looked at the Sieur de Corasse, who stood leaning against one of the posts of his chamber. They saw her no more, for she vanished, and no man could tell whither she had gone.

"Then the Sieur de Corasse entered into his room, pondering deeply, for he remembered the words of Orthon and said to himself: 'I fear me that I have seen my messenger. I repent me that I have set my dogs upon him, and the more that perhaps he will never visit me again, for he has told me, not once but many times, that if I angered him he would depart from me.'

"And in this he said well; for Orthon came no more to the castle of Corasse, and in less than a year its lord himself was dead."

---

1. Six o'clock.

How Gustavus Vasa won his Kingdom

Nearly four hundred years ago, on May 12, 1496, Gustavus Vasa was born in an old house in Sweden. His father was a noble of a well-known Swedish family, and his mother could claim as her sister one of the bravest and most unfortunate women of her time. Now, it was the custom in those days that both boys and girls should be sent when very young to the house of some great lord to be taught their duties as pages or ladies-in-waiting, and to be trained in all sorts of accomplishments. So when Gustavus Vasa had reached the age of six or seven, he was taken away from all his brothers and sisters and placed in the household of his uncle by marriage, whose name was Sten Sture. At that time Sweden had had no king of her own for a hundred years, when the kingdom had become united with Norway and Denmark in the reign of Queen Margaret by a treaty that is known in history as the Union of Calmar (1397). As long as Queen Margaret lived the three kingdoms were well-governed and happy; but her successors were by no means as wise as she, and at the period we are writing of the Danish stewards of King Hans and his son, Christian II, oppressed and ill-treated the Swedes in every possible way, and Sten Sture, regent though he was, had no power to protect them. From time to time the Danish kings came over to Sweden to look after their own interests, and on one of these visits King Hans saw little Gustavus Vasa at the house of Sten Sture in Stockholm. He is said to have taken notice of the boy, and to have exclaimed grimly that Gustavus would be a great man if he lived; and the Regent, thinking that the less attention the King paid to his unwilling subjects the safer their heads would be, at once sent the boy back to his father.

For some years Gustavus lived at home and had a merry time, learning to shoot by hitting a mark with his arrows before he was allowed any breakfast, and roaming all over the woods in his little coat of scarlet cloth. At thirteen he was sent for a time to school at Upsala, where he learned music as well as other things, and even taught himself to make musical instruments. One day, however, the Danish schoolmaster spoke scornfully of the Swedes, and Gustavus, dashing the sword which he carried through the book before him, vowed vengeance on all Danes, and walked out of the school for good.

As far as we know, Gustavus probably remained with his father for the next few years, and we next hear of him in 1514 at the Court of Sten

ANDREW LANG AND H. RIDER HAGGARD

Sture the younger. Already he had obtained a reputation among his friends both for boldness and caution, and though so young had learned experience by carefully watching all that was going on around him. His enemies, too, even the wicked Archbishop Trolle of Upsala, had begun to fear him without knowing exactly why, and he had already made a name for himself by his courage at the Swedish victory of Bränkyrka, when the standard was borne by Gustavus through the thickest of the fight. This battle dashed to the ground the King's hopes of getting Sten Sture, the Regent, into his power by fair means, so he tried treachery to persuade the Swede to enter his ship. But the men of Stockholm saw through his wiles and declined this proposal, and the King was driven to offer the Swedes a meeting in a church, on condition that Gustavus Vasa and five other distinguished nobles should be sent first on board as hostages. This was agreed to; but no sooner had the young men put off in their boat than a large Danish vessel cut off their retreat, and they were at once carried off to Denmark as prisoners.

For one moment it seemed likely that Gustavus would be hanged, and Sweden remain in slavery for many years longer, and indeed, if his life was spared, it was only because Christian thought it might be to his own advantage. Still, spared it was, and the young man was delivered to the care of a distant relation in Jutland, who was to forfeit 400l. in case of his escape. Here things were made as pleasant to him as possible, and he was allowed to hunt and shoot, though always attended by keepers.

One day, after he had behaved with such prudence that his keepers had almost given up watching him, he managed, while strolling in the great park, to give them the slip, and to hide himself where there was no chance of anyone finding him. He contrived somehow to get hold of a pilgrim's dress; then that of a cattle-driver, and in this disguise he made his way to the free city of Lübeck, and threw himself on the mercy of the burgomaster or mayor. By this time his enemies were on his track, and his noble gaoler, Sir Eric Bauer, claimed him as an escaped prisoner. But the people of Lübeck, who at that moment had a trade quarrel with Denmark, declared that the fugitive was not a prisoner who had broken his parole, but a hostage who had been carried off by treachery, and refused to give him up, though perhaps their own interest had more to do with their steadfastness than right and justice. As it was, Gustavus was held fast in Lübeck for eight months before they would let him go, and it was not until May 1520 that he crossed the Baltic in a little fishing-smack, and sailed for Stockholm, then besieged by Danish ships and defended by the widow of the Regent. But finding the town closely invested, he made for Calmar, and after a short stay in the castle he found his way into the heart of the country, learning sadly at every step how the worst enemies of Sweden were the Swedes themselves, who betrayed each other to their Danish foes for jealousy and gold. Like Prince Charlie, however, he was soon to find faithful hearts among his countrymen, and for every traitor there were at least a hundred who were true. While hiding on his father's property, he sent some of his tenants to Stockholm, to find out the state of affairs there. The news they brought was terrible. A fearful massacre, known in history as the Blood Bath, had taken place by order of the King. Citizens, bishops, nobles, and even servants had been executed in the public market, and the King's thirst for blood was not satisfied until some hundreds of Swedes had laid down their lives. Among those who fell on the first day was the father of Gustavus Vasa, who is said to have indignantly rejected the pardon offered him by the King for his fidelity to his country. "No," he exclaimed; "let me die with all these honest men." So he died, and his son-in-law after him, and his wife, her mother, sister, and three daughters were thrown into prison, where some of them were starved to death. To crown all, a price was set on the head of Gustavus.

On hearing this last news Gustavus resolved to take refuge in the province of Dalecarlia, and to trust to the loyalty of the peasants. By this time it was the end of November (1520), and the snow lay thick upon the ground; but this was rather in his favour, as his enemies would be less likely to pursue him. So he cut his hair short and put on the dress of a peasant, which in those days consisted of a short, thick jacket, breeches with huge buttons, and a low soft hat. Then he bought an axe and plunged into the forest. Here he soon made a friend for life in a very tall, strong woodcutter, known to his neighbours by the name of the "Bear-slayer." This woodcutter was employed by a rich man, Petersen by name, who had a large property near by, and had been at school with Gustavus Vasa at Upsala. But hearing that Danish spies were lurking around, Gustavus would not confide even in him, but patiently did what work was given him like a common servant. An accident betrayed him. A maid-servant happened one day to see the golden collar that Gustavus wore next his skin, and told her master. Petersen then recognised his old schoolfellow; but knowing that he would lose his own head if he gave him shelter, he advised the young noble to leave his hiding-place, and take shelter with another old friend, Arendt, who had once served under him. Here he was received with open arms; but this hospitality only concealed treachery, for his old comrade had formed a close friendship with the Danish stewards who ruled the land, and only wanted an opportunity to deliver Gustavus up to them. However, he was careful not to let his guest see anything of his plan, and even pretended to share his schemes for ridding the country of the enemy. So he hid Gustavus in an attic, where he assured him he would be perfectly safe, and left him, saying he would go round to all the neighbouring estates to enlist soldiers for their cause. But of course he was only going to give information about Gustavus, and to gain the reward.

Now, it was only an accident that prevented his treachery being successful. The first man he applied to, though a friend to the Danes, scorned to take a mean advantage of anyone, and told the traitor to go elsewhere.

Furiously angry, but greedy and determined as ever, the traitor set forth for the house of the Danish steward who lived nearest, well knowing that from him he would receive nothing but gratitude.

But the traitor's wife happened to be standing at her own door as her husband drove by, and guessed what had occurred and where he was going. She was an honest woman, who despised all that was base and underhand, so she stole out to one of her servants whom she could trust, and ordered him to make ready a sledge, for he would have to go on a journey. Then, in order that no one should know of Gustavus's escape until it was too late to overtake him, she let him down out of the window into the sledge, which drove off at once, across a frozen lake and past the copper-mines of Fahlun, to a little village at the far end, where Gustavus left his deliverer, giving him a beautiful silver dagger as a parting gift.

Sheltered by one person after another, and escaping many dangers on the way, Gustavus found himself at last in the cottage of one of the royal foresters, where he received a hospitable welcome from the man and his wife. But unknown to himself, Danish spies had been for some time on his track, and no sooner had Gustavus sat down to warm his tired limbs before the fire where the forester's wife was baking bread, than they entered and inquired if Gustavus Vasa had been seen to pass that way. Another moment and they might have become curious about the stranger sitting at the hearth, when the woman hastily turned round, and struck him on the shoulder with the huge spoon she held in her hand. "Lazy loon!" she cried. "Have you no work to do? Off with you at once and see to your threshing." The Danes only saw before them a common Swedish servant bullied by his mistress, and it never entered their heads to ask any questions; so once again Gustavus was saved.

Next day the forester hid him under a load of hay, and prepared to drive him through the forest to the houses of some friends—foresters like himself—who lived in a distant village. But Gustavus was not to reach even this place without undergoing a danger different from those he had met with before; for while they were jogging peacefully along the road they came across one of the numerous parties of Danes who were for ever scouring the country, and on seeing the cart a man stepped up, and thrust through the hay with his spear. Gustavus, though wounded, managed not to cry out, but reached, faint with loss of blood, his next resting-place.

After spending several days hidden among the boughs of a fir-tree, till the Danes began to think that their information must be false and Gustavus be looked for elsewhere, the fugitive was guided by one peasant after another through the forests till he found himself at the head of a large lake, and in the centre of many thickly-peopled villages. Here he assembled the dwellers in the country round, and spoke to them in the churchyard, telling of the wrongs that Sweden had suffered and of her children that had been slain. The peasants were moved by his words, but they did not wish to plunge into a war till they were sure of being successful, so they told Gustavus that they must find out something more before they took arms; meantime he was driven to seek a fresh hiding-place.

Gustavus was terribly dejected at the downfall of his hopes, for he had thought, with the help of the peasants, to raise at once the standard of rebellion; still he saw that flight was the only chance just now, and Norway seemed his best refuge. However, some fresh acts of tyranny on the part of their Danish masters did what Gustavus's own words had failed to do, and suddenly the peasants took their resolve and sent for Gustavus to be their leader.

The messengers found him at the foot of the Dovre-Fjeld Mountains between Norway and Sweden, and he joyfully returned with them, rousing the people as he went, till at last he had got together a force that far outnumbered the army which was sent to meet it.

Gustavus was not present at the first battle, which was fought on the banks of the Dale River, for he was travelling about preaching a rising among the Swedes of the distant provinces, but he arrived just after, to find that the peasants had gained an overwhelming victory. The fruits of this first victory were far-reaching. It gave the people confidence, thousands flocked to serve under Gustavus's banner, and within a few months the whole country, excepting Stockholm and Calmar, was in his hands. Then the nobles, in gratitude to their deliverer, sought to proclaim him king, but this he refused as long as a single Swedish castle remained beneath the Danish yoke, so for two more years he ruled Sweden under the title of Lord Protector. Then in 1523, when Stockholm and Calmar at last surrendered, Gustavus Vasa was crowned king.

Monsieur de Bayard's Duel

Now, when Monsieur de Bayard was fighting in the kingdom of Naples, he made prisoner a valiant Spanish captain, Don Alonzo de Soto-Mayor by name, who, not liking his situation, complained of the treatment he received, which he said was unworthy of his dignity as a knight. This was, however, quite absurd, and against all reason, for, as all the world knows, there never was a man more courteous than Monsieur de Bayard. At length, Monsieur de Bayard, wearied with the continued grumblings of the Spaniard, sent him a challenge. This was at once accepted, whether the duel should be fought on foot or on horseback, for Don Alonzo refused to withdraw anything that he had said of the French knight.

When the day arrived, Monsieur de la Palisse, accompanied by two hundred gentlemen, appeared on the ground, escorting their champion Monsieur de Bayard, mounted on a beautiful horse, and dressed all in white, as a mark of humility, the old chronicler tells us. But Don Alonzo, to whom belonged the choice of arms, declared that he preferred to fight on foot, because (he pretended) he was not so skilful a horseman as Monsieur de Bayard, but really because he knew that his adversary had that day an attack of malarial fever, and he hoped to find him weakened, and so to get the better of him. Monsieur de la Palisse and Bayard's other supporters advised him, from the fact of his fever, to excuse himself, and to insist on fighting on horseback; but Monsieur de Bayard, who had never trembled before any man, would make no difficulties, and agreed to everything, which astonished Don Alonzo greatly, as he had expected a refusal. An enclosure was formed by a few large stones piled roughly one on another. Monsieur de Bayard placed himself at one end of the ground, accompanied by several brave captains, who all began to offer up prayers for their champion. Don Alonzo and his friends took up a position at the other end, and sent Bayard the weapons that they had chosen—namely, a short sword and a poignard, with a gorget and coat of mail. Monsieur de Bayard did not trouble himself enough about the matter to raise any objection. For second he had an old brother-at-arms, Bel-Arbre by name, and for keeper of the ground Monsieur de la Palisse, who was very well skilled in all these things. The Spaniard also chose a second and a keeper of the ground. So when the combatants had taken their places, they both sank on their knees and prayed to God; but Monsieur de Bayard fell on his face and kissed the earth, then, rising, made the sign of the cross, and went straight for his enemy, as calmly, says the old chronicler, as if he were in a palace, and leading out a lady to the dance.

Don Alonzo on his side came forward to meet him, and asked, "Señor Bayardo, what do you want of me?" He answered, "To defend my honour," and without more words drew near; and each thrust hard with the sword, Don Alonzo getting a slight wound on his face. After that, they thrust at each other many times more, without touching. Monsieur de Bayard soon discovered the ruse of his adversary, who no sooner delivered his thrusts than he at once covered his face so that no hurt could be done him; and he bethought himself of a way to meet it. So, the moment Don Alonzo raised his arm to give a thrust, Monsieur de Bayard also raised his; but he kept his sword in the air, without striking a blow, and when his enemy's weapon had passed harmlessly by him, he could strike where he chose, and gave such a fearful blow at the throat that, in spite of the thickness of the gorget, the sword entered to the depth of four whole fingers, and he could not pull it out. Don Alonzo, feeling that he had got his death-blow, dropped his sword and grasped Monsieur de Bayard round the body, and thus wrestling they both fell to the ground. But Monsieur de Bayard, quick to see and to do, seized his sword, and, holding it to the nostrils of his enemy, he cried, "Surrender, Don Alonzo, or you are a dead man;" but he got no answer, for Don Alonzo was dead already. Then his second, Don Diego de Guignonnes, came forward and said, "Señor Bayardo, you have conquered him," which everyone could see for himself. But Monsieur de Bayard was much grieved, for, says the chronicler, he would have given a hundred thousand crowns, if he had had them, to have made Don Alonzo surrender. Still, he was grateful to God for having given him the victory, and gave thanks, and, kneeling down, kissed the earth three times. And after the body of Don Alonzo was carried from the ground, he said to the second, "Don Diego, my lord, have I done enough?" And Don Diego answered sadly, "Enough and too much, Señor Bayardo, for the honour of Spain." "You know," said Monsieur de Bayard, "that as the victor the body is mine to do as I will, but I yield it to you; and truly, I would that, my honour satisfied, it had fallen out otherwise." So the Spaniards bore away their champion with sobs and tears, and the French led off the conqueror with shouts of joy, and the noise of trumpets and clarions, to the tent of Monsieur de la

Palisse, after which Monsieur de Bayard went straight to the church to give thanks in that he had gained the victory. Thus it happened to the greater renown of Monsieur de Bayard, who was esteemed not only by the French, his countrymen, but by the Spaniards of the kingdom of Naples, to be a peerless knight, who had no equal look where you may.[1]

---

1. Brantôme.

Story of Gudbrand of the Dales[1]

There was a man named Gudbrand of the Dales, who was as good as king over the Dales though he had but the title of duke. He had one son, of whom this story makes mention. Now when Gudbrand heard that King Olaf was come to Loa and was compelling men to receive Christianity, he cut the war-arrow and summoned all the dalesmen to meet him at the village called Houndthorpe. Thither came they all in countless numbers, for the lake Lögr lies near, and they could come by water as well as by land.

There Gudbrand held an assembly with them, and said: "There is a man come to Loa named Olaf; he would fain offer us a faith other than we had before, and break all our gods in sunder. And he says that he has a God far greater and mightier. A wonder it is that the earth does not burst in sunder beneath him who dares to say such things; a wonder that our gods let him any longer walk thereon. And I expect that if we carry Thor out of our temple, wherein he stands and hath alway helped us, and he see Olaf and his men, then will Olaf's God and Olaf himself and all his men melt away and come to nought."

At this they all at once shouted loud, and said that Olaf should never escape alive if he came to meet them. "Never will he dare to go further south by the Dales," said they. Then they appointed seven hundred men to go and reconnoitre northwards to Breida. This force was commanded by Gudbrand's son, then eighteen years old, and many other men of renown with him; and they came to the village called Hof and were there for three nights, where they were joined by much people who had fled from Lesja Loa and Vagi, not being willing to submit to Christianity.

But King Olaf and Bishop Sigurd, after appointing teachers of religion at Loa and Vagi, crossed over the channel between Vagi and the land and came to Sil, and were there for the night; and they heard the tidings that a large force was before them. And the people of the country who were at Breida heard of the King's movements, and prepared for battle against him. But when the King rose in the morn, then he clad him for war, and marched south by Silfield, nor stayed till he came to Breida, where he saw a large army arrayed for battle.

---

1. From the Saga of King Olaf the Holy, or St. Olaf.

Then the King set his men in array and rode himself before them, and, addressing the country-folk, bade them embrace Christianity.

They answered: "Thou wilt have other work to do to-day than to mock us."

And they shouted a war-shout and smote their shields with their weapons. Then the King's men ran forward and hurled their spears; but the country-folk turned and fled, few of them standing their ground. Gudbrand's son was there taken prisoner; but King Olaf gave him quarter and kept him near himself. Three nights the King was there. Then spake he with Gudbrand's son, saying: "Go thou back now to thy father and tell him that I shall come there soon."

Whereupon he went back home and told his father the ill tidings, how they had met the King and fought with him; "but our people all fled at the very first," said he, "and I was taken prisoner. The King gave me quarter, and bade me go and tell thee that he would come here soon. Now have we left no more than two hundred men out of that force with which we met him, and I advise thee, father, not to fight with that man."

"One may hear," said Gudbrand, "that all vigour is beaten out of thee. Ill luck went with thee, and long will thy journey be spoken of. Thou believest at once those mad fancies which that man brings who hath wrought foul shame on thee and thine."

In the following night Gudbrand dreamed a dream. A man came to him, a shining one, from whom went forth great terror. And thus he spake: "Thy son went not on a path of victory against King Olaf; and far worse wilt thou fare if thou resolvest to do battle with the King, for thou wilt fall, thyself and all thy people, and thee and thine will wolves tug and ravens rend."

Much afraid was Gudbrand at this terror, and told it to Thord Fatpaunch, a chief man of the Dales.

He answered: "Just the same vision appeared to me."

And on the morrow they bade the trumpet-blast summon an assembly, and said that they thought it good counsel to hold a conference with that man who came from the north with new doctrine, and to learn what proofs he could bring.

After this Gudbrand said to his son: "Thou shalt go to the King who spared thy life, and twelve men shall go with thee." And so it was done.

And they came to the King and told him their errand—that the country-folk would fain hold a conference with him, and would have a truce between them. The King liked that well, and they settled it so by a treaty between them till the appointed meeting should be; and this done they went back and told Gudbrand and Thord of the truce. The King then went to the village called Lidsstadir, and stayed there five nights. Then he went to meet the country-folk, and held a conference with them; but the day was very wet.

As soon as the conference was met, the King stood up and said that the dwellers in Lesja Loa and Vagi had accepted Christianity and broken down their heathen house of worship, and now believed in the true God who made heaven and earth and knew all things. Then the King sat down; but Gudbrand answered:

"We know not of whom thou speakest. Thou callest him God whom neither thou seest nor anyone else. But we have that god who may be seen every day, though he is not out to-day because the weather is wet: and terrible will he seem to you, and great fear will, I expect, strike your hearts if he come into our assembly. But since thou sayest that your God is so powerful, then let Him cause that to-morrow the weather be cloudy but without rain, and meet we here again."

Thereafter the King went home to his lodging, and with him Gudbrand's son as a hostage, while the King gave them another man in exchange. In the evening the King asked Gudbrand's son how their god was made. He said that he was fashioned to represent Thor: he had a hammer in his hand, and was tall of stature, hollow within, and there was a pedestal under him on which he stood when out-of-doors; nor was there lack of gold and silver upon him. Four loaves of bread were brought to him every day, and flesh-meat therewith. After this talk they went to bed. But the King was awake all night and at his prayers.

With dawn of day the King went to mass, then to meat, then to the assembly. And the weather was just what Gudbrand had bargained for. Then stood up the bishop in his gown, with mitre on head and crozier in hand; and he spoke of the faith before the country-folk, and told of the many miracles which God had wrought, and brought his speech to an eloquent conclusion.

Then answered Thord Fat-paunch: "Plenty of words has that horned one who holds a staff in his hand crooked at the top like a wether's horn. But seeing that you, my good fellows, claim that your God works so many miracles, bespeak of Him for to-morrow that He let it be bright sunshine; and meet we then, and do one of the twain, either agree on this matter or do battle."

And with that they broke up the assembly for the time.

There was a man with King Olaf named Kolbein Strong; he was from the Firths by kin. He had ever this gear, that he was girded with a sword, and had a large cudgel or club in his hand. The King bade Kolbein be close to him on the morrow. And then he said to his men:

"Go ye to-night where the country-folk's ships are, and bore holes in them all, and drive away from their farm-buildings their yoke-horses." And they did so.

But the King spent the night in prayer, praying God that He would solve this difficulty of His goodness and mercy. And when service times were over (and that was towards daybreak) then went he to the assembly. When he came there but few of the country-folk had come. But soon they saw a great multitude coming to the assembly; and they bare among them a huge image of a man, all glittering with gold and silver; which when those who were already at the assembly saw, they all leapt up and bowed before this monster. Then was it set up in the middle of the place of assembly: on the one side sat the folk of the country, on the other the King and his men.

Then up stood Gudbrand of the Dales and spake: "Where is now thy God, O King? Methinks now He boweth His beard full low; and, as I think, less is now thy bragging and that of the horned one whom ye call bishop, and who sits beside thee yea, less than it was yesterday. For now is come our god who rules all, and he looks at you with keen glance, and I see that ye are now full of fear and hardly dare to lift your eyes. Lay down now your superstition and believe in our god, who holds all your counsel in his hand." And so his words were ended.

The King spake with Kolbein Strong, so that the country-folk knew it not: "If it so chance while I am speaking that they look away from their god, then strike him the strongest blow thou canst with thy club."

Then the King stood up and spake: "Plenty of words hast thou spoken to us this morning. Thou thinkest it strange that thou canst not see our God; but we expect that He will soon come to us. Thou goest about to terrify us with thy god, who is blind and deaf and can neither help himself nor others, and can in no way leave his place unless he be carried; and I expect now that evil is close upon him. Nay, look now and see toward the east, there goeth now our God with great light."

Just then up sprang the sun, and toward the sun looked the country-folk all. But in that moment Kolbein dealt such a blow on their god that he burst all asunder, and thereout leapt rats as big as cats, and vipers and snakes.

But the country-folk fled in terror, some to their ships, which when they launched, the water poured in and filled them, nor could they so get away, and some who ran for their horses found them not. Then the King had them called back and said he would fain speak with them; whereupon the country-folk turned back and assembled.

Then the King stood up and spake.

"I know not," said he, "what means this tumult and rushing about that ye make. But now may well be seen what power your god has, whom ye load with gold and silver, meat and food, and now ye see what creatures have enjoyed all this—rats and snakes, vipers and toads. And worse are they who believe in such things, and will not quit their folly. Take ye your gold and jewels that are here now on the field and carry them home to your wives, and never put them again on stocks or stones. But now there are two choices for us: that you accept Christianity or do battle with me to-day. And may those win victory to whom it is willed by the God in whom we believe."

Then stood up Gudbrand of the Dales and spake: "Much scathe have we gotten now in our god; but, as he cannot help himself, we will now believe in the God in whom thou believest." And so they all accepted Christianity.

Then did the bishop baptize Gudbrand and his son. King Olaf and Bishop Sigurd left religious teachers there, and they parted friends who before were foes. And Gudbrand had a church built there in the Dales.

Sir Richard Grenville

S ir Richard Grenville, of Bideford, in Devon, was one of the most noted admirals in the reign of Queen Elizabeth. Although he had large estates, and was very rich, he liked better to go abroad to the new countries just then discovered, or to fight for his country, than to stay at home.

From his wonderful courage and determination never to fly from an enemy, however great the odds might be against him, he had the good fortune to win glory in the most glorious sea-fight that has ever been fought.

In 1591 he was vice-admiral of a small fleet consisting of six line of battle ships, six victuallers, and two or three pinnaces, under the command of Lord Thomas Howard. In the month of August in that year, they lay at anchor off the island of Flores, where they had put in for a fresh supply of water, and to take in ballast, as well as to refresh the crew, for many of them were sick.

Half of the crew of Grenville's ship were disabled and were on shore, when news was brought that a Spanish Armada, consisting of fifty-three ships, was near at hand.

When the admiral heard it, knowing himself to be at a disadvantage, he instantly signalled to the rest of the fleet to cut or weigh their anchors and to follow him out to sea.

All the commanders obeyed his summons but Sir Richard Grenville, whose duty as vice-admiral was to follow at the rear of the fleet; he also waited until his men who were on shore could rejoin him.

Meanwhile he had everything set in readiness to fight, and all the sick were carried to the lower hold.

The rest of the English ships were far away, hull down on the horizon, and the Spaniards, who had come up under cover of the island, were already bearing down in two divisions on his weatherbow before the "Revenge" was ready to sail. Then the master and others, seeing the hopelessness of their case, begged Sir Richard to trust to the good sailing of his ship, "to cut his maine saile and cast about, and to follow the admiral."

But Sir Richard flew into a terrible passion, and swore he would hang any man who should then show himself to be a coward. "That he would rather choose to dye than to dishonour himselfe, his countrie, and her maiestie's shippe."

ANDREW LANG AND H. RIDER HAGGARD

He boldly told his men that he feared no enemy, that he would yet pass through the squadron and *force* them to give him way.

Then were the hundred men on the "Revenge" who were able to fight and to work the ship, fired with the spirit of their commander, and they sailed out to meet the foe with a cheer.

All went well for a little time, and the "Revenge" poured a broadside into those ships of the enemy that she passed. But presently a great ship named "San Felipe" loomed over her path and took the wind out of her sails, so that she could no longer answer to her helm.

While she lay thus helplessly, all her sails of a sudden slack and sweeping the yards, she fired her lower tier, charged with crossbar shot, into the "San Felipe." Then the unwieldy galleon of a thousand and five hundred tons, which bristled with cannon from stem to stern, had good reason to repent her of her temerity, and "shifted herselfe with all dilligence from her sides, utterly misliking her entertainment." It is said she foundered shortly afterwards.

Meanwhile four more Spanish vessels had come up alongside the "Revenge," and lay two on her larboard and two on her starboard. Then a hand to hand fight began in terrible earnest. As those soldiers in the ships alongside were repulsed or thrown back into the sea, yet were their places filled with more men from the galleons around, who brought fresh ammunition and arms. The Spanish ships were filled with soldiers, in some were two hundred besides mariners, in some five hundred, in others eight hundred.

"And a dozen times we shook "em off as a dog that shakes his ears when he leaps from the water to the land."

Grenville was severely hurt at the beginning of the fight, but he paid no heed to his wound, and stayed on the upper decks to cheer and encourage his men. Two of the Spanish ships were sunk by his side, yet two more came in their places, and ever and ever more as their need might be.

Darkness fell upon the scene, and through the silence the musketry fire crackled unceasingly, and the heavy artillery boomed from time to time across the sea. About an hour before midnight Grenville was shot in the body, and while his wound was being dressed, the surgeon who attended him was killed, and at the same time Grenville was shot again in the head.

Still he cried to his men, "Fight on, fight on!"

Before dawn the Spaniards, weary of the fight that had raged for fifteen hours, that had cost them fifteen ships and fifteen hundred men, had drawn off to a little distance, and lay around her in a ring.

Daylight discovered the little "Revenge" a mere water-logged hulk, with rigging and tackle shot away, her masts overboard, her upper works riddled, her pikes broken, all her powder spent, and forty of her best men slain.

The glow that heralded sunrise shot over the sky and stained the placid waters beneath to crimson. In this sea of blood the wreck lay, her decks ruddy with the stain of blood sacrificed for honour.

She lay alone at the mercy of the waves, and unable to move save by their rise and fall, alone with her wounded and dying and her dead to whom could come no help.

Then Sir Richard Grenville called for the master gunner, whom he knew to be both brave and trusty, and told him to sink the ship, so that the Spaniards might have no glory in their conquest. He besought his sailors to trust themselves to the mercy of God, and not to the mercy of men, telling them that for the honour of their country the greater glory would be theirs if they would consent to die with him.

The gunner and many others cried, "Ay, ay, sir," and consented to the sinking of the ship.

But the captain and master would not agree to it: they told Sir Richard that the Spanish admiral would be glad to listen to a composition, as themselves were willing to do. Moreover there were still some men left who were not mortally wounded, and who might yet live to do their country good service. They told him too that the Spaniard could never glory in having taken the ship, for she had six feet of water in the hold already, as well as three leaks from shot under water, that could not be stopped to resist a heavy sea.

But Sir Richard would not listen to any of their reasoning. Meanwhile the master had gone to the general of the Armada, Don Alfonso Baffan, who, knowing Grenville's determination to fight to the last, was afraid to send any of his men on board the "Revenge" again, lest they should be blown up or sink on board of her.

The general yielded that "all their lives should be saved, the companie sent for England, and the better sorte to pay such reasonable ransome as their estate would beare, and in the meane season to be free from galley or imprisonment."

After the men had heard what the captain said they became unwilling to die, and with these honourable terms for surrender they drew back from Sir Richard and the master gunner. "The maister gunner, finding himselfe prevented and maistered by the greater number, would have slaine himselfe with a sword had he not beene by force withhold and locked into his cabben."

Then the Spanish general sent to the "Revenge" to bring Sir Richard to his own ship; for he greatly admired his wonderful courage.

Sir Richard told him they might do what they chose with his body, for he did not care for it; and as he was being carried from his ship in a fainting state, he asked those of his men near him to pray for him.

He only lived for three days after this, but was treated with the greatest courtesy and kindness by the Spaniards. He did not speak again until he was dying, when he said:

"Here am I, Richard Grenville, with a joyful and quiet mind, for that I have ended my life as a true soldier ought to do, that hath fought for his country, Queen, religion, and honour. Whereby my soul most joyfully departeth out of this body, and shall always leave behind it an everlasting fame of a valiant and true soldier, that hath done his dutie as he was bound to do."

The Story of Molly Pitcher

It is a strange and interesting thing to see how history repeats itself in a series of noble and picturesque incidents which are so much alike that they might be easily mistaken for one another. Perhaps in the years to come they will be mistaken for one another, and then those learned scholars who love to deny all the things that are worth believing will say, as they say now of William Tell and the apple: "Whenever an event is represented as happening in different countries and among different nations, we may be sure that it never happened at all." Yet to Spain belongs Augustina, the Maid of Saragossa; to England, brave Mary Ambree; and to America, Molly Pitcher, the stout-hearted heroine of Monmouth; and these three women won for themselves honour and renown by the same valorous exploits. Augustina is the most to be envied, for her praises have been sung by a great poet; Mary Ambree has a noble ballad to perpetuate her fame; Molly Pitcher is still without the tribute of a verse to remind her countrymen occasionally of her splendid courage in the field.

The Spanish girl was of humble birth, young, poor, and very handsome. When Saragossa was besieged by the French during the Peninsular War, she carried food every afternoon to the soldiers who were defending the batteries. One day the attack was so fierce, and the fire so deadly, that by the gate of Portillo not a single man was left alive to repulse the terrible enemy. When Augustina reached the spot with her basket of coarse and scanty provisions, she saw the last gunner fall bleeding on the walls. Not for an instant did she hesitate; but springing over a pile of dead bodies, she snatched the match from his stiffening fingers and fired the gun herself. Then calling on her countrymen to rally their broken ranks, she led them back so unflinchingly to the charge that the French were driven from the gate they had so nearly captured, and the honour of Spain was saved. When the siege was lifted and the city free a pension was settled on Augustina, together with the daily pay of an artilleryman, and she was permitted to wear upon her sleeve an embroidered shield bearing the arms of Saragossa. Lord Byron, in his poem "Childe Harold," has described her beauty her heroism, and the desperate courage with which she defended the breach:

"Who can avenge so well a leader's fall?
What maid retrieve when man's flushed hope is lost!

> *Who hang so fiercely on the flying Gaul,*
> *Foiled by a woman's hand before a battered wall?"*

For the story of Mary Ambree we must leave the chroniclers—who to their own loss and shame never mention her at all—and take refuge with the poets. From them we learn all we need to know, and it is quickly told. Her lover was slain treacherously in the war between Spain and Holland, the English being then allies of the Dutch; and, vowing to avenge his death, she put on his armour and marched to the siege of Ghent, where she fought with reckless courage on its walls. Fortune favours the brave, and wherever the maiden turned her arms the enemy was repulsed, until at last the gallant Spanish soldiers vied with the English in admiration of this valorous foe:

> *"If England doth yield such brave lassies as thee.*
> *Full well may she conquer, faire Mary Ambree."*

Even the Great Prince of Parma desired to see this dauntless young girl, and finding her as chaste as she was courageous and beautiful, he permitted her to sail for home without any molestation from his army.

> *"Then to her own country she back did returne,*
> *Still holding the foes of faire England in scorne;*
> *Therefore English captaines of every degree*
> *Sing forth the brave valours of Mary Ambree."*

And now for Molly Pitcher, who, unsung and almost unremembered, should nevertheless share in the honours heaped so liberally upon the Spanish and English heroines. "A red-haired, freckled-faced young Irishwoman," without beauty and without distinction, she was the newly-wedded wife of an artilleryman in Washington's little army. On June 28, 1778, was fought the battle of Monmouth, famous for the admirable tactics by which Washington regained the advantages lost through the negligence of General Charles Lee, and also for the splendid charge and gallant death of Captain Moneton, an officer of the English grenadiers. It was a Sunday morning, close and sultry. As the day advanced, the soldiers on both sides suffered terribly from that fierce, unrelenting heat in which America rivals India. The thermometer stood at 96 in the shade. Men fell dead in their ranks without a wound, smitten by sunstroke, and the sight of them filled their comrades with dismay. Molly Pitcher, regardless of everything save the anguish of the sweltering, thirsty troops, carried buckets of water from a neighbouring spring, and passed them along the line. Back and forward she trudged, this strong, brave, patient young woman, while the sweat poured down her freckled face, and her bare arms blistered in the sun. She was a long time in reaching her husband—so many soldiers begged for drink as she toiled by—but at last she saw him, parched, grimy, spent with heat, and she quickened her lagging steps. Then suddenly a ball whizzed past, and he fell dead by the side of his gun before ever the coveted water had touched his blackened lips. Molly dropped her bucket, and for one dazed moment stood staring at the bleeding corpse. Only for a moment, for, amid the turmoil of battle, she heard the order given to drag her husband's cannon from the field. The words roused her to life and purpose. She seized the rammer from the trodden grass, and hurried to the gunner's post. There was nothing strange in the work to her. She was too well versed in the ways of war for either ignorance or alarm. Strong, skilful, and fearless, she stood by the weapon and directed its deadly fire until the fall of Moneton turned the tide of victory. The British troops under Clinton were beaten back after a desperate struggle, the Americans took possession of the field, and the battle of Monmouth was won.

On the following day, poor Molly, no longer a furious Amazon, but a sad-faced widow, with swollen eyes, and a scanty bit of crape pinned on her broad young bosom, was presented to Washington, and received a sergeant's commission with half-pay for life. It is said that the French officers, then fighting for the freedom of the colonies, that is, against the English, were so delighted with her courage that they added to this reward a cocked hat full of gold pieces, and christened her "La Capitaine." What befell her in after-years has never been told. She lived and died obscurely, and her name has well-nigh been forgotten in the land she served. But the memory of brave deeds can never wholly perish, and Molly Pitcher has won for herself a little niche in the temple of Fame, where her companions are fair Mary Ambree and the dauntless Maid of Saragossa.

The Voyages, Dangerous Adventures, and Imminent Escapes of Captain Richard Falconer[1]

I was born at a town called Bruton, in Somersetshire, and my parents were well-to-do people. My mother died when I was very young; my father, who had been a great traveller in his days, often told me of his adventures, which gave me a strong desire for a roving life. I used to beg my father to let me go to sea with some captain of his acquaintance; but he only warned me solemnly against the dangers to which sailors were exposed, and told me I should soon wish to be at home again.

But at last, through my father's misfortunes, my wish was gratified, for he was robbed of a large sum of money, and found himself unable to provide for me as he wished. Disaster followed disaster till he was compelled to recommend to me the very life he had warned me against. I left him for Bristol, carrying with me a letter he had written to a captain there, begging him to give me all the help in his power, and never saw him again. But Captain Pultney, his friend, welcomed me like a son, and before long got me a berth on the "Albion" frigate, in which I set sail for Jamaica on May 2, 1699.

When we were in the Bay of Biscay a terrible storm came on; the billows ran mountains high, and our vessel was the sport of the waves. A ship that had overtaken and followed us the day before seemed to be in yet worse distress, and signalled to us for aid; but we could not get very near them without danger to ourselves. We sent out our long-boat, with two of our men; but the rope that held her to the ship broke with the violence of the waves, and she was carried away, nor did we ever hear what became of our unhappy comrades. Very soon, in spite of the labour of the crew, the vessel we were trying to help went down, and out of fifty-four men, only four were saved who had the good fortune to catch the ropes we threw out to them. When they told us their story, however, we could not help wondering at the escape we had had, for the lost ship belonged to a pirate, who had only been waiting till the storm was over to attack us, and the men we had saved had, according to their own account, been compelled against their will to serve the pirates.

---

1. London, 1720.

Very soon the storm abated, and we continued our voyage. It was not long before we had another adventure with pirates, and the next time they caught us at midnight, and, hailing us, commanded us to come on board their ship with our captain. We answered that we had no boat, and asked them to wait till the morning. At this, the pirate captain threatened to sink us, and therewith fired a gun at our vessel.

But we, being on our guard, had already mustered our guns and our forces, thirty-eight men, counting the passengers, who were as ready to fight as any of us. So we sent them back a broadside, which surprised them and did them some damage. Then we tacked about, and with six of our guns raked the enemy fore and aft; but we were answered very quickly with a broadside that killed two of our men and wounded a third. Presently they boarded us with about fourscore men, and we found all our resistance idle, for they drove us into the forecastle, where we managed to barricade ourselves, and threatened to turn our own guns against us if we did not surrender immediately. But our captain being resolute, ordered us to fire on them with our small-arms. Now close to our steerage was a large cistern lined with tin, where several cartridges of powder happened to be; and, happily for us, in the tumult of the firing this powder took fire, and blew part of the quarter-deck and at least thirty of the enemy into the air. On this we sallied out, and drove the rest into their own vessel again with our cutlasses, killing several. But, alas! with the explosion and the breach of the quarter-deck our powder-room was quite blocked up, and we had to go on fighting with what powder we had by us. Fight we did, nevertheless, for at least four hours, when dawn broke, and to our great joy we saw another ship not far away, and distinguished English colours. At this sight we gave a great shout and fired our small-arms again; but our enemies very quickly cut away their grappling irons, and did their best to make off. Their rigging, however, was so shattered that they could not hoist sail, and in the meantime up came the English ship, and without so much as hailing the pirate, poured a broadside into her. Then followed a desperate fight. As for us, we steered off, to clear away the lumber from our powder-room, as we had nothing left to charge our guns with. In half-an-hour we had loaded again, and returned to the fight; but as we approached we saw the pirate sinking. The English ship had torn a hole in her between wind and water, so that she sank in an instant, and only eight men were saved. They told us that their captain was a pirate from Guadaloupe, and when they sank they had not more than twenty men left out of a hundred and fifty. On board our ship seven sailors and two passengers were killed, while the Guernsey frigate that rescued us had lost sixteen men and three wounded.

I need now relate no more of our adventures on the voyage till I come to a very sad one which befell me in October. We were sailing towards Jamaica, and one day I went into the boat astern which had been hoisted overboard in the morning to look after a wreck we had seen on the water. I pulled a book out of my pocket and sat reading in the boat; but before I was aware, a storm began to rise, so that I could not get up the ship side as usual, but called for the ladder of ropes in order to get back that way. Now, whether the ladder was not properly fastened above, or whether, being seldom used, it broke through rottenness, I cannot tell, but down I fell into the sea, and though, as I heard afterwards, the ship tacked about to take me up, I lost sight of it in the dusk of the evening and the gathering storm.

Now my condition was terrible. I was forced to drive with the wind and current, and after having kept myself above water for about four hours, as near as I could guess in my fright, I felt my feet touch ground every now and then, and at last a great wave flung me upon the sand. It was quite dark, and I knew not what to do; but I got up and walked as well as my tired limbs would carry me. For I could discover no trace of firm land, and supposed I was on some sandbank which the sea would overflow at high tide. But by-and-by I had to sit down out of sheer exhaustion, though I only looked for death. All my sins came before me, and I prayed earnestly, and at last recovered calm and courage.

In spite of all my efforts to keep awake, I fell fast asleep before dawn came.

In the morning I was amazed to find myself among four or five very low sandy islands, all separated half-a-mile or more, as I guessed, by the sea. With that I became more cheerful, and walked about to see if I could find anything eatable. To my grief I found nothing but a few eggs, that I was obliged to eat raw, and this almost made me wish that the sea had engulfed me rather than thrown me on this desert island, which seemed to me inhabited only by rats and several kinds of birds.

A few bushes grew upon it, and under these I had to shelter at night, but though I searched through the island, I could not find a drop of fresh water. Nor could I have continued to live, having only the eggs I found, if I had not succeeded in knocking down some birds with a stick, which made me a grand banquet. This gave me heart to try to make a fire after the fashion of the blacks by rubbing two sticks together, and I managed to do this after a while, and cooked my birds on the fire I had lit.

That night came a great storm, with the reddest lightning I had ever seen, and rain that drenched me through. But in the morning I had the joy of finding several pools of rain-water; and this put it into my mind to make a kind of well, that I might keep a supply of water by me.

With my hands and a stick I dug a hollow place, large enough to hold a hogshead of water, and when it was dug I paved it with stones, and, getting in, stamped them down hard, and beat the sides close with my stick so that the well would hold water a long time. But how to get it there was a difficulty, till by soaking my shirt, which was pretty fine, in water, I found that I could make it fairly water-tight, and with this holland bucket carry two gallons at a time, which only leaked out about a pint in two hundred yards. By this contrivance, in two days I had filled my well.

I next made myself a cupboard of earth by mixing water with it; but unhappily it lasted only four days, the sun drying it so fast that it cracked.

I had a small Ovid, printed by Elzevir, which fortunately I had put in my pocket as I was going up the ladder of ropes. This was a great solace, for I could entertain myself with it under a bush till I fell asleep. Moreover, I had good health, though at first I was troubled with headache for want of my hat, which I had lost in the water. But I made myself a wooden cap of green sprigs, and lined it with one of the sleeves of my shirt.

The island I was upon seemed about two miles round, and perfectly deserted. Often did I wish to have companions in my misfortune, and even—Heaven forgive me!—hoped for a wreck. I fancied that if I stayed there long alone I should lose the power of speech, so I talked aloud, asked myself questions, and answered them. If anybody had been by to hear they would certainly have thought me bewitched, I used to ask myself such odd questions!

But one morning a violent storm arose, which continued till noon, when I caught sight of a ship labouring with the waves. At last, with the fury of the tempest, it was completely thrown out of the water upon the shore, a quarter of a mile from the place where I was watching. I ran to see if there was anyone I could help, and found four men, all who were in the vessel, trying to save what they could out of her. When I came up and hailed them in English they were mightily surprised, and asked me how I came there. I told them my story, and they were greatly distressed for themselves as well as for me, since they found there was no hope of getting their vessel off the sands; so we began to bemoan each other's misfortunes. But I must confess that I was never more rejoiced in my whole life, for they had on board plenty of everything for a twelvemonth, and nothing spoiled. We worked as hard as we could, and got out whatever would be useful to us before night. Then, taking off the sails, we built a tent big enough to hold twenty men, and now I thought myself in a palace.

The names of my four companions were Thomas Randal, Richard White, William Musgrave, and Ralph Middleton. When we had been together some time we began to be very easy, and to wait contentedly till we should get out of this strait. But at last it came into our minds that a determined effort might free us, and at once we set to work to clear the sand from the ship. We laboured at the task for sixteen days, resting only on Sundays, and by that time we had thrown up the sand on each side, making a passage for our vessel right to the surface of the water where it was lowest. We next got poles to put under the vessel to launch her out, and resolved on the day following, God willing, to thrust her into the water. But we were prevented by the illness of Mr. Randal, who had been the guide and counsellor of our whole party. It soon became evident that he could not recover, and the week after he died.

After this we succeeded in launching our vessel, but again a terrible misfortune happened. We had made the ship fast with two anchors the night before we intended to begin our voyage, and my companions resolved to stay on shore, while I, as for some nights had been my custom, slept on board.

I rested very contentedly, and in the morning went on deck ready to call my companions. To my horror the sea surrounded the vessel; there was not a glimpse of land! The shock was so terrible that I fell down on the deck unconscious. How long I continued so I know not, but when I came to myself a little reflection told me what had happened. A hurricane had risen and torn away the vessel while I slept heavily, for the night before we had all drunk too freely, and my remorse was the more bitter for remembering Mr. Randal, the good man whose warnings, had he lived, would have prevented this misfortune.

But fate was kinder to me than I deserved. For a fortnight I was tossed upon the sea without discovering land, and with only the company of the dog that had been poor Mr. Randal's. But three days later I saw land right ahead, to my great joy, though joy was not unmixed with fear, as I did not know into whose hands I might fall. It was on January 30 that I reached the bay and town of Campeche, where I was met by two canoes, with a Spaniard and six Indians, who, on learning something of my story, I speaking in broken French, which the Spaniard understood, immediately took me on shore to the Governor. He, on hearing of my arrival, sent for me where he sat at dinner, and received me with the utmost kindness.

These generous Spaniards not only feasted me while I remained there, but soon collected among themselves money enough to fit out my vessel ready to go and rescue my poor companions left on the desert island. On February 15 we sailed from Campeche Bay, after I, having nothing else to give, had offered my Ovid to the Governor. He took it kindly, saying that he should prize it very highly, not only for its own sake, but in memory of my misfortunes.

Fifteen days after we reached the island, and found my three companions, but in a miserable condition. For they were left without provisions and with hardly any fresh water, every necessary being on board the ship; and when we arrived they had been five days without eating or drinking, and were too weak to crawl in search of food. But now, for the time being, their misfortunes were ended, and I cannot describe the joy with which they welcomed us after having almost despaired of any human help.

We soon set out again in the Spanish ship, and by-and-by, not without a number of adventures on the way, we reached Jamaica, where I met with my old shipmates, who were very much surprised to see me, thinking that I had been lost in the sea many months ago. The ship had hung lights out for several hours that I might know where to swim, but all to no purpose, as I could see nothing through the darkness of the storm. I found that the captain was very ill, and went to visit him on shore. He told me that he did not expect to live long, and was glad I had come to take charge of the ship, which would have sailed before if he had been fit to command her. A week after he died, entrusting me with the management of his affairs, and messages to his wife, who lived at Bristol.

We set sail for England on June 1, 1700, and on August 21 we discovered the Land's End. How rejoiced I was to see England once more, let them judge that have escaped so many perils as I had done.

My first task when I reached Bristol was to inquire for my father; but a bitter disappointment awaited me. He was dead, broken down before his time by grief and misfortune. I could not bear to stay on shore, where everything reminded me of him, and, for all my delight in coming back to England, it was not long before I set sail again in quest of fresh adventures.

Marbot's March

I have now (says General Marbot, speaking of his Spanish campaign) reached one of the most terrible experiences of my military career. Marshal Lannes had just won a great victory, and the next day, after having received the reports of the generals, he wrote his despatch for one of our officers to take to the Emperor. Napoleon's practice was to give a step to the officer who brought him the news of an important success, and the marshals on their side entrusted such tasks to officers for whose speedy promotion they were anxious. It was a form of recommendation which Napoleon never failed to recognise. Marshal Lannes did me the honour of appointing me to carry the news of the victory of Tudela, and I could indulge the hope of being major before long. But, alas! I had yet much blood to lose before I reached that rank.

The high road from Bayonne to Madrid by Vittoria, Miranda del Ebro, Burgos, and Aranda forks off at Miranda from that leading to Saragossa by Logroño. A road from Tudela to Aranda across the mountains about Soria forms the third side of a great triangle. While Lannes was reaching Tudela the Emperor had advanced from Burgos to Aranda. It was, therefore, much shorter for me to go from Tudela to Aranda than by way of Miranda del Ebro. The latter road, however, had the advantage of being covered by the French armies; while the other, no doubt, would be full of Spanish fugitives who had taken refuge after Tudela in the mountains. The Emperor, however, had informed Lannes that he was sending Ney's corps direct from Aranda to Tudela; so thinking Ney to be at no great distance, and that an advanced force which he had pushed on the day after the battle to get touch of him at Taragona would secure me from attack as far as Aranda, Lannes ordered me to take the shortest road. I may frankly admit that if I had had my choice I should have preferred to make the round by Miranda and Burgos; but the marshal's orders were positive, and how could I express any fear for my own person in the presence of a man who knew no more fear for others than he did for himself?

The duties of marshal's aide-de-camp in Spain were terrible. During the revolutionary wars the generals had couriers paid by the state to carry their despatches; but the Emperor, finding that these men were not capable of giving any intelligible account of what they had seen, did away with them, and ordered that in future despatches should be carried by aides-de-camp. This was all very well as long as we were at war among the good Germans, to whom it never occurred to attack a French messenger; but the Spaniards waged fierce war against them. This was of great advantage to the insurgents, for the contents of our despatches informed them of the movements of our armies. I do not think I am exaggerating when I say that more than two hundred staff officers were killed or captured during the Peninsular War. One may regret the death of an ordinary courier, but it is less serious than the loss of a promising officer, who, moreover, is exposed to the risks of the battlefield in addition to those of a posting journey. A great number of vigorous men well skilled in their business begged to be allowed to do this duty, but the Emperor never consented.

Just as I was starting from Tudela, Major Saint-Mars hazarded a remark intended to dissuade Lannes from sending me over the mountains. The marshal, however, answered, "Oh, he will meet Ney's advance guard to-night, and find troops echelonned all the way to the Emperor's head-quarters." This was too decided for any opposition, so I left Tudela November 4, at nightfall, with a detachment of cavalry, and got without any trouble as far as Taragona, at the foot of the mountains. In this little town I found Lannes' advance guard. The officer in command, hearing nothing of Ney, had pushed an infantry post six leagues forward towards Agreda. But as this body was detached from its supports, it had been ordered to fall back on Taragona if the night passed without Ney's scouts appearing.

After Taragona there is no more high road. The way lies entirely over mountain paths covered with stones and splinters of rock. The officer commanding our advanced guard had, therefore, only infantry and a score of hussars of the 2nd (Chamborant) Regiment. He gave me a troop horse and two orderlies, and I went on my way in brilliant moonlight. When we had gone two or three leagues we heard several musket-shots, and bullets whistled close past us. We could not see the marksmen, who were hidden among the rocks. A little farther on we found the corpses of two French infantry soldiers, recently killed. They were entirely stripped, but their shakoes were near them, by the numbers on which I could see that they belonged to one of the regiments in Ney's corps. Some little distance farther we saw a horrible sight. A young officer of the 10th Mounted Chasseurs, still wearing his uniform, was nailed by his hands and feet, head downwards, to a barn door. A small fire had been lighted beneath him. Happily, his tortures had been ended by death; but as the blood was still flowing from his wounds, it was clear that the murderers were not far off. I drew my sword; my two hussars handled their carbines. It was just as well that we were on our guard, for a few moments later seven or eight Spaniards, two of them mounted, fired upon us from behind a bush. We were none of us wounded, and my two hussars replied to the fire, and killed each his man. Then, drawing their swords, they dashed at the rest. I should have been very glad to follow them, but my horse had lost a shoe among the stones and was limping, so that I could not get him into a gallop. I was the more vexed because I feared that the hussars might let themselves be carried away in the pursuit and get killed in some ambush. I called them for five minutes; then I heard the voice of one of them saying, in a strong Alsatian accent, "Ah! you thieves! you don't know the Chamborant Hussars yet. You shall see that they mean business." My troopers had knocked over two more Spaniards, a Capuchin mounted on the horse of the poor lieutenant, whose haversack he had put over his own neck, and a peasant on a mule, with the clothes of the slaughtered soldiers on his back. It was quite clear that we had got the murderers. The Emperor had given strict orders that every Spanish civilian taken in arms should be shot on the spot; and, moreover, what could we do with these two brigands, who were already seriously wounded, and who had just killed three Frenchmen so barbarously? I moved on, therefore, so as not to witness the execution, and the hussars shot the monk and the peasant, repeating, "Ah, you don't know the Chamborant!" I could not understand how an officer and two privates of Ney's corps could be so near Taragona when their regiments had not come that way; but most probably they had been captured elsewhere, and were being taken to Saragossa, when their escort learned the defeat of their countrymen at Tudela, and massacred their prisoners in revenge for it.

After this not very encouraging start I continued my journey. We had gone for some hours, when we saw a bivouac fire of the detachment belonging to the advance guard which I had left at Taragona. The sub-lieutenant in command, having no tidings of Ney, was prepared to return to Taragona at daybreak, in pursuance of his orders. He knew that we were barely two leagues from Agreda, but did not know of which side that town was in possession. This was perplexing for me. The infantry detachment would return in a few hours, and if I went back with it, when it might be that in another league I should fall in with Ney's column, I should be giving a poor display of courage, and laying myself open to reproach from Lannes. On the other hand, if Ney was still a day or two's march away, it was almost certain that I should be murdered by the peasants of the mountains or by fugitive soldiers. What was more, I had to travel alone, for my two brave hussars had orders to return to Taragona when we had found the infantry detachment. No matter; I determined to push on; but then came the difficulty of finding a mount. There was no farm or village in this deserted place where I could procure a horse. That which I was riding was dead lame; and even if the hussars had been able, without incurring severe punishment, to lend me one of theirs, theirs were much fatigued. The horse that had belonged to the officer of chasseurs had received a bullet in the thigh during the fighting. There was only the peasant's mule left. This was a handsome beast, and, according to the laws of war, belonged to the two hussars, who, no doubt, reckoned on selling her when they got back to the army. Still the good fellows made no demur about lending her to me, and put my saddle on her back. But the infernal beast, more accustomed to the pack than to the saddle, was so restive that directly I tried to get her away from the group of horses and make her go alone she fell to kicking, until I had to choose between being sent over a precipice and dismounting.

So I decided to set out on foot. After I had taken farewell of the infantry officer, this excellent young man, M. Tassin by name—he had been a friend of my poor brother Felix at the military school— came running after me, and said that he could not bear to let me thus expose myself all alone, and that though he had no orders, and his men were raw recruits, with little experience in war, he must send one with me, so that I might at least have a musket and some cartridges in case of an attack. We agreed that I should send the man back with Ney's corps; and I went off, with the soldier accompanying me. He was a slow-speaking Norman, with plenty of slyness under an appearance of good nature. The Normans are for the most part brave, as I learnt when I commanded the 23rd Chasseurs, where I had five or six hundred of them. Still, in order to know how far I could rely on my follower, I chatted with him as we went along, and asked if he would stand his ground if we were attacked. He said neither yes nor no, but answered, "Well, sir, we shall see." Whence I inferred that when the moment of danger arrived my new companion was not unlikely to go and see how things were getting on in the rear.

The moon had just set, and as yet daylight had not appeared. It was pitch-dark, and at every step we stumbled over the great stones with which these mountain paths are covered. It was an unpleasant situation, but I hoped soon to come upon Ney's troops, and the fact of having seen the bodies of soldiers belonging to his corps increased the hope. So I went steadily on, listening for diversion to the Norman's stories of his country. Dawn appeared at last, and I saw the first houses of a large village. It was Agreda. I was alarmed at finding no outposts, for it showed that not only did no troops of the marshal's occupy the place, but that his army corps must be at least half a day further on. The map showed no village within five or six leagues of Agreda, and it was impossible that the regiments could be quartered in the mountains, far from any inhabited place. So I kept on my guard, and before going any farther reconnoitred the position.

Agreda stands in a rather broad valley. It is built at the foot of a lofty hill, deeply escarped on both sides. The southern slope, which reaches the village, is planted with large vineyards. The ridge is rough and rocky, and the northern slope covered with thick coppice, a torrent flowing at the foot. Beyond are seen lofty mountains, uncultivated and uninhabited. The principal street of Agreda runs through the whole length of the place, with narrow lanes leading to the vineyards opening into it. As I entered the village I had these lanes and the vineyards on my right. This is important to the understanding of my story.

Everybody was asleep in Agreda; the moment was favourable for going through it. Besides, I had some hope—feeble, it is true—that when I reached the farther end I might perhaps see the fires of Marshal Ney's advance guard. So I went forward, sword in hand, bidding my soldier cock his musket. The main street was covered with a thick bed of damp leaves, which the people placed there to make manure; so that our footsteps made no sound, of which I was glad. I walked in the middle of the street, with the soldier on my right; but, finding himself no doubt in a too conspicuous position, he gradually sheered off to the houses, keeping close to the walls so that he might be less visible in case of an attack, or better placed for reaching one of the lanes which open into the country. This showed me how little I could rely on the man; but I made no remark to him. The day was beginning to break. We passed the whole of the main street without meeting any one. Just as I was congratulating myself on reaching the last houses of the village, I found myself at twenty-five paces' distance, face to face with four Royal Spanish Carabineers on horseback with drawn swords. Under any other circumstances I might have taken them for French gendarmes, their uniforms being exactly similar, but the gendarmes never march with the extreme advanced guard. These men, therefore, could not belong to Ney's corps, and I at once perceived they were the enemy. In a moment I faced about, but just as I had turned round to the direction from which I had come I saw a blade flash six inches from my face. I threw my head sharply back, but nevertheless got a severe sabre-cut on the forehead, of which I carry the scar over my left eyebrow to this day. The man who had wounded me was the corporal of the carabineers, who, having left his four troopers outside the village, had according to military practice gone forward to reconnoitre. That I had not met him was probably due to the fact that he had been in some side lane, while I had passed through the main street. He was now coming back through the street to rejoin his troopers, when, seeing me, he had come up noiselessly over a layer of leaves and was just going to cleave my head from behind, when, by turning round, I presented to him my face and received his blow on my forehead. At the same moment the four carabineers, who seeing that their corporal was all ready for me had not stirred, trotted up to join him, and all five dashed upon me. I ran mechanically towards the houses on the right in order to get my back against a wall; but by good luck I found, two paces off, one of the steep and narrow lanes, which went up to the vineyards. The soldier had already reached it. I flew up there too with the five carabineers after me; but at any rate they could not attack me all at once, for there was only room for one horse to pass. The brigadier went in front; the other four filed after him. My position, although not as unfavourable as it would have been in the street, where I should have been surrounded, still remained alarming; the blood flowing freely from my wound had in a moment covered my left eye, with which I could not see at all, and I felt that it was coming towards my right eye, so that I was compelled by fear of getting blinded to keep my head bent over the left shoulder so as to bring the blood to that side. I could not staunch it, being obliged to defend myself against the corporal, who was cutting at me heavily. I parried as well as I could, going up backwards all the time. After getting rid of my scabbard and my busby, the weight of which hampered me, not daring to turn my head for fear of losing sight of my adversary, whose sword was crossed with mine, I told the light infantry man, whom I believed to be behind me, to place his musket on my shoulder, and fire at the Spanish corporal. Seeing no barrel, however, I leapt a pace back and turned my head quickly. Lo and behold, there was my scoundrel of a

Norman soldier flying up the hill as fast as his legs would carry him. The corporal thereupon attacked with redoubled vigour, and, seeing that he could not reach me, made his horse rear so that his feet struck me more than once on the breast. Luckily, as the ground went on rising the horse had no good hold with his hind legs, and every time that he came down again I landed a sword cut on his nose with such effect that the animal presently refused to rear at me any more. Then the brigadier, losing his temper, called out to the trooper behind him, "Take your carbine: I will stoop down, and you can aim at the Frenchman over my shoulders." I saw that this order was my death-signal; but as in order to execute it the trooper had to sheathe his sword and unhook his carbine, while all this time the corporal never ceased thrusting at me, leaning right over his horse's neck, I determined on a desperate action, which would be either my salvation or my ruin. Keeping my eye fixed on the Spaniard, and seeing in his that he was on the point of again stooping over his horse to reach me, I did not move until the very instant when he was lowering the upper part of his body towards me; then I took a pace to the right, and leaning quickly over to that side, I avoided my adversary's blow, and plunged half my sword-blade into his left flank. With a fearful yell the corporal fell back on the croup of his horse; he would probably have fallen to the ground if the trooper behind him had not caught him in his arms. My rapid movement in stooping had caused the despatch which I was carrying to fall out of the pocket of my pelisse. I picked it up quickly, and at once hastened to the end of the lane where the vines began. There I turned round and saw the carabineers busy round their wounded corporal, and apparently much embarrassed with him and with their horses in the steep and narrow passage.

This fight took less time than I have taken to relate it. Finding myself rid, at least for the moment, of my enemies, I went through the vines and reached the edge of the hill. Then I considered that it would be impossible for me to accomplish my errand and reach the Emperor at Aranda. I resolved, therefore, to return to Marshal Lannes, regaining first the place where I had left M. Tassin and his picket of infantry. I did not hope to find them still there; but at any rate the army which I had left the day before was in that direction. I looked for my soldier in vain, but I saw something that was of more use to me—a spring of clear water. I halted there a moment, and, tearing off a corner of my shirt, I made a compress which I fastened over my wound with my handkerchief. The blood spurting from my forehead had stained the despatches which I held in my hand, but I was too much occupied with my awkward position to mind that.

The agitations of the past night, my long walk over the stony paths in boots and spurs, the fight in which I had just been engaged, the pain in my head, and the loss of blood had exhausted my strength. I had taken no food since leaving Tudela, and here I had nothing but water to refresh myself with. I drank long draughts of it, and should have rested longer by the spring had I not perceived three of the Spanish carabineers riding out of Agreda and coming towards me through the vines. If they had been sharp enough to dismount and take off their long boots, they would probably have succeeded in reaching me; but their horses, unable to pass between the vine stocks, ascended the steep and rocky paths with difficulty. Indeed, when they reached the upper end of the vineyards they found themselves brought up by the great rocks, on the top of which I had taken refuge, and unable to climb any farther. Then the troopers, passing along the bottom of the rocks, marched parallel with me a long musket-shot off. They called to me to surrender, saying that as soldiers they would treat me as a prisoner of war, while if the peasants caught me I should infallibly be murdered. This reasoning was sound, and I admit that if I had not been charged with despatches for the Emperor, I was so exhausted that I should perhaps have surrendered.

However, wishing to preserve to the best of my ability the precious charge which had been entrusted to me, I marched on without answering. Then the three troopers, taking their carbines, opened fire upon me. Their bullets struck the rocks at my feet but none touched me, the distance being too great for a correct aim. I was alarmed, not at the fire, but at the notion that the reports would probably attract the peasants who would be going to their work in the morning, and I quite expected to be attacked by these fierce mountaineers. My presentiment seemed to be verified, for I perceived some fifteen men half a league away in the valley advancing towards me at a run. They held in their hands something that flashed in the sun. I made no doubt that they were peasants armed with their spades, and that it was the iron of these that shone thus. I gave myself up for lost, and in my despair I was on the point of letting myself slide down over the rocks on the north side of the hill to the torrent, crossing it as best I could, and hiding myself in some chasm of the great mountains which arose on the farther side of the gorge. Then, if I was not discovered, and if I still had the strength, I should set out when night came in the direction of Taragona.

This plan, though offering many chances of failure, was my last hope. Just as I was about to put it into execution, I perceived that the three carabineers had given up firing on me, and gone forward to reconnoitre the group which I had taken for peasants. At their approach the iron instruments which I had taken for spades or mattocks were lowered, and I had the inexpressible joy of seeing a volley fired at the Spanish carabineers. Instantly turning, they took flight towards Agreda, as it seemed, with two of their number wounded. "The newcomers, then, are French!" I exclaimed. "Here goes to meet them!" and, regaining a little strength from the joy of being delivered, I descended, leaning on my sword. The French had caught sight of me; they climbed the hill, and I found myself in the arms of the brave Lieutenant Tassin.

This providential rescue had come about as follows. The soldier who had deserted me while I was engaged with the carabineers in the streets of Agreda had quickly reached the vines; thence, leaping across the vine stocks, ditches, rocks, and hedges, he had very quickly run the distance which lay between him and the place where we had left M. Tassin's picket. The detachment was on the point of starting for Taragona, and was eating its soup, when my Norman came up all out of breath. Not wishing, however, to lose a mouthful, he seated himself by a cooking-pot and began to make a very tranquil breakfast, without saying a word about what had happened at Agreda. By great good luck he was noticed by M. Tassin, who, surprised at seeing him returned, asked him where he had quitted the officer whom he had been told off to escort. "Good Lord, sir," replied the Norman, "I left him in that big village with his head half split open, and fighting with Spanish troopers, and they were cutting away at him with their swords like anything." At these words Lieutenant Tassin ordered his detachment to arms, picked the fifteen most active, and went off at the double towards Agreda. The little troop had gone some way when they heard shots, and inferred from them that I was still alive but in urgent need of succour. Stimulated by the hope of saving me, the brave fellows doubled their pace, and finally perceived me on the ridge of the hill, serving as a mark for three Spanish troopers.

M. Tassin and his men were tired, and I was at the end of my strength. We halted, therefore, for a little, and meanwhile you may imagine that I expressed my warmest gratitude to the lieutenant and his men, who were almost as glad as I was. We returned to the bivouac where M.

Tassin had left the rest of his people. The *cantinière* of the company was there with her mule carrying two skins of wine, bread, and ham. I bought the lot and gave them to the soldiers, and we breakfasted, as I was very glad to do, the two hussars whom I had left there the night before sharing in the meal. One of these mounted the monk's mule and lent me his horse, and so we set out for Taragona. I was in horrible pain, because the blood had hardened over my wound. At Taragona I rejoined Lannes' advance guard: the general in command had my wound dressed, and gave me a horse and an escort of two hussars. I reached Tudela at midnight, and was at once received by the marshal, who, though ill himself, seemed much touched by my misfortune. It was necessary, however, that the despatch about the battle of Tudela should be promptly forwarded to the Emperor, who must be impatiently awaiting news from the army on the Ebro. Enlightened by what had befallen me in the mountains, the marshal consented that the officer bearing it should go by Miranda and Burgos, where the presence of French troops on the roads made the way perfectly safe. I should have liked very much to be the bearer, but I was in such pain and so tired that it would have been physically impossible for me to ride hard. The marshal therefore entrusted the duty to his brother-in-law, Major Guéhéneuc. I handed him the despatches stained with my blood. Major Saint-Mars, the secretary, wished to re-copy them and change the envelope. "No, no," cried the marshal, "the Emperor ought to see how valiantly Captain Marbot has defended them." So he sent off the packet just as it was, adding a note to explain the reason of the delay, eulogising me, and asking for a reward to Lieutenant Tassin and his men, who had hastened so zealously to my succour, without reckoning the danger to which they might have been exposed if the enemy had been in force.

The Emperor did, as a matter of fact, a little while after, grant the Cross both to M. Tassin and to his sergeant, and a gratuity of 100 francs to each of the men who had accompanied them. As for the Norman soldier, he was tried by court martial for deserting his post in the presence of the enemy, and condemned to drag a shot for two years, and to finish his time of service in a pioneer company.

Eylau. The Mare Lisette

General Marbot, one of Napoleon's most distinguished soldiers, thus describes his adventures at the battle of Eylau. "To enable you to understand my story, I must go back to the autumn of 1805, when the officers of the Grand Army, among their preparations for the battle of Austerlitz, were completing their outfits. I had two good horses, the third, for whom I was looking, my charger, was to be better still. It was a difficult thing to find, for though horses were far less dear than now, their price was pretty high, and I had not much money; but chance served me admirably. I met a learned German, Herr von Aister, whom I had known when he was a professor at Sorèze. He had become tutor to the children of a rich Swiss banker, M. Scherer, established at Paris in partnership with M. Finguerlin. He informed me that M. Finguerlin, a wealthy man, living in fine style, had a large stud, in the first rank of which figured a lovely mare, called Lisette, easy in her paces, as light as a deer, and so well broken that a child could lead her. But this mare, when she was ridden, had a terrible fault, and fortunately a rare one: she bit like a bulldog, and furiously attacked people whom she disliked, which decided M. Finguerlin to sell her. She was bought for Mme. de Lauriston whose husband, one of the Emperor's aides-de-camp, had written to her to get his campaigning outfit ready. When selling the mare M. Finguerlin had forgotten to mention her fault, and that very evening a groom was found disembowelled at her feet. Mme. de Lauriston, reasonably alarmed, brought an action to cancel the bargain; not only did she get her verdict, but, in order to prevent further disasters, the police ordered that a written statement should be placed in Lisette's stall to inform purchasers of her ferocity, and that any bargain with regard to her should be void unless the purchaser declared in writing that his attention had been called to the notice. You may suppose that with such a character as this the mare was not easy to dispose of, and thus Herr von Aister informed me that her owner had decided to let her go for what anyone would give. I offered 1,000 francs, and M. Finguerlin delivered Lisette to me, though she had cost him 5,000. This animal gave me a good deal of trouble for some months. It took four or five men to saddle her, and you could only bridle her by covering her eyes and fastening all four legs; but once you were on her back, you found her a really incomparable mount.

"However, since while in my possession she had already bitten several people, and had not spared me, I was thinking of parting with her. But I had meanwhile engaged in my service Francis Woirland, a man who was afraid of nothing, and he, before going near Lisette, whose bad character had been mentioned to him, armed himself with a good hot roast leg of mutton. When the animal flew at him to bite him, he held out the mutton; she seized it in her teeth, and burning her gums, palate, and tongue, gave a scream, let the mutton drop, and from that moment was perfectly submissive to Woirland, and did not venture to attack him again. I employed the same method with a like result. Lisette became as docile as a dog, and allowed me and my servant to approach her freely. She even became a little more tractable towards the stablemen of the staff, whom she saw every day, but woe to the strangers who passed near her! I could quote twenty instances of her ferocity, but I will confine myself to one. While Marshal Augereau was staying at the château of Bellevue, near Berlin, the servants of the staff, having observed that when they went to dinner someone stole the sacks of corn that were left in the stable, got Woirland to unfasten Lisette and leave her near the door. The thief arrived, slipped into the stable, and was in the act of carrying off a sack, when the mare seized him by the nape of the neck, dragged him into the middle of the yard, and trampled on him till she broke two of his ribs. At the shrieks of the thief people ran up, but Lisette would not let him go till my servant and I compelled her, for in her fury she would have flown at anyone else. She had become still more vicious ever since the Saxon hussar officer, of whom I have told you, had treacherously laid open her shoulder with a sabre-cut on the battlefield of Jena.

"Such was the mare which I was riding at Eylau at the moment when the fragments of Augereau's army corps, shattered by a hail of musketry and cannon-balls, were trying to rally near the great cemetery. You will remember how the 14th of the line had remained alone on a hillock, which it could not quit except by the Emperor's order. The snow had ceased for the moment; we could see how the intrepid regiment, surrounded by the enemy, was waving its eagle in the air to show that it still held its ground and asked for support. The Emperor, touched by the grand devotion of these brave men, resolved to try to save them, and ordered Augereau to send an officer to them with orders to leave the hillock, form a small square, and make their way towards us, while a brigade of cavalry should march in their direction and assist their efforts. This was before Murat's great charge. It was almost impossible to carry out the Emperor's wishes, because a swarm of Cossacks was between us and the 14th, and it was clear that any officer who was sent towards the unfortunate regiment would be killed or captured before he could get to it. But the order was positive, and the marshal had to comply.

"It was customary in the Imperial army for the aides-de-camp to place themselves in file a few paces from their general, and for the one who was in front to go on duty first: then, when he had performed his mission, to return and place himself last, in order that each might carry orders in his turn, and dangers might be shared equally. A brave captain of engineers named Froissard, who, though not an aide-de-camp, was on the marshal's staff, happened to be nearest to him, and was bidden to carry the order to the 14th. M. Froissard galloped off; we lost sight of him in the midst of the Cossacks, and never saw him again nor heard what had become of him. The marshal, seeing that the 14th did not move, sent an officer named David; he had the same fate as Froissard: we never heard of him again. Probably both were killed and stripped, and could not be recognised among the many corpses which covered the ground. For the third time the marshal called, 'The officer for duty.' It was my turn.

"Seeing the son of his old friend, and I venture to say his favourite aide-de-camp, come up, the kind marshal's face changed and his eyes filled with tears, for he could not hide from himself that he was sending me to almost certain death. But the Emperor must be obeyed. I was a soldier; it was impossible to make one of my comrades go in my place, nor would I have allowed it; it would have been disgracing me. So I dashed off. But though ready to sacrifice my life I felt bound to take all necessary precautions to save it. I had observed that the two officers who went before me had gone with swords drawn, which led me to think that they had purposed to defend themselves against any Cossacks who might attack them on the way. Such defence, I thought, was ill-considered, since it must have compelled them to halt in order to fight a multitude of enemies, who would overwhelm them in the end. So I went otherwise to work, and leaving my sword in the scabbard, I regarded myself as a horseman who is trying to win a steeplechase, and goes as quickly as possible and by the shortest line towards the appointed goal, without troubling himself with what is to right or left of his path. Now, as my goal was the hillock occupied by the 14th, I resolved to get there without taking any notice of the Cossacks, whom in thought I abolished. This plan answered perfectly. Lisette, lighter than a swallow and flying rather than running, devoured the intervening space, leaping the piles of dead men and horses, the ditches, the broken gun-carriages, the half-extinguished bivouac fires. Thousands of Cossacks swarmed over the plain. The first who saw me acted like sportsmen who, when beating, start a hare, and announce its presence to each other by shouts of 'Your side! Your side!' but none of the Cossacks tried to stop me, first, on account of the extreme rapidity of my pace, and also probably because, their numbers being so great, each thought that I could not avoid his comrades farther on; so that I escaped them all, and reached the 14th regiment without either myself or my excellent mare having received the slightest scratch.

"I found the 14th formed in square on the top of the hillock, but as the slope was very slight the enemy's cavalry had been able to deliver several charges. These had been vigorously repulsed, and the French regiment was surrounded by a circle of dead horses and dragoons, which formed a kind of rampart, making the position by this time almost inaccessible to cavalry; as I found, for in spite of the aid of our men, I had much difficulty in passing over this horrible entrenchment. At last I was in the square. Since Colonel Savary's death at the passage of the Wkra, the 14th had been commanded by a major. While I imparted to this officer, under a hail of balls, the order to quit his position and try to rejoin his corps, he pointed out to me that the enemy's artillery had been firing on the 14th for an hour, and had caused it such loss that the handful of soldiers which remained would inevitably be exterminated as they went down into the plain, and that, moreover, there would not be time to prepare to execute such a movement, since a Russian column was marching on him, and was not more than a hundred paces away. 'I see no means of saving the regiment,' said the major; 'return to the Emperor, bid him farewell from the 14th of the line, which has faithfully executed his orders, and bear to him the eagle which he gave us, and which we can defend no longer: it would add too much to the pain of death to see it fall into the hands of the enemy.' Then the major handed me his eagle, saluted for the last time by the glorious fragment of the intrepid regiment with cries of 'Vive l'Empereur!' they were going to die for him. It was the *Cæsar morituri te salutant* of Tacitus,[1] but in this

---

1. As a matter of fact, Suetonius, "The destined to die salute thee."

case the cry was uttered by heroes. The infantry eagles were very heavy, and their weight was increased by a stout oak pole on the top of which they were fixed. The length of the pole embarrassed me much, and as the stick without the eagle could not constitute a trophy for the enemy, I resolved with the major's consent to break it and only carry off the eagle. But at the moment when I was leaning forward from my saddle in order to get a better purchase to separate the eagle from the pole, one of the numerous cannon-balls which the Russians were sending at us went through the hinder peak of my hat, less than an inch from my head. The shock was all the more terrible since my hat, being fastened on by a strong leather strap under the chin, offered more resistance to the blow. I seemed to be blotted out of existence, but I did not fall from my horse; blood flowed from my nose, my ears, and even my eyes; nevertheless I still could hear and see, and I preserved all my intellectual faculties, although my limbs were paralysed to such an extent that I could not move a single finger.

"Meanwhile the column of Russian infantry which we had just perceived was mounting the hill; they were grenadiers wearing mitre-shaped caps with metal ornaments. Soaked with spirits, and in vastly superior numbers, these men hurled themselves furiously on the feeble remains of the unfortunate 14th, whose soldiers had for several days been living only on potatoes and melted snow; that day they had not had time to prepare even this wretched meal. Still our brave Frenchmen made a valiant defence with their bayonets, and when the square had been broken, they held together in groups and sustained the unequal fight for a long time.

"During this terrible struggle several of our men, in order not to be struck from behind, set their backs against my mare's flanks, she, contrary to her practice, remaining perfectly quiet. If I had been able to move I should have urged her forward to get away from this field of slaughter. But it was absolutely impossible for me to press my legs so as to make the animal I rode understand my wish. My position was the more frightful since, as I have said, I retained the power of sight and thought. Not only were they fighting all round me, which exposed me to bayonet-thrusts, but a Russian officer with a hideous countenance kept making efforts to run me through. As the crowd of combatants prevented him from reaching me, he pointed me out to the soldiers around him, and they, taking me for the commander of the French, as I was the only mounted man, kept firing at me over their comrades' heads, so that bullets were constantly whistling past my ear. One of them would certainly have taken away the small amount of life that was still in me had not a terrible incident led to my escape from the *mêlée*.

"Among the Frenchmen who had got their flanks against my mare's near flank was a quartermaster-sergeant, whom I knew from having frequently seen him at the marshal's, making copies for him of the 'morning states.' This man, having been attacked and wounded by several of the enemy, fell under Lisette's belly, and was seizing my leg to pull himself up, when a Russian grenadier, too drunk to stand steady, wishing to finish him by a thrust in the breast, lost his balance, and the point of his bayonet went astray into my cloak, which at that moment was puffed out by the wind. Seeing that I did not fall, the Russian left the sergeant and aimed a great number of blows at me. These were at first fruitless, but one at last reached me, piercing my left arm, and I felt with a kind of horrible pleasure my blood flowing hot. The Russian grenadier with redoubled fury made another thrust at me, but, stumbling with the force which he put into it, drove his bayonet into my mare's thigh. Her ferocious instincts being restored by the pain, she sprang at the Russian, and at one mouthful tore off his nose, lips, eyebrows, and all the skin of his face, making of him a living death's-head, dripping with blood. Then hurling herself with fury among the combatants, kicking and biting, Lisette upset everything that she met on her road. The officer who had made so many attempts to strike me tried to hold her by the bridle; she seized him by his belly, and carrying him off with ease, she bore him out of the crush to the foot of the hillock, where, having torn out his entrails and mashed his body under her feet, she left him dying on the snow. Then, taking the road by which she had come, she made her way at full gallop towards the cemetery of Eylau. Thanks to the hussar's saddle on which I was sitting, I kept my seat. But a new danger awaited me. The snow had begun to fall again, and great flakes obscured the daylight when, having arrived close to Eylau, I found myself in front of a battalion of the Old Guard, who, unable to see clearly at a distance, took me for an enemy's officer leading a charge of cavalry. The whole battalion at once opened fire on me; my cloak and my saddle were riddled, but I was not wounded nor was my mare. She continued her rapid course, and went through the three ranks of the battalion as easily as a snake through a hedge. But this last spurt had exhausted Lisette's strength; she had lost much blood, for one of the large veins in her thigh had been divided, and the poor animal collapsed suddenly and fell on one side, rolling me over on the other.

"Stretched on the snow among the piles of dead and dying, unable to move in any way, I gradually and without pain lost consciousness. I felt as if I was being gently rocked to sleep. At last I fainted quite away without being revived by the mighty clatter which Murat's ninety squadrons advancing to the charge must have made in passing close to me and perhaps over me. I judge that my swoon lasted four hours, and when I came to my senses I found myself in this horrible position. I was completely naked, having nothing on but my hat and my right boot. A man of the transport corps, thinking me dead, had stripped me in the usual fashion, and wishing to pull off the only boot that remained, was dragging me by one leg with his foot against my body. The jerks which the man gave me no doubt had restored me to my senses. I succeeded in sitting up and spitting out the clots of blood from my throat. The shock caused by the wind of the ball had produced such an extravasation of blood, that my face, shoulders, and chest were black, while the rest of my body was stained red by the blood from my wound. My hat and my hair were full of bloodstained snow, and as I rolled my haggard eyes I must have been horrible to see. Anyhow, the transport man looked the other way, and went off with my property without my being able to say a single word to him, so utterly prostrate was I. But I had recovered my mental faculties, and my thoughts turned towards God and my mother.

"The setting sun cast some feeble rays through the clouds. I took what I believed to be a last farewell of it. 'If,' thought I, 'I had only not been stripped, some one of the numerous people who pass near me would notice the gold lace on my pelisse, and, recognising that I am a marshal's aide-de-camp, would perhaps have carried me to the ambulance. But seeing me naked, they do not distinguish me from the corpses with which I am surrounded, and, indeed, there soon will be no difference between them and me. I cannot call help, and the approaching night will take away all hope of succour. The cold is increasing: shall I be able to bear it till to-morrow, seeing that I feel my naked limbs stiffening already?' So I made up my mind to die, for if I had been saved by a miracle in the midst of the terrible *mêlée* between the Russians and the 14th, could I expect that there would be a second miracle to extract me from my present horrible position? The second miracle did take place in the following manner. Marshal Augereau had a valet named Pierre Dannel, a very intelligent and very faithful fellow, but somewhat given to arguing. Now it happened during our stay at La Houssaye that Dannel, having answered his master, got dismissed. In despair, he begged me to plead for him. This I did so zealously that I succeeded in getting him taken back into favour. From that time the valet had been devotedly attached to me. The outfit having been all left behind at Landsberg, he had started all out of his own head on the day of battle to bring provisions to his master. He had placed these in a very light waggon which could go everywhere, and contained the articles which the marshal most frequently required. This little waggon was driven by a soldier belonging to the same company of the transport corps as the man who had just stripped me. This latter, with my property in his hands, passed near the waggon, which was standing at the side of the cemetery, and, recognising the driver, his old comrade, he hailed him, and showed him the splendid booty which he had just taken from a dead man.

"Now you must know that when we were in cantonments on the Vistula the marshal happened to send Dannel to Warsaw for provisions, and I commissioned him to get the trimming of black astrachan taken from my pelisse, and have it replaced by grey, this having recently been adopted by Prince Berthier's aides-de-camp, who set the fashion in the army. Up to now, I was the only one of Augereau's officers who had grey astrachan. Dannel, who was present when the transport man made his display, quickly recognised my pelisse, which made him look more closely at the other effects of the alleged dead man. Among these he found my watch, which had belonged to my father and was marked with his cypher. The valet had no longer any doubt that I had been killed, and while deploring my loss, he wished to see me for the last time. Guided by the transport man he reached me and found me living. Great was the joy of this worthy man, to whom I certainly owed my life. He made haste to fetch my servant and some orderlies, and had me carried to a barn, where he rubbed my body with rum. Meanwhile someone went to fetch Dr. Raymond, who came at length, dressed the wound in my arm, and declared that the release of blood due to it would be the saving of me.

"My brother and my comrades were quickly round me; something was given to the transport soldier who had taken my clothes, which he returned very willingly, but as they were saturated with water and with blood, Marshal Augereau had me wrapped in things belonging to himself. The Emperor had given the marshal leave to go to Landsberg, but as his wound forbad him to ride, his aides-de-camp had procured a sledge, on which the body of a carriage had been placed. The marshal, who could not make up his mind to leave me, had me fastened up beside him, for I was too weak to sit upright.

"Before I was removed from the field of battle I had seen my poor Lisette near me. The cold had caused the blood from her wound to clot, and prevented the loss from being too great. The creature had got on to her legs and was eating the straw which the soldiers had used the night before for their bivouacs. My servant, who was very fond of Lisette, had noticed her when he was helping to remove me, and cutting up into bandages the shirt and hood of a dead soldier, he wrapped her leg with them, and thus made her able to walk to Landsberg. The officer in command of the small garrison there had had the forethought to get quarters ready for the wounded, so the staff found places in a large and good inn.

"In this way, instead of passing the night without help, stretched naked on the snow, I lay on a good bed surrounded by the attention of my brother, my comrades, and the kind Dr. Raymond. The doctor had been obliged to cut off the boot which the transport man had not been able to pull off, and which had become all the more difficult to remove owing to the swelling of my foot. You will see presently that this very nearly cost me my leg, and perhaps my life.

"We stayed thirty-six hours at Landsberg. This rest, and the good care taken of me, restored me to the use of speech and senses, and when on the second day after the battle Marshal Augereau started for Warsaw I was able to be carried in the sledge. The journey lasted eight days. Gradually I recovered strength, but as strength returned I began to feel a sensation of icy cold in my right foot. At Warsaw I was lodged in the house that had been taken for the marshal, which suited me the better that I was not able to leave my bed. Yet the wound in my arm was doing well, the extravasated blood was becoming absorbed, my skin was recovering its natural colour. The doctor knew not to what he could ascribe my inability to rise, till, hearing me complaining of my leg, he examined it, and found that my foot was gangrened. An accident of my early days was the cause of this new trouble. At Sorèze I had my right foot wounded by the unbuttoned foil of a schoolfellow with whom I was fencing. It seemed that the muscles of the part had become sensitive, and had suffered much from cold while I was lying unconscious on the field of Eylau; thence had resulted a swelling which explained the difficulty experienced by the soldier in dragging off my right boot. The foot was frost-bitten, and as it had not been treated in time, gangrene had appeared in the site of the old wound from the foil. The place was covered with an eschar as large as a five-franc piece. The doctor turned pale when he saw the foot: then, making four servants hold me, and taking his knife, he lifted the eschar, and dug the mortified flesh from my foot just as one cuts the damaged part out of an apple. The pain was great, but I did not complain. It was otherwise, however, when the knife reached the living flesh, and laid bare the muscles and bones till one could see them moving. Then the doctor, standing on a chair, soaked a sponge in hot sweetened wine, and let it fall drop by drop into the hole which he had just dug in my foot. The pain became unbearable. Still, for eight days I had to undergo this torture morning and evening, but my leg was saved.

"Nowadays, when promotions and decorations are bestowed so lavishly, some reward would certainly be given to an officer who had braved danger as I had done in reaching the 14th regiment; but under the Empire a devoted act of that kind was thought so natural that I did not receive the cross, nor did it ever occur to me to ask for it. A long rest having been ordered for the cure of Marshal Augereau's wound, the Emperor wrote to bid him return for treatment to France, and sent to Italy for Masséna, to whom my brother, Bro, and several of my comrades were attached. Augereau took me with him, as well as Dr. Raymond and his secretary. I had to be lifted in and out of the carriage; otherwise I found my health coming back as I got away from those icy regions towards a milder climate. My mare passed the winter in the stables of M. de Launay, head of the forage department. Our road lay through Silesia. So long as we were in that horrible Poland, it required twelve, sometimes sixteen, horses to draw the carriage at a walk through the bogs and quagmires; but in Germany we found at length civilisation and real roads.

"After a halt at Dresden, and ten or twelve days' stay at Frankfort, we reached Paris about March 15. I walked very lame, wore my arm in a sling, and still felt the terrible shaking caused by the wind of the cannon-ball; but the joy of seeing my mother again, and her kind care of me, together with the sweet influences of the spring, completed my cure. Before leaving Warsaw I had meant to throw away the hat which the ball had pierced, but the marshal kept it as a curiosity and gave it to my mother. It still exists in my possession, and should be kept as a family relic."

How Marbot crossed the Danube

After crossing the Traun, burning the bridge at Mauthhausen, and passing the Enns, the army advanced to Mölk, without knowing what had become of General Hiller. Some spies assured us that the archduke had crossed the Danube and joined him, and that we should on the morrow meet the whole Austrian army, strongly posted in front of Saint-Pölten. In that case, we must make ready to fight a great battle; but if it were otherwise, we had to march quickly on Vienna in order to get there before the enemy could reach it by the other bank. For want of positive information the Emperor was very undecided. The question to be solved was, Had General Hiller crossed the Danube, or was he still in front of us, masked by a swarm of light cavalry, which, always flying, never let us get near enough to take a prisoner from whom one might get some enlightenment?

Still knowing nothing for certain, we reached, on May 7, the pretty little town of Mölk, standing on the bank of the Danube, and overhung by an immense rock, on the summit of which rises a Benedictine convent, said to be the finest and richest in Christendom. From the rooms of the monastery a wide view is obtained over both banks of the Danube. There the Emperor and many marshals, including Lannes, took up their quarters, while our staff lodged with the parish priest. Much rain had fallen during the week, and it had not ceased for twenty-four hours, and still was falling, so that the Danube and its tributaries were over their banks. That night, as my comrades and I, delighted at being sheltered from the bad weather, were having a merry supper with the parson, a jolly fellow, who gave us an excellent meal, the aide-de-camp on duty with the marshal came to tell me that I was wanted, and must go up to the convent that moment. I was so comfortable where I was that I found it annoying to have to leave a good supper and good quarters to go and get wet again, had but I to obey.

All the passages and lower rooms of the monastery were full of soldiers, forgetting the fatigues of the previous days in the monks'j good wine. On reaching the dwelling-rooms, I saw that I had been sent for about some serious matter, for generals, chamberlains, orderly officers, said to me repeatedly, "The Emperor has sent for you." Some added, "It is probably to give you your commission as major." This I did not believe, for I did not think I was yet of sufficient importance to the sovereign for him to send for me at such an hour to give me my commission with his own hands. I was shown into a vast and handsome gallery, with a balcony looking over the Danube; there I found the Emperor at dinner with several marshals and the abbot of the convent, who has the title of bishop. On seeing me, the Emperor left the table, and went towards the balcony, followed by Lannes. I heard him say in a low tone, "The execution of this plan is almost impossible; it would be sending a brave officer for no purpose to almost certain death." "He will go, sir," replied the marshal; "I am certain he will go, at any rate we can but propose it to him." Then, taking me by the hand, the marshal opened the window of the balcony over the Danube. The river at this moment, trebled in volume by the strong flood, was nearly a league wide; it was lashed by a fierce wind, and we could hear the waves roaring. It was pitch-dark, and the rain fell in torrents, but we could see on the other side a long line of bivouac fires. Napoleon, Marshal Lannes, and I, being alone on the balcony, the marshal said, "On the other side of the river, you see an Austrian camp. Now, the Emperor is keenly desirous to know whether General Hiller's corps is there, or still on this bank. In order to make sure he wants a stout-hearted man, bold enough to cross the Danube, and bring away some soldier of the enemy's, and I have assured him that you will go." Then Napoleon said to me, "Take notice that I am not giving you an order; I am only expressing a wish. I am aware that the enterprise is as dangerous as it can be, and you can decline it without any fear of displeasing me. Go, and think it over for a few moments in the next room; come back and tell us frankly your decision."

I admit that when I heard Marshal Lannes' proposal I had broken out all over in a cold sweat; but at the same moment, a feeling, which I cannot define, but in which a love of glory and of my country was mingled, perhaps, with a noble pride, raised my ardour to the highest point, and I said to myself, "The Emperor has here an army of 150,000 devoted warriors, besides 25,000 men of his guard, all selected from the bravest. He is surrounded with aides-de-camp and orderly officers, and yet when an expedition is on foot, requiring intelligence no less than boldness, it is I whom the Emperor and Marshal Lannes choose." "I will go, sir," I cried without hesitation. "I will go; and if I perish, I leave my mother to your Majesty's care." The Emperor pulled my ear to mark his satisfaction; the marshal shook my hand, "I was quite right to tell your Majesty that he would go. There's what you may call a brave soldier."

My expedition being thus decided on, I had to think about the means of executing it. The Emperor called General Bertrand, his aide-de-camp, General Dorsenne, of the guard, and the commandant of the imperial head-quarters, and ordered them to put at my disposal whatever I might require. At my request an infantry picket went into the town to find the burgomaster, the syndic of the boatmen, and five of his best hands. A corporal and five grenadiers of the old guard who could all speak German, and had still to earn their decoration, were also summoned, and voluntarily agreed to go with me. The Emperor had them brought in first, and promised that on their return they should receive the Cross at once. The brave men replied by a "Vive l'Empereur!" and went to get ready. As for the five boatmen, on its being explained to them through the interpreter that they had to take a boat across the Danube, they fell on their knees and began to weep. The syndic declared that they might just as well be shot at once, as sent to certain death. The expedition was absolutely impossible, not only from the strength of the current, but because the tributaries had brought into the Danube a great quantity of fir trees recently cut down in the mountains, which could not be avoided in the dark, and would certainly come against the boat and sink it. Besides, how could one land on the opposite bank among willows which would scuttle the boat, and with a flood of unknown extent? The syndic concluded, then, that the operation was physically impossible. In vain did the Emperor tempt them with an offer of 6,000 francs per man; even this could not persuade them, though, as they said, they were poor boatmen with families, and this sum would be a fortune to them. But, as I have already said, some lives must be sacrificed to save those of the greater number, and the knowledge of this makes commanders sometimes pitiless. The Emperor was inflexible, and the grenadiers received orders to take the poor men, whether they would or not, and we went down to the town.

The corporal who had been assigned to me was an intelligent man. Taking him for my interpreter, I charged him as we went along to tell the syndic of the boatmen that as he had got to come along with us, he had better in his own interest show us his best boat, and point out everything that we should require for her fitting. The poor man obeyed; so we got an excellent vessel, and we took all that we wanted from the others. We had two anchors, but as I did not think we should be able to make use of them, I had sewn to the end of each cable a piece of canvas with a large stone wrapped in it. I had seen in the south of

France the fishermen use an apparatus of this kind to hold their boats by throwing the cord over the willows at the water's edge. I put on a cap, the grenadiers took their forage caps, we had provisions, ropes, axes, saws, a ladder,—everything, in short, which I could think of to take.

Our preparations ended, I was going to give the signal to start, when the five boatmen implored me with tears to let the soldiers escort them to their houses, to take perhaps the last farewell of their wives and children; but, fearing that a tender scene of this kind would further reduce their small stock of courage, I refused. Then the syndic said, "Well, as we have only a short time to live, allow us five minutes to commend our souls to God, and do you do the same, for you also are going to your death." They all fell on their knees, the grenadiers and I following their example, which seemed to please the worthy people much. When their prayer was over, I gave each man a glass of the monks' excellent wine, and we pushed out into the stream.

I had bidden the grenadiers follow in silence all the orders of the syndic who was steering; the current was too strong for us to cross over straight from Mölk: we went up, therefore, along the bank under sail for more than a league, and although the wind and the waves made the boat jump, this part was accomplished without accident. But when the time came to take to our oars and row out from the land, the mast, on being lowered, fell over to one side, and the sail, dragging in the water, offered a strong resistance to the current and nearly capsized us. The master ordered the ropes to be cut and the masts to be sent overboard: but the boatmen, losing their heads, began to pray without stirring. Then the corporal, drawing his sword, said, "You can pray and work too; obey at once, or I will kill you." Compelled to choose between possible and certain death, the poor fellows took up their hatchets, and with the help of the grenadiers, the mast was promptly cut away and sent floating. It was high time, for hardly were we free from this dangerous burden when we felt a fearful shock. A pine-stem borne down by the stream had struck the boat. We all shuddered, but luckily the planks were not driven in this time. Would the boat, however, resist more shocks of this kind? We could not see the stems, and only knew that they were near by the heavier tumble of the waves. Several touched us, but no serious accident resulted. Meantime the current bore us along, and as our oars could make very little way against it to give us the necessary slant, I feared for a moment that it would sweep us below the enemy's camp, and that my expedition would fail. By dint of hard rowing, however, we had got three-quarters of the way over, when I saw an immense black mass looming over the water. Then a sharp scratching was heard, branches caught us in the face, and the boat stopped. To our questions the owner replied that we were on an island covered with willows and poplars, of which the flood had nearly reached the top. We had to grope about with our hatchets to clear a passage through the branches, and when we had succeeded in passing the obstacle, we found the stream much less furious than in the middle of the river, and finally reached the left bank in front of the Austrian camp. This shore was bordered with very thick trees, which, overhanging the bank like a dome, made the approach difficult no doubt, but at the same time conccaled our boat from the camp. The whole shore was lighted up by the bivouac fires, while we remained in the shadow thrown by the branches of the willows. I let the boat float downwards, looking for a suitable landing-place. Presently I perceived that a sloping path had been made down the bank by the enemy to allow the men and horses to get to the water. The corporal adroitly threw into the willows one of the stones that I had made ready, the cord caught in a tree, and the boat brought up against the land a foot or two from the slope. It must have been just about midnight. The Austrians, having the swollen Danube between them and the French, felt themselves so secure that except the sentry the whole camp was asleep.

It is usual in war for the guns and the sentinels always to face towards the enemy, however far off he may be. A battery placed in advance of the camp was therefore turned towards the river, and sentries were walking on the top of the bank. The trees prevented them from seeing the extreme edge, while from the boat I could see through the branches a great part of the bivouac. So far my mission had been more successful than I had ventured to hope, but in order to make the success complete I had to bring away a prisoner, and to execute such an operation fifty paces away from several thousand enemies, whom a single cry would rouse, seemed very difficult. Still, I had to do something. I made the five sailors lie down at the bottom of the boat under guard of two grenadiers, another grenadier I posted at the bow of the boat which was close to the bank, and myself disembarked, sword in hand, followed by the corporal and two grenadiers. The boat was a few feet from dry land; we had to walk in the water, but at last we were on the slope. We went up, and I was making ready to rush on the nearest sentry, disarm him, gag him, and drag him off to the boat, when the ring of metal and the sound of singing in a low voice fell on my ears. A man, carrying a great tin pail, was coming to draw water, humming a song as he went; we quickly went down again to the river to hide under the branches, and as the Austrian stooped to fill his pail my grenadiers seized him by the throat, put a handkerchief full of wet sand over his mouth, and placing their sword-points against his body threatened him with death if he resisted or uttered a sound. Utterly bewildered, the man obeyed, and let us take him to the boat; we hoisted him into the hands of the grenadiers posted there, who made him lie down beside the sailors. While this Austrian was lying captured, I saw by his clothes that he was not strictly speaking a soldier, but an officer's servant. I should have preferred to catch a combatant, who could have given me more precise information; but I was going to content myself with this capture for want of a better, when I saw at top of the slope two soldiers carrying a cauldron between them, on a pole. They were only a few paces off. It was impossible for us to re-embark without being seen. I therefore signed to my grenadiers to hide themselves again, and as soon as the two Austrians stooped to fill their vessel, powerful arms seized them from behind, and plunged their heads under water. We had to stupefy them a little, since they had their swords, and I feared that they might resist. Then they were picked up in turn, their mouths covered with a handkerchief full of sand, and sword-points against their breasts constrained them to follow us. They were shipped as the servant had been, and my men and I got on board again.

So far all had gone well. I made the sailors get up and take their oars, and ordered the corporal to cast loose the rope which held us to the bank. It was, however, so wet, and the knot had been drawn so tight by the force of the stream, that it was impossible to unfasten. We had to saw the rope, which took us some minutes. Meanwhile, the rope, shaking with our efforts, imparted its movement to the branches of the willow round which it was wrapped, and the rustling became loud enough to attract the notice of the sentry. He drew near, unable to see the boat, but perceiving that the agitation of the branches increased, he called out, "Who goes there?" No answer. Further challenge from the sentry. We held our tongues, and worked away. I was in deadly fear; after facing so many dangers, it would have been too cruel if we were wrecked in sight of port. At last, the rope was cut and the boat pushed off. But hardly was it clear of the overhanging willows than the light of the bivouac fires made it visible to the sentry, who, shouting, "To arms," fired at us. No one was hit but at the sound the whole camp was astir in a moment, and the gunners, whose pieces were ready loaded and trained on the river, honoured my boat with some cannon-shots. At the report my heart leapt for joy, for I knew that the Emperor and marshal would hear it. I turned my eyes towards the convent, with its lighted windows, of which I had, in spite of the distance, never lost sight. Probably all were open at this moment, but in one only could I perceive any increase of brilliancy; it was the great balcony window, which was as large as the doorway of a church, and sent from afar a flood of light over the stream. Evidently it had just been opened at the thunder of the cannon, and I said to myself, "The Emperor and the marshals are doubtless on the balcony; they know that I have reached the enemy's camp, and are making vows for my safe return." This thought raised my courage, and I heeded the cannon-balls not a bit. Indeed, they were not very dangerous, for the stream swept us along at such a pace that the gunners could not aim with any accuracy, and we must have been very unlucky to get hit. One shot would have done for us, but all fell harmless into the Danube. Soon I was out of range, and could reckon a successful issue to my enterprise. Still, all danger was not yet at an end; We had still to cross among the floating pine-stems, and more than once we struck on submerged islands, and were delayed by the branches of the poplars. At last we reached the right bank, more than two leagues below Mölk, and a new terror assailed me. I could see bivouac fires, and had no means of learning whether they belonged to a French regiment. The enemy had troops on both banks, and I knew that on the right bank Marshal Lannes' outposts were not far from Mölk, facing an Austrian corps, posted at Saint-Pölten.

Our army would doubtless go forward at daybreak, but was it already occupying this place? And were the fires that I saw those of friends or enemies? I was afraid that the current had taken me too far down, but the problem was solved by French cavalry trumpets sounding the reveillé. Our uncertainty being at an end, we rowed with all our strength to the shore, where in the dawning light we could see a village. As we drew near, the report of a carbine was heard, and a bullet whistled by our ears. It was evident that the French sentries took us for a hostile crew. I had not foreseen this possibility, and hardly knew how we were to succeed in getting recognised, till the happy thought struck me of making my six grenadiers shout, "Vive l'Empereur Napoléon!" This was, of course, no certain evidence that we were French, but it would attract the attention of the officers, who would have no fear of our small numbers, and would no doubt prevent the men from firing on us before they knew whether we were French or Austrians. A few moments later I came ashore, and I was received by Colonel Gautrin and the 9th Hussars, forming part of Lannes' division. If we had landed half a league lower down we should have tumbled into the enemy's pickets. The colonel lent me a horse, and gave me several wagons, in which I placed the grenadiers, the boatmen, and the prisoners, and the little cavalcade went off towards Mölk. As we went along, the corporal, at my orders, questioned the three Austrians, and I learnt with satisfaction that the camp whence I had brought them away belonged to the very division, General Killer's, the position of which the Emperor was so anxious to learn. There was, therefore, no further doubt that that general had joined the archduke on the other side of the Danube. There was no longer any question of a battle on the road which we held, and Napoleon, having only the enemy's cavalry in front of him, could in perfect safety push his troops forward towards Vienna, from which we were but three easy marches distant. With this information I galloped forward, in order to bring it to the Emperor with the least possible delay.

When I reached the gate of the monastery, it was broad day. I found the approach blocked by the whole population of the little town of Mölk, and heard among the crowd the cries of the wives, children, and friends of the sailors whom I had carried off. In a moment I was surrounded by them, and was able to calm their anxiety by saying, in very bad German, "Your friends are alive, and you will see them in a few moments." A great cry of joy went up from the crowd, bringing out the officer in command of the guard at the gate. On seeing me he ran off in pursuance of orders to warn the aides-de-camp to let the Emperor know of my return. In an instant the whole palace was up. The good Marshal Lannes came to me, embraced me cordially, and carried me straight off to the Emperor, crying out, "Here he is, sir; I knew he would come back. He has brought three prisoners from General Hiller's division." Napoleon received me warmly, and though I was wet and muddy all over, he laid his hand on my shoulder, and did not forget to give his greatest sign of satisfaction by pinching my ear. I leave you to imagine how I was questioned! The Emperor wanted to know every incident of the adventure in detail, and when I had finished my story said, "I am very well pleased with you, 'Major' Marbot." These words were equivalent to a commission, and my joy was full. At that moment, a chamberlain announced that breakfast was served, and as I was calculating on having to wait in the gallery until the Emperor had finished, he pointed with his finger towards the dining-room, and said, "You will breakfast with me." As this honour had never been paid to any officer of my rank, I was the more flattered. During breakfast I learnt that the Emperor and the marshal had not been to bed all night, and that when they heard the cannon on the opposite bank they had all rushed on to the balcony. The Emperor made me tell again the way in which I had surprised the three prisoners, and laughed much at the fright and surprise which they must have felt.

At last, the arrival of the wagons was announced, but they had much difficulty in making their way through the crowd, so eager were the people to see the boatmen. Napoleon, thinking this very natural, gave orders to open the gates, and let everybody come into the court. Soon after, the grenadiers, the boatmen, and the prisoners were led into the gallery. The Emperor, through his interpreter, first questioned the three Austrian soldiers, and learning with satisfaction that not only General Hiller's corps, but the whole of the archduke's army, were on the other bank, he told Berthier to give the order for the troops to march at once on Saint-Pölten. Then, calling up the corporal and the five soldiers, he fastened the Cross on their breast, appointed them knights of the Empire, and gave them an annuity of 1,200 francs apiece. All the veterans wept for joy. Next came the boatmen's turn. The Emperor told them that, as the danger they had run was a good deal more than he had expected, it was only fair that he should increase their reward; so, instead of the 6,000 francs promised, 12,000 in gold were given to them on the spot. Nothing could express their delight; they kissed the hands of the Emperor and all present, crying, "Now we are rich!" Napoleon laughingly asked the syndic if he would go the same journey for the same price the next night. But the man answered that, having escaped by miracle what seemed certain death, he would not undertake such a journey again even if his lordship, the abbot of Mölk, would give him the monastery and all its possessions. The boatmen withdrew, blessing the generosity of the French Emperor, and the grenadiers, eager to show off their decoration before their comrades, were about to go off with their three prisoners, when Napoleon perceived that the Austrian servant was weeping bitterly. He reassured him as to his safety, but the poor lad replied, sobbing, that he knew the French treated their prisoners well, but that, as he had on him a belt, containing nearly all his captain's money, he was afraid that the officer would accuse him of deserting in order to rob him, and he was heart-broken at the thought. Touched by the worthy fellow's distress, the Emperor told him that he was free, and as soon as we were before Vienna, he would be passed through the outposts, and be able to return to his master. Then, taking a rouleau of 1,000 francs, he put it in the man's hand, saying, "One must honour goodness wherever it is shown." Lastly, the Emperor gave some pieces of gold to each of the other two prisoners, and ordered that they too should be sent back to the Austrian outposts, so that they might forget the fright which we had caused them, and that it might not be said that any soldiers, even enemies, had spoken to the Emperor of the French without receiving some benefit.

The piteous Death of Gaston, Son of the Count of Foix

More than five hundred years ago, on St. Catherine's Day, 1388, Master Jean Froissart, a priest of Hainault, rode into the little town of Orthez. He was in search of information about battles and tournaments, for he was writing his famous "History and Chronicle." To get news of all kinds he rode gaily about, with a white greyhound in a leash, and carrying a novel which he had begun for the entertainment of ladies and princes. Arriving at Orthez (where, long afterwards, the Duke of Wellington fought the French on the borders of Spain), Master Froissart alighted at the hotel with the sign of the Moon. Meanwhile a knight who had travelled with Froissart went up to the castle, and paid his court to Gaston Phoebus, Count of Foix. He found the Count in the gallery of the palace just after dinner, for this prince always went to bed at midday and took supper at midnight. He was a great and powerful noble, of stately and beautiful presence, though now he was nearly sixty years old. A wise knight he was, bold in enterprise, and of good counsel. Never did he suffer any unbeliever in his company, and he was very pious, every day making many and long prayers, and giving alms to the poor folk at his gate. He took much delight in minstrelsy, and at his midnight supper songs and virelays were chanted to him. Till about three o'clock in the morning he listened while Master Froissart read aloud his poems, tales, or histories, while the courtiers yawned, no doubt, and wished for bedtime. But it was the good Count's manner to turn night into day. He was sometimes melancholy, and, as is told in the story of Orthon, men believed that he saw and knew events far distant, but in what manner none could tell. This great prince dwelt at peace while the wars of France, England, Portugal, and Spain raged outside his dominions. Rich, powerful, handsome, and deeply religious, he seemed to have everything that could make him happy, but he had no son and heir; his lands, on his death, would go to a distant cousin. Nor did the lady his wife live with the Count of Foix. Concerning this, and the early death of the Count's one son, Gaston, Master Froissart was very curious, but he found that people did not care to speak of the matter. At length an old squire told him the story of the death of Gaston.

The Countess of Foix was the sister of the King of Navarre, and between the Count her husband, and the King her brother, a quarrel arose on a question of money. The Count therefore sent his wife to her brother at Pampeluna, that she might arrange the matter; but the end of it was that she stayed in Navarre, and did not return to her lord. Meanwhile her son Gaston grew up at Orthez, and married a daughter of the Count of Armagnac, being now a lad of sixteen, a good squire, and in all things very like his father. He had a desire to see his mother, and so rode into Navarre, hoping to bring home his mother, the Countess of Foix. But she would not leave Navarre for all that he could say, and the day came when he and the young squires of his company must return. Then the King of Navarre led him apart into a secret chamber, and there gave him a little purse. Now the purse was full of a powder of such sort that no living creature could taste of it and live, but must die without remedy.

"Gaston, fair nephew," said the King, "you see how your father, the Count, holds your mother in bitter hate—a sore grief to me and to you also. Now to change all this, and bring your father and mother back to their ancient love, you must watch your chance and sprinkle a little of this powder on any food that your father is about to eat, taking good care that no man sees you. And the powder is a charm so strong that your father, as soon as he has tasted it, will desire nothing so much as to be friends with your mother again, and never will they leave each other. But you must take heed that no man knows of this purpose, or all is lost."

The young Count, believing, in his innocence, what his uncle said, made answer that he would gladly do as he was bidden. Then he rode back to Orthez, and showed his father all the presents and jewels that had been given to him in Navarre, except the little purse.

Now it was the custom of the young Count to be much in the company of his brother by another mother, and, as they played together one day, this boy, named Yvain, caught hold of the little purse which Gaston wore about his neck under his coat, and asked him what it was. But Gaston made no answer. Three days later the lads quarrelled over a stroke at tennis, and Gaston struck Yvain a blow. Yvain ran weeping to his father, the Count, who asked what ailed him.

"Gaston struck me," said he, "but it is Gaston, not I, who deserves a blow."

"What has he done?" asked the Count.

"Ever since he came from his mother's in Navarre he carries about his neck a little purse full of a powder. But I only know that he says you and his mother will soon be good friends once more."

"Ha!" cried the Count, "do you be silent."

That day at dinner, as Gaston served the meats, for this was his duty, the Count called to him, seized his coat, opened it, and, with his knife, cut the purse from the boy's neck. Gaston said no word, but grew pale and trembled. The Count opened the purse, spread the powder on a piece of bread, and threw it to a dog. No sooner had the dog eaten the bread than his eyes turned round, and he fell dead.

The Count leaped up, a knife in his hand, and would have slain his son as a traitor, but the knights and esquires, kneeling, prayed him to hold his hand.

"Perchance," said they, "Gaston knew not the nature of that which was in the purse, and is guiltless in this matter."

"So be it," said the Count. "Hold him prisoner in the tower at your own peril."

Then he seized all the companions and friends of Gaston, for they must have known, he said, that his son carried a purse secretly. Fifteen of the fairest and noblest of the boys he put to death with horrible tortures, but they knew nothing and could tell nothing. Then he called together all his nobles and bishops, and told them that Gaston also must die. But they prayed for his life, because they loved him dearly, and he was the heir of all the Count's lands. So the Count decided to keep Gaston in prison for some months, and then send him to travel for two or three years. The Pope sent a cardinal to the Count, bidding him spare Gaston, but, before the Cardinal reached Orthez, Gaston was dead.

One day the servant who took meat and drink into the boy's dark dungeon saw that he had not tasted food for many days. All the dishes lay full of mouldering meat in a row along the wall. Then the servant ran and warned the Count that Gaston was starving himself to death. The Count was trimming his nails with a little knife, and he sped in great anger to the dungeon.

"Traitor, why dost thou not eat?" he cried, dealt the boy a cuff, and rushed out again, and so went to his chamber.

But the point of the little knife, which was in his hand, had cut a vein in Gaston's neck, and, being weak with hunger and grief, Gaston died, for the vein could not be staunched. Then the Count made great lament, and had his head shaven, and wore mourning for many days.

Thus it chanced that the Count of Foix lived without an heir, turning night into day, praying much, and listening to minstrels, giving alms, and hearkening to strange messages of death and war that were borne

ANDREW LANG AND H. RIDER HAGGARD

to him how no man knew. And his brother, Pierre, was a good knight and wise by day, yet at night madness fell on him, and he raved, beating the air with a naked sword. And this had been his manner ever since he fought with and slew a huge bear on the hills. Now when his wife saw that bear brought home dead she fainted, and in three days she fled with her children, and came back no more. For her father had once pursued that bear, which cried to him: "Thou huntest me who wish thee no harm, but thou shalt die an ill death." He then left off pursuing the bear; but the Count's brother slew the beast on another day, and thereafter he went mad in the night, though by day he was wise enough.

These tales were told to Master Froissart by the old squire at Orthez.

Rolf Stake[1]

There was once a king in Denmark named Rolf Stake; right famous is he among the kings of yore, foremost for liberality, daring, and courtesy. Of his courtesy one proof celebrated in story is this.

A poor little boy named Vögg came into King Rolf's hall: the King was then young and slender of build. Vögg went near and looked up at him. Then said the King: "What wouldst thou say, boy, that thou lookest at me so?"

Vögg answered: "When I was at home, I heard tell that King Rolf at Hleidr was the tallest man in Northland; but now here sits in the high seat a thin stake, and they call him their king."

Then answered the King: "Thou, boy, hast given me a name to be known by—Rolf Stake to wit. 'Tis custom to follow a naming with a gift. But now I see that thou hast not with the naming any gift to give me such as would beseem me to accept, wherefore he of us who hath must give to the other." With that the King drew a gold ring from his own hand and gave it to him.

Then said Vögg: "Blessed above all kings be thou who givest! And by this vow I bind me to be that man's bane who shall be thine."

Then said the King with a laugh: "With small gain is Vögg fain."

Further, this proof is told of Rolf Stake's daring.

There ruled over Upsala a king named Adils, who had to wife Yrsa, Rolf Stake's mother. He was at war with Ali, the king who then ruled Norway. They appointed to meet in battle upon the ice of the lake called Venir. King Adils sent a message to Rolf Stake, his stepson, that he should come to help him, and promised pay to all his force so long as they should be on the campaign, but the King himself was to receive for his own three costly things from Sweden, whatsoever he should choose. King Rolf could not go himself by reason of a war that he had against the Saxons; but he sent to Adils his twelve Berserks, of whom were Bödvar Bjarki, Hjalti Stoutheart, Whiteserk Bold, Vött, Vidseti, and the brothers Svipdag and Beigud.

In the battle then fought fell King Ali and a great part of his host. And King Adils took from the dead prince the helmet Battleboar and his horse Raven. Then the Berserks of Rolf Stake asked for their wage,

---

1. From Snorri's *Edda*, cap. 44.

three pounds of gold apiece; and further they asked to carry to Rolf Stake those costly things which they in his behalf should choose. These were the helmet Battleboar, and the corslet Finnsleif, which no weapon could pierce, and the gold ring called Sviagriss, an heirloom from Adils' forefathers. But the King denied them all the costly things, nor did he even pay their wage.

The Berserks went away ill-content with their lot, and told Rolf Stake what had been done.

At once he started for Upsala, and when he came with his ships into the river Fyri he then rode to Upsala, and with him his twelve Berserks, without any truce guaranteed. Yrsa, his mother, welcomed him, and led him, not to the King's hall, but to a lodging. There fires were lighted for them and ale given them to drink.

Then some men of King Adils came in and threw billets of wood on the fire, and made such a blaze that it scorched the clothes of Rolf's company. And they said: "Is it true that Rolf Stake and his Berserks flee neither fire nor iron?" Then up leapt Rolf and all his twelve, and he crying,

> *"Heap we yet higher*
> *Adils' house-fire,"*

took his shield and cast it on the fire, and leapt thereover, crying yet again,

> *"He fleeth not the flame*
> *Who leapeth o'er the same."*

Likewise one after the other did all his men. Then they seized those who had heaped up the fire, and cast them thereon.

And now came Yrsa and gave to Rolf Stake a deer's horn filled with gold, and therewith the ring Sviagriss, and bade them ride away to their fleet. They leapt on their horses and rode down to Fyris-field. Soon they saw that King Adils rode after them with his force fully armed, purposing to slay them. Whereupon Rolf Stake, plunging his right hand into the horn, took of the gold and sowed it all over the path. But when the Swedes saw that, they leapt from their saddles and gathered each what he could get; but King Adils bade them ride on, and himself rode at speed. Slungnir his horse was named, of all horses the fleetest.

Then Rolf Stake, when he saw that King Adils rode near him, took the ring Sviagriss and threw it to him, and bade him accept the gift. King Adils rode to the ring, and lifting it on his lowered spear-point slid it up along the shaft. Then did Rolf Stake turn him back, and, seeing how he louted low, cried: "Now have I made Sweden's greatest grovel swine-wise."

So they parted.

For this reason gold is by poets called "the seed of Stake" or "of Fyris-field."

The Wreck of the "Wager"

The Honourable John Byron, grandfather of the poet, was a celebrated British Admiral who in almost all his voyages fell in with such rough weather that his sailors nicknamed him "Foul-weather Jack."

When he was seventeen years old he served as midshipman in the "Wager," a vessel attached to the squadron under the command of Commodore Anson which sailed out to the Spanish Settlements in the Pacific in 1740.

From the set-out the expedition was unfortunate. Almost all the ships were ill-fitted and ill-provisioned for so long a voyage. Moreover they were delayed until long after the proper season for their departure was past, which was regarded by the soldiers and sailors as an evil omen. This neglect affected the "Wager" more than any other ship, as she was an old East Indiaman, and had been bought into the service for the voyage, and fitted out for it as a man-of-war.

Besides this, when under sail she listed to one side, as she was top-laden with heavy military gear and stores for the use of the other vessels, while the lower holds were filled with light merchandise for bartering with the Indians.

Her crew were men who had been pressed on their return from long voyages, and the marines a small troop of invalids from the Chelsea Hospital, who were all alike very miserably depressed at the prospect of the long voyage which lay before them.

Even Captain Kid, under whose command the "Wager" sailed out of port, when on his death-bed shortly after, foretold her ill-success.

Upon his death Captain Cheap took command, and was able to keep with the squadron until they were about to enter the Straits la Marie, where the wind shifted to the south, and with the turn of the tide the "Wager" was separated from the other ships, and very narrowly escaped being wrecked off Staten Island.

However, she regained her station with the rest of the fleet until a few days later, when they were caught by a deep roll of a hollow sea, and lost their mizzen mast, and all the windward chain plates were broken.

They tried to rig up a substitute for the mizzen mast, but failed, as hard westerly gales set in with a tremendous short chopping swell, which raised the waves to a mountainous height, while from time to time a heavy sea broke over the ship. The boats on the davits were cast from their lashings, and filled with water, and the ship in all parts was soon in a most shattered and crazy state.

They had now lost sight of the squadron, and from the numbers of birds, and the drifting seaweed in the waters, they found they were being borne on to a lee shore. The heavy clouds that lowered above them, or the blinding sleet and snow, hid the sun and prevented the officers from taking sights; and at night no moon or stars by which they could steer their course were visible in the wild gloom through which they tossed.

When the officers at last found they were out of their bearings, they tried to persuade the captain to alter the course, but this he refused to do, as he believed he was making directly for the Island of Socoro, which was the place arranged for the squadron to meet, and whence it was intended they should make their first attack upon the Spaniards.

At this time, when all but twelve men on the "Wager" were disabled by fatigue or sickness, there loomed against the dull clouds a yet heavier cloud, which was that of mountainous masses of land. Then Captain Cheap at last realised their danger, and gave orders to wear ship to the southward, hoping that they might crowd her off the land.

But the fury of the gale increased as night fell upon them, while to add to their dismay, as each sail was set with infinite labour, it was set only to be blown or rent immediately from the yard.

At four o'clock in the morning the ship struck, then again for the second time more violently; and presently she lay helpless on her beam ends—while the sea every now and then broke over her.

Everyone who could move rushed to the quarter-deck, but those who were dying of scurvy and who could not leave their hammocks were drowned in them.

In the uncertain light of dawn they could see nothing around them but leaden breakers from whose foam-crested manes the wind swept the blinding spray. The ship lay in this terrible plight for some little time, while every soul on board counted each moment as his last.

In this scene of wild disorder the men lost all reason and restraint, some gave themselves up to death like logs, and were rolled hither and thither with each jerk and roll of the shivering ship.

One man in the exaltation of his despair stalked about the deck, and flourished a cutlass over his head, and struck at anyone who came near him with it—meanwhile shouting that he was the "king of the country."

Another, and a brave man, was so overcome by the fury of the seething waters, that he tried to throw himself from the rails at the quarter-deck, and to end in death a scene he felt too shocking to look upon.

The man at the helm still kept his post, though both rudder and tiller had been carried away; and applied himself to his duty with the same respect and coolness as though the ship were in the greatest safety.

Then Mr. Jones, the mate, spoke to the men, saying, "My friends! have you never seen a ship amongst breakers before? Lend a hand, boys, and lay on to the sheets and braces. I have no fear but that we shall stick her near enough to the land to save our lives."

Although he said these gallant words without hope of saving a single soul, he gave courage to many of the men, and they set to work in earnest.

They steered as best they could by the sheets and braces, and presently ran her in between an opening in the breakers, and soon found themselves wedged fast between two great rocks.

With the break of day the weather cleared sufficiently to give them a glimpse of the land. They then set to work to get out the boats. The first one that was launched was so overladen by those anxious to save themselves, that they were almost swamped before they reached the shore.

On the day before the ship was wrecked, the captain had had his shoulder dislocated by a fall, and was lying in his berth when John Byron, whose duty it was to keep him informed of all that passed on deck, went to ask if he would not like to land. But the captain refused to leave the ship until everyone else had gone.

Throughout the ship, the scene was now greatly changed. The men who but a few moments before had been on their knees praying for mercy, when they found themselves not in immediate danger, became very riotous, rushed to the cabins and stores, and broke open every chest and box they could find, as well as casks of wine and brandy. And by drinking it some of them were rendered so helpless that they were drowned on board by the seas that continually swept over them.

The boatswain and five other men refused to leave the ship while there was any liquor to be got; then at last the captain consented to be helped from his bed, and to be taken on shore.

ALTHOUGH THEY WERE THANKFUL TO escape from the wreck, when they reached the land they found themselves in a scene desolate enough to quell the bravest soul.

The bay in which they had been cast away was open to the full force of the ocean, and was formed by rocky headlands and cliffs with here and there a stretch of beach, while rising abruptly from the sea a rock-bound steep frowned above them, which they afterwards named Mount Misery. Stretching back from the beach lay stagnant lagoons and dreary flats of morass and swamp, the edges of which were drained by the roots of heavy forest trees whose impenetrable gloom clothed the intervening country and hillsides.

And out before them in the tempestuous waters the wreck lay, from whose stores must come their only present chance of life.

With nightfall presently at hand, though they were cold and wet and hungry, they had to try to find a shelter, and at last chanced upon an Indian hut at a little distance from the beach. Into this poor refuge the men packed themselves in a voluntary imprisonment, while, to add to their distress, they were afraid of being attacked by Indians.

One of the officers died in this miserable place during the night, and of those left outside who were unable from want of room to press in, two more perished from cold.

The next morning found them cramped with starvation and cold, with no food but some fragments of biscuit, a solitary seagull someone had killed, and the stalks of wild celery that grew upon the beach. This they made into soup, and served as far as it would go to the hundred and forty men who clamoured for food.

The men who had remained on the wreck were now anxious to be brought on shore, and repeatedly made signals to that effect; but the sea was running high and it was not possible at once to set out to their relief. In their rage at the delay they fired one of the quarter-deck guns upon the camp, while on board they destroyed everything they could lay hands on. In his brutality and greed for spoil, a man named James Mitchell murdered one of their number. When at last they were brought to land they came dressed in laced clothes and officers' suits which they had put on over their own dirty clothes.

These men Captain Cheap instantly had stripped of their finery and arms, and enforced the most strict discipline upon them and all the crew.

In a few days they had a shelter made with boats turned keel upwards, and placed on props, while the sides were lined with canvas and boughs.

Then followed five weary months, during which these hunger-driven men roamed the wretched island rocks both night and day, searching for shell-fish for food—men who were even thankful at the times when they were able to kill and eat the carrion crows that fed upon the flesh of their drowned comrades cast up by the tide. Some Indians surprised them by a visit, and stayed for several days, and with them they were able to barter cloth and beads for some dogs, and these they killed and ate.

The Indians were very short and black, and had long coarse hair that hung over their faces, and were almost without clothing of any kind.

The shipwrecked men grew more and more discontented as the months went by, and several of them threatened to take the life of the captain, whose strict discipline and guard over the stores made them very angry.

James Mitchell, who had murdered a man on the wreck, and had since committed another murder on Mount Misery, where his victim was found shockingly stabbed and mangled, was amongst this set. They had determined to leave the others, and on the night before their departure had placed a barrel of gunpowder close to the captain's hut, intending to blow it up, but were dissuaded from doing this by one of their number. After wandering about the island for some time they went up one of the lagoons on a punt they had made, and were never heard of again.

Captain Cheap was very jealous of his authority, and hasty in suspecting both officers and men of a desire to mutiny, and this suspicion on his part led to the unfortunate shooting by him of a midshipman named Mr. Cozens, whom he heard one day disputing with the purser as to the disposal of some stores he was at the time receiving from the wreck. The captain already had a personal dislike to Mr. Cozens, and hearing high words immediately rushed out of his hut and shot him. Mr. Cozens did not die until several days after, but the captain would not allow him to be attended to by the surgeon, or to have any care from the other men, though they begged to be allowed to carry him to their tent, but ordered that he should be left upon the ground, under a bit of canvas thrown over some bushes, until he died. This inhumanity on the part of Captain Cheap much embittered the men against him.

Their numbers were now lessened, chiefly by famine, to one hundred souls; the weather was still tempestuous and rainy, and the difficulty of finding food daily increased.

They had saved the long-boat from the wreck, and about this time John Bulkely, who had been a gunner on the "Wager," formed a plan of trying to make the voyage home through the Straits of Magellan. The plan was proposed to the captain, and though he thought it wiser to pretend to fall in with it, he had no intention of doing so. And when Bulkely and his followers suggested that there should be some restrictions on his command, or that at least he should do nothing without consulting his officers, the captain refused to consent to this; whereupon they imprisoned him, intending to take him to England on the charge of having murdered Mr. Cozens.

But when the boats were ready for sailing they found there would not be enough room for everybody. So the captain, Mr. Hamilton, and the doctor were left on the island.

John Byron did not know they were going to do this until the last moment. There were eighty-one men who left the island, who were distributed in the long-boat, the cutter, and the barge.

After they had been out about two days it was thought necessary to send back to the old station for some spare canvas. John Byron was sent back with the barge on this errand. When he was well away from the long-boat he told those with him he did not mean to return, but to rejoin Captain Cheap; and they agreed to do so too.

Although they were welcomed by those left on the island, there was little food for so many mouths, as almost everything had been carried off by the voyagers, and for a considerable time they were forced to live upon a kind of seaweed called slaugh, which with the stalks of wild celery they fried in the tallow of some candles they had saved.

This poor food reduced them to a terrible condition of weakness.

At last a really fair day broke upon them, when they went out to the remains of the wreck, and had the good fortune to hook up out of the bottom, three casks of beef which they brought safely to shore. The good food gave them renewed strength and energy, and again they became very anxious to leave the island.

Accordingly they launched both boats on December 15. The captain, Lieutenant Hamilton, and John Byron were in the barge with nine men, and Mr. Campbell in the yawl with six. And thus they set out on their journey northward.

Then followed weary days, during which they rowed over high seas, and weary nights of exposure and cold, when they landed on some barren shore for rest and to wait for daylight.

On Christmas Eve they found themselves tossing on a wide bay, and unable by the force of the currents to double the rocky headlands that lay in front of them. Unable, too, by the fury of the breakers to make the land or to find harbour, they were forced to lie outside all that night upon their oars.

They were so hungry then that they ate their shoes, which were made of raw sealskin.

On Christmas Day some of them landed, and had the good fortune to kill a seal. Though the two men who were left in each boat to take care of it could see their companions on shore eating seal, they were unable to have any themselves, as again when night came on the wind blew very hard, and the mighty breakers beat with pulse-like regularity on the shore.

John Byron, who had fallen into a comfortless sleep in the boat, was suddenly awakened by a shriek, and saw the yawl turned bottom upwards and go down.

One man was drowned, the other was thrown up by the breakers on the beach and saved by the people there.

At this place Mr. Hamilton, who was with the shore party, shot at a large sea-lion, which he hit with two balls; and when the brute presently charged at him with open mouth, he thrust his bayonet down its throat, as well as a great part of the barrel of his gun. But the sea-lion bit this in two with the greatest ease, and in spite of all its wounds, and all other efforts to kill it, got away.

As they had lost the yawl there was not enough of room to take all the men away from this place, therefore four of the marines agreed to remain and to try to make their way on foot to a more habitable country.

The captain gave them guns and food, and as the boat put off, they stood upon the beach and gave three cheers, and shouted "God bless the King."

The others made another attempt to double the cape, but the wind, the sea, and currents were too strong for them, and again they failed. So disheartened were they now, that caring little for life, they agreed to return to their original station on Wager's Island, and to end their days in miserable existence there.

They went back to the place where they had left the four marines in order to try to get some seal for their return passage and to take these men back with them, but when they searched all traces of them had gone.

It was here that the surgeon found in a curious cave the bodies of several Indians that were stretched out on a kind of platform. The flesh on the bodies had become perfectly dry and hard, and it was thought that it must be the kind of burial given to the great men or Caciques of the Indians.

After a terrible journey back to Wager's Island they reached it alive, though again worn out by hunger and fatigue.

The first thing they did on reaching their old station was to bury the corpse of the man who had been murdered on Mount Misery by James Mitchell, for the men thought that all their misfortunes had arisen from the neglect of this proper duty to the dead, and they were sure that the restless spirit of this person haunted the waters around them at night, as they heard strange and unearthly cries from the sea. And one night, in bright moonlight, they saw and heard something which looked like a human being swimming near the shore.

Inconsistent as this may seem, they were soon so terribly driven by hunger that the last dreadful suggestion for food was beginning to be whispered amongst them, when fortunately some Indians from the island of Chiloc appeared. It was supposed they had heard of the wreck from those first Indians who had visited them, and had come to collect old iron and nails, which they value very much.

They were able to persuade the Cacique, who was a Christian named Martini, to promise to show them the safest and best way to some of the Spanish Settlements. Once more the barge was launched, with the fifteen souls on board who now remained on the island of the shipwrecked crew.

They followed their Indian guide by day for some time, during which their sufferings were so terrible that it was no unusual thing for one of their number to fall back dying from the oars, meanwhile beseeching his comrades for two or three mouthfuls of food which they had not.

Captain Cheap, who was always well provided with seal by the Indians, again showed how regardless he could be of the sufferings of others, and often though he could have relieved his men by giving up a small portion of his own food when he heard their heartrending appeals for it, let them die at their posts unheedful of their want and misery.

They were rather taken in by their Christian Indian Martini. He made them row the heavy barge a very long way up a river and then deserted them for several days. They found he wished to secure the barge here, which was to be a part of his reward, and which was too heavy to be carried over the rocks of the headlands in the way they carried their own canoes—and by which they escaped the heavy seas that ran round those places.

However, the Cacique returned again, and after a time he consented to take the captain with John Byron to row his canoe on to another part of the coast where there were more Indians.

They reached this camp late one evening, and while the captain was at once taken by Martini to a wigwam, Byron was left outside to shift for himself as best he could. He was so exhausted that all he could do was to creep into the shelter of a wigwam, and chance what fate might bring him.

These wigwams were built of branches of trees placed in a circle, which are bound at the top by a kind of creeper called supple-jack. The frame of the wigwam is covered with boughs and bark. The fire is lit in the very centre, round which the Indians lie. As there is no outlet for the smoke, it is not a very comfortable place to sleep in.

There were only two Indian women in the wigwam into which John Byron crept, who were very astonished to see him. However, they were kind to him and made up a good fire, and presently, when he made them understand that he was hungry, they gave him some fish to eat. But when he had finished it he was still so hungry that he made signs for more. Then they went out into the night, taking their dogs with them, and came back in an hour or two shivering and with water dripping from their hair. They had caught two more fish, which after they had cooked slightly they gave him to eat.

These people live only on what they can take from the sea, and train their dogs to dive for fish and their women for sea-eggs. While collecting these the women stay under water a wonderfully long time; they have really the hardest work to do, as they have to provide food for their husbands and children. They are not allowed to touch any food themselves until the husband is satisfied, when he gives them a very small portion, generally that which he does not care to eat himself.

Martini then told them that they would have to return in the canoe by which they had come to their companions, and that the Indians they were leaving would join them in a few days, after which they would all set out together on the journey northwards. They found Mr. Elliot, the surgeon, very ill, and Mr. Hamilton and Mr. Campbell were almost starved, having had only a few sea-eggs to eat since they had left.

About the middle of March they re-embarked with the other Indians, and soon afterwards Mr. Elliot died. He had been one of the strongest of the party, and one of the most useful and self-denying, and had never spared himself in trying to provide food for the others. He was also one of the best shots of the party.

Most of them were now reduced to rags and without shoes, and when they had to cross the stony headlands and swamps, and to carry heavy burdens, their feet were often terribly torn.

The Cacique had now become a very hard master to all but the captain, and forced them to row like galley slaves when they were in the boats. Indeed, the captain seemed to encourage the Indian in this conduct. He had become more selfish and cunning in keeping all the food he could lay hands on for himself, and was accustomed to sleep with his head pillowed on a dirty piece of canvas in which he wrapped portions of seal or sea-eggs. Thorough cleanliness had become an impossibility to them: they were now terribly emaciated and covered by vermin. The captain particularly was a most shocking sight. His legs had become tremendously swelled, probably from the disease known as "beri-beri," while his body was almost a skeleton, his beard had grown very long, and his face was covered with train oil and dirt.

When at last they were within a few miles of the island of Chiloc, they found they had to cross a most dangerous bay. After waiting for two days for fair weather they started, although the Cacique even then seemed terrified, and there was every reason for it, as the sea ran so strong and their boat was most crazy, the bottom plank having opened, and ceaseless bailing had to be carried on all the time. It was early in June when they reached this place.

Directly the Cacique landed he buried all the things he had brought from the wreck, for he knew that the Spaniards would take everything from him.

That same evening, as they drew near to a settlement of Chiloc Indians the Cacique asked them to load their one remaining gun with the last charge of powder, and to show him how to fire it off. Holding the gun as far away from his head as he could he fired, and fell back into the bottom of the canoe.

When the Chiloc Indians found out who they were, they brought fish and potatoes for them to eat, and this was the nicest meal they had had for more than a year.

These Indians are very strong and nice-looking people; they are extremely neat in their dress. The men wear what is called a puncho, which is a square piece of cloth in stripes of different colours, with a slit in the centre wide enough to put their heads through, and it hangs from their shoulders.

After a little time the shipwrecked men were sent on by these people to the Spaniards at Castro. There they were met by a number of soldiers, with three or four officers, who surrounded them fiercely as though they were a most formidable enemy instead of the four poor helpless creatures left of the fifteen men that had set out from Wager's Island.

Though they had had much better food since they had been with the kindly Indians, they were so weak that they could hardly walk up the hill to the shed in which they were to be lodged.

Numbers of people came to look at them in this place, as though they were wild beasts or curiosities; and when they heard they had been starved for more than a year, they brought quantities of chicken and all kinds of good things for them to eat.

John Byron then began to feel more comfortable. He was always ready to make a meal, and used to carry food in his pockets so that he need not wait a second for it if he felt hungry. Even the captain owned that he ate so much that he felt quite ashamed of himself.

In a little time an old Jesuit priest came to see them. He did not come because he was sorry for them, but because he had heard from the Indian Cacique that they had things of great value about them. The priest began by producing a bottle of brandy, and gave them all some to open their hearts.

Captain Cheap told him he had nothing, not remembering that Martini had seen his gold repeater watch; but at the same time he said that Mr. Campbell had a silver watch, which he at once ordered him to make a present of to the priest.

Soon after the Spanish governor sent for them to be brought to Chaco, where they were very well treated by the people. Whilst here John Byron was asked to marry the niece of a very rich old priest.

The lady made the suggestion through her uncle, saying that first she wished him to be converted, and then he might marry her.

When the old priest made the offer, he took John Byron into a room where there were several large chests full of clothes. Taking from one of them a large piece of linen, he told him it should be made up into shirts for him at once if he would marry the lady.

The thought of new shirts was a great temptation to John Byron, as he had only the one in which he had lived ever since he had been wrecked.

However, he denied himself this luxury, and excused himself for not being able to accept the honour of the lady's hand.

On *this* occasion he managed to speak Spanish sufficiently well to make himself understood.

In January 1742 they were sent on to Valparaiso as English prisoners. Only Captain Cheap and Mr. Campbell were recognised as officers, as they had saved their commissions, and they were sent to St. Jago, while John Byron and Mr. Hamilton were kept in prison. However, when they were released they were permitted to rejoin the others at St. Jago, and found them living with a Scotch physician named Don Patricio Gedd.

When Dr. Gedd heard of the four English prisoners, he had begged the President to allow them to live at his house.

This was granted, and during the two years they lived there with him, he treated them most hospitably, and would hear of no return being made for his kindness.

Mr. Campbell changed his religion while they were at St. Jago, and left his companions.

At the end of two years the President sent for them, and told them that they were at liberty to leave the country in a French ship bound for Spain.

Accordingly, in the end of December 1744, they sailed in the frigate bound for Conception, where she was to join three more French ships that were homeward bound.

On October 27 they reached Cape Ortegal, and after lying at anchor there for several days they were taken to Landernan, where they lived on parole for three months, until an order came from the Court of Spain to allow them to return home by the first ship that sailed. After arranging with the captain of a Dutch lugger to land them at Dover they embarked in her and had a very uncomfortable passage.

When they got well up Channel they found the Dutchman had no intention of landing them at Dover, as he was making his way up off the coast of France. In the midst of their indignation at this breach of faith, an English man-of-war appeared to windward, and bore down upon them. This was the "Squirrel," commanded by Captain Masterton. He at once sent them off in one of his cutters, and they arrived at Dover that afternoon.

ANDREW LANG AND H. RIDER HAGGARD

They agreed to start for London the next morning. Captain Cheap and Mr. Hamilton were to drive in a post-chaise, and John Byron was to ride. But when they came to divide the little money they had left, it was found there would be barely enough to pay for horses. There was not a farthing left for John Byron to buy any food he might want on the way, nothing even to pay for the turnpikes. However, he boldly cheated these by riding as hard as he could through them all, and paid no attention to the shouts of the men when they tried to stop him. The want of food he had to put up with.

When he got to the Borough he took a coach and drove to Marlborough Street, where his people had lived before he left England. But when he came to the house he found it shut up. He had been away for five years, and had not heard a word from home all that time, therefore he was at a loss to know what to do for a few minutes until he remembered a linen draper's shop near by which his family had used. He drove there, and told them who he was. They paid his coachman for him, and told him that his sister was married to Lord Carlisle, and was living in Soho Square.

He went at once to her house; but the porter would not admit him for a long time. He was strangely dressed; half in Spanish, and half in French clothing, and besides, he wore very large and very mud-bespattered boots. The porter was about to shut the door in his face when John Byron persuaded him to let him in.

Then at last his troubles were over. His sister was delighted to see him, and at once gave him money with which to buy new clothes. And until he looked like an Englishman again, he did not feel he had come to the end of all the strange scenes and adventures that he had experienced for more than five years.

Peter Williamson[1]

I was born in Hirulay, in the county of Aberdeen. My parents, though not rich, were respectable, and so long as I was under their care all went well with me. Unhappily, I was sent to stay with an aunt at Aberdeen, where, at eight years old, when playing on the quay, I was noticed as a strong, active little fellow by two men belonging to a vessel in the harbour. Now this vessel was in the employ of certain merchants of Aberdeen, who used her for the villainous purpose of kidnapping— that is, stealing young children from their parents, and selling them as slaves in the plantations abroad.

These impious monsters, marking me out for their prey, tempted me on board the ship, which I had no sooner entered than they led me between the decks to some other boys whom they had kidnapped in like manner. Not understanding what a fate was in store for me, I passed the time in childish amusement with the other lads in the steerage, for we were never allowed to go on deck while the vessel stayed in the harbour, which it did till they had imprisoned as many luckless boys as they needed.

Then the ship set sail for America. I cannot remember much of the voyage, being a mere child at the time, but I shall never forget what happened when it was nearly ended. We had reached the American coast when a hard gale of wind sprang up from the south-east, and about midnight the ship struck on a sandbank off Cape May, near Delaware. To the terror of all on board, it was soon almost full of water. The boat was then hoisted out, and the captain and his fellow-villains, the crew, got into it, leaving me and my deluded companions, as they supposed, to perish. The cries, shrieks, and tears of a throng of children had no effect on these merciless wretches.

But happily for us the wind abated, and the ship being on a sandbank, which did not give way to let her deeper, we lay here till morning, when the captain, unwilling to lose all his cargo, sent some of the crew in a boat to the ship's side to bring us ashore. A sort of camp was made, and here we stayed till we were taken in by a vessel bound to Philadelphia.

At Philadelphia people soon came to buy us. We were sold for 16*l*.

---

1. Glasgow, 1758. Written by himself.

apiece. I never knew what became of my unhappy companions, but I was sold for seven years to one of my countrymen, Hugh Wilson, who in his youth had suffered the same fate as myself in being kidnapped from his home.

Happy was my lot in falling into his power, for he was a humane, worthy man. Having no children of his own, and pitying my sad condition, he took great care of me till I was fit for business, and at twelve years old set me about little things till I could manage harder work. Meanwhile, seeing my fellow-servants often reading and writing, I felt a strong desire to learn, and told my master that I should be glad to serve a year longer than the bond obliged me if he would let me go to school. To this he readily agreed, and I went every winter for five years, also learning as much as I could from my fellow-servants.

With this good master I stayed till I was seventeen years old, when he died, leaving me a sum of money, about 120*l.* sterling, his best horse, and all his wearing apparel.

I now maintained myself by working about the country, for anyone who would employ me, for nearly seven years, when I determined to settle down. I applied to the daughter of a prosperous planter, and found my suit was acceptable both to her and her father, so we married. My father-in-law wishing to establish us comfortably, gave me a tract of land which lay, unhappily for me, as it has since proved, on the frontiers of Pennsylvania. It contained about two hundred acres, with a good house and barn.

I was now happy in my home with a good wife; but my peace did not last long, for about 1754 the Indians in the French interest, who had formerly been very troublesome in our province, began to renew their old practices. Even many of the Indians whom we supposed to be in the English interest joined the plundering bands; it was no wonder, for the French did their utmost, to win them over, promising to pay 15*l.* for every scalp of an Englishman!

Hardly a day passed but some unhappy family fell a victim to French bribery and savage cruelty. As for me, though now in comfortable circumstances, with an affectionate and amiable wife, it was not long before I suddenly became the most pitiable of mankind. I can never bear to think of the last time I saw my dear wife, on the fatal 2nd of October, 1754. That day she had left home to visit some of her relations, and, no one being in the house but myself, I stayed up later than usual, expecting her return. How great was my terror when, at eleven o'clock at night, I heard the dismal war-whoop of the savages, and, flying to the window, saw a band of them outside, about twelve in number.

They made several attempts to get in, and I asked them what they wanted. They paid no attention, but went on beating at the door, trying to get it open. Then, having my gun loaded in my hand, I threatened them with death if they would not go away. But one of them, who could speak a little English, called out in return that if I did not come out they would burn me alive in the house. They told me further—what I had already found out—that they were no friends to the English, but that if I would surrender myself prisoner they would not kill me.

My horror was beyond all words. I could not depend on the promises of such creatures, but I must either accept their offer or be burnt alive. Accordingly I went out of my house with my gun in my hand, not knowing what I did or that I still held it. Immediately, like so many tigers, they rushed on me and disarmed me. Having me now completely in their power, the merciless villains bound me to a tree near the door, and then went into the house and plundered what they could. Numbers of things which they were unable to carry away were set fire to with the house and consumed before my eyes. Then they set fire to my barn, stable, and outhouses, where I had about two hundred bushels of wheat, and cows, sheep, and horses. My agony as I watched all this havoc it is impossible to describe.

When the terrible business was over, one of the monsters came to me, a tomahawk in his hand, threatening me with a cruel death if I would not consent to go with them. I was forced to agree, promising to do all that was in my power for them, and trusting to Providence to deliver me out of their hands. On this they untied me, and gave me a great load to carry on my back, under which I travelled all that night with them, full of the most terrible fear lest my unhappy wife should likewise have fallen into their clutches. At daybreak my master ordered me to lay down my load, when, tying my hands round a tree with a small cord, they forced the blood out of my finger ends. They then kindled a fire near the tree to which I was bound, which redoubled my agony, for I thought they were going to sacrifice me there.

When the fire was made, they danced round me after their manner, with all kinds of antics, whooping and crying out in the most horrible fashion. Then they took the burning coals and sticks, flaming with fire at the ends; and held them near my face, head, hands and feet, with fiendish delight, at the same time threatening to burn me entirely if I called out or made the least noise. So, tortured as I was, I could make no sign of distress but shedding silent tears, which, when they saw, they took fresh coals, and held them near my eyes, telling me my face was wet, and they would dry it for me. I have often wondered how I endured these tortures; but at last they were satisfied, and sat down round the fire and roasted the meat which they had brought from my dwelling!

When they had prepared it they offered some to me, and though it may be imagined that I had not much heart to eat, I was forced to seem pleased, lest if I refused it they should again begin to torture me. What I could not eat I contrived to get between the bark and the tree—my foes having unbound my hands till they supposed I had eaten all they gave me. But then they bound me as before, and so I continued all day. When the sun was set they put out the fire, and covered the ashes with leaves, as is their custom, that the white people may find no signs of their having been there.

Travelling thence, by the river, for about six miles, I being loaded heavily, we reached a spot near the Blue Hills, where the savages hid their plunder under logs of wood. Thence, shocking to relate, they went to a neighbouring house, that of Jacob Snider, his wife, five children, and a young man, a servant. They soon forced their way into the unhappy man's dwelling, slew the whole family, and set fire to the house.

The servant's life was spared for a time, since they thought he might be of use to them, and forthwith loaded him with plunder. But he could not bear the cruel treatment that we suffered; and though I tried to console him with a hope of deliverance, he continued to sob and moan. One of the savages, seeing this, instantly came up, struck him to the ground, and slew him.

The family of John Adams next suffered. All were here put to death except Adams himself, a good old man, whom they loaded with plunder, and day after day continued to treat with the most shocking cruelty, painting him all over with various colours, plucking the white hairs from his beard, and telling him he was a fool for living so long, and many other tortures which he bore with wonderful composure, praying to God.

One night after he had been tortured, when he and I were sitting together, pitying each other's misfortunes, another party of Indians arrived, bringing twenty scalps and three prisoners, who gave us terrible accounts of what tragedies had passed in their parts, on which I cannot bear to dwell.

These three prisoners contrived to escape, but unhappily, not knowing the country, they were recaptured and brought back. They were then all put to death, with terrible tortures.

A great snow now falling, the savages began to be afraid that the white people would follow their tracks upon it and find out their skulking retreats, and this caused them to make their way to their winter quarters, about two hundred miles further from any plantations or English inhabitants. There, after a long and tedious journey, in which I was almost starved, I arrived with this villainous crew. The place where we had to stay, in their tongue, was called Alamingo, and there I found a number of wigwams full of Indian women and children. Dancing, singing, and shooting were their general amusements, and they told what successes they had had in their expeditions, in which I found myself part of their theme. The severity of the cold increasing, they stripped me of my own clothes and gave me what they usually wear themselves—a blanket, a piece of coarse cloth, and a pair of shoes made of deer-skin.

The better sort of Indians have shirts of the finest linen they can get; and with these some wear ruffles, but they never put them on till they have painted them different colours, and do not take them off to wash, but wear them till they fall into pieces. They are very proud, and delight in trinkets, such as silver plates round their wrists and necks, with several strings of *wampum*, which is made of cotton, interwoven with pebbles, cockle-shells, &c. From their ears and noses they have rings and beads, which hang dangling an inch or two.

The hair of their heads is managed in different ways: some pluck out and destroy all except a lock hanging from the crown of the head, which they interweave with wampum and feathers. But the women wear it very long, twisted down their backs, with beads, feathers, and wampum, and on their heads they carry little coronets of brass or copper.

No people have a greater love of liberty or affection for their relations, yet they are the most revengeful race on earth, and inhumanly cruel. They generally avoid open fighting in war, yet they are brave when taken, enduring death or torture with wonderful courage. Nor would they at any time commit such outrages as they do, if they were not tempted by drink and money by those who call themselves civilised.

At Alamingo I was kept nearly two months, till the snow was off the ground—a long time to be among such creatures! I was too far from any plantations or white people to try to escape; besides, the bitter cold made my limbs quite benumbed. But I contrived to defend myself more or less against the weather by building a little wigwam with the bark of the trees, covering it with earth, which made it resemble a cave, and keeping a good fire always near the door.

Seeing me outwardly submissive, the savages sometimes gave me a little meat, but my chief food was Indian corn. Having liberty to go about was, indeed, more than I had expected; but they knew well it was impossible for me to escape.

At length they prepared for another expedition against the planters and white people, but before they set out they were joined by many other Indians from Fort Duquesne, well stored with powder and ball that they had received from the French.

As soon as the snow was quite gone, so that no trace of their footsteps could be found, they set out on their journey towards Pennsylvania, to the number of nearly a hundred and fifty. Their wives and children were left behind in the wigwams. My duty was to carry whatever they entrusted to me; but they never gave me a gun. For several days we were almost famished for want of proper provisions: I had nothing but a few stalks of Indian corn, which I was glad to eat dry, and the Indians themselves did not fare much better.

When we again reached the Blue Hills, a council of war was held, and we agreed to divide into companies of about twenty men each, after which every captain marched with his party where he thought proper. I still belonged to my old masters, but was left behind on the mountains with ten Indians, to stay till the rest returned, as they did not think it safe to carry me nearer to the plantations.

Here being left, I began to meditate on my escape, for I knew the country round very well, having often hunted there. The third day after the great body of the Indians quitted us my keepers visited the mountains in search of game, leaving me bound in such a way that I could not get free. When they returned at night they unbound me, and we all sat down to supper together, feasting on two polecats which they had killed. Then, being greatly tired with their day's excursion, they lay down to rest as usual.

Seeing them apparently fast asleep, I tried different ways of finding out whether it was a pretence to see what I should do. But after making a noise and walking about, sometimes touching them with my feet, I found that they really slept. My heart exulted at the hope of freedom, but it sank again when I thought how easily I might be recaptured. I resolved, if possible, to get one of their guns, and if discovered to die in self-defence rather than be taken; and I tried several times to take one from under their heads, where they always secure them. But in vain; I could not have done so without rousing them.

So, trusting myself to the divine protection, I set out defenceless. Such was my terror, however, that at first I halted every four or five yards, looking fearfully towards the spot where I had left the Indians, lest they should wake and miss me. But when I was about two hundred yards off I mended my pace, and made all the haste I could to the foot of the mountains.

Suddenly I was struck with the greatest terror and dismay, hearing behind me the fearful cries and howlings of the savages, far worse than the roaring of lions or the shrieking of hyænas; and I knew that they had missed me. The more my dread increased the faster I hurried, scarce knowing where I trod, sometimes falling and bruising myself, cutting my feet against the stones, yet, faint and maimed as I was, rushing on through the woods. I fled till daybreak, then crept into a hollow tree, where I lay concealed, thanking God for so far having favoured my escape. I had nothing to eat but a little corn.

But my repose did not last long, for in a few hours I heard the voices of the savages near the tree in which I was hid threatening me with what they would do if they caught me, which I already guessed too well. However, at last they left the spot where I heard them, and I stayed in my shelter the rest of that day without any fresh alarms.

At night I ventured out again, trembling at every bush I passed, and thinking each twig that touched me a savage. The next day I concealed myself in the same manner, and at night travelled forward, keeping off the main road, used by the Indians, as much as possible, which made my journey far longer, and more painful than I can express.

But how shall I describe my terror when, on the fourth night, a party of Indians lying round a small fire which I had not seen, hearing the rustling I made among the leaves, started from the ground, seizing their arms, and ran out into the wood? I did not know in my agony of fear whether to stand still or rush on. I expected nothing but a terrible death; but at that very moment a troop of swine made towards the place where the savages were. They, seeing the hogs, guessed that their alarm had been caused by them, and returned merrily to their fire and lay down to sleep again. As soon as this happened I pursued my way more cautiously and silently, but in a cold perspiration with terror at the peril I had just escaped. Bruised, cut, and shaken, I still held on my path till break of day, when I lay down under a huge log, and slept undisturbed till noon. Then, getting up, I climbed a great hill, and, scanning the country round, I saw, to my unspeakable joy, some habitations of white people, about ten miles distant.

My pleasure was somewhat damped by not being able to get among them that night. But they were too far off; therefore, when evening fell, I again commended myself to Heaven, and lay down, utterly exhausted. In the morning, as soon as I woke, I made towards the nearest of the cleared lands which I had seen the day before; and that afternoon I reached the house of John Bull, an old acquaintance. I knocked at the door, and his wife, who opened it, seeing me in such a frightful condition, flew from me like lightning, screaming, into the house.

This alarmed the whole family, who immediately seized their arms, and I was soon greeted by the master with his gun in his hand. But when I made myself known—for at first he took me for an Indian—he and all his family welcomed me with great joy at finding me alive; since they had been told I was murdered by the savages some months ago.

No longer able to bear up, I fainted and fell to the ground. When they had recovered me, seeing my weak and famished state, they gave me some food, but let me at first partake of it very sparingly. Then for two days and nights they made me welcome, and did their utmost to bring back my strength, with the kindest hospitality. Finding myself once more able to ride, I borrowed a horse and some clothes of these good people, and set out for my father-in-law's house in Chester county, about a hundred and forty miles away. I reached it on January 4, 1755; but none of the family could believe their eyes when they saw me, having lost all hope on hearing that I had fallen a prey to the Indians.

They received me with great joy; but when I asked for my dear wife I found she had been dead two months, and this fatal news greatly lessened the delight I felt at my deliverance.

A WONDERFUL VOYAGE

This is a story of a man who, when in command of his ships and when everything went prosperously with him, was so overbearing and cruel that some of his men, in desperation at the treatment they received, mutinied against him. But the story shows another side of his character in adversity which it is impossible not to admire.

In 1787 Captain Bligh was sent from England to Otaheite in charge of the "Bounty," a ship which had been specially fitted out to carry young plants of the breadfruit tree, for transplantation to the West Indies.

"The breadfruit grows on a spreading tree, about the size of a large apple tree; the fruit is round, and has a thick tough rind. It is gathered when it is full-grown, and while it is still green and hard; it is then baked in an oven until the rind is black and scorched. This is scraped off, and the inside is soft and white like the crumb of a penny loaf."

The Otaheitans use no other bread but the fruit kind. It is, therefore, little wonder that the West Indian planters were anxious to grow this valuable fruit in their own islands, as, if it flourished there, food would be provided with little trouble for their servants and slaves.

In the passage to Otaheite, Captain Bligh had several disturbances with his men. He had an extremely irritable temper, and would often fly into a passion and make most terrible accusations, and use most terrible language to his officers and sailors.

On one occasion he ordered the crew to eat some decayed pumpkins, instead of their allowance of cheese, which he said they had stolen from the ship's stores.

The pumpkin was to be given to the men at the rate of one pound of pumpkin to two pounds of biscuits.

The men did not like accepting the substitute on these terms. When the captain heard this, he was infuriated, and ordered the first man of each mess to be called by name, at the same time saying to them, "I'll see who will dare refuse the pumpkin or anything else I may order to be served out." Then, after swearing at them in a shocking way, he ended by saying, "I'll make you eat grass, or anything else you can catch before I have done with you," and threatened to flog the first man who dared to complain again.

While they were at Otaheite several of the sailors were flogged for

ANDREW LANG AND H. RIDER HAGGARD

small offences, or without reason, and on the other hand, during the seven months they stayed at the island, both officers and men were allowed to spend a great deal of time on shore, and were given the greatest possible liberty.

Therefore, when the breadfruit plants were collected, and they weighed anchor on April 4 in 1787, it is not unlikely they were loth to return to the strict discipline of the ship, and to leave an island so lovely, and where it was possible to live in the greatest luxury without any kind of labour.

From the time they sailed until April 27, Christian, the third officer, had been in constant hot water with Captain Bligh. On the afternoon of that day, when the captain came on deck, he missed some cocoanuts that had been heaped up between the guns. He said at once that they had been stolen, and that it could not have happened without the officers knowing of it. When they told him they had not seen any of the crew touch them, he cried, "Then you must have taken them yourselves!" After this he questioned them separately; when he came to Christian, he answered, "I do not know, sir, but I hope you do not think me so mean as to be guilty of stealing yours."

The captain swore terribly, and said, "You must have stolen them from me, or you would be able to give a better account of them!" He turned to the others with much more abuse, and saying, "D—n you! you scoundrels, you are all thieves alike, and combine with the men to rob me. I suppose you'll steal my yams next, but I'll sweat you for it, you rascals! I'll make half of you jump overboard before you get through Endeavour Straits!"

Then he turned to the clerk, giving the order to "stop the villains' grog, and to give them but half a pound of yams to-morrow: if they steal *them*, I'll reduce them to a quarter."

That night Christian, who was hardly less passionate and resentful than the captain, told two of the midshipmen, Stewart and Hayward, that he intended to leave the ship on a raft, as he could no longer endure the captain's suspicion and insults. He was very angry and excited, and made some preparations for carrying out his plan, though these had to be done with the greatest secrecy and care.

It was his duty to take the morning watch, which is from four to eight o'clock, and this time he thought would he a good opportunity to make his escape. He had only just fallen into a restless slumber when he was called to take his turn.

He got up with his brain still alert with the sense of injury and wrong, and most curiously alive to seize any opportunity which might lead to an escape from so galling a service.

On reaching the deck, he found the mate of the watch had fallen asleep, and that the other midshipman was not to be seen.

Then he made a sudden determination to seize the ship, and rushing down the gangway ladder, whispered his intention to Matthew Quintal and Isaac Martin, seamen, both of whom had been flogged. They readily agreed to join him, and several others of the watch were found to be quite as willing.

Someone went to the armourer for the keys of the arm chest, telling him they wanted to fire at a shark alongside.

Christian then armed those men whom he thought he could trust, and putting a guard at the officers' cabins, went himself with three other men to the captain's cabin.

It was just before sunrise when they dragged him from his bed, and tying his hands behind his back, threatened him with instant death if he should call for help or offer any kind of resistance. He was taken up to the quarter deck in his nightclothes, and made to stand against the mizzen mast with four men to guard him.

Christian then gave orders to lower the boat in which he intended to cast them adrift, and one by one the men were allowed to come up the hatchways, and made to go over the side of the ship into it. Meanwhile no heed was given to the remonstrances, reasoning, and prayers of the captain, saving threats of death unless he was quiet.

Some twine, canvas, sails, a small cask of water, and a quadrant and compass were put into the boat, also some bread and a small quantity of rum and wines. When this was done the officers were brought up one by one and forced over the side. There was a great deal of rough joking at the captain's expense, who was still made to stand by the mizzen-mast, and much bad language was used by everybody.

When all the officers were out of the ship, Christian said, "Come, Captain Bligh, your officers and men are now in the boat, and you must go with them; if you make the least resistance you will be instantly put to death."

He was lowered over the side with his hands still fastened behind his back, and directly after the boat was veered astern with a rope.

Someone with a little pity for them threw in some pieces of pork and some clothes, as well as two or three cutlasses; these were the only arms given.

There were altogether nineteen men in this pitiful strait. Although much of the conduct of the mutineers is easily understood with regard to the captain, the wholesale crime of thrusting so many innocent persons out on to the mercy of the winds and waves, or out to the death from hunger and thirst which they must have believed would inevitably overtake them, is incomprehensible.

As the "Bounty" sailed away, leaving them to their fate, those in the boat cast anxious looks to the captain as wondering what should then be done. At a time when his mind must have been full of the injury he had received, and the loss of his ship at a moment when his plans were so flourishing and he had every reason to congratulate himself as to the ultimate success of the undertaking, it is much in his favour that he seems to have realised their unfortunate position and to have been determined to make the best of it.

His first care was to see how much food they had. On examining it they found there was a hundred and fifty pounds of bread, thirty-two pounds of pork, six quarts of rum, six bottles of wine, and twenty-eight gallons of water.

As they were so near Tofoa they determined to put in there for a supply of breadfruit and water, so that they might keep their other provisions. But after rowing along the coast for some time, they only discovered some cocoanut trees on the top of a stony cliff, against which the sea beat furiously. After several attempts they succeeded in getting about twenty nuts. The second day they failed to get anything at all.

However, some natives came down to the boat and made inquiries about the ship; but the captain unfortunately told the men to say she had been lost, and that only they were saved.

This proved most disastrous; for the treacherous natives, finding they were defenceless, at first brought them presents of breadfruit, plantains and cocoanuts, rendering them all more hopeful and cheerful by their kindness. But towards night their numbers increased in a most alarming manner, and soon the whole beach was lined by them.

Presently they began knocking stones together, by which the men knew they intended to make an attack upon them. They made haste to get all the things into the boat, and all but one, named John Norton, succeeded in reaching it. The natives rushed upon this poor man and stoned him to death.

Those in the boat put to sea with all haste, but were again terribly alarmed to find themselves followed by natives in canoes from which they renewed the attack.

Many of the sailors were a good deal hurt by stones, and they had no means at all with which to protect themselves. At last they threw some clothes overboard; these tempted the enemy to stop to pick them up, and as soon as night came on they gave up the chase and returned to the shore.

All the men now begged Captain Bligh to take them towards England; but he told them there could be no hope of relief until they reached Timor, a distance of full twelve hundred leagues; and that, if they wished to reach it, they would have to content themselves with one ounce of bread and a quarter of a pint of water a day. They all readily agreed to this allowance of food, and made a most solemn oath not to depart from their promise to be satisfied with the small quantity. This was about May 2. After the compact was made, the boat was put in order, the men divided into watches, and they bore away under a reefed lug-foresail.

A fiery sun rose on the 3rd, which is commonly a sign of rough weather, and filled the almost hopeless derelicts with a new terror.

In an hour or two it blew very hard, and the sea ran so high that their sail was becalmed between the waves; they did not dare to set it when on the top of the sea, for the water rushed in over the stern of the boat, and they were obliged to bale with all their might.

The bread was in bags, and in the greatest danger of being spoiled by the wet. They were obliged to throw some rope and the spare sails overboard, as well as all the clothes but what they wore, to lighten the boat, then the carpenter's tool-chest was cleared and the bread put into it.

They were all very wet and cold, and a teaspoonful of rum was served to each man, with a quarter of a breadfruit which was so bad that it could hardly be eaten; but the captain was determined at all risks to keep to the compact they had entered into, and to make their provisions last eight weeks.

In the afternoon the sea ran even higher, and at night it became very cold; but still they did not dare to leave off baling for an instant, though their legs and arms were numb with fatigue and wet.

In the morning a teaspoonful of rum was served to all, and five small cocoanuts divided for their dinner, and everyone was satisfied.

ANDREW LANG AND H. RIDER HAGGARD

When the gale had subsided they examined the bread, and found a great deal of it had become mouldy and rotten; but even this was carefully kept and used. The boat was now near some islands, but they were afraid to go on shore, as the natives might attack them; while being in sight of land, where they might replenish their poor stock of provisions and rest themselves, added to their misery. One morning they hooked a fish, and were overjoyed at their good fortune; but in trying to get it into the boat it was lost, and again they had to content themselves with the damaged bread and small allowance of water for their supper.

They were dreadfully cramped for room, and were obliged to manage so that half their number should lie down in the bottom of the boat or upon a chest, while the others sat up and kept watch: their limbs became so stiff from being constantly wet, and from want of space to stretch them in, that after a few hours' sleep they were hardly able to move.

About May 7 they passed what the captain supposed must be the Fiji Islands, and two large canoes put off and followed them for some time, but in the afternoon they gave up the chase. It rained heavily that day, and everyone in the boat did his best to catch some water, and they succeeded in increasing their stock to thirty-four gallons, besides having had enough to drink for the first time since they had been east adrift; but the rain made them very cold and miserable, and as they had no dry things their shiverings were terrible.

The next morning they had an ounce and a half of pork, a teaspoonful of rum, half a pint of cocoanut milk, and an ounce of bread for breakfast, which was quite a large meal for them. The rum, though (or because) in such small quantities, is said to have been of the greatest service to them.

Through fifteen weary days and nights of ceaseless rain they toiled, sometimes through fierce storms of thunder and lightning, and before terrific seas lashed into foam and fury by swift and sudden squalls, with only their miserable pittance of bread and water to keep body and soul together. Now and then a little rum was given after any extra fatigue of baling, but only at the times set apart for meals.

In this rain and storm the little sleep they got only added to their discomfort, save for the brief forgetfulness it brought; for they had to lie down in water in the bottom of the boat, and with no covering but the streaming clouds above them.

The captain then advised them to wring their clothes through sea-water, which they found made them feel much warmer for a time.

On May 17 everyone was ill and complaining of great pain, and begging for more food; but the captain refused to increase their allowance, though he gave them all a small quantity of rum.

Until the 24th they flew before the wild seas that swept over stem and stern of their boat, and kept them constantly baling.

Some of them now looked more than half dead from starvation, but no one suffered from thirst, as they had absorbed so much water through the skin.

A fine morning dawned on the 25th, when they saw the sun for the first time for fifteen days, and were able to eat their scanty allowance in more comfort and warmth. In the afternoon there were numbers of birds called boobies and noddies near, which are never seen far from land.

The captain took this opportunity to look at the state of their bread, and found if they did not exceed their allowance there was enough to last for twenty-nine days, when they hoped to reach Timor. That afternoon some noddies came so near the boat that one was caught. These birds are about the size of a small pigeon; it was divided into eighteen parts and given by lot. The men were much amused when they saw the beak and claws fall to the lot of the captain. The bird was eaten, bones and all, with bread and water, for dinner.

Now they were in calmer seas they were overtaken by a new trouble. The heat of the sun became so great that many of them were overcome by faintness, and lay in the bottom of the boat in an apathetic state all day, only rousing themselves towards evening, when the catching of birds was attempted.

On the morning of the 28th the sound of breakers could be heard plainly; they had reached the Great Barrier Beef, which runs up much of the east coast of Australia.

After some little time a passage nearly a quarter of a mile in width was discovered through the reef, and they were carried by a strong current into the peaceful waters which lie within the Barrier.

For a little time they were so overjoyed that their past troubles were forgotten. The dull blue-grey lines of the mainland, with its white patches of glaring sandhills, could be seen in the distance, and that afternoon they landed on an island.

They found the rocks around it were covered with oysters and huge clams, which could easily be got at low tide. Some of their party sent out to reconnoitre returned greatly pleased at having found plenty of fresh water.

A fire was made by help of a small magnifying-glass. Among the things thrown into the boat from the ship was a small copper pot; and thus with a mixture of oysters, bread, and pork a stew was made, and everyone had plenty to eat.

The day after they landed was the 29th of May, the anniversary of the restoration of King Charles II, and as the captain thought it applied to their own renewed health and strength, he named it Restoration Island.

After a few days' rest, which did much to revive the men, and when they had filled all their vessels with water and had gathered a large supply of oysters, they were ready to go on again.

As they were about to start everybody was ordered to attend prayers, and as they were embarking about twenty naked savages came running and shouting towards them, each carrying a long barbed spear, but the English made all haste to put to sea.

For several days they sailed over the lake-like stillness of the Barrier reef-bound waters, and past the bold desolations of the Queensland coast, every headland and bay there bearing the names Cook gave them only a few years before, and which still tell us by that nomenclature each its own story of disappointment and hope.

Still making way to the north, they passed many more islands and keys, the onward passage growing hot and hotter, until on June 3, when they doubled Cape York, the peninsula which is all but unique in its northward bend, they were again in the open sea.

By this time many of them were ill with malaria, then for the first time some of the wine which they had with them was used.

But the little boat still bravely made its way with its crew, whose faces were so hollow and ghastly that they looked like a crew of spectres, sailing beneath the scorching sun that beat down from the pale blue of the cloudless sky upon a sea hardly less blue in its greater depths. Only the hope that they would soon reach Timor seemed to rouse them from a state of babbling delirium or fitful slumber.

On the 11th the captain told them they had passed the meridian of the east of Timor; and at three o'clock on the next morning they sighted the land.

It was on Sunday, June 14, when they arrived at Company Bay, and were received with every kindness by the people.

Thus ended one of the most remarkable voyages that has ever been made. They had been sent out with provisions only sufficient for their number for *five* days, and Captain Bligh had, by his careful calculation, and determination to give each man only that equal portion they had agreed to accept, made it last for *fifty* days, during which time they had come three thousand six hundred and eighteen nautical miles.

There had been days when the men were so hunger-driven that they had besought him with pitiful prayers for more to eat, and when it was his painful duty to refuse it; and times, as they passed those islands where plentiful food could be got, when he had to turn a deaf ear to their longings to land. He had to endure the need of food, the cramped position, the uneasy slumber, as did his men; as well as the more perfect knowledge of their dangers. There had been days and nights while he worked out their bearings when he had to be propped up as he took the stars or sun.

It was, therefore, Captain Bligh's good seamanship, his strict discipline and fairness in the method of giving food and wine to those who were sick, that enabled them to land at Timor with the whole of their number alive, with the exception of the one man who was stoned to death by the savages at Tofoa.

THE PITCAIRN ISLANDERS

I t will be remembered that nothing had been heard of the "Bounty" since she was seen off Point Venus on the morning of September 22, 1789.

In 1809, just twenty years after, when Captain Folger, of the American ship "Topaz," landed at Pitcairn Island, one of the most remote of the islands in the Pacific, he found there a solitary Englishman and five Otaheitan women and nineteen children. The man, who gave his name as Alexander Smith, said he was the only remaining person of the nine who had escaped in the "Bounty."

Although this information was given to the Admiralty shortly after, it was not until the year 1814, when the "Briton," under the command of Sir Thomas Staines, and the "Tagus," under that of Captain Pipon, were cruising in the Pacific, that one day on which the ships were sailing in the same direction about six leagues apart, both commanders were greatly surprised to see an island in lat. 24° 40′ and long. 130° 24′ W.

They were puzzled to know what it could be, as Pitcairn Island (named after a son of Major Pitcairn who was lost in the "Aurora"), the only one known in the neighbourhood, was marked on their charts as in long. 133° 24′ W., more than three degrees out.

They thought they had made a new discovery, and as they ran in for the land they were astonished to see some neatly-built huts surrounded by gardens and plantations.

Some people were seen coming down the cliff with canoes on their shoulders. Presently one was launched and made off through the heavy surf towards the ships. They were more surprised than ever when one of the young men in it cried out in English as they came alongside, "Won't you heave us a rope, now?"

He sprang up the side of the ship swiftly. When on deck he told Sir Thomas Staines and Captain Pipon, when they asked him who he was, that his name was Thursday October Christian, and that he was the son of the late Fletcher Christian by an Otaheitan mother; that he was the first born on the island, and his name was given him as he had been born on a Thursday in October. He was now twenty-four years of age, and had a fine muscular figure, dark hair, and a brownish complexion, and "in his good-natured and benevolent countenance he had all the features of an honest English face." He wore no clothing except a small piece of cloth about his loins and a straw hat trimmed with cock's feathers. He spoke English correctly and pleasantly both as to grammar and pronunciation. He also told them he was married to a woman much older than himself, one of those who had come with his father from Otaheite. His companion was a fine boy of about seventeen or eighteen years, named George Young, son of Young the midshipman.

The islanders were much surprised at the many things new to them in the ship, at the guns, and everything around them. They were greatly entertained at the sight of a little dog. "Oh, what a pretty little thing it is!" exclaimed Young. "I know it is a dog, for I have heard of such an animal."

The young men told the captains of many of the events that had happened among the first settlers; but said that John Adams, now an old man, could tell them much more. He was the only surviving Englishman that came away in the "Bounty," and at that time he was called Alexander Smith.

The captains determined to go on shore to see Adams, and to hear from him the true story of Christian's fate, and of that of his companions.

Adams, who had been concealed since the arrival of the ships, when he found that the two captains had landed and were not armed, and that they did not intend to take him prisoner, came to the beach to meet them, and brought his wife with him, who was a very old woman and nearly blind.

After so many years the sight of the King's uniform no doubt brought back the scene of the "Bounty" to Adams, for at first he was very nervous and ill at ease.

However, when Sir Thomas Staines assured him they were not there with any intention of taking him away, that they were not even aware that such a person as himself existed, he regained confidence, and then told them he had taken the name of John Adams since the sole care of the women and children on the island had fallen upon him. He pretended he had not taken any great share in the mutiny, that he was sick in bed when it took place, and that he had been roused up and compelled to take a musket in his hand. He said he was now ready and willing to go back to England in one of the ships.

When the islanders heard him say this, all the women and children wept bitterly, and the young men stood motionless and absorbed in grief. When the officers again assured them that he should on no account be molested, the people were overcome with joy and gratitude. Adams then told them of the fate of the "Bounty" and of the rest of the mutineers.

It is easy to suppose that when Christian sailed for the last time from Otaheite his mind was full of misgiving; that he bitterly repented the rash act by which the ship had fallen into his hands and by which in all probability nineteen men had lost their lives, and also the wrecked and criminal lives of his followers. The picture of the derelict crew in their little boat was ever in his mind as he had last seen them watching with despairing eyes their ship sail away; and again as distance blurred all form, and it lay a blot on the sunny waters, immediately before it was hidden by the horizon line.

That blot became ever blacker and heavier to his mental vision as one by one his projects failed. A sullen and morose outcast for ever from civilisation, he sailed out into the unknown seas with his little band of desperate followers, to find if possible some solitary island, some unknown spot, where they might be lost for ever from the world.

Curiously, the place which he pictured, the object for which he sought, was soon after given to him to find.

Its steep cliffs rise from the sea precipitously, and beyond and above them a ridge of rocky hills runs from north to south, from which, again, two mountainous peaks of a thousand feet and more in height stand up like sentinels.

At a little distance from the coast-line a white wall of surf lashes itself into fury, and breaks everlastingly over the hidden reefs that raise so formidable a guard around the island as to render safe landing impossible save only at particular places and times.

Encouraged by this forbidding coast-line, after they had sailed all round the island they effected a landing, and finding it uninhabited, they decided to make it their home. The "Bounty" was run into an inlet between the cliffs, and after she had been dismantled and her materials used for building houses, in 1790 they burnt her, as they feared she might attract the notice of any ship that should chance to pass.

The first thing they did after their arrival was to divide the land into nine equal parts, giving none to the Otaheitan men, who it is said had been carried off from their own island by force. At first they were kindly treated by the white men; but afterwards they made them their slaves.

When they had been on the island a few weeks Christian became more gloomy and taciturn, and his conduct to the others grew more overbearing and unreasonable day by day.

Fear entered into his soul, and he looked with dislike and suspicion upon all around him, shunned their companionship and sought a place where he could be alone with his dark thoughts. Up at the extreme end of the ridge of hills that runs across the island the almost inaccessible cave may still be seen to which he carried a store of provisions and ammunition, and thus shut himself off from the others, and with only the sound of the roaring breakers as they beat on the shore below to disturb his solitude, the madman dwelt alone with his terrible history of the past.

One story is that in a fit of maniacal insanity he flung himself over the rocks into the sea. Another that he was shot by one of the mutineers whilst digging in a plantation.

The accounts are contradictory. But whether from suicide or murder, his death happened within a year after he landed at Pitcairn Island.

For about two years, while they all worked at the building of the houses and at cultivating the ground, the Otaheitan men toiled without a murmur. But when Williams, who had lost his wife, insisted that he would take one of theirs or leave the island in one of the "Bounty's" boats, the other Englishmen, who did not want to part with him, compelled one of the Otaheitans to give his wife to him.

From this time the Otaheitans became discontented, until the man whose wife had been taken away was murdered in the woods; then things went on more quietly for a year or two longer, when two of the most desperate and cruel of the mutineers, Quintal and M'Koy, at last drove them to form a plot to destroy their oppressors. A day was fixed by them to attack and put to death all the Englishmen when they were at work in the yam plots.

They killed Martin and Brown, one with a maul, the other with a musket, while Adams made his escape, though he was wounded in the shoulder by a bullet.

Young, who was a great favourite with the women, was hidden by them during the attack, while M'Koy and Quintal fled to the woods.

That night all the native men were murdered by the widows of the Europeans. This happened in 1793. From that time till 1798 the colonists went on quietly, until M'Koy, who had once been employed in a Scotch distillery, and had for some time been making experiments on the *ti* root, succeeded in extracting from it an intoxicating liquor.

After this Quintal also gave his whole time to making the spirit, and in consequence the two men were constantly drunk, and in one of his fits of delirium M'Koy threw himself from a cliff, and was instantly killed. Quintal became more and more unmanageable, and frequently threatened to destroy Adams and Young—who, knowing that he would carry out his threat, determined to kill him. This they did by felling him with an axe as they would an ox.

Thus it was that at last only two men were left on the island, Adams and Young. The latter, who was of a quiet and studious nature, resolved to have prayers every morning and evening, and regular services on Sunday, and to teach the children, of whom there were nineteen, several of them then being between the ages of seven and nine years. Young, however, did not live long, but died of asthma about a year after the murder of Quintal.

In their beautiful island of the sea, where the lordly banyans grow, and where the feathery cocoanut palms stand boldly along the cliffs, or here and there fringe the rocky beach—for in this temperate climate just without the tropics there are but few trees and vegetables that will not grow—there, unknown for many years to the world, and far away from its busy jar and fret, the simple and kindly natures that these children of Pitcairn Island must have inherited from their Otaheitan mothers were trained to an almost perfect sense of duty and piety by old John Adams.

With a Bible and Prayer-book to aid him he persevered with his self-imposed task. It was a task that must often have cost him much labour and patient study, for though he could read he was not able to write until he was a very old man.

Though in the eyes of the law his crime can never be wiped out, in the eyes of humanity, his sincere repentance and long and tender devotion to his charge—a charge that ended only on the day of his death—will for ever render the last of the mutineers a character to be remembered with admiration and respect.

A Relation of three years' Suffering of Robert Everard upon the Island of Assada, near Madagascar, in a Voyage to India, in the year 1686[1]

When I was a boy, my father, Mr. William Everard, apprenticed me to the captain of a ship bound for Bombay in India, and thence to Madagascar, for blacks. I left London on August 5, 1686, and after different adventures on the voyage, of which I need not here speak, our ship reached Madagascar.

The King of Madagascar received us kindly enough, and promised in about a month to furnish the captain with as many negroes as he desired. This satisfied us very well, and, mooring the ship, we stayed some days, trading with the negroes for rice and hens and bananas.

Now one day the supercargo and six of the men and myself went ashore, taking guns and powder, and knives and scissors to trade with, and the ship's dog went with us. And, carrying our chest of goods to the house of one of the natives, we traded, and the negroes brought us such things as they had in exchange.

But presently we heard a great noise, and a crowd began to gather, so that we thought the King was coming. But, alas! we soon found that the people of the town had risen against us, and ten or twelve broke in with their lances, and killed five of the boat's crew and the man who took care of the boat! The supercargo, running out of the house to get to the King, was thrust through by one of these murderous natives, and died immediately. I myself, being knocked down by the fall of the others, lay among the dead like one dead.

When the blacks took them up, however, they saw I was alive, and did not kill me in cold blood, but carried me to the King's house, which was just by the house where they had killed our men, whose bodies I saw them carrying down to fling into the sea as I looked out at the King's door.

He bade me sit down, and ordered the women to bring me some boiled rice on a plantain leaf, but in my terrible condition I could not

---

1. Taken from the Churchill Collection, 1732. Written by himself.

eat. At night the King's men showed me my lodging in a small hut among the slaves, where I remained till the morning.

That morning our ship sailed. All the night as she lay there she had kept firing her great guns, and one shot came into the middle of the King's house, and went through it.

But when she had sailed I saw some of the blacks with bottles of wine taken out of the great cabin, which I myself had filled the morning I went ashore. They had also the captain's sword and the ship's compass, and some great pieces of the flag tied round their waists. So I asked those negroes who understood a little English if they had killed any on board. They said "Yes," and told me that the blacks in a canoe that went to our ship to trade had lances hidden, and fell upon the captain and the mate, who suspected nothing, and killed them and some others of our men, but the rest had time to arm themselves, and so drove the blacks away.

I asked them also why they killed our men, and they told the King, who answered that an English ship had been before, and played the rogue with them, and killed some of the natives, and they had therefore taken revenge.

After this the King went to visit his towns, and bid me go along with him; and I went first to one place and then another, to be shown to the people. But the women when they saw me shrieked and ran away in a fright—never having seen a white man, and thinking I was a spirit.

Then the King and his army went to the other side of the island, and carried me with them and our dog, and there he began mustering together a greater army, taking more men out of every town he visited. As soon as the women saw the King and his army coming, they got their sticks and came dancing for joy. And when he came into a town a mat was laid on the ground for him to sit on. When he sat down the wife of the chief of the town came out with some white stuff upon a stone, and dipped her finger in it, and put one spot on the King's forehead, and one on each cheek, and one on his chin; and so they did to his four wives who went with him. Then, when the women had done spotting them, the captain of the town and all his men came before the King, some with great calabashes full of liquor, and he bid the captain get his men ready to go along with the army, which was done in a day's time. Thus he went from town to town.

The dog belonging to our ship went too, and when he saw any hogs, he ran and barked at them till the negroes came and killed them with their lances. And sometimes he would fetch a young pig and bring it to me.

It was six or seven weeks before they reached the town of the enemy, and rushed into it, firing and striking with their lances, and killing or taking prisoners all who did not run away. Then marching further up the country they met with the enemy's whole army; and for about a month they fought with them day after day, our side nearly always getting the better of it.

When as many prisoners had been taken as the King needed for slaves, we marched back again through the towns, and the people brought great parcels of rice made up in plantain leaves, and pots of boiled fish for the King and his men to eat with their rice. They used to sit four, and six, or eight together; they also gave me some by myself, on a plantain leaf. This they did at every town where the King came. But as I was coming back with them I was taken lightheaded, so that sometimes I fell down, and could not stir without extreme pain.

About a week after we reached our own town the King asked me if I could make powder. I told him "No;" he then asked if I could make shot. I said "Yes;" and he told his men to fetch some lead, and clay for the moulds, and as well as I could I made three or four hundred shot. The King was pleased with these, and while I was making them I had victuals given me, and some of their best drink.

But afterwards the King bid me go about the island with some of his men to find flint stones; and when I could find none he took no more notice of me, but turned me out of his house, and would not let me come into it any more. Then I had to seek for my own food to save myself from being starved, and it pleased God that I found such food as the natives eat—yams and potatoes, which I dug out of the earth with a piece of sharp stone, having neither knife nor any other tool. And I made fire as the natives did, rubbing together two pieces of stick, and roasted my yams, and gathered bananas and oranges and other fruit. Then sometimes I caught fish with a small, sharp-pointed stick, and crabs, and now and then a turtle. I also found turtles' eggs. I used to keep yams and potatoes by me to serve five or six days, and when they were gone I hunted for more.

My lodging was under a tree on the hard ground, where I slept for two years and nine months and sometimes in the year it would rain for three months together, or only become fine for an hour or so—yet for all that I lay under the tree still. I always had a fire on each side of me to keep me warm, because I had no covering but the branches and leaves of the tree. Sometimes in the night I crept outside the cottage of one of the natives for shelter, but I was forced to be gone before they were up for fear they would do me harm.

When I wanted water I went almost a mile for a drink, and had nothing to bring back a little water in to keep by me and drink whenever I was thirsty. Also, I had to see that there were no blacks near the water, lest they should set upon me.

Two years after I had come to the country I suffered terrible pain with sores that broke out upon me, but finding some honey in a rock by the seaside, I made a kind of salve which gave me a little ease. But now the time of my worst distress was drawing to an end.

For when I had been three years in the island there came Arabs to buy negroes, and I pleaded with them to take me away, telling them how it was that I, an English boy, was left in this condition. Then the chief merchant of the Arabs said he could not carry me away without the King's leave, for it would spoil their trade; but he would try to get me clear, and as long as the Arabian vessel lay there I might come to his house and get food and drink.

About six weeks after the merchant sent for me, and told me he had bought me of the King for twenty dollars, and that he would carry me to my own country people again.

The ship lay there about ten weeks, and when they had got all their negroes we sailed from Madagascar. But all the history of my voyaging with the Arabs, who treated me with much kindness, and sold me at last to Englishmen, would be too long to relate. When I first saw my own countrymen I had forgotten English, so that I could only speak to them in the language of Madagascar; but by the time I had been among them six or seven days my English came back, and I could tell them my story.

At last I was taken on board an English ship called the "Diana," and, sailing in this, I reached Yarmouth and afterwards Blackwall, where I met my father, to the great joy of us both. Thus I conclude my narrative, with humble thanks to God for His wonderful preservation of me through so many hardships and dangers.

The Fight at Svolder Island (A.D. 1000)

Olaf Tryggvason, King of Norway, had sailed with a large fleet eastwards to Wendland, passing through the Danish king's dominion without his goodwill, and was now returning thence. He sailed with a light breeze and fair weather for Denmark, the smaller ships going before, and the larger ships following behind because they needed more wind.

At an island off Wendland were gathered many great chiefs: the island is called Svolder. In this fleet was Sweyn, King of the Danes, who had many charges against King Olaf—one being that Olaf had taken to wife Sweyn's sister without his leave; another that he had established himself in Norway, a land tributary to Sweyn and subdued by King Harold his father. Earl Sigvaldi was there with the Danish king because he was his earl. And in this combined fleet was a mighty chief, Olaf the Swede, King of the Swedes, who deemed he had to avenge on King Olaf of Norway great dishonour; for he had broken betrothals with, and smitten with his glove, Olaf the Swede's mother. This same woman Sigridr Sweyn, the Danish king, had now to wife, and she was strongly urging on Sweyn to do King Olaf hurt or dishonour. With this fleet, too, was Earl Eric, Hacon's son, who deemed he had very great charges against King Olaf and his men, because they had been present at the slaying of his father, Earl Hacon, and had driven out of the land all his sons; and Olaf had established himself in the kingdom afterwards.

These chiefs had an overwhelming host, and lay in a harbour on the inner side of the island; but King Olaf's ships were sailing past outside, and the chiefs were on the high ground of the island, and saw where the fleet was sailing from the east. They saw that the small craft sailed in front.

Soon they saw a ship large and splendid. Then said King Sweyn: "Get we to our ships with all speed; there sails Long Snake from the east."

Answered Earl Eric: "Bide we awhile, sire; they have more big ships than Long Snake alone."

And so it was. This ship belonged to Styrkar of Gimsa.

Now saw they yet another ship, large and well-equipped, a ship with a figure-head.

Said King Sweyn: "Now here will be sailing Long Snake; and take we heed that we be not too late in meeting them."

Then answered Earl Eric: "That will not be Long Snake; few of their big ships have passed as yet; there are many more to come."

And it was even as the Earl said.

Now sailed a ship with striped sails, a long-ship built for speed, and much larger than the others that had gone by. And when King Sweyn saw that this ship had no figure-head on her, then stood he up and said, laughing the while: "Olaf Tryggvason is afraid now; he dares not to sail with his dragon's head; go we and attack him."

Answered then Earl Eric: "That is not Olaf Tryggvason. I know the ship, for I have often seen it; it belongs to Erling Skjalgsson. And 'tis better that we go astern of him to this battle. Brave wights are on board there, as we shall surely know if we meet Olaf Tryggvason. Better is a gap in the King's fleet than a ship thus well-manned."

Then said Olaf, the Swedish king, to the Earl: "We ought not to fear joining battle with Olaf, though he have many ships. And it is great shame and disgrace for men to hear in other lands, if we lie by with an overwhelming host while he sails the high road of the seas outside."

Earl Eric answered: "Sire, let this swift long-ship pass if she will. I can tell you good tidings: that Olaf Tryggvason has not sailed by us, and this day you will have the chance of fighting with him. There are here now many chiefs, and I expect of this bout that we shall all have plenty of work."

Still they said, when this long-ship and many craft had gone by: "That must have been Long Snake. And Earl Eric," said the Danes, "will never fight to avenge his father if he do not so now."

The Earl answered much in wrath, and said that the Danes would not be found less loath to fight than himself and his men.

They waited not long ere three ships came sailing, whereof one, by far the largest, bore a golden dragon's head. Then all said that the Earl had spoken truth, and there now was Long Snake.

Earl Eric answered: "That is not Long Snake." But he bade them attack if they would.

And at once Sigvaldi took his long-ship and rowed out to the ships, holding up a white shield; they, on the other hand, lowered their sails and waited. But that large ship was the Crane, steered by Thorkell Dydrill, the King's kinsman. They asked of Sigvaldi what tidings he had to tell them. He declared he could tell them tidings of Sweyn, the Danish king, which it were right Olaf Tryggvason should know—he was setting a snare for him if he were not on his guard. Then Thorkell and his men let their ship float, and waited for the King.

Then saw King Sweyn four ships of great size sailing, and one by far the largest, and on it a dragon's head conspicuous, all of gold. And they all at once said: "A wondrous big ship and a beautiful one is the Long Snake. There will be no long-ship in the world to match her for beauty, and much glory is there in causing to be made such a treasure."

Then said Sweyn, the Danish king, out loud: "The Long Snake shall bear me; I shall steer it this evening before set of sun."

Whereat Earl Eric said, but so that few men heard: "Though Olaf Tryggvason had no more ships than may now be seen, never will Danish king steer this ship if they two and their forces have dealings together."

Sigvaldi, when he saw where the ships were sailing, bade Thorkell Dydrill draw his ship under the island; but Thorkell said the wind sat better for them to sail out at sea than to keep under the land with large ships and light breeze. But they gathered them under the island, these last four, because they saw some of their ships rowing under the island, and suspected that there might be some new tidings; so they tacked and stood in close to the island, and lowered their sails and took to their oars. The large ship of this group was named Short Snake.

And now the chiefs saw three very large ships sailing, and a fourth last of all. Then said Earl Eric to King Sweyn and to Olaf, the Swedish king: "Now stand ye up and to your ships; none will now deny that Long Snake sails by, and there ye may meet Olaf Tryggvason."

Whereat silence fell on the chiefs, and none spake; and great fear was on the crews, and many a one there dreaded his bane.

Olaf Tryggvason saw where his men had laid them under the island, and, feeling sure that they must have heard some tidings, he also turned these ships inwards to the island, and they lowered sail. Earl Sigvaldi steered his ship inwards along the island to meet the fleet of the other kings that was coming out from the harbour inside. Therefore sang Stefnir about Sigvaldi, the foul traitor who drew Tryggvason into a trap.

Sweyn, the Danish king, and Olaf, the Swedish king, and Earl Eric had made this agreement between them, that, if they slew Olaf Tryggvason, he of them who should be nearest at the time should own the ship and all the share of booty taken in the battle; but of the realm of the Norse king they should each have a third.

Then saw Olaf Tryggvason and all his men that they were betrayed, for lo the whole sea about them was covered with ships; but Olaf had a small force, as his fleet had sailed on before him. And now lay in his place each one of those three chiefs, Sweyn, King of Danes, with his force; Olaf, King of Swedes, with his host; while in the third place Earl Eric set his men in array.

Then talked with King Olaf a wise man, Thorkell Dydrill, and said: "Here are overwhelming odds to fight against. Hoist we our sails, and sail we after our fleet out to sea; for in no man is it cowardice to know his own measure."

King Olaf answered with loud voice: "Bind we our ships together with ropes, and let men don their war apparel and draw their swords; my men must not think of flight."

And Olaf Tryggvason asked his men: "Who is chief over this force that lies here nearest to us?"

They answered:

"We think it be Sweyn, King of Danes."

Then said King Olaf: "We need not fear that force; never did Danes win victory in battle when fighting on shipboard against Norsemen."

Again asked King Olaf: "Who lies there out beyond with so many ships?"

He was told that it was Olaf Ericsson, King of Swedes.

Then answered King Olaf: "We need not fear Swedish horse-eaters;[1] they will be more eager to lick up what is in their sacrificial bowls than to board Long Snake under our weapons."

And yet again asked King Olaf Tryggvason: "Who owns those large ships that lie out beyond the other squadrons?"

He was told that it was Earl Eric, Hacon's son, with the Iron Earn, of all ships the largest.

Then said King Olaf: "Many high-born men are arrayed against us in that host, and with that force we may expect a stubborn battle: they are Norsemen as are we, and have often seen bloody swords and exchange of blows, and they will think they meet their match in us, as in truth they do."

So these four chiefs, two kings and two earls, joined battle with Olaf Tryggvason. Sigvaldi indeed took little part in the fight, but Skuli Thorsteinsson in his short poem says that Sigvaldi was there. Very sharp and bloody was this contest, and the Danes fell most because they were nearest the Norsemen. Soon they did not hold their ground,

---

1. The Swedes were still heathens, and ate horses, meat then forbidden to Christians.

but withdrew out of shot range; and this fleet, as Olaf had said, came off with no glory. But none the less the battle raged fierce and long, and numbers fell on either side—of the Swedes, however, most—till it came about that Olaf the Swede saw this to be the best counsel for himself and his fleet, to make as if they shunned the fight. And so he bade his ships drop away sternwards; and then Earl Eric lay broadside on.

King Olaf Tryggvason had laid the Long Snake between Short Snake and the Crane, and the smallest ships outside them. But Earl Eric, as each of these was disabled, caused it to be cut away, and pressed on to those that were behind. Now, when the small ships of King Olaf were cleared, the men leapt from them and went up on the larger ships. There was in this bout much loss of life in either party; but ever, as men fell in Earl Eric's ships, others took their place, Swedes and Danes; whereas none took the place of the men who fell on Olaf's side. All his ships were cleared presently except Long Snake; this held out because it was highest inboard and best manned. And while there were men to do so, they had gone thither aboard, and though some of the crew had perished, the ship had maintained its full numbers. But when Short Snake and Crane were disabled, then Earl Eric had them cut away, and thereafter Iron Ram lay broadside to broadside with Long Snake.

This battle was so stubborn as to stir wonder, first for the brave attack, but still more for the defence. When ships made at the Snake from all sides yet the defenders so hasted to meet them that they even stepped over the bulwarks into the sea and sank with their weapons, heedless of all else save, as in a land fight, to press ever forwards.

The men fell there first in the ship's waist, where the board was lowest, while forward about the prow and aft in the space next the poop they held out longest. And when Earl Eric saw that the Snake was defenceless amidships he boarded it with fifteen men. But when Wolf the Red and other forecastlemen saw that, then they advanced from the forecastle and charged so fiercely on where the Earl was that he had to fall back to his ship. And when he came on board the Ram the Earl roused his men to attack bravely; and they boarded the Snake a second time with a large force.

By this time Wolf and all the forecastlemen had come to the poop, and all the foreship was disabled, Earl Eric's force attacking King Olaf's on every side. Earl Eric with his men then charged aft on the space next the poop, and a stubborn resistance was there. King Olaf had been all that day on the poop of the Snake; he bare a golden shield and helm, heavy ring-mail, strong so that nought could pierce it, though 'tis said that there was no stint of missiles showered on the poop, for all men knew the King, as his armour was easily recognised and he stood high on the stern-castle. And by him stood Kolbjorn, his marshal, clad in armour like to the King's.

Now, this battle went as might be looked for when brave men on both sides met: those lost who were fewer in numbers. And when all King Olaf's force had fallen, then leapt he overboard himself, holding his shield above his head; and so did Kolbjorn, his marshal, but his shield was under him on the sea, and he could not manage to dive, wherefore the men who were in the small ships took him, but he received quarter from the Earl. And after this all leapt overboard who yet lived; but most of these were wounded, and those who received quarter were taken as they swam: these were Thorkell Netja, Karlshead, Thorstein, and Einar Bowstring-shaker.

But after the battle was ended Earl Eric took for his own Long Snake and the other ships of King Olaf, and the weapons of many men who had wielded them manfully to the death.

Most famous has been this battle in Northland; first by reason of the brave defence, next for the attack and victory, wherein that ship was overcome on the deep sea which all had deemed invincible, but chiefly because there fell a chief famous beyond any of the Danish tongue. So greatly did men admire King Olaf and seek his friendship, that many would not hear of his being dead, but declared that he was yet alive in Wendland or in the south region. And about that many stories have been made.

The Death of Hacon the Good (a.d. 961)

(Eric Bloodaxe, Harold Fairhair's favourite son, ruled Norway for a year or so after his father's death. Then he and his queen Gunnhilda became so hated by the people that they welcomed as king his brother Hacon, who returned from England, where he had been brought up. Eric was forced to flee. For some time he was in Northumberland; he fell in the west while freebooting, about A.D. 950. Gunnhilda and her sons went to Denmark; they made many attempts to recover Norway; the issue of the last is here told.)

KIng Hacon, Athelstan's foster-son, long ruled over Norway; but in the latter part of his life Eric's sons came to Norway, and strove with him for the kingdom. They had battles together, wherein Hacon ever won the victory. The last battle was fought in Hordaland, on Stord Island, at Fitjar: there Hacon won the victory, but also got his death-wound.

And this battle came about in this wise. Gunnhilda's sons sailed northward from Denmark, taking the outer way, nor came they to land oftener than for men to get knowledge of their goings, while they also got knowledge of the public banquets given to King Hacon. They had ships well-found in men and weapons; and in their company was a mighty viking named Eyvind Skreyja; he was a brother of Queen Gunnhilda.

Hacon was at a banquet at Fitjar on Stord Island when they came thither; but he and all his men were unaware of their coming till the ships were sailing up from the south and had now gotten close to the island. King Hacon was even then sitting at table.

Now came a rumour to the King's guard that ships were seen sailing; wherefore some who were keenest of sight went out to look. And each said to his fellows that this would be an enemy, and each bade other to tell the King; but for this task none was found save Eyvind Finnsson, who was nicknamed Skald-spoiler.

He went in before the King, and spake thus: "Fleeting hour is short, sire, but meal-time long."

Said the King: "Skald, what news?"

Eyvind answered:

> *"Vengers ('tis said) of Bloodaxe crave*
> *The battle-shock of belted glaive;*
> *Our sitting-time is done.*
> *Hard task, but 'tis thine honour, King,*
> *I seek, who here war tidings bring.*
> *Arm swiftly, every one!"*

Then answered the King: "Eyvind, thou art a brave wight and a wise; thou wouldst not tell war tidings unless they were true." Whereupon all said that this was true, that ships were sailing that way, and within short space of the island. And at once the tables were taken up, and the King went out to see the fleet.

But when he had seen it he called to him his counsellors, and asked what should be done.

"Here be sailing many ships from the south: we have a force small but goodly. Now, I wish not to lead my best friends into overwhelming danger; but surely would be willing to flee, if wise men should not deem that this were great shame or folly."

Then made answer each to other that everyone would rather fall dead across his fellow than flee before Danes.

Whereat the King said: "Well spoken for heroes as ye are! And let each take his weapons, nor care how many Danes there be to one Norseman."

Thereafter the King took his shield, and donned his coat of ring-mail, and girded him with the sword Millstone-biter, and set a golden helm on his head. Then did he marshal his force, putting together his bodyguard and the guests of the feast.

Gunnhilda's sons now came up on land, and they likewise marshalled their force, and it was by far the larger. The day was hot and sunny; so King Hacon slipped off his mail coat and raised his helm, and egged on his men to the onset laughing, and thus cheered his warriors by his blithe bearing. Then the fight began, and it was most stubborn. When the missiles were all thrown, King Hacon drew sword and stood in front under the banner, and hewed right and left; never did he miss, or, if he missed his man, the sword bit another.

Eyvind Skreyja went fiercely forward in the battle, challenging the Norsemen's courage. And chiefly pressed he on where Hacon's banner was, crying, "Where is the Norsemen's king? Why doth he hide him? Why dares he not come forth and show himself? Who can point me to him?"

Then answered King Hacon: "Hold thou on forward, if thou wilt find the Norsemen's king."

And Hacon cast his shield by his side, and gripped his sword's mid-hilt with both hands, and ran forth from under the banner.

But Thoralf Skumsson said, "Suffer me, sire, to go against Eyvind."

The King answered: "Me he wished to find; wherefore me he shall first meet." But when the King came where Eyvind was, he hewed on either side of him, and then, with Millstone-biter in both hands, hewed at Eyvind's head, and clove him through helm and head right down to the shoulders.

This battle was not good for men weak in strength, weapons, or courage. Nor was it long after the fall of Eyvind Skreyja ere the whole Danish force turned and fled to their ships. Great numbers fell on the side of Eric's sons; but they themselves escaped.

King Hacon's men followed them far that day, and slew all whom they might; but the King bade his swift ship be launched, and rowed northwards along the coast, meaning to seek his house at Alrekstead, for he had gotten a wound by an arrow that pierced his arm while he drove before him the flying foe. And he lost so much blood that he swooned away. And when he came to the place called Hacon's Stone (it was where he was born), there he stayed for the night, bidding his land tent be set up and himself be carried ashore.

And as soon as King Hacon knew that his wound was mortal, he called to him his counsellors, and talked at large with his friends about those things that had been done in his days. And of this he then repented, that he had done much against God and Christian men's laws during his rule.

His friends offered to convey his body westwards to England, and bury it there in Church ground.

But the King answered: "Of this I am not worthy; I lived as heathen men live, so, too, shall ye bury me."

He bewailed the quarrels of himself and his kin; and having but one daughter, a child, and no son, he sent a letter to Gunnhilda's sons, wherein it was written that he gave to his kinsman Harold Grayfell his guard and his kingdom.

After this King Hacon died: he had ruled Norway for twenty-six years. He was mourned both by friends and foes. As Eyvind Skald-spoiler says:

"The King is born in blessed day
Such love who gains:
Of his fair age ever and aye
Good fame remains."

His men carried his body to Soeheim in North Hordaland, and raised a mound over it.

I

The Boyhood of Prince Charlie

In 1734 the city of Gaeta, in the kingdom of Naples, was held by an Austrian force, and was besieged by a mixed army of French, Walloons, Spaniards, and Italians, commanded by the Duke of Liria. Don Carlos, a Spanish prince, was doing his best, by their aid, to conquer the kingdom of Naples for himself. There is now no kingdom of Naples: there are no Austrian forces in Italy, and there is certainly, in all the armies of Europe, no such officer as was fighting under the Duke of Liria. This officer, in the uniform of a general of artillery, was a slim, fair-haired, blue-eyed boy of thirteen. He seemed to take a pleasure in the sound of the balls that rained about the trenches. When the Duke of Liria's quarters had been destroyed by five cannon shots, this very young officer was seen to enter the house, and the duke entreated, but scarcely commanded, him to leave. The boy might be heard shouting to the men of his very mixed force in all their various languages. He was the darling of the camp, and the favourite of the men, for his courage and pleasant manners.

This pretty boy with a taste for danger, Charles Edward Stuart, was called by his friends "the Prince of Wales." He was, indeed, the eldest son of James VIII of Scotland and Third of England, known to his enemies as "the Pretender." James, again, was the son of James II, and was a mere baby when, in 1688, his father fled from England before the Prince of Orange.

The child (the son of James II) grew up in France: he charged the English armies in Flanders, and fought not without distinction. He invaded Scotland in 1715, where he failed, and now, for many years, he had lived in Rome, a pensioner of the Pope. James was an unfortunate prince, but is so far to be praised that he would not change his creed to win a crown. He was a devout Catholic—his enemies said "a bigoted Papist"—he was the child of bad luck from his cradle; he had borne many disappointments, and he was never the man to win back a kingdom by the sword. He had married a Polish princess, of the gallant House of Sobieski, and at Gaeta his eldest son, though only a boy, showed that he had the courage of the Sobieskis and the charm of the Stuarts. The spies of the English Government confessed that the boy was more dangerous than the man, Prince Charles than King James.

While Charles, at Gaeta, was learning the art of war, and causing his cousin, the Duke of Liria, to pass some of the uneasiest moments of his life, at home in Rome his younger brother Henry, Duke of York, aged nine, was so indignant with his parents for not allowing him to go to the war with his brother, that he flung away his little sword in a temper. From their cradle these boys had thought and heard of little else but the past glories of their race; it was the dream of their lives to be restored to their own country. In all he did, the thought was always uppermost with Charles. On the way from Gaeta to Naples, leaning over the ship's side, the young Prince lost his hat; immediately a boat was lowered in the hope of saving it, but Charles stopped the sailors, saying with a peculiar smile, "I shall be obliged before long to go and fetch myself a hat in England."

Every thought, every study, every sport that occupied the next few years of Charles' life in Rome, had the same end, namely, preparing himself in every way for the task of regaining his kingdom. Long days of rowing on the lake of Albano, and boar-hunting at Cisterna, made him strong and active. He would often make marches in shoes without stockings, hardening his feet for the part he played afterwards on many a long tramp in the Highlands. Instead of enjoying the ordinary effeminate pleasures of the Roman nobility, he shot and hunted; and in the Borghese Gardens practised that royal game of golf, which his ancestors had played long before on the links at St. Andrews and the North Inch of Perth. His more serious studies were, perhaps, less ardently pursued. Though no prince ever used a sword more gallantly and to more purpose, it cannot be denied that he habitually spelled it "sord," and though no son ever wrote more dutiful and affectionate letters to a father, he seldom got nearer the correct spelling of his parent's name than "Gems. In lonely parts of Rome the handsome lad and his melancholy father might often have been seen talking eagerly and confidentially, planning, and for ever planning, that long-talked-of descent upon their lost kingdom.

If his thoughts turned constantly to Britain, many hearts in that country were thinking of him with anxious prayers and hopes. In England, in out-of-the-way manor-houses and parsonages, old-fashioned, high-church squires and clergymen still secretly toasted the exiled family. But in the fifty years that had passed since the Revolution, men had got used to peace and the blessings of a settled government. Jacobitism in England was a sentiment, hereditary in certain Tory families; it was not a passion to stir the hearts of the people and engage them in civil strife. It was very different with the Scots. The Stuarts were, after all, their old race of kings; once they were removed and unfortunate, their tyranny was forgotten, and the old national feeling centred round them. The pride of the people had suffered at the Union (1707); the old Scots nobility felt that they had lost in importance; the people resented the enforcement of new taxes. The Presbyterians of the trading classes were Whigs; but the persecuted Episcopalians and Catholics, with the mob of Edinburgh, were for "the auld Stuarts back again." This feeling against the present Government and attachment to the exiled family were especially strong among the fierce and faithful people of the Highlands. Among families of distinction, like the Camerons of Lochiel, the Oliphants of Gask, and many others, Jacobitism formed part of the religion of gallant, simple-minded gentlemen and of high-spirited, devoted women. In many a sheiling and farmhouse old broadswords and muskets, well-hidden from the keen eye of the Government soldiers, were carefully cherished against the brave day when "the king should have his own again."

In 1744 that day seemed to have dawned to which Charles had all his life been looking forward. France, at war with England, was preparing an invasion of that country, and was glad enough to use the claims of the Stuarts for her own purposes. A fleet was actually on the point of starting, and Charles, in the highest spirits, was already on shipboard, but the English admiral was alert. A storm worked havoc among the French ships, and it suited the French Government to give up the expedition. Desperate with disappointment, Charles proposed to his father's friend, the exiled Lord Marischall, to sail for Scotland by himself in a herring-boat, and was hurt and indignant when the old soldier refused to sanction such an audacious plan.

Charles had seen enough of hanging about foreign courts and depending on their wavoring policy; he was determined to strike a blow for himself. In Paris he was surrounded by restless spirits like his own; Scots and Irish officers in the French service, and heart-broken exiles like old Tullibardine, eager for any chance that would restore them to their own country. Even prudent men of business lent themselves to Charles's plans. His bankers in Paris advanced him 180,000 livres for the purchase of arms, and of two Scottish merchants at Nantes, Walsh and Routledge, one undertook to convey him to Scotland in a brig of eighteen guns, the "Doutelle," while the other chartered a French man-of-war, the "Elizabeth," to be the convoy, and to carry arms and ammunition. To provide these Charles had pawned his jewels, jewels which "on *this* side I could only wear with a very sad heart," he wrote to his father; for the same purpose he would gladly have pawned his shirt. On June 22 he started from the mouth of the Loire in all haste and secrecy, only writing for his father's blessing and sanction when he knew it would be too late for any attempt to be made to stop him. The companions of his voyage were the old Marquis of Tullibardine, who had been deprived of his dukedom of Athol in the '15; the Prince's tutor and cousin, Sir Thomas Sheridan, a rather injudicious Irishman; two other Irishmen in the French and Spanish services; Kelly, a young English divine; and Æneas Macdonald, a banker in Paris, and younger brother of the chieftain Macdonald of Kinloch Moidart, a prudent young man, who saw himself involved in the Prince's cause very much against his will and better judgment.

II

Prince Charlie's Landing

ENGLAND AND FRANCE BEING AT war at this time, the Channel was constantly swept by English men-of-war. The "Doutelle" and her convoy were hardly four days out before the "Elizabeth" was attacked by an English frigate, the "Lion." Knowing *who* it was he had on board, Walsh, the prudent master of the "Doutelle," would by no means consent to join in the fray, and sheered off to the north in spite of the commands and remonstrances of the Prince. The unfortunate "Elizabeth" was so much disabled that she had to return to Brest, taking with her most of the arms and ammunition for the expedition. At night the "Doutelle" sailed without a light and kept well out to sea, and so escaped further molestation. The first land they sighted was the south end of the Long Island. Gazing with eager eyes on the Promised Land, old Lord Tullibardine was the first to notice a large Hebridean eagle which flew above the ship as they approached. "Sir," he said, "it is a good omen; the king of birds has come to welcome your royal highness to Scotland."

Charles had need of all happy auguries, for on his arrival in Scotland things did not seem very hopeful. With his usual rash confidence he had very much exaggerated the eagerness of his friends and supporters to welcome him in whatever guise he might come. Never had fallen kings more faithful and unselfish friends than had the exiled Stuarts in the Highland chiefs and Jacobite lairds of Scotland, but even they were hardly prepared to risk life and property with a certainty of failure and defeat. Let the Prince appear with 5,000 French soldiers and French money and arms, and they would gather round him with alacrity, but they were prudent men and knew too well the strength of the existing Government to think that they could overturn it unaided.

The first man to tell the Prince this unwelcome truth was Macdonald of Boisdale, to whom he sent a message as soon as he landed in Uist. This Boisdale was brother of the old Clanranald, chief of the loyal clan Macdonald of Clanranald. If these, his stoutest friends, hesitated to join his expedition Charles should have felt that his cause was desperate indeed. But his mind was made up with all the daring of his five-and-twenty years, and all the ill-fated obstinacy of his race. For hours he argued with the old Highlander as the ship glided over the waters of the Minch. He enumerated the friends he could count on, among them the two most powerful chiefs of the North, Macdonald of Sleat, and the Macleod. "They have both declared for the existing Government," was the sad reply. Before taking leave of the Prince, Boisdale again urged his returning "home." "I am come *home*," replied Charles passionately, "and can entertain no notion of returning. I am persuaded that my faithful Highlanders will stand by me."

On July 19 the "Doutelle" cast anchor in Loch na-Nuagh, in the country of the loyal Macdonalds. The first thing Charles did was to send a letter to the young Clanranald to beg his immediate presence. The next day four of the chief men of the clan waited on Charles, Clanranald, Kinloch Moidart, Glenaladale, and another who has left us a lively picture of the meeting. For three hours, in a private interview, Clanranald tried in vain to dissuade the Prince. Then Charles—still preserving his incognito—appeared among the assembled gentlemen on deck. "At his first appearance I found my heart swell to my very throat "writes the honest gentleman who narrates the story. His emotion was fully shared by a younger brother of Kinloch Moidart's who stood on deck silent from youth and modesty, but with his whole heart looking out of his eyes. His brother and the other chiefs walked up and down the deck arguing and remonstrating with Charles, proving the hopelessness of the undertaking. As he listened to their talk the boy's colour came and went, his hand involuntarily tightened on his sword. Charles caught sight of the eager young face, and, turning suddenly towards him cried, "Will *you* not assist me?" "I will, I will; though not another man in the Highlands should draw a sword, I will die for you." Indeed, years after all had failed, young Clanranald prepared a new rising, and had 9,000 stand of arms concealed in the caves of Moidart.

The boy's words were like flint to tinder. Before they left the ship the hesitating chieftains had pledged themselves to risk property, influence, freedom, and life itself in the Prince's cause. These gallant Macdonalds were now willing to run all risks in receiving the Prince even before a single other clan had declared for him. Old Macdonald of Boisdale entertained Charles as an honoured guest in his bare but hospitable Highland house. All the people of the district crowded to see him as he sat at dinner. The young Prince delighted all present by his geniality and the interest he showed in everything Highland, and when he insisted on learning enough Gaelic to propose the king's health in their native language, the hearts of the simple and affectionate people were completely gained.

Meanwhile young Clanranald had gone to Skye to try and persuade Macleod and Sir Alexander Macdonald to join the Prince. It was all in vain; these two powerful chiefs were too deeply committed to the Government. Next to these two, the most influential man in the Highlands was Cameron of Locheil. Indeed, such was the respect felt by all his neighbours for his gentle and chivalrous character, that there was no one whose example would carry such weight. It was all-important to gain him to the cause. No one saw more clearly than Locheil the hopelessness of the undertaking, no one was more unwilling to lead his clansmen to what he knew was certain destruction. He would see the Prince, he said, and warn him of the danger and entreat him to return. "Write to him," urged Locheil's brother, "but do not see him. I know you better than you know yourself. If this Prince once sets eyes on you he will make you do whatever he pleases." It was but too true a prophecy. When all argument had failed to move Locheil's prudent resolution, Charles exclaimed passionately, "In a few days, with a few friends, I will raise the Royal Standard and proclaim to the people of Britain that Charles Stuart is come over to claim the crown of his ancestors, to win it or perish in the attempt. Locheil, who, my father has often told me, was our firmest friend, may stay at home and learn from the newspapers the fate of his Prince." It was more than the proud, warm heart of the chief could stand. "No," he cried with emotion, "I will share the fate of my Prince, and so shall every man over whom nature and fortune has given me any power."

Even before the Royal Standard was raised an unexpected success crowned the rebel arms. The Government had troops stationed both at Fort Augustus and Fort William. The latter being in the heart of the disaffected district, the commanding officer at Fort Augustus despatched two companies of newly-raised men to its assistance. This body, under a Captain Scott, was approaching the narrow bridge which crossed the Spean some seven miles from Fort William; all at once a body of Highlanders appeared, occupying the bridge and barring further passage. Had the troops plucked up courage enough to advance they would have found only some dozen Macdonalds; but the wild sound of the pipes, the yells of the Highlanders, and their constant movement which gave the effect of a large body, struck terror into the hearts of the recruits; they wavered and fell back, and their officer, though himself a brave man, had to order a retreat. But the sound of firing had attracted other bodies of Macdonalds and Camerons in the neighbourhood. All at once the steep, rough hillside seemed alive with armed Highlanders; from rock and bush they sprung up, startling the echoes by their wild shouts. In vain the disordered troops hurried along the road and rushed across the isthmus to the further side of the lakes; there a new party of Macdonalds, led by Keppoch, met them in front, and the whole body surrendered with hardly a blow struck. They were carried prisoners to Locheil's house, Achnacarry. In default of medical aid, the wounded captain was sent to Fort William, in that spirit of generous courtesy which characterised all Charles's behaviour to his defeated enemies.

On August 19 the Royal Standard was raised at Glenfinnan, a deep rocky valley between Loch Eil and Loch Sheil, where the Prince's monument now stands. Charles, with a small body of Macdonalds, was the first to arrive, early in the morning. He and his men rowed up the long narrow Loch Sheil. The valley was solitary—not a far-off bagpipe broke the silence, not a figure appeared against the skyline of the hills. With sickening anxiety the small party waited, while the minutes dragged out their weary length. At last, when suspense was strained to the utmost, about two in the afternoon, a sound of pipes was heard, and a body of Camerons under Lochiel appeared over the hill, bringing with them the prisoners made at the Bridge of Spean. Others followed: Stewarts of Appin, Macdonalds of Glencoe and Keppoch, till at least 1,500 were present. Then the honoured veteran of the party, old Tullibardine, advanced in solemn silence and unfurled the royal banner, with the motto *Tandem Triumphans*. As its folds of white, blue, and red silk blew out on the hill breeze, huzzas rent the air, and the sky was darkened by the bonnets that were flung up. An English officer, a prisoner taken at Spean, stood by, an unwilling spectator of the scene. "Go, sir," cried the Prince in exultation, "go to your general; tell him what you have seen, and say that I am coming to give him battle."

III

The March South

FOR A FULL MONTH PRINCE Charles had been in Scotland. During that time a body of men, amounting to a small army, had collected round him; his manifestoes had been scattered all over the country (some were even printed in Edinburgh), and yet the Government had taken no steps to oppose him. News travelled slowly from the Highlands; it was August 9 before any *certain* account of the Prince's landing was received in Edinburgh. One bad fruit of the Union was that Scotch questions had to be settled in London, and London was three days further away. Moreover, at that greater distance, men had more difficulty in realising the gravity of the situation. Conflicting rumours distracted the authorities in Edinburgh; now it was declared that the Prince had landed with 10,000 French soldiers, at another time men ridiculed the idea of his getting a single man to rise for him. Those who knew the country best took the matter most seriously. The question of defence was not an easy one. At that time almost all the available British troops were in Flanders, fighting the French; the soldiers that were left in Scotland were either old veterans, fit only for garrison duty, newly raised companies whose mettle was untried, or local militias which were not to be trusted in all cases. If the great lords who had raised and who commanded them chose to declare for the Stuarts, they would carry their men with them.

The commander-in-chief, Sir John Cope, was not the man to meet so sudden and so peculiar a crisis. He had nothing of a real general's love of responsibility and power of decision. To escape blame and to conduct a campaign according to the laws of war was all the old campaigner cared for. When it was decided that he was to march with all the available forces in Scotland into the Highlands he willingly obeyed, little guessing what a campaign in the Highlands meant. Almost at once it was found that it would be impossible to provide food for horses as well as men. So the dragoons under Colonel Gardiner were left at Stirling. We shall hear of them again. But his 1,500 infantry were weighted heavily enough; a small herd of black cattle followed the army to provide them with food, and more than 100 horses carried bread and biscuit. Confident that the loyal clans would come in hundreds to join his standard, Cope carried 700 stand of arms. By the time he reached Crieff, however, not a single volunteer had come in, and the stand of arms was sent back. Cope followed one of the great military roads which led straight to Fort Augustus, and had been made thirty years before by General Wade. Now across that road, some ten miles short of the fort, lies a high precipitous hill, called Corryarack. Up this mountain wall the road is carried in seventeen sharp zigzags; so steep is it that the country people call it the "Devil's Staircase." Any army holding the top of the pass would have an ascending enemy at its mercy, let alone an army of Highlanders, accustomed to skulk behind rock and shrub, and skilled to rush down the most rugged hillsides with the swiftness and surefootedness of deer.

While still some miles distant, Cope learned that the Highlanders were already in possession of Corryarack. The rumour was premature, but it thoroughly alarmed the English general. He dared not attempt the ascent; to return south was against his orders. A council of war, hastily summoned, gave him the advice he wished for, and on the 28th the army had turned aside and was in full retreat on Inverness.

Meanwhile, the Prince's army was pressing forward to meet Cope. The swiftest-footed soldiers that ever took the field, the Highlanders were also the least heavily-weighted. A bag of oatmeal on his back supplied each man's need, Charles himself burned his baggage and marched at the head of his men as light of foot and as stout of heart as the best of them. On the morning of the 27th they were to ascend Corryarack. The Prince was in the highest spirits. As he laced his Highland brogues he cried, "Before I take these off I shall have fought with Mr. Cope!" Breathless the Highland army reached the top of the hill; they had gained *that* point of vantage. Eagerly they looked down the zigzags on the further side; to their amazement not a man was to be seen, their road lay open before them! When they learned from deserters the course Cope's army had taken, they were as much disappointed as triumphant.

A body of Highlanders was despatched to try and take the barracks at Ruthven, where twelve soldiers, under a certain Sergeant Molloy, held the fort for the Government. This man showed a spirit very different from that of his superior officer's. This is his own straightforward account of the attack and repulse:

> *"Noble General,—They summoned me to surrender,*
> *but I told him I was too old a soldier to part*
> *with so strong a place without bloody noses. They*
> *offered me honourable terms of marching out bag*
> *and baggage, which I refused. They threatened to*
> *hang me and my party. I said I would take my*
> *chance. They set fire to the sally-port which I*
> *extinguished; and failing therein, went off asking*
> *leave to take their dead man, which I granted."*

Honour to Molloy, whatever the colour of his cockade!

Though unsuccessful at Ruthven, some members of this party, before rejoining the Prince's army at Dalwhinnie, made an important capture. Macpherson of Cluny was one of the most distinguished chiefs in the Highlands, ruling his clan with a firm hand, and repressing all thieving amongst them. As captain of an independent company, he held King George's commission; his honour kept him faithful to the Government, but his whole heart was on the other side. He was taken prisoner in his own house by a party "hardly big enough to take a cow," and once a prisoner in the Highland army, it was no difficult task to persuade him to take service with the Prince.

The army now descended into the district of Athol. With curious emotion old Tullibardine approached his own house of Blair from which he had been banished thirty years before. The brother who held his titles and properties fled before the Highland army, and the noble old exile had the joy of entertaining his Prince in his own halls. The Perthshire lairds were almost all Jacobites. Here at Blair, and later at Perth, gentlemen and their following flocked to join the Prince.

One of the most important of these was Tullibardine's brother, Lord George Murray, an old soldier who had been "out in the '15." He had real genius for generalship, and moreover understood the Highlanders and their peculiar mode of warfare. He was no courtier, and unfortunately his blunt, hot-tempered, plain speaking sometimes ruffled the Prince, too much accustomed to the complacency of his Irish followers. But all that was to come later. On the march south there were no signs of divided counsels. The command of the army was gladly confided to Lord George.

Another important adherent who joined at this time was the Duke of Perth, a far less able man than Lord George, but endeared to all his friends by his gentleness and courage and modesty. Brought up in France by a Catholic mother, he was an ardent Jacobite, and the first man to be suspected by the authorities. As soon as the news spread that the Prince had landed in the West, the Government sent an officer to arrest the young duke. There was a peculiar treachery in the way this was attempted. The officer, a Mr. Campbell of Inverawe, invited himself to dinner at Drummond Castle, and, after being hospitably entertained, produced his warrant. The duke retained his presence of mind, appeared to acquiesce, and, with habitual courtesy, bowed his guest first out of the room; then suddenly shut the door, turned the key and made his escape through an ante-room, a backstairs, and a window, out into the grounds. Creeping from tree to tree he made his way to a paddock where he found a horse, without a saddle but with a halter. He mounted, and the animal galloped off. In this fashion he reached the house of a friend, where he lay hid till the time he joined the Prince.

No Jacobite family had a nobler record of services rendered to the Stuarts than the Oliphants of Gask. The laird had been "out in the '15," and had suffered accordingly, but he did not hesitate a moment to run the same risks in the '45. He brought with him to Blair his high-spirited boy, young Lawrence, who records his loyal enthusiasm in a journal full of fine feeling and bad spelling! Indeed, one may say that bad spelling was, like the "white rose," a badge of the Jacobite party. Mistress Margaret Oliphant, who with her mother and sisters donned the white cockade and waited on their beloved Prince at her aunt's, Lady Nairne's, house, also kept a journal wherein she regrets in ill-spelt, fervent words that being "only a woman" she cannot carry the Prince's banner. This amiable and honourable family were much loved among their own people. "Oliphant is king to us" was a by-word among retainers who had lived on their land for generations. But at this crisis the shrewd, prosperous Perthshire farmers refused to follow their landlord on such a desperate expedition. Deeply mortified and indignant, the generous, hot-tempered old laird forbade his tenants to gather in the harvest which that year was early and abundant. As Charles rode through the Gask fields he noticed the corn hanging over-ripe and asked the cause. As soon as he was told, he jumped from his horse, cut a few blades with his sword and, in his gracious princely way, exclaimed "There, *I* have broken the inhibition! Now every man may gather in his own." It was acts like this that gained the hearts of gentle and simple alike, and explain that passionate affection for Charles that remained with many to the end of their days as part of their religion. The strength of this feeling still touches our hearts in many a Jacobite song. "I pu'ed my bonnet ower my eyne, For weel I loued Prince Charlie," and the yearning refrain, "Better loued ye canna be, Wull ye no come back again?" On the 3rd Charles entered Perth, at the head of a body of troops, in a handsome suit of tartan, but with his last guinea in his pocket! However, requisitions levied on Perth and the neighbouring towns did much to supply his exchequer, and it was with an army increased in numbers and importance, as well as far better organised—thanks to Lord G. Murray—that Charles a week later continued his route to Edinburgh. Having no artillery the Highland army avoided Stirling, crossed the Forth at the Fords of Frew entirely unopposed, and marched to Linlithgow, where they expected to fight with Gardiner's dragoons. That body however did not await their arrival, but withdrew to Corstorphine, a village two miles from Edinburgh.

The next halt of the Prince's army was at Kirkliston. In the neighbourhood lay the house of New Liston, the seat of Lord Stair, whose father was so deeply and disgracefully implicated in the massacre of Glencoe. It was remembered that a grandson of the murdered Macdonald was in the army with the men of his clan. Fearing that they would seize this opportunity of avenging their cruel wrong, the general proposed placing a guard round the house. Macdonald hearing this proposal, went at once to the Prince. "It is right," he said, "that a guard should be placed round the house of New Liston, but that guard must be furnished by the Macdonalds of Glencoe. If they are not thought worthy of this trust they are not fit to bear arms in your Royal Highness' cause, and I must withdraw them from your standard." The passion for revenge may be strong in the heart of the Highlander, but the love of honour and the sense of loyalty are stronger still. The Macdonalds, as we shall see, carried their habit of taking their own way to a fatal extent.

IV

Edinburgh

Meanwhile nothing could exceed the panic that had taken possession of the town of Edinburgh. The question of the hour was, could the city be defended *at all*, and if so, could it, in case of siege, hold out till Cope might be expected with his troops? That dilatory general, finding nothing to do in the North, was returning to Edinburgh by sea, and might be looked for any day. There could be no question of the strength of the Castle. It was armed and garrisoned, and no army without large guns need attempt to attack it. But with the town it was different. The old town of Edinburgh, as everybody knows, is built along the narrow ridge of a hill running from the hollow of Holyrood, in constant ascent, up to the Castle rock. On each side narrow wynds and lanes descend down steep slopes, on the south side to the Grassmarket and the Cowgate, on the north—at the time of which we write—the sides of the city sloped down to a lake called the Norloch, a strong position, had the city been properly fortified. More than two hundred years before, in the desolate and anxious days that followed Flodden, the magistrates of the city, hourly expecting to be invaded, had hastily built a high wall round the whole city as it then was. For the time the defence was sufficient. But the wall had been built without reference to artillery, it had neither towers nor embrasures for mounting cannons. It was simply a very high, solid, park wall, as may be seen to this day by the curious who care to visit the last remnants of it, in an out-of-the-way corner near the Grassmarket.

If the material defences were weak, the human defenders were weaker still. The regular soldiers were needed for the Castle; Hamilton's dragoons, stationed at Leith, were of no use in the defence of a city, the town guard was merely a body of rather inefficient policemen, the trained bands mere ornamental volunteers who shut their eyes if they had to let off a firearm in honour of the king's birthday. As soon as it seemed certain that the Highland army was approaching Edinburgh, preparations, frantic but spasmodic, were made to put the city in a state of defence.

The patriotic and spirited Maclaurin, professor of mathematics, alone and unaided, tried to mount cannons on the wall, but not with much success. The city determined to raise a regiment of volunteers;

funds were not lacking; it was more difficult to find the men. Even when companies were formed, their ardour was not very great. Rumour and ignorance had exaggerated the numbers and fierceness of the Highland army; quiet citizens, drawn from desk or shop, might well shrink from encountering them in the field. Parties were divided in the town; the Prince had many secret friends among the citizens. In back parlours of taverns "douce writers," and advocates of Jacobite sympathies, discussed the situation with secret triumph; in many a panelled parlour high up in those wonderful old closes, spirited old Jacobite ladies recalled the adventures of the '15, and bright-eyed young ones busied themselves making knots of white satin. "One-third of the men are Jacobite," writes a Whig citizen, "and two-thirds of the ladies."

On Saturday, 14th, the news reached Edinburgh that the Prince had arrived at Linlithgow, and that Gardiner had retired on Corstorphine, a village two miles from Edinburgh. Consternation was general; advice was sought from the law officers of the Crown, and it was found that they had all retired to Dunbar. The Provost was not above suspicion. His surname was Stuart; no Scotsman could believe that he really meant to oppose the chief of his name.

On Sunday, as the townsfolk were at church about eleven o'clock, the firebell rang out its note of alarm, scattering the congregation into the streets. It was the signal for the mustering of the volunteers. The officer in command at the Castle was sending the dragoons from Leith to reinforce Gardiner at Corstorphine, and the volunteers were ordered to accompany them. They were standing in rank in the High Street, when the dragoons rattled up the Canongate at a hard trot; as they passed they saluted their brothers in arms with drawn swords and loud huzzas, then swept down the West Bow and out at the West Port. For a moment military ardour seized the volunteers, but the lamentations and tears of their wives and children soon softened their mood again. A group of Jacobite ladies in a balcony mocked and derided the civic warriors, but had finally to close their windows to prevent stones being hurled at them.

One of the volunteer companies was composed of University students. Among them was, doubtless, more than one stout young heart, eager for fame and fighting, but most were more at home with their books than their broadswords. "Oh, Mr. Hew, Mr. Hew," whispered one youth to his comrade, "does not this remind you of the passage in Livy where the Gens of the Fabii marched out of the city, and the matrons and maids of Rome were weeping and wringing their hands?" "Hold your tongue," said Mr. Hew, affecting a braver spirit, "you'll discourage the men." "Recollect the end, Mr. Hew," persisted his trembling comrade; "*they all perished to a man!*" This was not destined to be the fate of the Edinburgh volunteers. On the march down the West Bow, one by one they stole off, up the narrow wynds and doorways, till by the time they reached the West Port, only the student corps remained, and even its ranks were sadly thinned. The remnant were easily persuaded that their lives were too precious to their country to be rashly thrown away, and quietly marched back to the college yards.

There was no alarm that night. At one o'clock the Provost, accompanied by a few of the city guard, carrying a lantern before him, visited the outposts and found all at their places. In the narrow streets of Edinburgh the people were accustomed to transact all their business out of doors. Next morning (Monday, 16th), the streets were already crowded at an early hour with an anxious, vociferous crowd. At 10 o'clock a man arrived with a message from the Prince, which he incautiously proclaimed in the street. If the town would surrender it should be favourably treated; if it resisted it must expect to be dealt with according to the usages of war. Greatly alarmed, the people clamoured for a meeting, but the Provost refused; he trusted to the dragoons to defend the city. A little after noon, the citizens looking across from the Castle and the northern windows of their houses, saw the dragoons in retreat from Coltbridge As they watched the moving figures, the pace quickened and became a regular flight; by the time the dragoons were opposite the city on the other side of the Norloch, they were running like hares. They made at first for their barracks at Leith, but the distance still seemed too short between them and the terrifying Highlanders; they never drew rein till they had reached Prestonpans, nor did they rest there longer than an hour or two, but galloped on, and were at Dunbar before nightfall. And yet they had not exchanged a blow with their foes! At the first sight of a reconnoitring party of horsemen, panic had seized them and they had fled. This was the celebrated "Canter of Coltbridge."

The effect on the city was disturbing in the extreme. A tumultuous meeting was held in the council chamber, the volunteers were drawn up in the streets. As they stood uncertain what to do a man on horseback— it was never known who he was—galloped up the Bow, and as he passed along the ranks, shouted "The Highlanders are coming, sixteen thousand strong."

It was too much for the volunteers, they marched up to the Castle and gave in their arms! Meanwhile, a packet was handed into the council chamber signed C. P., and offering the same terms as in the morning, only adding that the town must open its gates by two o'clock next morning. The cry was unanimous to surrender, but to gain time deputies were sent to the Prince at Gray's Mill, two miles from Edinburgh, to ask for further delay. Hardly had the deputies gone when, in through the opposite gate galloped a messenger from Dunbar, to say that Cope had landed there with his troops. Opinion now swung round the other way, and men's courage rose to the point of *speaking* about resistance. The deputies returned at ten at night; Charles, they said, was inexorable and stuck to his conditions. To cause a delay, a new set of deputies were sent forth at a very late hour, and went out by the West Bow *in a hackney coach*.

To gain time, and then steal another march on Cope, was even more important to the Prince than to his enemies. There were weak points in the wall that might be attacked. The chief gate of the city, the Netherbow, lay midway up the High Street, dividing the real borough of Edinburgh from the Canongate; on each side of this gate the wall descended sharply down hill, running along Leith Wynd on the north side and St. Mary's Wynd on the south. The houses of the latter— Edinburgh houses numbering their ten or twelve stories—were actually built on to the wall. By entering one of these, active and determined men might clear the wall by a fire of musketry from the upper windows, and then make an escalade. Another weak point was at the foot of Leith Wynd, where the wall met the Norloch. About midnight Locheil and five hundred of his men started to make a night attack. They were guided by Mr. Murray of Broughton (the Prince's secretary, afterwards a traitor), who had been a student in Edinburgh and knew the town well. To avoid chance shots from the guns of the Castle, they made a wide circle round the town, but so still was the night that across the city they could hear the watches called in the distant fortress. Swift and silent as Red Indians, the Highlanders marched in the shadow cast by the high, dark houses of the suburbs without arousing the sleeping inmates. They could see cannons on the walls, but no sentinels were visible. They determined to try fraud before resorting to force. Twenty Camerons placed themselves in hiding on each side of the gate, sixty stood in the dark recess of the Wynd, the rest were at the bottom of the slope. One of the number, disguised as the servant of an English officer of dragoons, knocked loudly at the gate, demanding admission. The watch refused to open and threatened to fire. So this stratagem was not successful. Already the dawn was beginning to break, and a council was held among the leaders of the band in low hurried whispers. They were deliberating whether they should not retreat, when all at once a heavy rumbling noise from within the city broke the silence of the night. The hackney coach before mentioned had deposited its load of deputies at the council chamber and was returning to its stable-yard in the Canongate. A word to the watchmen within and the gates swung on their heavy hinges. In rushed the body of Camerons, secured the bewildered watchmen, and in a few minutes had seized the city guard-house and disarmed the soldiers. Then they struck up the wild pibroch "We'll awa' to Sheriffmuir to haud the Whigs in order," and startled citizens rushing to their windows saw in the dim twilight the streets filled with plaids and bonnets. The conquerors visited all the outposts as quietly as if they were troops relieving guard. A citizen strolling along by the wall early next morning found a Highland soldier astride on one of the cannons, "Surely you are not the same soldiers who were here yesterday?" "Och no!" was the answer with a grave twinkle, "she be relieved."

At noon Prince Charles rode to Holyrood by way of Arthur's Seat and Salisbury Crags. He was on foot as he approached the ancient home of his race, but the large and enthusiastic crowd which came out to meet him pressed so closely upon him in their eagerness to kiss his hand, that he had to mount a horse, and rode the last half mile between the Duke of Perth and Lord Elcho. A gallant young figure he must have appeared at that moment—tall and straight and fresh-coloured, in a tartan coat and blue bonnet, with the cross of St. Andrew on his breast. As he was about to enter the old palace of Holyrood, out of the crowd stepped the noble and venerable figure of Mr. Hepburn of Keith. He drew his sword, and, holding it aloft, with grave enthusiasm marshalled the Prince up the stairs. It was surely a good omen; no man in Scotland bore a higher character for learning, goodness, and patriotism than Mr. Hepburn; he was hardly less respected by the Whigs than the Jacobites.

That same afternoon, at the old Cross in the High Street, with pomp of heralds and men-at-arms, James VIII was proclaimed king, and his son's commission as regent was read aloud to the listening crowd. Loud huzzas almost drowned the wild music of the bagpipes, the Highlanders in triumph let off their pieces in the air, and from every window in the high houses on each side ladies fluttered their white handkerchiefs. Beside the Cross, beautiful Mrs. Murray of Broughton sat on horseback, a drawn sword in one hand, while with the other she distributed white cockades to the crowd. Even grave Whig statesmen like the Lord President Forbes were disturbed by the enthusiastic Jacobitism that possessed all the Scotch ladies. More than one followed the example of the high-spirited Miss Lumsden, who let her lover clearly understand that she would have nothing more to say to him unless he took up arms for the Prince, and doubtless more young gallants than Robert Strange joined the rebels for no better reason than their ladies' command.

A ball was given at Holyrood that same evening, and surrounded by all that was bravest and most beautiful and brilliant in Scottish society, it was no wonder that Charles felt that this was but the beginning of a larger and more complete triumph.

V

Prestonpans

IN LESS THAN A MONTH Prince Charles had marched through a kingdom, and gained a capital, but he felt his triumph insecure till he had met his enemies in fair fight. Nor were his followers less eager for battle. In a council of war held at Holyrood, Charles declared his intention of leading the army against Cope, and of charging in person at its head. *That*, however, the chiefs would not hear of; the Prince's life was all-important to their cause, and must not be rashly exposed to danger. The arms that the Edinburgh trained bands had used to so little purpose—about a thousand muskets—had fallen into the hands of their enemies; but even with this addition, the Highland soldiers were insufficiently accoutred. The gentlemen, who marched in the front ranks, were, it is true, completely armed with broadsword, musket, pistol, and dirk, but in the rank and file many an unkempt, half-clothed, ill-fed cateran carried merely a bill-hook or scytheblade fixed into a long pole. It was the swiftness and splendid daring of their onset that made these ill-armed, untrained clansmen the equals or more than the equals of the regular army that opposed them.

In the meantime Cope, with his army of 2,000 foot, reinforced by the fugitive dragoons, some 600 men under Gardiner, were marching from Dunbar. Gardiner, as brave a soldier as he was a good and devout Christian, was full of foreboding. The "canter of Coltbridge" had broken his heart; a "most foul flight," he called it, and added, to a friend who tried to comfort him, that there were not ten men in his troop whom he could trust not to run away at the first fire. No such misgiving seems to have disturbed Sir John Cope. On Friday the 20th the Hanoverian army reached Prestonpans, and formed its ranks on a plain between the sea on the north and the ridge of Carberry Hill on the south. The road from Edinburgh to Haddington passed through this plain, and the simple old general argued that the advancing army would be sure to take the easiest road. Fortunately Lord George Murray knew better where the peculiar strength of the Highlanders lay.

Early on Friday morning the Prince's army broke up from their camp at Duddingstone. Charles himself was the first man on the field. As the troops began their march, he drew his sword and cried: "Gentlemen, I have thrown away the scabbard;" high-spirited words which found an echo in the hearts of all the brave men present.

The army marched in column, three abreast, the various clans holding together under their own chiefs. Two miles short of Prestonpans Lord George learned the position of Cope's army, and at once led his light-footed soldiers up the slopes that commanded the plain. The English general was hourly expecting to see his enemies approach from the west by the road, and he was fully prepared to meet them at that point. At two in the afternoon, to his amazement, they suddenly appeared from the south, marching over the ridge of the hill.

The Hanoverian soldiers had enough spirit to receive them with cheers, to which the Highlanders responded by wild yells. They longed ardently to sweep down the slope and give instant battle, but the nature of the ground made this impossible even to a Highland army. Intersecting the hillside were high stone walls, which would have to be scaled under a hot fire from below, and at the bottom was a swamp, a wide ditch, and a high hedge. A certain gentleman in the Prince's army—Mr. Ker of Gordon—rode over the ground on his pony to examine its possibilities. He went to work as coolly as if he were on the hunting-field, making breaches in the wall and leading his pony through, in spite of a dropping fire from the Hanoverians. He reported that to charge over such ground was impossible. The Highlanders were bitterly disappointed; their one fear was that Cope should again slip away under cover of darkness. To prevent this Lord Nairne and 600 Perthshire men were sent to guard the road to Edinburgh. Seeing that nothing more could be done that night, both armies settled down to rest; General Cope lay in comfort at Cockenzie, Prince Charles on the field; a bundle of peastraw served for his pillow; a long white cloak thrown over his plaid for a covering.

Among the volunteers who had recently joined the Prince was an East Lothian laird called Anderson. He had often shot over the fields about Prestonpans. During the night he suddenly remembered a path which led from the heights, down through the morass on to the plain, slightly to the east of Cope's army. He sought out Lord George and told him of this path, and he, struck with the possibility of making immediate use of the information, took him without delay to the Prince. Charles was alert on the instant, entered into the plan proposed, and the next moment the word of command was passed along the sleeping lines. A few moments later the whole army was moving along the ridge in the dim starlight. But here a difficulty occurred. At Bannockburn, and in all great battles afterwards, except Killiekrankie, the Macdonalds had held the place of honour on the right wing of the army. They claimed that position now with haughty tenacity. The other clans, equally brave and equally proud, disputed the claim. It was decided to draw lots to settle the question. Lots were drawn, and the place of honour fell to the Camerons and Stewarts. An ominous cloud gathered on the brows of the Macdonald chiefs, but Locheil, as sagacious as he was courteous, induced the other chiefs to waive their right, and, well content, the clan Macdonald marched on in the van.

Up on the hill the sky was clear, but a thick white mist covered the plain. Under cover of this the Highlanders passed the morass in the one fordable place. In the darkness the Prince missed a stepping-stone and slipped into the bog, but recovered so quickly that no one had time to draw a bad omen from the accident. A Hanoverian dragoon, standing sentinel near this point, heard the march of the soldiers while they were still invisible in the dusk, and galloped off to give the alarm, but not before the Highland army was free from the swamp and had formed in two lines on the plain. Macdonalds and Camerons and Stewarts were in the first line; behind, at a distance of fifty yards, the Perthshiremen and other regiments led by Charles himself.

Learning that the enemy was now approaching from the east side of the plain, Cope drew up his men to face their approach. In the centre was the infantry—the steadiest body in his army—on his left, near the sea and opposite the Macdonalds, Hamilton's dragoons, on the right, the other dragoons under Gardiner, and in front of these the battery of six cannon. This should have been a formidable weapon against the Highlanders, who, unfamiliar with artillery, had an almost superstitious fear of the big guns, but they were merely manned by half-a-dozen feeble old sailors. There was a brief pause as the two armies stood opposite each other in the sea of mist. The Highlanders muttered a short prayer, drew their bonnets down on their eyes, and moved forward at a smart pace. At that moment a wind rose from the sea and rolled away the curtain of mist from between the two armies. In front of them the Highlanders saw their enemy drawn up like a hedge of steel. With wild yells they came on, their march quickening to a run, each clan charging in a close compact body headed by its own chief. Even while they rushed on, as resistless as a torrent, each man fired his musket deliberately and with deadly aim, then flung it away and swept on, brandishing his broadsword. A body of Stewarts and Camerons actually stormed the battery, rushing straight on the muzzles of the guns. The old men who had them in charge had fled at the first sight of the Highlanders; even the brave Colonel Whiteford, who alone and unassisted stood to his guns, had to yield to their furious onset. Gardiner's dragoons standing behind the battery were next seized by the panic; they made one miserable attempt to advance, halted, and then wheeling round, dashed wildly in every direction. Nor could Hamilton's dragoons on the other wing stand the heavy rolling fire of the advancing Macdonalds. Mad with terror, man and horse fled in blind confusion, some backwards, confounding their own ranks, some along the shore, some actually through the ranks of the enemy.

Only the infantry in the centre stood firm and received the onset of the Highlanders with a steady fire. A small band of Macgregors, armed only with scytheblades, charged against this hedge of musketry. This curious weapon was invented by James More, a son of Rob Roy Macgregor. He was the leader of this party, and fell, pierced by five bullets. With undaunted courage he raised himself on his elbow, and shouted, "Look ye, my lads, I'm not dead; by Heaven I shall see if any of you does not do his duty." In that wild charge, none of the clansmen failed to "do his duty." Heedless of the rain of bullets, they rushed to close quarters with the Hanoverian infantry, who, deserted by the dragoons, were now attacked on both sides as well as in front. A few stood firm, and the gallant Colonel Gardiner put himself at their head. A blow from a scytheblade in the hands of a gigantic Macgregor ended his life, and spared him the shame and sorrow of another defeat. The Park walls at their back prevented the infantry from seeking ignoble security in flight, after the fashion of the dragoons, and they were forced to lay down their weapons and beg for quarter. Some 400 of them fell, struck down by the broadswords and dirks of their enemy, more than 700 were taken prisoners, and only a few hundreds escaped.

The battle was won in less than five minutes. Charles himself commanded the second column, which was only fifty yards behind the first, but, by the time he arrived on the scene of action, there was nothing left to be done. Nothing, that is, in securing the victory, but Charles at once occupied himself in stopping the carnage and protecting the wounded and prisoners. "Sir," cried one of his staff, riding up to him, "there are your enemies at your feet." "They are my father's subjects," answered Charles sadly, turning away.

In vain did Sir John Cope and the Earl of Home try to rally the dragoons. Holding pistols to the men's heads, they succeeded in collecting a body in a field near Clement's Wells, and tried to form a squadron; but the sound of a pistol-shot renewed the panic and off they started again at the gallop. There was nothing for it but for the officers to put themselves at the head of as many fugitives as they could collect, and conduct the flight. Hardly did they draw rein till they were safe at Berwick. There the unfortunate general was received by Lord Mark Ker with the well-known sarcasm—'Sir, I believe you are the first general in Europe who has brought the first news of his own defeat."[1]

In the meantime, the wounded they had left on the field were being kindly cared for by the victorious army. Charles despatched a messenger to bring medical aid—an errand not without danger to a single horseman on roads covered with straggling bodies of dragoons. But the adventure just suited the gallant spirit of young Lawrence Oliphant. At Tranent the sight of him and his servant at their heels sent off a body of dragoons at the gallop. Single fugitives he disarmed and dismounted, sending the horses back to the Prince by the hands

1. Others were Frederick the Great, and David Leslie!

of country lads. Once he had to discharge his pistol after a servant and pony, but for the most part the terrified soldiers yielded at a word.

Entering the Netherbow, he galloped up the streets of Edinburgh shouting, "Victory! victory!" From every window in the High Street and Luckenbows white caps looked out, while the streets were crowded with eager citizens, and joyful hurrahs were heard on every side. At Lucky Wilson's, in the Lawn Market, the young gentleman alighted, called for breakfast, and sent for the magistrates to deliver his orders that the gates were to be closed against any fugitive dragoons. Hat in hand, the magistrates waited on the Prince's aide-de-camp, but at that moment the cry arose that dragoons and soldiers were coming up the street. Up jumps Mr. Oliphant and out into the street, faces eight or nine dragoons, and commands them to dismount in the Prince's name. This the craven Hanoverians were quite prepared to do. Only one presented his piece at the young officer. Mr. Oliphant snapped his pistol at him, forgetting that it was empty. Immediately half a dozen shots were fired at him, but so wildly that none did him any harm beyond shattering his buckle, and he retreated hastily up one of the dark steep lanes that led into a close.

The commander of the Castle refused to admit the fugitives, threatened even to fire on them as deserters, and they had to gallop out at the West Port and on to Stirling. Another of the Prince's officers, Colquhoun Grant, drove a party of dragoons before him all the way into Edinburgh, and stuck his bloody dirk into the Castle gates as a defiance.

Sadder was the fate of another Perthshire gentleman, as young and as daring as Lawrence Oliphant. David Thriepland, with a couple of servants, had followed the dragoons for two miles from the field; they had fled before him, but, coming to a halt, they discovered that their pursuers numbered no more than three. They turned on them and cut them down with their swords. Many years afterwards, when the grass was rank and green on Mr. Thriepland's grave, a child named Walter Scott, sitting on it, heard the story from an old lady who had herself seen the death of the young soldier.

The next day (Sunday) the Prince held his triumphant entry up the High Street of Edinburgh. Clan after clan marched past, with waving plaids and brandished weapons; the wild music of the pipes sounded as full of menace as of triumph. From every window in the dark, high houses on each side, fair faces looked down, each adorned with the white cockade. In their excitement the Highlanders let off their pieces into the air. By an unfortunate accident one musket thus fired happened to be loaded, and the bullet grazed the temple of a Jacobite lady, Miss Nairne, inflicting a slight wound. "Thank God that this happened to *me*, whose opinions are so well known," cried the high-spirited girl. "Had a Whig lady been wounded, it might have been thought that the deed had been intentional."[2]

VI

The March to Derby

A SUCCESSFUL ARMY, ESPECIALLY AN insurgent army, should never pause in its onward march. If Prince Charles could have followed the flying dragoons over the Border into England he would have found no preparations made to resist him in the Northern counties. Even after the King and Government were alarmed by the news of the battle of Preston, a full month was allowed to pass before an army under General Wade arrived at Newcastle on the 29th of October. Dutch, Hessian, and English troops were ordered home from Flanders and regiments were raised in the country, though at first no one seems to have seriously believed in anything so daring as an invasion of England by Prince Charles and his Highlanders.

So far there had come no word of encouragement from the English Jacobites. Still, Charles never doubted but that they would hasten to join him as soon as he crossed the Border. On the very morrow of Prestonpans he sent messengers to those whom he considered his friends in England, telling of his success and bidding them be ready to join him. In the meantime he waited in Edinburgh till his army should be large and formidable enough to undertake the march South. After the battle numbers of his soldiers had deserted. According to their custom, as soon as any clansman had secured as much booty as he could conveniently carry, he started off home to his mountains to deposit his spoil. A stalwart Highlander was seen staggering along the streets of Edinburgh with a pier glass on his back, and ragged boys belonging to the army adorned themselves with gold-laced hats, or any odd finery they could pick up.

---

2. In *Waverley* this generous speech is attributed to Flora Macivor.

Many new adherents flocked to join the Prince. Among these was the simple-minded old Lord Pitsligo. He commanded a body of horse, though at his age he could hardly bear the fatigues of a campaign. In Aberdeenshire—always Jacobite and Episcopalian—Lord Lewis Gordon collected a large force; in Perthshire Lord Ogilvy raised his clan, though neither of these arrived in time to join the march South. Even a Highland army could not start in mid-winter to march through a hostile country without any preparations. Tents and shoes were provided by the city of Edinburgh, and all the horses in the neighbourhood were pressed for the Prince's service.

On the first day of November the army, numbering 6,000 men, started for the Border. Lord George led one division, carrying the supplies by Moffat and Annandale to the West Border. Charles himself commanded the other division. They pretended to be moving on Newcastle, marched down Tweedside and then turned suddenly westward and reached England through Liddesdale.

On the 8th they crossed the Border. The men unsheathed their swords and raised a great shout. Unfortunately, as he drew his claymore, Locheil wounded his hand, and his men, seeing the blood flow, declared it to be a bad omen.

But fortune still seemed to follow the arms of the Adventurer. Carlisle was the first strong town on the English Border, and though insufficiently garrisoned, was both walled and defended by a Castle. The mayor, a vain-glorious fellow, was ambitious of being the first man to stay the victorious army, and published a proclamation saying that he was not "Patterson, a Scotchman, but Pattieson, a true-hearted Englishman, who would defend his town against all comers."

A false report that Wade was advancing from the West made Charles turn aside and advance to Brampton in the hope of meeting him, but the roads were rough, the weather was wild and cold, the Hanoverian general was old, and again, as at Corryarack, Charles prepared to meet an enemy that never appeared.

In the meantime a division of the army had returned to Carlisle and was laying siege to it with great vigour. Lord George Murray and the Duke of Perth worked in the trenches in their shirt sleeves. The sound of bullets in their ears, the sight of formidable preparations for an assault, were too much for the mayor and his citizens; on the 13th, the "true-hearted Englishmen" hung out a white flag, and the Prince's army marched in and took possession. It was another success, as sudden and complete as any of the former ones. But there were ominous signs even at this happy moment. The command of the siege of Carlisle had been given to the Duke of Perth, and Lord George Murray, the older and abler general, resented the slight. He sent in his resignation of the command of the forces, but with proud magnanimity offered to serve as a volunteer. Charles accepted the resignation, but the idea of losing the one general of any experience they had, created consternation among the chiefs. The crisis would have become serious but for the generous good sense and modesty of the Duke of Perth, who sent in his resignation also to the Prince. A more ominous fact was that they had been almost a week in England and no one had declared for them. Charles refused to let anything damp his hopefulness. Lancashire was the stronghold of Jacobitism. Once in Lancashire, gentlemen and their following would flock to join him.

The road between Carlisle and Preston lies over bare, stony heights, an inhospitable country in the short, bleak days and long nights of November. Charles shared every hardship with his soldiers. He had a carriage but he never used it, and it was chiefly occupied by Lord Pitsligo. With his target on his shoulder he marched alongside of the soldiers, keeping up with their rapid pace, and talking to them in his scanty Gaelic. He seldom dined, had one good meal at night, lay down with his clothes on, and was up again at four next morning. No wonder that the Highlanders were proud of "a Prince who could eat a dry crust, sleep on pease-straw, dine in four minutes, and win a battle in five." Once going over Shap Fell he was so overcome by drowsiness and cold that he had to keep hold of one of the Ogilvies by the shoulderbelt and walked some miles half asleep. Another time the sole of his boot was quite worn out, and at the next village he got the blacksmith to nail a thin iron plate to the boot. "I think you are the first that ever shod the son of a king," he said, laughing as he paid the man.

Still entire silence on the part of the English Jacobites. The people in the villages and towns through which they passed looked on the uncouth strangers with ill-concealed aversion and fear. Once going to his quarters in some small town the "gentle Locheil" found that the good woman of the house had hidden her children in a cupboard, having heard that the Highlanders were cannibals and ate children!

The town of Preston was a place of ill omen to the superstitious Highlanders. There, thirty years before, their countrymen had been disastrously defeated. They had a presentiment that they too would never get beyond that point. To destroy this fear, Lord George Murray marched half his army across the river and encamped on the further side.

Manchester was the next halting-place, and there the prospects were rather brighter. An enterprising Sergeant Dickson hurried on in front of the army with a girl and a drummer boy at his side. He marched about the streets recruiting, and managed to raise some score of recruits. In Manchester society there was a certain Jacobite element; on Sunday the church showed a crowd of ladies in tartan cloaks and white cockades, and a nonjuring clergyman preached in favour of the Prince's cause. Among the officers who commanded the handful of men calling itself the Manchester Regiment, were three brothers of the name of Deacon, whose father, a nonjuring clergyman, devoted them all gladly to the cause. Another, Syddel, a wig-maker, had as a lad of eleven seen his father executed as a Jacobite in the '15, and had vowed undying vengeance against the house of Hanover. Manchester was the only place in England that had shown any zeal in the Prince's cause, and it only contributed some few hundred men and 3,000*l.* of money.

The situation seemed grave to the leaders of the Prince's army. He himself refused to recognise any other fact than that every day brought him nearer to London. On October 31 the army left Manchester. At Stockport they crossed the Mersey, the Prince wading up to the middle. Here occurred a very touching incident. A few Cheshire gentlemen met Charles at this point, and with them came an aged lady, Mrs. Skyring. As a child she remembered her mother lifting her up to see Charles II land at Dover. Her parents were devoted Cavaliers, and despite the ingratitude of the royal family, loyalty was an hereditary passion with their daughter. For years she had laid aside half her income and had sent it to the exiled family, only concealing the name of the donor, as being of no interest to them. Now, she had sold all her jewels and plate, and brought the money in a purse as an offering to Charles. With dim eyes, feeble hands, and feelings too strong for her frail body, she clasped Charles's hand, and gazing at his face said, "Lord, now lettest Thou Thy servant depart in peace."

The Highland forces were in the very centre of England and had not yet encountered an enemy, but now they were menaced on two sides. General Wade—'Grandmother Wade" the Jacobite soldiers called him—by slow marches through Yorkshire had arrived within three days' march of them on one side, while, far more formidable, in front of them at Stafford lay the Duke of Cumberland with 10,000 men. He was a brave leader, and the troops under him were seasoned and experienced. At last the English Government had wakened up to the seriousness of the danger which they had made light of as long as it only affected Scotland. When news came that the Scots had got beyond Manchester, a most unmanly panic prevailed in London. Shops were shut, there was a run on the Bank, it has even been asserted that George II himself had many of his valuables removed on to yachts in the Thames, and held himself in readiness to fly at any moment.

The Duke of Cumberland and his forces were the only obstacle between the Prince's army and London. Lord George Murray, with his usual sagacity, determined to slip past this enemy also, as he had already slipped past Wade. While the Prince, with one division of the army, marched straight for Derby, he himself led the remaining troops apparently to meet the Duke of Cumberland. That able general fell into the snare and marched up his men to meet the Highlanders at Congleton. Then Lord George broke up his camp at midnight (of December 2), and, marching across country in the darkness, joined the Prince at Leek, a day's journey short of Derby. By this clever stratagem the Highland army got a start of at least a day's march on their way to London.

On the 4th, the Highland army entered Derby, marching in all day in detachments. Here Charles learned the good news from Scotland that Lord John Drummond had landed at Montrose with 1,000 French soldiers and supplies of money and arms. Never had fortune seemed to shine more brightly on the young Prince. He was sure now of French assistance, he shut his eyes to the fact that the English people were either hostile or indifferent; if it came to a battle he was confident that hundreds of the enemy would desert to his standard. The road to London and to a throne lay open before him! That night at mess he seriously discussed how he should enter London in triumph. Should it be in Highland or English dress? On horseback or on foot? Did he notice, one wonders, that his gay anticipations were received in ominous silence by the chiefs? At least the private soldiers of his army shared his hopes. On the afternoon of the 5th many had their broadswords and dirks sharpened, and some partook of the Sacrament in the churches. They all felt that a battle was imminent.

Next morning a council of war was held. Charles was eager to arrange for an immediate advance on London. Success seemed to lie within his grasp. Lord George Murray rose as spokesman for the rest. He urged immediate retreat to Scotland! Two armies lay one on either hand, a third was being collected to defend London. Against 30,000 men what could 5,000 avail? He had no faith in a French invasion, he was convinced that nothing was to be looked for from the English Jacobites. "Rather than go back, I would I were twenty feet underground," Charles cried in passionate disappointment. He argued, he commanded, he implored; the chiefs were inexorable, and it was decided that the retreat should begin next morning before daybreak. This decision broke the Prince's heart and quenched his spirit; never again did his buoyant courage put life into his whole army. Next morning he rose sullen and enraged, and marched in gloomy silence in the rear.

All the private soldiers and many of the officers believed that they were being led against the Duke of Cumberland. When returning daylight showed that they were retreating by the same road on which they had marched so hopefully two days before, they were filled with grief and rage. "Would God," writes a certain brave Macdonald, "we had pushed on though we had all been cut to pieces, when we were in a condition for fighting and doing honour to our noble Prince and the glorious cause we had taken in hand." The distrust caused in the Prince's mind by Lord George's action had, later, the most fatal effect.

VII

The Retreat

Never, perhaps, in any history was there a march more mournful than that of the Highland army from Derby. These soldiers had never known defeat, and yet there they were, in full retreat through a hostile country. So secret and rapid were their movements that they had gained two full days' march before the Duke of Cumberland had any certain news of their retreat. Though he started at once in pursuit, mounting a body of infantry on horses that they might keep up with the cavalry, and though all were fresh and in good condition, it was not till the 18th that he overtook the Prince's army in the wilds of Cumberland. Lord George Murray, looking upon himself as responsible for the safety of the army, had sent on the first division under the Prince, and himself brought up the rear with the baggage and artillery. In the hilly country of the North of England, it was no light task to travel with heavy baggage. The big wagons could not be dragged up the steep ill-made roads, and the country people were sullenly unwilling to lend their carts. The general was reduced to paying sixpence for every cannon ball that could be carried up the hills. The Prince was already at Penrith on the 17th, but Lord George had been obliged to stop six miles short of that point. Marching before daybreak on the 18th, he reached a village called Clifton as the sun rose. A body of horsemen stood guarding the village; the Highlanders, exhilarated at meeting a foe again, cast their plaids and rushed forward. On this the Hanoverians—a mere body of local yeomanry—fled. Among a few stragglers who were taken prisoner was a footman of the Duke of Cumberland, who told his captors that his master with 4,000 cavalry was following close behind them. Lord George resolved to make a stand, knowing that nothing would be more fatal than allowing the dragoons to fall suddenly on his troops when they had their backs turned. He had a body of Macdonalds and another of Stuarts with him; he found also some two hundred Macphersons, under their brave commander Cluny, guarding a bridge close to the village. The high road here ran between a wall on one side, and fields enclosed by high hedges and ditches on the other. On either side he could thus place his soldiers under cover. As evening fell he learned that the Hanoverian soldiers were drawn up on the moor, about a mile distant. He sent some of his men to a point where they should be partly visible to the enemy over a hedge; these he caused to pass and repass, so as to give a delusive idea of numbers. When the night fell the Highland soldiers were drawn up along the wall on the road, and in the enclosures behind the hedges; Lord George and Cluny stood with drawn swords on the highway. Every man stood at his post on the alert, in the breathless silence. Though the moon was up, the night was cloudy and dark, but in a fitful gleam the watchful general saw dark forms approaching in a mass behind a hedge. In a rapid whisper he asked Cluny what was to be done. "I will charge sword in hand if you order me," came the reply, prompt and cheery. A volley from the advancing troops decided the question. "There is no time to be lost; we must charge," cried Lord George, and raising the Highland war cry, "Claymore, Claymore," he was the first to dash through the hedge (he lost his hat and wig among the thorns, and fought the rest of the night bareheaded!). The dragoons were forced back on to the moor, while another body of horse was similarly driven back along the high road by the Stuarts and Macdonells of Glengarry. About a dozen Highlanders, following too eagerly in pursuit, were killed on this moor, but the loss on the other side was far greater. Nor did the Duke of Cumberland again attack the retreating enemy; he had learned, like the other generals before him, the meaning of a Highland onset.[3]

A small garrison of Highlanders had been left in Carlisle, but these rejoined the main army as it passed through the town. There was an unwillingness among the soldiers to hold a fort that was bound to be taken by the enemy. Finally the Manchester regiment consented to remain, probably arguing, in the words of one of the English volunteers, that they "might as well be hanged in England as starved in Scotland."

The Esk was at this time in flood, running turbid and swift. But the Highlanders have a peculiar way of crossing deep rivers. They stand shoulder to shoulder, with their arms linked, and so pass in a continuous chain across. As Charles was fording the stream on horseback, one man was swept away from the rest and was being rapidly carried down. The Prince caught him by the hair, shouting in Gaelic, "Cohear, cohear!" "Help, help!"

They were now again on Scottish ground, and the question was, whither were they to go next? Edinburgh, immediately after the Prince's departure, had gladly reverted to her Whig allegiance. She was garrisoned and defended; any return thither was practically out of the question. It was resolved that the army should retire to the Highlands through the West country.

Dumfries, in the centre of the Covenanting district, had always been hostile to the Stuarts. Two months before, when the Highland army marched south, some of her citizens had despoiled them of tents and baggage. To revenge this injury, Charles marched to Dumfries and levied a large fine on the town. The Provost, Mr. Carson, was noted for his hostility to the Jacobites. He was warned that his house was to be burned, though the threat was not carried out. He had a little daughter of six years old at the time; when she was quite an old lady she told Sir Walter Scott that she remembered being carried out of the house in the arms of a Highland officer. She begged him to point out

---

3. Readers of *Waverley* will remember that in this fight Fergus Macivor was taken prisoner.

ANDREW LANG AND H. RIDER HAGGARD

the *Pretender* to her. This he consented to do, after the little girl had solemnly promised always to call him the *Prince* in future.

An army which had been on the road continuously for more than two winter months, generally presents a sufficiently dilapidated appearance; still more must this have been the case with the Highland army, ill-clad and ill-shod to begin with. The soldiers—hardly more than 4,000 now—who on Christmas day marched into Glasgow, had scarcely a whole pair of boots or a complete suit of tartans among them. This rich and important town was even more hostile than Dumfries to the Jacobites, but it was necessity more than revenge that forced the Prince to levy a heavy sum on the citizens, and exact besides 12,000 shirts, 6,000 pairs of stockings, and 6,000 pairs of shoes.

At Stirling, whither the Prince next led his army, the prospects were much brighter. Here he was joined by the men raised in Aberdeenshire under Lord Lewis Gordon, Lord Strathallan's Perthshire regiment, and the French troops under Lord John Drummond. The whole number of his army must have amounted to not much less than 9,000 men.

The Duke of Cumberland had given up the pursuit of the Highland army after Carlisle; an alarm of a French invasion having sent him hurrying back to London. In his stead General Hawley had been sent down to Scotland and was now in Edinburgh at the head of 8,000 men. He was an officer trained in the Duke of Cumberland's school, severe to his soldiers and relentlessly cruel to his enemies. A vain and boastful man, he looked with contempt on the Highland army, in spite of the experience of General Cope. On the 16th he marched out of Edinburgh with all his men, anticipating an easy victory. Lord George Murray was at Linlithgow, and slowly retreated before the enemy, but not before he had obtained full information of their numbers and movements. On the nights of January 15 and 16, the two armies lay only seven miles apart, the Prince's at Bannockburn and General Hawley's at Falkirk. From the one camp the lights of the other were visible. The Highland army kept on the alert, expecting every hour to be attacked.

All the day of the 16th they waited, but there was no movement on the part of the English forces. On the 17th the Prince's horse reconnoitred and reported perfect inactivity in Hawley's camp. The infatuated general thought so lightly of the enemy that he was giving himself up to amusement.

The fair and witty Lady Kilmarnock lived in the neighbourhood at Callender House. Her husband was with the Prince, and she secretly favoured the same cause. By skilful flattery and hospitality, she so fascinated the English general that he recklessly spent his days in her company, forgetful of the enemy and entirely neglectful of his soldiers.

Charles knew that the strength of his army lay in its power of attack, and so resolved to take the offensive. The high road between Bannockburn and Falkirk runs in a straight line in front of an old and decaying forest called Torwood. Along this road, in the face of the English camp, marched Lord John Drummond, displaying all the colours in the army, and making a brave show with the cavalry and two regiments. Their advance was only a feint. The main body of the army skirted round to the south of the wood, then marched across broken country—hidden at first by the trees and later by the inequalities of the ground—till they got to the back of a ridge called Falkirk Muir, which overlooked the English camp. Their object was to gain the top of this ridge before the enemy, and then to repeat the manoeuvres of Prestonpans.

Meanwhile, the English soldiers were all unconscious, and their general was enjoying himself at Callender House. At eleven o'clock General Huske, the second in command, saw Lord John Drummond's advance, and sent an urgent message to his superior officer. He, however, refused to take alarm, sent a message that the men might put on their accoutrements, and sat down to dinner with his fascinating hostess. At two o'clock, General Huske, looking anxiously through his spy-glass, saw the bulk of the Highland army sweeping round to the back of the ridge.

A messenger was instantly despatched to Callender House. At last Hawley was aroused to the imminence of the danger. Leaving the dinner table, he leaped on his horse and arrived in the camp at a gallop, breathless and bare-headed. He trusted to the rapidity of his cavalry to redeem the day. He placed himself at the head of the dragoons, and up the ridge they rode at a smart trot. It was a race for the top. The dragoons on their horses were the first to arrive, and stood in their ranks on the edge of the hill. From the opposite side came the Highlanders in three lines; first the clans (the Macdonalds, of course, on the right), then the Aberdeenshire and Perthshire regiments, lastly cavalry and Lord John Drummond's Frenchmen. Undismayed, nay, rather exhilarated by the sight of the three regiments of dragoons drawn up to receive them, they advanced at a rapid pace. The dragoons, drawing their sabres, rode on at full trot to charge the Highlanders. With the steadiness of old soldiers, the clans came on in their ranks, till within ten yards of the enemy. Then Lord George gave the signal by presenting his own piece, and at once a withering volley broke the ranks of the dragoons. About 400 fell under this deadly fire and the rest fled, fled as wildly and ingloriously as their fellows had done at Coltbridge or Prestonpans. A wild storm of rain dashing straight in their faces during the attack added to the confusion and helplessness of the dragoons. The right and centre of Hawley's infantry were at the same instant driven back by the other clans, Camerons and Stewarts and Macphersons. The victory would have been complete but for the good behaviour of three regiments at the right of Hawley's army, Price's, Ligonier's, and Barrel's. From a point of vantage on the edge of a ravine they poured such a steady fire on the left wing of the Highlanders, that they drove them back and forced them to fly in confusion. Had the victorious Macdonalds only attacked these three steady regiments, the Highland army would have been victorious all along the line. Unfortunately they had followed their natural instinct instead of the word of command, and flinging away their guns, were pursuing the fugitive dragoons down the ridge. The flight of the Hanoverians was so sudden that it caused suspicion of an ambush. The Prince was lost in the darkness and rain. The pipers had thrown their pipes to their boys, had gone in with the claymore, and could not sound the rally. It was not a complete victory for Charles, but it was a sufficiently complete defeat for General Hawley, who lost his guns. The camp at Falkirk was abandoned after the tents had been set on fire, and the general with his dismayed and confused followers retired first to Linlithgow and then to Edinburgh. Hawley tried to make light of his defeat and to explain it away, though to Cumberland he said that his heart was broken; but the news of the battle spread consternation all over England, and it was felt that no one but the Duke of Cumberland was fit to deal with such a stubborn and daring enemy.

The Prince's army did not reap so much advantage from their victory as might have been expected; their forces were in too great confusion to pursue the English general, and on the morrow of the battle many deserted to their own homes, carrying off their booty. A more serious loss was the defection of the clan Glengarry. The day after the battle a young Macdonald, a private soldier of Clanranald's company, was withdrawing the charge from a gun he had taken on the field. He had abstracted the bullet, and, to clean the barrel, fired off the piece. Unfortunately it had been double loaded, and the remaining bullet struck Glengarry's second son, Æneas, who was in the street at the time. The poor boy fell, mortally wounded, in the arms of his comrades, begging with his last breath that no vengeance should be exacted for what was purely accidental. It was asking too much from the feelings of the clansmen. They indignantly demanded that blood should atone for blood. Clanranald would gladly have saved his clansman, but dared not risk a feud which would have weakened the Prince's cause. So another young life as innocent as the first was sacrificed to clan jealousy. The young man's own father was the first to fire on his son, to make sure that death should be instantaneous. Young Glengarry was buried with all military honours, Charles himself being chief mourner; but nothing could appease the angry pride of the clan, and the greater part of them returned to their mountains without taking any leave.

VIII

In the Highlands

ON JANUARY 30 THE DUKE OF Cumberland arrived in Edinburgh. His reception was a curious parody of Charles's brilliant entry four months before. The fickle mob cheered the one as well as the other; the Duke occupied the very room at Holyrood that had been Charles's; where the one had danced with Jacobite beauties, the other held a reception of Whig ladies. Both were fighting their father's battle; both were young men of five-and-twenty. But here likeness gives way to contrast; Charles was graceful in person, and of dignified and attractive presence; his cousin, Cumberland, was already stout and unwieldy, and his coarse and cruel nature had traced unpleasant lines on his face. He was a poor general but a man of undoubted courage. Yet he had none of that high sense of personal honour that we associate with a good soldier. In Edinburgh he found many of the English officers who had been taken prisoner at Prestonpans. They had been left at large on giving their word not to bear arms against the Prince. Cumberland declared that this "parole" or promise was not binding, and ordered them to return to their regiments. A small number—it is right that we should know and honour their names—Sir Peter Halket, Mr. Ross, Captain Lucy Scott, and Lieutenants Farquharson and Cumming, thereupon sent in their resignations, saying that the Duke was master of their commissions but not of their honour.

On the 30th the Duke and his soldiers were at Linlithgow, and hoped to engage the Highland army next day near Falkirk. But on the next day's march they learned from straggling Highlanders that the enemy had already retired beyond the Forth. They had been engaged in a futile siege of Stirling Castle. The distant sound of an explosion which was heard about midday on the 1st, proved to be the blowing up of the powder magazine, the last act of the Highlanders before withdrawing from Stirling. This second, sudden retreat was as bitter to the Prince as the return from Derby. After the battle at Falkirk he looked forward eagerly and confidently to fighting Cumberland on the same ground. But there was discontent and dissension in the camp. Since Derby the Prince had held no councils, and consulted with no one but Secretary Murray and his Irish officers. The chiefs were dispirited and deeply hurt, and, as usual, the numbers dwindled daily from desertion. In the midst of his plans for the coming battle, Charles was overwhelmed by a resolution on the part of the chiefs to break up the camp and to retire without delay to the Highlands. Again he saw his hopes suddenly destroyed, again he had to yield with silent rage and bitter disappointment.

The plan of the chiefs was to withdraw on Inverness, there to attack Lord Loudon (who held the fort for King George); to rest and recruit, each clan in its own country, till in the spring they could take the field again with a fresher and larger army. Lord George Murray led one division by the east coast and Aberdeen, to the rendezvous near Inverness, Charles led the other by General Wade's road through Badenoch and Athol. Cumberland with his heavy troops and baggage could not overtake the light-footed Highlanders; by the time he reached Perth he was six days' march behind them. He sent old Sir Andrew Agnew to garrison the house of Blair, and other small companies to occupy all the chief houses in Athol. He himself retired with the main body to Aberdeen, and there waited for milder weather.

In the neighbourhood of Inverness lies the country of the Mackintoshes. The laird of that ilk was a poor-spirited, stupid man. It was his simple political creed that that king was the right one who was willing and able "to give a half-guinea to-day and another to-morrow." That was probably the pay he drew as officer in one of King George's Highland companies. Of a very different spirit was his wife. Lady Mackintosh was a Farquharson of Invercauld; in her husband's absence she raised a body of mixed Farquharsons and Mackintoshes, several hundred strong, for the Prince. These she commanded herself, riding at their head in a tartan habit with pistols at her saddle. Her soldiers called her "Colonel Anne." Once in a fray between her irregular troops and the militia, her husband was taken prisoner and brought before his own wife. She received him with a military salute, "Your servant, captain;" to which he replied equally shortly, "Your servant, colonel."

This high-spirited woman received Charles as her guest on February 16 at the castle of Moy, twelve miles from Inverness.

Having learnt that Charles was staying there with a small guard, Lord Loudon conceived the bold plan of capturing the Prince, and so putting an end to the war once for all. On Sunday the 16th, at nightfall, he started with 1,500 men with all secrecy and despatch. Still the secret had oozed out, and the dowager Lady Mackintosh sent a boy to warn her daughter-in-law and the Prince. The boy was both faithful and sagacious. Finding the high road already full of soldiers, he skulked in a ditch till they were past, then, by secret ways, over moor and moss, running at the top of his pace, he sped on, till, faint and exhausted, he reached the house at five o'clock in the morning, and panted out the news that Loudon's men were not a mile away! The Prince was instantly aroused, and in a few minutes was out of the house and off to join Lochiel not more than a mile distant. As it happened, Lord Loudon's troops had already been foiled and driven back by a bold manoeuvre of some of "Colonel Anne's" men. A blacksmith with some half-dozen men—two pipers amongst them—were patrolling the woods near the high road, when in the dim morning twilight they saw a large body of the enemy approaching. They separated, planted themselves at intervals under cover, fired rapidly and simultaneously, shouted the war cries of the various clans, Lochiel, Keppoch, Glengarry, while the pipers blew up their pipes furiously behind. The advancing soldiers were seized with panic, and flying wildly back, upset the ranks of the rear and filled them with the same consternation. The "Rout of Moy" was hardly more creditable to the Hanoverian arms than the "Canter of Coltbridge." In this affair only one man fall, MacRimmon, the hereditary piper of the Macleods. Before leaving Skye he had prophesied his own death in the lament, "Macleod shall return, but MacRimmon shall never."

The next day, February 18, Charles, at the head of a body of troops, marched out to besiege Inverness. He found that town already evacuated: Lord Loudon had too little faith in his men to venture another meeting with the enemy. Two days later Fort George also fell into the Prince's hands.

During the next six weeks the Highland army was employed in detachments against the enemies who surrounded them on all sides. Lord John Drummond took Fort Augustus, Lochiel and others besieged—but in vain—the more strongly defended Fort William. Lord Cromarty pursued Lord Loudon into Sutherland. But the most notable and gallant feat of arms was performed by Lord George Murray. He marched a body of his own Athol men, and another of Macphersons under Cluny—700 men in all—down into his native district of Athol. At nightfall they started from Dalwhinnie, before midnight they were at Dalnaspidal, no one but the two leaders having any idea of the object of the expedition. It was the middle of March; at that season they might count on five hours of darkness before daybreak. It was then explained to the men that they were to break up into some thirty small companies, and each was to march to attack one of the English garrisons placed in all the considerable houses in the neighbourhood. It was necessary that each place should be attacked at the same time, that the alarm might not spread. By daybreak all were to reassemble at the Falls of Bruar, within a mile or two of Castle Blair. One after the other the small parties moved off swiftly and silently in the darkness, one marching some ten miles off to the house of Faskally, others attacking Lude, Kinnachin, Blairfettie, and many other houses where the English garrisons were sleeping in security. Meanwhile Lord George and Cluny, with five-and-twenty men and a few elderly gentlemen, went straight to the Falls of Bruar. In the grey of the morning a man from the village of Blair came up hastily with the news that Sir Andrew Agnew had got the alarm, and with several hundred men was scouring the neighbourhood and was now advancing towards the Falls! Lord George might easily have escaped up the pass, but if he failed to be at the rendezvous, each small body as it came in would be surrounded and overpowered by the enemy. The skilful general employed precisely the same ruse as had been so successful at the Rout of Moy.

He put his followers behind a turf wall at distant intervals, displayed the colours in a conspicuous place, and placed his pipers to advantage. As Sir Andrew came in sight, the sun rose, and was flashed back by brandished broadswords behind the turf wall. All along the line plaids seemed to be waving, and heads appeared and disappeared as if a large body of men were behind; while the pipes blew up a clamorous pibroch, and thirty men shouted for three hundred. Sir Andrew fell into the snare, and promptly marched his men back again. One by one the other parties came in: some thirty houses had yielded to them, and they brought three hundred prisoners with them.

After this success Lord George actually attempted to take the House of Blair. It was a hopeless enterprise; the walls of the house were seven feet thick, and Lord George had only two small cannons. "I daresay the man's mad, knocking down his own brother's house," said the stout old commander, Sir Andrew, watching how little effect the shot had on the walls. Lord George sent to Charles for reinforcements when it began to seem probable that he could reduce the garrison by famine, but Charles, embittered and resentful, and full of unjust suspicion against his general, refused any help, and on March 31 Lord George had to abandon the siege and withdraw his men. The Prince's suspicions, though unjust, were not unnatural. Lord George had twice advised retreat, where audacity was the only way to success.

IX

Culloden

In the meantime the weeks were rolling on. The grey April of the North, if it brought little warmth, was at least lengthening the daylight, and melting the snow from the hills, and lowering the floods that had made the rivers impassable. Since the middle of February the Duke of Cumberland and his army of at least eight thousand men—horse and infantry—had been living at free quarters in Aberdeen. He bullied the inhabitants, but he made careful provision for his army. English ships keeping along the coast were ready to supply both stores and ammunition as soon as the forces should move. With the savage content of a wild animal that knows that his prey cannot escape, the duke was in no hurry to force on an engagement till the weather should be more favourable.

To the Highland army every week's delay was a loss. Many of the clansmen had scattered to their homes in search of subsistence, for funds were falling lower and lower at Inverness. Fortune was treating Charles harshly at this time. Supplies had been sent once and again from France, but the ships that had brought them had either fallen into the enemy's hands, or had been obliged to return with their errand unaccomplished.

His soldiers had now to be paid in meal, and that in insufficient quantities. There was thus discontent in the ranks, and among the chiefs there was a growing feeling of discouragement. Charles treated with reserve and suspicion the men who were risking property and life for his cause, and consulted only with Secretary Murray and his Irish officers.

On April 8 the Duke of Cumberland began his march from Aberdeen. Between the two armies lay the river Spey, always deep and rapid, almost impassable when the floods were out. A vigilant body of men commanding the fords from either bank would have any army at its mercy that might try to cross the stream under fire. Along the west bank Lord John Drummond and his men had built a long, low barrack of turf and stone. From this point of vantage they had hoped to pour their fire on the Hanoverian soldiers in mid-stream, but the vigilant Duke of Cumberland had powerful cannons in reserve on the opposite bank, and Lord John and his soldiers drew off before the enemy got across.

On Monday the 15th this retreating party arrived at Inverness, bringing the news that the Duke was already at Nairne, and would probably next day approach to give battle. Prince Charles was in the highest spirits at the news. In the streets of Inverness the pipers blew the gatherings of the various clans, the drums beat, and with colours flying the whole army marched out of the town and encamped on the plain of Culloden.

The Prince expected to be attacked next morning, Tuesday the 16th, and at six o'clock the soldiers were drawn up in order of battle. There was an ominous falling away in numbers. The Macphersons with Cluny had scattered to their homes in distant Badenoch; the Frasers were also absent. (Neither of these brave and faithful clans was present at the battle the next day.) The Keppoch Macdonalds and some other detachments only came in next morning.

By the most fatal mismanagement no provision had been made for feeding the soldiers that day, though there was meal and to spare at Inverness. A small loaf of the driest and coarsest bread was served out to each man. By the afternoon, the starving soldiers had broken their ranks and were scattering in search of food. Lord Elcho had reconnoitred in the direction of Nairne, twelve miles off, and reported that the English army would not move that day; they were resting in their camp and celebrating their commander's birthday. Charles called a council of war at three in the afternoon. Lord George Murray gave the daring counsel that instead of waiting to be attacked they should march through the night to Nairne, and while it was still dark surprise and overwhelm the sleeping enemy. By dividing the Highland forces before reaching Nairne they might attack the camp in front and rear at the same moment; no gun was to be fired which might spread the alarm; the Highlanders were to fall on with dirk and broadsword. The Prince had meant to propose this very plan: he leaped up and embraced Lord George. It was a dangerous scheme; but with daring, swiftfooted, enterprising men it did not seem impossible. Yes! but with men faint and dispirited by hunger? At the review that morning the army had numbered about 7,000 men, but hardly more than half that number assembled in the evening on the field, the rest were still scattered in search of food. By eight o'clock it was dark enough to start. The attack on the enemy's camp was timed for two in the morning, six hours was thus allowed for covering the twelve miles. The army was to march in three columns, the clans first in two divisions, Lochiel and Lord George at the head with 30 of the Mackintoshes as guides. The Prince himself commanded the third column, the Lowland troops, and the French and Irish regiments. The utmost secrecy was necessary; the men marched in dead silence. Not only did they avoid the high roads, but wherever a light showed the presence of a house or sheiling they had to make a wide circuit round it. The ground they had to go over was rough and uneven; every now and then the men splashed into unexpected bogs or stumbled over hidden stones. Add to this that the night was unusually dark. Instead of marching in three clear divisions, the columns got mixed in the darkness and mutually kept each other back. Soon the light-footed clansmen got ahead of the Lowland and French and Irish regiments unused to such heavy walking. Every few minutes messengers from the rear harassed the leaders of the van by begging them to march more slowly. It was a cruel task to restrain the pace while the precious hours of darkness were slipping past. At Kilravock House the van halted. This was the point where it was arranged that the army was to divide, one part marching straight on the English camp, the other crossing the river so as to fall on the enemy from the opposite side. The rear had fallen far behind, and there was more than one wide gap between the various troops. The Duke of Perth galloped up from behind and told Lord George that it was necessary that the van should wait till the others came up; other officers reported that the men were dropping out of their ranks, and falling asleep by the roadside. Watches were now consulted. It was already two o'clock and there were still four miles to be covered. Some of the officers begged that, at all risks, the march might be continued. As they stood consulting an aide-de-camp rode up from the rear saying that the Prince desired to go forward, but was prepared to yield to Lord George's judgment. Just then through the darkness there came from the distance the rolling of drums! All chance of surprising the English camp was at an end. With a heavy heart Lord George gave the order to march back. This affair increased the Prince's suspicions of Lord George, which were fostered by his Irishry.

In the growing light the retreat was far more rapid than the advance had been. It was shortly after five that the army found themselves in their old quarters at Culloden. Many fell down where they stood, overpowered with sleep; others dispersed in search of food. Charles himself and his chief officers found nothing to eat and drink at Culloden House but a little dry bread and whisky. Instead of holding a council of war, each man lay down to sleep where he could, on table or floor.

But the sleep they were able to snatch was but short. At about eight a patrol coming in declared that the Duke of Cumberland was already advancing, his main body was within four miles, his horse even nearer.

In the utmost haste the chiefs and officers of the Highland army tried to collect their men. Many had straggled off as far as Inverness, many were still overpowered with sleep; all were faint for lack of food. When the ranks were arrayed in order of battle, their numbers only amounted to 5,000 men. They were drawn up on the open plain; on the right, high turf walls, enclosing a narrow field, protected their flank (though, as it proved, quite ineffectually), on their left lay Culloden House. In spite of hunger and fatigue, the old fighting instinct was so strong in the clans that they took up their positions in the first line with all their old fire and enthusiasm, *all but the Macdonalds*. By extraordinary mismanagement the clans Glengarry, Keppoch, and Clanranald—they who had so nobly led the right wing at Prestonpans and Falkirk—were placed on the left. It was a slight that bitterly hurt their pride; it was also, to their superstitious minds, a fatal omen. Who was the cause of the blunder? This does not seem to be certainly known. On the right, where the Macdonalds should have been, were the Athol men, the Camerons, the Stewarts of Appin, Macleans, Mackintoshes, and other smaller clans, each led by their own chiefs, and all commanded by Lord George. At the extremities of the two wings the guns were placed, four on each side, the only artillery on the Prince's side. The second line consisted of the French, Irish, and Lowland regiments. The Prince and his guards occupied a knoll at the rear, from which the whole action of the fight was visible. His horse was later covered with mud from the cannon balls striking the wet moor, and a man was killed behind him. By one o'clock the Hanoverian army was drawn up within five hundred paces of their enemies. The fifteen regiments of foot were placed in three lines, so arranged that the gaps in the first line were covered by the centres of the regiments in the second line. Between each regiment in the first line two powerful cannons were placed, and the three bodies of horse were drawn up, flanking either wing. The men were fresh, well fed, confident in their general, and eager to retrieve the dishonour of Prestonpans and Falkirk.

A little after one, the day clouded over, and a strong north-easterly wind drove sudden showers of sleet in the faces of the Highland army. They were the first to open fire, but their guns were small, and the firing ill-directed; the balls went over the heads of the enemy and did little harm. Then the great guns on the other side poured out the return fire, raking the ranks of the Highlanders, clearing great gaps, and carrying destruction even into the second line. For half an hour the Highlanders stood exposed to this fire while comrade after comrade fell at their side. It was all they could do to keep their ranks; their white, drawn faces and kindling eyes spoke of the hunger for revenge that possessed their hearts. Lord George was about to give the word to charge, when the Mackintoshes impatiently rushed forward, and the whole of the centre and left wing followed them. On they dashed blindly, through the smoke and snow and rattling bullets. So irresistible was the onset that they actually swept through two regiments in the first line, though almost all the chiefs and front rank men had fallen in the charge. The regiment in the second rank—Sempill's—was drawn up three deep— the first rank kneeling, the third upright—all with bayonets fixed. They received the onrushing Highlanders with a sharp fire. This brought the clansmen to a halt, a few were forced back, more perished, flinging themselves against the bayonets. Their bodies were afterwards found in heaps three or four deep.

While the right and centre perished in this wild charge, the Macdonalds on the left remained sullenly in their ranks, rage and angry pride in their souls. In vain the Duke of Perth urged them to charge. "Your courage," he cried, "will turn the left into the right, and I will henceforth call myself Macdonald."

In vain Keppoch, with some of his kin, charged alone. "My God! have the children of my tribe forsaken me?" he cried, looking back to where his clansmen stood stubborn and motionless. The stout old heart was broken by this dishonour. A few minutes later he fell pierced by many bullets.

In the meantime the second line had been thrown into confusion. A detachment of the Hanoverians—the Campbells, in fact—had broken down the turf walls on the Prince's right. Through the gaps thus made, there rode a body of dragoons, who fell on the rear and flanks of the Lowland and French regiments, and scattered them in flight. Gillie MacBane held a breach with the claymore, and slew fourteen men before he fell. But the day was lost. All that courage, and pride, and devotion, and fierce hate could do had been done, and in vain.

Charles had, up to the last, looked for victory. He offered to lead on the second line in person; but his officers told him that Highlanders would never return to such a charge. Two Irish officers dragged at his reins; his army was a flying mob, and so he left his latest field, unless, as was said, he fought at Laffen as a volunteer, when the Scots Brigade nearly captured Cumberland. He had been eager to give up Holyrood to the wounded of Prestonpans; *his* wounded were left to die, or were stabbed on the field. He had refused to punish fanatics who tried to murder him; his faithful followers were tortured to extract information which they never gave. He lost a throne, but he won hearts, and, while poetry lives and romance endures, the Prince Charles of the Forty-Five has a crown more imperishable than gold. This was the ending of that Jacobite cause, for which men had fought and died, for which women had been content to lose homes and husbands and sons.

It was the end of that gifted race of Stuart kings who, for three centuries and more of varying fortunes, had worn the crown of Scotland.

But it was not the end of the romance of the Highland clans. Crushed down, scattered, and cruelly treated as these were in the years that followed Culloden, nothing could break their fiery spirit nor kill their native aptitude for war. In the service of that very government which had dealt so harshly with them, they were to play a part in the world's history, wider, nobler, and not less romantic than that of fiercely faithful adherents to a dying cause. The pages of that history have been written in imperishable deeds on the hot plains of India, in the mountain passes of Afghanistan, in Egypt, in the Peninsula, on the fields of Waterloo and Quatre Bras, and among the snows of the Crimea. And there may be other pages of this heroic history of the Highland regiments that our children and our children's children shall read with proud emotion in days that are to be.

The Burke and Wills
Exploring Expedition

O n August 21, 1860, in the most lovely season of the year—that of early spring—the citizens of Melbourne crowded to the Royal Park to witness the departure of the most liberally equipped exploring party that had yet set out to penetrate the unknown regions of Australia. Their object was to cross the land from the South to the Northern Seas, a task which had never before been accomplished, as well as to add to the scientific knowledge of the interior.

The expedition started under the leadership of Robert O'Hara Burke, who began his career as a cadet at Woolwich, but left at an early age to enter a regiment of Hussars in the Austrian service, in which he subsequently held a captaincy.

When this regiment was disbanded, in 1848, he obtained an appointment in the Irish Constabulary, which he exchanged for the Police Force of Victoria in 1853, and in this he was at once made an inspector.

A Mr. Landells, in charge of the camels, went as second in command, and William John Wills, an astronomer and surveyor, as third.

Wills was the son of Dr. William Wills, and was born at Totnes, in Devonshire, in 1834; he was cousin to Lieutenant Le Viscomte, who perished with Sir John Franklin in the "Erebus."

In 1852 the news of the wonderful gold discoveries induced him to try his fortune in Victoria; but he soon became attached to the staff of the Melbourne Observatory, where he remained until selected for the post of observer and surveyor to the exploring expedition.

From the time that the expedition first took shape the names of these leaders were associated in the minds of the people with those of other brave men who had toiled to solve the mystery that lay out in the great thirsty wilderness of the interior. Some of them had tried, and, failing, had returned broken in health by the terrible privations they had met with. Others, having failed, had tried again; but the seasons and years had rolled on since, and had brought back no story of their fate.

Therefore, as late in the afternoon Burke, mounted on a pretty grey, rode forth at the head of the caravan, cheer after cheer rang out from either side of the long lane formed by the thousands of sympathetic colonists who were eager to get a last glimpse of the adventurers.

Immediately following the leader came a number of pack horses led by the European servants on foot; then Landells and Dr. Beckler mounted on camels; and in their train sepoys, leading two by two twenty-four camels, each heavily burdened with forage and provisions, and a mounted sepoy brought up the rear.

At intervals after these several wagons rolled past, and finally when nearly dusk, Wills and Fergusson, the foreman, rode out to their first camping-ground at the village of Essendon, about seven miles distant.

Before the evening star, following close the crescent moon, had dropped below the dark and distant hill range, the green near the church was crowded by the picturesque confusion of the camp.

Above the fires of piled gum-tree bark and sticks rose soft plumes of white smoke that scented the air fragrantly, and the red light of the flames showed, as they would show many times again, the explorers' tents in vivid relief against the coming night.

The horses and camels were unloaded and picketed, and the men sat at the openings of their tents eating their supper, or stood in groups talking to those anxious friends who had come out from Melbourne to say the last good speed, or to repeat fears, to which imagination often lent the wildest colouring, of perils that awaited the adventurers in the great unknown land.

The wet weather which set in soon after their start made travelling very slow as they crossed Victoria, though at that time all seemed to go well with the party.

On fine days Wills found he was able to write his journal and do much of his work whilst riding his camel; he sat behind the hump, and had his instruments packed in front of it; thus he only needed to stop when the bearings had to be carefully taken.

They halted for several days at Swan Hill, which was their last resting-place before leaving the Colony. They were very hospitably entertained there by the people.

This may have had something to do with the ill-content of some of the party when on the march again, as at Balranald, beyond the Murray, Burke found himself obliged to discharge the foreman, Fergusson.

The plan of their route had to be changed here, as they were told that all along the Lower Darling, where they intended to travel, there was absolutely no food for their horses, but a plant called the Darling Pea, which made the animals that ate it mad.

Burke was at this time constantly irritated by Landells refusing to allow the camels to travel the distance of a day's march, or to carry their proper burden; he was naturally full of anxiety to push on while the season was favourable, and impatient and hasty when anything occurred to hinder their progress.

Landells insisted upon taking a quantity of rum for the use of the camels, as he had heard of an officer who took two camels through a two years' campaign in Cabul, the Punjab, and Scind by allowing them arrack. He had also been sowing dissension in the camp for some time; and, in short, the camels and the officer in charge of them seemed likely to disorganise the whole of the enterprise.

Complaints were now continually reaching Burke from the managers of the sheep stations through which they passed, that their shearers had got drunk on some of the camels' rum, which had been obtained from the wagons. He therefore, at last, determined to leave the rum behind. Landells, of course, would not agree to this, and in the end sent in his resignation.

In the course of the same day Dr. Beckler followed his example, giving as his reason that he did not like the manner in which Burke spoke to Landells, and that he did not consider the party safe without him to manage the camels. Burke did not, however, accept the Doctor's resignation.

This happened shortly before they left Menindie, the last station of the settled districts, and it was impossible to find anyone to take Landells' place. Wills was, however, at once promoted to be second in charge.

Burke now divided the expedition into two parts—one to act with him as an exploring party to test the safety of the route to Cooper's Creek, which was about four hundred miles farther on; the other to remain at Menindie with the heavy stores, under the care of Dr. Beckler, until arrangements were made to establish a permanent depôt in the interior.

The advance party of eight started on October 29, under the guidance of a man named Wright, who was said to have practical knowledge of the "back country."

They were Burke, Wills, Brahé, Patten, M'Donough, King, Gray, and Dost Mahomet, with fifteen horses and sixteen camels.

When this journey was made it was immediately after one of those wonderful seasons that transform these parts of Central Australia from a treeless and grassless desert to a land where the swelling plains that stretch from bound to bound of the horizon are as vast fields of ripening corn in their yellow summertide.

Riding girth high through the lovely natural grass, from which the ripe seed scattered as they passed, or camping at night surrounded by it, the horses and camels improved in condition each day, and were never at a loss for water. Sometimes they found a sufficiency in a natural well or claypan; or again they struck for some creek towards the west or north, whose irregular curves were outlined on the plain by the gum-trees growing closely on its banks.

Nowhere did they experience great difficulty or serious obstacle on their northward way, though sometimes, as they crossed the rough ironstone ranges which crop up now and then on this great and ever rising table-land, there was little feed, and the sharp stones cut the feet of the animals as they trod with faltering footsteps down the precipitous gulleys, out of which the floods had for ages torn a path. As they followed the dry bed of such a path leading to rich flats, they would come upon quiet pools deeply shaded by gums and marsh mallow, that had every appearance of being permanent.

After they had been out ten days and had travelled over two hundred miles, Burke had formed so good an opinion of Wright that he made him third in charge, and sent him back to Menindie to replace Dr. Beckler—whose resignation was now accepted—in command of the portion of the expedition at that place. Wright took with him despatches to forward to Melbourne, and his instructions were to follow up the advance party with the heavy stores immediately.

Burke now pushed on to Cooper's Creek; and though the last part of their journey led them over many of those tracts of country peculiar to Australia where red sandy ridges rise and fall for many miles in rigid uniformity, and are clothed for the most part in the monotonous grey of salt and cotton-bush leafage, yet they saw before them what has since proved to be one of the finest grazing lands in the world.

Still, as they went on, though the creeks and watercourses were more frequent, everywhere they showed signs of rapid drying up.

The party reached the Cooper on November 11, and after resting for a day, they set about preparing the depôt. For about a fortnight from this point Burke or Wills made frequent short journeys to the north or north-east, to feel their way before starting for the northern coast.

On one occasion Wills went out taking with him M'Donough and three camels, and when about ninety miles from the head camp he walked to a rising ground at some distance from where they intended to stop to make some observations, leaving M'Donough in charge of the camels and to prepare tea.

On his return he found that the man had fallen asleep, and that the camels had gone. Night closing in almost directly prevented any search for the missing animals.

Next morning nothing could be seen of them, though their tracks were followed for many miles, and though Wills went to some distant hills and searched the landscape on all sides with his field-glasses.

With a temperature of 112° in the shade, and the dazzling sun-rays beating from a pallid and cloudless sky, they started on their homeward walk of eighty miles, with only a little bread and a few johnny cakes to eat, each carrying as much water as he could.

They feared to light a fire even at night, as it might have attracted the blacks; therefore they took it in turn to sleep and watch when the others rested; while the dingoes sneaked from their cover in the belts of scrub, and howled dismally around them.

They reached the depôt in three days, having found only one pool of stagnant water, from which they drank a great deal and refilled the goatskin bag.

Wills was obliged to return afterwards with King to recover the saddles and things that were left when the camels strayed.

For some time Wright had been expected to arrive with the caravan from Menindie; yet a whole month passed and he did not come.

Burke who had now become very impatient at the loss of opportunity and time, determined to make a dash across the continent to the sea.

He therefore left Brahé, a man who could travel by compass and observation, in charge at Cooper's Creek depôt until Wright should arrive, giving him positive instructions to remain there until the return of the exploring party from the Gulf of Carpentaria, which he thought would be in about three or four months.

Burke started northwards on December 16, in company with Wills, King, and Gray, taking with them six camels, one horse, and provisions for three months, while Brahé, three men, and a native were left at the Creek with the rest of the horses and camels.

THE EXPEDITION WAS NOW IN three parts, and Wright, who perhaps knew more about the uncertainty of the seasons and the terrible consequences of drought than any of the party, still delayed leaving Menindie with his contingent, though he well knew that as the summer advanced the greater would be the difficulty to travel.

He had become faint-hearted, and every day invented some new excuse for not leaving. One day it was that there were not enough camels and horses to carry the necessary provision; the next, that the country through which they must pass was infested by blacks; the next, that he waited for his appointment to be confirmed by the authorities at Melbourne; and all this time he knew that Burke depended solely upon him to keep up communication with the depôt from the Darling.

Finally he started at the end of January (summer in Australia), more than a month after his appointment was officially confirmed, and more than two months after his return from Menindie.

For the first few days after Burke and Wills set off they followed up the creek, and though the banks were rugged and stony, there was plenty of grass and soft bush near. They soon fell in with a large tribe of blacks, the first they had seen, who followed them for some time, and constantly tried to entice them to their camp to dance. When they refused to go the natives became very troublesome, until they threatened to shoot them.

They were fine-looking men, but easily frightened, and only carried as a means of defence a shield and a large kind of boomerang.

The channel of the Creek was often quite dry for a great distance; then a chain of magnificent water-holes followed, from whose shady pools pelicans, black swans, and many species of duck flew up in flocks at the approach of the travellers.

After a few days they reached what seemed to be the end of Cooper's Creek, and, steering a more north-easterly course, they journeyed for some time over great plains covered by dry grass-stalks or barren sandy ridges, on the steep sides of which grew scant tufts of porcupine grass; sometimes following the lines of a creek, or, again, travelling along the edge of a splendid lagoon that stretched its placid waters for miles over the monotonous landscape.

Even the stony desert they found far from bad travelling ground, and but little different from much of what they had already crossed.

Yet ever before them there, from the sunrise to its setting, the spectral illusive shapes of the mirage floated like restless spirit betwixt heaven and earth on the quivering heat-haze.

On January 7 they crossed the Tropic of Capricorn, and their way beyond it soon began to improve.

In the excitement of exploring fine country Burke rushed on with almost headlong feverishness, travelling in every available hour of the day, and often by night, even grudging the necessary time for food and rest. He walked with Wills in front, taking it in turn with him to steer by a pocket compass.

Before they left each camp its number was cut deeply into the bark of some prominent tree. Wills kept the little record there is of their journey, and as they went it was the duty of King or Gray to blaze a tree to mark their route.

They passed now over many miles of the richly grassed slopes of a beautiful open forest, intersected by frequent watercourses where the land trended gradually upward to the distant mountain-range. Sometimes they had to go out of their course in order to avoid the tangle of tropic jungle; but onward north by east they went, beneath the shade of heavy-fruited palms, their road again made difficult by the large and numerous anthills that give these northern latitudes so strange a solemnity and appearance of desolation.

After leaving Cooper's Creek they often crossed the paths the blacks made for themselves, but had hitherto seen nothing of the natives. One day Golah, one of the camels (who were all now beginning to show great signs of fatigue), had gone down into the bed of a creek to drink, and could not be made to climb its steep sides again.

After several unsuccessful attempts to get him up, they determined to try bringing him down until an easier ascent could be found. King thereupon went on alone with him, and had great difficulty in getting him through some of the deeper water-holes.

But after going in this way for two or three miles they were forced to leave him behind, as it separated King from the rest of the party, and they found that a number of blacks were hiding in the box-trees on the banks, watching, and following them with stealthy footsteps.

It now became a very difficult matter for the camels to travel as the heavy rains that had fallen made the land so wet and boggy that with every footstep they sank several inches into it.

At Camp 119 Burke left them in charge of Gray and King, and walked on to the shores of Carpentaria with Wills, and took only the horse Billy to carry their provisions.

They followed the banks of a river which Burke named the Cloncurry. A few hundred yards below the camp Billy got bogged in a quicksand bank so deeply as to be unable to stir, and they had to undermine him on the creek side and pull him into the water. About five miles farther on he bogged again, and afterwards was so weak that he could hardly crawl.

After floundering along in this way for some time they came upon a native path which led through a forest; following it, they reached a large patch of sandy ground where the blacks had been digging yams and had left numbers lying on the surface; and these the explorers were glad enough to eat.

A little farther on they saw a black lying coiled round his camp fire, and by him squatted his lubra and piccaninny yabbering at a great rate. They stopped to take out their pistols in case of need before disturbing them; almost immediately the black got up to stretch his limbs, and presently saw the intruders.

He stared at them for some time, as if he thought he must be dreaming, then, signing to the others, they all dropped on their haunches, and shuffled off in the quietest manner.

Near their fire was a worley (native hut) large enough to shelter a dozen blacks; it was on the northern outskirt of the forest, and looked out across a marsh which is sometimes flooded by sea-water. Upon this were hundreds of wild geese, plover, and pelicans. After they crossed it they reached a channel through which the sea-water enters, and there passed three blacks, who silently and unasked pointed out the best way to go.

Next day, Billy being completely tired, they short-hobbled and left him, going forward again at daybreak in the hope of at last reaching the open sea. After following the Flinders (this country had already been explored by Gregory) for about fifteen miles, and finding that the tide ebbed and flowed regularly, and that the water was quite salt, they decided to go back, having successfully accomplished one great object of their mission, by crossing the Australian continent from south to north.

After rejoining Gray and King on February 13, the whole party began the return march. The incessant and heavy rains that had set in rendered travelling very difficult; but the provisions were running short, and it was necessary to try to get back to the depôt without delay.

The damp and suffocating heat that brooded in the air overpowered both man and beast, who were weak and weary from want of rest; and to breast the heavy rains and to swim the rapid creeks in flood well-nigh exhausted all their strength.

Day after day they stumbled listlessly onward; while the poor camels, sweating, bleeding, and groaning from fear, had their feet at almost every step entangled by the climbing plants that clung to the rank grasses, which had rushed in magical growth to a height of eight or ten feet.

If for a moment they went to windward of their camp fires they were maddened by swarms of mosquitoes, and everywhere were pestered by ants.

Wonderful green and scarlet ants dropped upon them from the trees as they passed; from every log or stick gathered for the fires a new species crept; inch-long black or brown "bulldogs" showed fight at them underfoot: midgets lurked in the cups of flowers; while the giant white ant ate its stealthy way in swarms through the sap of the forest trees from root to crown.

Every night fierce storms of thunder crashed and crackled overhead, and the vivid lightning flaring across the heavens overpowered the moonlight.

Gray, who had been ailing for some time, grew worse, though probably, as they were all in such evil plight, they did not think him really ill.

One night Wills, returning to a camp to bring back some things that had been left, found him hiding behind a tree eating skilligolee. He explained he was suffering from dysentery, and had taken the flour without leave.

It had already been noticed that the provisions disappeared in an unaccountable way; therefore Wills ordered him back to report himself to Burke. But Gray was afraid to tell, and got King to do so for him. When Burke heard of it, he was very angry, and flogged him.

On March 20 they overhauled the packs, and left all they could do without behind, as the camels were so exhausted.

Soon after this they were again beyond the line of rainfall, and once more toiling over the vast plains and endless stony rises of the interior.

At the camp called Boocha's Rest they killed the camel Boocha, and spent the whole day cutting up and jerking the flesh—that is, removing all bone and fat and drying the lean parts in the sun; they also now made use of a plant called portulac as a vegetable, and found it very good, and a great addition to their food.

For more than a week it had become very troublesome to get Gray to walk at all; he was still in such bad odour from his thieving that the rest of the party thought he pretended illness, and as they had to halt continually to wait for him when marching, he was always in mischief.

The faithful Billy had to be sacrificed in the Stony Desert, as he was so reduced and knocked up that there seemed little chance of his reaching the other side; and another day was taken to cut up and jerk his flesh.

At dawn on the fourth day before they reached the depôt, when they were preparing to start they were shocked to find poor Gray was dying.

His companions, full of remorse for bygone harshness, their better natures stirred to the depths of humanity by his pitiful case, knelt around to support him in those last moments as he lay stretched speechless on his desolate sand bed. Thus comforted, his fading eyes closed for ever as the red sun rose above the level plain.

The party remained in camp that day to bury him, though they were so weak that they were hardly able to dig a grave in the sand sufficiently deep for the purpose.

They had lived on the flesh of the worn-out horse for fifteen days, and once or twice were forced to camp without water. Though the sun was always hot, at night a gusty wind blew from the south with an edge like a razor, which made their fire so irregular as to be of little use to them. The sudden and cruel extremes of heat and cold racked the exhausted frames of the explorers with pain, and Burke and King were hardly able to walk. They pushed on, only sustained by the thought that but a few hours, a few miles, now separated them from the main party, where the first felicitations on the success of their exploit awaited them, and, what was of greater importance to men shattered by hardships and privation, wholesome food, fresh clothing, and the comfort of a properly organised camp.

On the morning of April 21, with every impatient nerve strung to its utmost tension, and full of hope, they urged their two remaining camels forward for the last thirty miles; and Burke, who rode a little in advance of the others, shouted for joy when they struck Cooper's Creek at the exact spot where Brahé had been left in charge of the depôt.

"I think I see their tents," he cried, and putting his weary camel to its best speed, he called out the names of the men he had left there.

"There they are! There they are!" he shouted eagerly, and with a last spurt left the others far behind.

When Wills and King reached the depôt they saw Burke standing by the side of his camel in a deserted camp, *alone*.

He was standing, lost in amazement, staring vacantly around. Signs of recent departure, of a final packing-up, everywhere met the eye: odd nails and horseshoes lay about, with other useful things that would not have been left had the occupants merely decamped to some other spot. Then, as one struck by some terrible blow, Burke reeled and fell to the ground, overcome by the revulsion of feeling from exultant hope to sudden despair.

Wills, who had ever the greater control of himself, now walked in all directions to make a careful examination, followed at a little distance by King.

Presently he stopped, and pointing to a tree, into the bark of which had been newly cut the words—

"DIG.
"April 21, 1861"

he said:—

"*King, they are gone!* They have only gone to-day—there are the things they have left!"

The two men immediately set to work to uncover the earth, and found a few inches below the surface a box containing provisions and a bottle.

In the bottle was a note, which was taken to Burke at once, who read it aloud:—

Depôt, Cooper's Creek,
April 21, 1861

The depôt party of the Victorian Exploring
Expedition leaves this camp to-day to return to the
Darling.

"I intend to go S.E. from Camp 60, to get into our old track near Bulloo. Two of my companions and myself are quite well; the third—Patten—has been unable to walk for the last eighteen days, as his leg has been severely hurt when thrown by one of the horses.

"No person has been up here from the Darling.

"We have six camels and twelve horses in good working condition.

WILLIAM BRAHÉ

When the leader had finished reading it, he turned to the others and asked if they would start next day to try to overtake Brahé's party.

They replied that they could not. With the slightest exertion all felt the indescribable languor and terrible aching in back and legs that had proved fatal to poor Gray. And, indeed, it was as much as any one of them could do to crawl to the side of the creek for a billy of water.

They were not long in getting out the stores Brahé had left, and in making themselves a good supper of oatmeal porridge and sugar.

This and the excitement of their unexpected position did much to revive them. Burke presently decided to make for a station on the South Australian side which he believed was only one hundred and twenty miles from the Cooper. Both Wills and King wanted to follow down their old track to the Darling, but afterwards gave in to Burke's idea. Therefore it was arranged that after they had rested they would proceed by gentle stages towards the Mount Hopeless sheeprun.

Accordingly, on the next day Burke wrote and deposited in the cache a letter giving a sketch of the exploration, and added the following postscript:

"The camels cannot travel, and we cannot walk, or we should follow the other party. We shall move very slowly down the Creek."

The cache was again covered with earth, and left as they had found it, though nothing was added to the word "Dig," or to the date on the tree; which curious carelessness on the part of men accustomed to note every camping-ground in this way seems unaccountable.

A few days after their return they started with the month's supply of provisions that had been left.

They had every reason to hope, with the help of the camels, they might easily reach Mount Hopeless in time to preserve their lives and to reap the reward of their successful exertions.

It will be remembered that when Burke formally appointed Brahé as officer in command of the depôt until Wright should arrive, he was told to await his leader's return to Cooper's Creek, *or not to leave it until obliged by absolute necessity*. Day after day, week after week passed, and Wright, with the rest of the stores from Menindie, never came. It was more than four months since Burke's party went north, and every day for the last six weeks Brahé had looked out anxiously for their return.

On one hand he was worried by Patten, who was dying, and who wanted to go back to the Darling for advice; on the other, by M'Donough's continually pouring into his ears the assurance that Burke would not return that way, but had doubtless by this time made for some port on the Queensland coast, and had returned to Melbourne by sea; and that if they stayed at the depôt they would all get scurvy, and in the end die of starvation. Though they had sufficient provisions to keep them for another month, they decided to start on the morning of April 21, leaving the box of stores and the note hidden in the earth which the explorers found on their return.

Following their former route towards the Darling, they fell in with Wright's party at Bulloo, where they had been stationary for several weeks, and where three of the men had died of scurvy.

Brahé at once put himself under Wright's orders; but he did not rest until Wright consented to go to Cooper's Creek with him, so that before abandoning the expedition he might feel assured that the explorers had not returned.

Wright and Brahé reached the depôt on May 8, a fortnight after the others had left, and Brahé seeing nothing above ground in the camp to lead him to think anyone had been there, did not trouble to disturb the box which he had originally planted—as Wright suggested the blacks would be more likely to find it; therefore, running their horses several times over the spot, they completed by their thoughtless stupidity the most terrible blunder the explorers had begun.

Wright and Brahé then rejoined the camp at Bulloo, when all moved back to Menindie, and reached that place on June 18.

Brahé at once set off for Melbourne, and by this time everyone there seemed to be alive to the necessity of sending out to look for the explorers.

Two steamers were despatched to the Gulf of Carpentaria, and a relief party, in charge of Alfred Howitt, up to the Cooper.

From South Australia an organised expedition of twenty-six men, with McKinlay as leader, was already engaged in the search, as well as several smaller parties from the neighbouring colonies.

Burke, Wills, and King, much revived with the rest of a few days and the food they had found at the depôt, left for Mount Hopeless, with the intention of following as nearly as possible the route taken by Gregory many years before.

Shortly after their departure Landa, one of the camels, bogged at the side of a water-hole and sank rapidly, as the ground beneath was a bottomless quicksand; all their efforts to dig him out were useless, and they had to shoot him where he lay, and cut off what flesh they could get at to jerk.

They made a fresh start next day with the last camel, Rajah, only loaded with the most useful and necessary articles; and each of the men now carried his own swag of bed and clothing.

In addition to these misfortunes they had now to contend with the blast of drought that lay over the land; with the fiery sun, that streamed from cloudless skies, beneath which the very earth shrunk from itself in gaping fissures; with the wild night wind, that shrieked and skirled with devastating breath over the wilderness beneath the cold light of the crowding stars.

For a few days they followed the Creek, but found that it split up into sandy channels which became rapidly smaller as they advanced, and sent off large billabongs (or backwaters) to the south, slightly changing the course of the Creek each time, until it disappeared altogether in a north-westerly direction. Burke and Wills went forward alone to reconnoitre, and found that the land as far as they could see stretched away in great earthy plains intersected by lines of trees and empty watercourses.

Next day they retraced their steps to the last camp, and realised that their rations were rapidly diminishing and their boots and clothing falling to pieces.

Rajah was very ill and on the point of dying, when Burke ordered him to be shot, his flesh being afterwards dried in the usual manner.

Some friendly blacks, whom they amused by lighting fires with matches, gave them some fish and a kind of bread called nardoo.

At various times they had tried to learn from the blacks how to procure the nardoo grain, which is the seed of a small clover-like plant, but had failed to make them understand what they wanted.

Then Wills went out alone to look for it; but as he expected to find it growing on a tree, was of course unsuccessful, and the blacks had again moved off to some other branch of the Creek.

The terrible fate of death from starvation awaited them if they could not obtain this knowledge, and for several days they all persevered with the search, until quite by chance King at last caught sight of some seeds which proved to be nardoo lying at the foot of a sandhill, and they soon found the plain beyond was black with it.

ANDREW LANG AND H. RIDER HAGGARD

With the reassurance that they could now support themselves they made another attempt to reach Mount Hopeless. Burke and King each carried a billy of water, and the last of the provisions was packed up in their swags; but after travelling for three days they found no water, and were forced to turn back to the Creek, at a point where—though they knew it not—scarce fifty miles remained to be accomplished, and just as Mount Hopeless would have appeared above the horizon had they continued their route for even another day.

Wearily they retraced their footsteps to the water and to the prospect of existence. They at once set about collecting nardoo; two of them were employed in gathering it, while one stayed in camp to clean and crush it.

In a few days Burke sent Wills back to the depôt to bury the field-books of their journey north in the cache, and another letter to tell of their present condition.

When Wills reached the spot he could see no trace of anyone having been there but natives, and that the hiding-place had not been touched.

Having deposited the field-books and a note, with an account of their sufferings and a pitiful and useless appeal for food and clothing, he started back to rejoin Burke, terribly fatigued and weak from his long walk.

It had taken him eleven days to cover the seventy miles to and fro, and he had had very little to eat.

However, to his surprise, one morning, on his way back he heard a cooee from the opposite bank of the Creek, and saw Pitchery, the chief of the friendly blacks, beckoning to him to come to their camp. Pitchery made him sit down by a fire, upon which a large pile of fish was cooking.

This he thought was to provide a breakfast for the half-dozen natives who sat around; but to his astonishment they made him eat the whole lot, while they sat by extracting the bones.

Afterwards a supply of nardoo was given him; at which he ate until he could eat no more. The blacks then asked him to stay the night with them; but as he was anxious to rejoin Burke and King, he went on.

In his absence Burke, while frying some fish that the natives had given him, had set fire to the mia-mia (a shelter made by the blacks of bushes and trees).

It burnt so quickly that every remnant of their clothing was destroyed, and nothing saved but a gun.

In a few days they all started back towards the depôt, in the hope that they could live with the blacks; but they found they had again disappeared.

On again next morning to another of the native camps; but, finding it empty, the wanderers took possession of the best mia-mia, and Wills and King were sent out to collect nardoo.

This was now absolutely their only food, with the exception of two crows which King shot; he alone seemed to be uninjured by the nardoo. Wills had at last suddenly collapsed, and could only lie in the mia-mia, and philosophically contemplate the situation.

He strongly advised Burke and King to leave him, as the only chance for the salvation of any one of them now was to find the blacks.

Very reluctantly at last Burke consented to go; and after placing a large supply of nardoo, wood, and water within easy reach, Burke said again:

"I will not leave you, Wills, under any other circumstance than that of your own wish."

And Wills, again repeating "It is our only chance," gave him a letter and his watch for his father.

King had already buried the rest of the field-books near the mia-mia.

THE FIRST DAY AFTER THEY left Wills Burke was very weak, and complained sadly of great pain in his back and legs. Next day he was a little better, and walked for about two miles, then lay down and said he could go no farther.

King managed to get him up, but as he went he dropped his swag and threw away everything he had to carry.

When they halted he said he felt much worse, and could not last many hours longer, and he gave his pocket-book to King, saying:—

"I hope you will remain with me till I am quite dead—it is a comfort to know someone is by; but when I am dying, it is my wish that you should place the pistol in my right hand, and that you leave me unburied as I lie."

Doubtless he thought of King's weak state, and wished to spare him the labour of digging a grave.

The last of the misfortunes that had followed the enterprise from the outset, misfortunes in many cases caused by the impatient zeal of its leader, was drawing to its close.

Tortured by disappointment and despair, racked by starvation and disease, he lay in the desert dying.

Flinging aside the last poor chance of succour, renouncing all hope that he might yet live to reap the reward of his brilliant dash across the continent, he met death

> *"With the pistol clenched in his failing hand,*
> *With the death mist spread o'er his fading eyes*
> *He saw the sun go down on the sand,*
> *And he slept—and never saw it rise."*

King lingered near the spot for a few hours; but at last, feeling it to be useless, he went on up the Creek to look for the natives.

In one of their deserted mia-mias he found a large store of the nardoo seed, and, carrying it with him, returned to Wills.

On his way back he shot three crows. This addition to their food would, he felt, give them a chance of tiding over their difficulties until the blacks could again be found. But as he drew near the mia-mia where he and poor Burke had left Wills a few days before, and saw his lonely figure in the distance lying much as they had left him, a sudden fear came upon him.

Hitherto the awful quiet of these desolate scenes had little impressed him, and now it came upon him heavily. The shrilling of a solitary locust somewhere in the gums, the brisk crackle of dry bark and twigs as he trod, the melancholy sighing of the wind-stirred leafage, offered him those inexplicable contrasts that give stress to silence.

Anxious to escape thoughts so little comprehended, King hurried on, and essayed a feeble "cooee" when a few yards from the sleeper. No answering sound or gesture greeted him.

Wills had fallen peacefully asleep for ever.

Footprints on the sand showed that the blacks had already been there, and after King had buried the corpse with sand and rushes as well as he was able, he started to follow their tracks.

Feeling desperately lonely and ill, he went on, and as he went he shot some more crows. The blacks, hearing the report of the gun, came to meet him, and taking him to their camp gave him food.

The next day they talked to him by signs, putting one finger in the ground and covering it with sand, at the same time pointing up the Creek, saying "White fellow."

By this they meant that one white man was dead.

King, by putting two fingers in the sand and covering them, made them understand that his second companion was also dead.

Finding he was now quite alone, they seemed very sorry for him, and gave him plenty to eat. However, in a few days they became tired of him, and by signs told him they meant to go up the Creek, pointing in the opposite direction to show that that must be his way. But when he shot some more crows for them they were very pleased. One woman to whom he gave a part of a crow gave him a ball of nardoo, and, showing him a wound on her arm, intimated that she would give him more, but she was unable to pound it. When King saw the wound he boiled some water in his billy and bathed it. While the whole tribe sat round, watching and yabbering excitedly, he touched it with some lunar caustic; she shrieked and ran off, crying "mokow! mokow!" (fire! fire!) She was, however, very grateful for his kindness, and from that time she and her husband provided him with food.

ABOUT TWO MONTHS LATER THE relief party reached the depôt, where they found the letters and journals the explorers had placed in the cache. They at once set off down the Creek, in the hope still of finding Burke and Wills. They met a black who directed them to the native camp. Here they found King sitting alone in the mia-mia the natives had made for him, wasted and worn to a shadow, almost imbecile from the terrible hardships he had suffered.

He turned his hopeless face upon the new-comers, staring vacantly at them, muttering indistinctly words which his lips refused to articulate. Only the remnants of his clothing marked him as a civilised being. The blacks who had fed him sat round to watch the meeting with most gratified and delighted expressions.

Howitt waited for a few days to give King an opportunity of recovering his strength, that he might show them where the bodies of his unfortunate leaders lay, that the last sad duty to the dead might be performed before they left the place.

Burke's body had been dragged a short distance from where it originally lay, and was partly eaten by the dingoes (wild dogs). The remains were carefully collected, wrapped in a Union Jack, and placed in a grave dug close to the spot.

A FEW WEEKS LATER THE citizens of Melbourne, once again aroused to extravagant enthusiasm, lined the streets through which the only survivor of the only Victorian Exploration Expedition was to pass.

ANDREW LANG AND H. RIDER HAGGARD

"Here he comes! Here he comes!" rang throughout the crowd as King was driven to the Town Hall to tell his narrative to the company assembled there.

"There is a man!" shouted one—"There is a man who has lived in hell."

A FEW MONTHS LATER HOWITT was again sent to Cooper's Creek to exhume the bodies of Burke and Wills and bring them to Melbourne. They were honoured by a public funeral, and a monument was erected to their memory—

> *"A statue tall, on a pillar of stone,*
> *Telling its story to great and small*
> *Of the dust reclaimed from the sand-waste lone."*

The Story of Emund (a.d. 1020)

There was a man named Emund of Skara; lawman in Western Gautland, and very wise and eloquent. Of high birth he was, had a numerous kin, and was very wealthy. Men deemed him cunning, and not very trusty. He passed for the man of most weight in West Gautland now that the Earl was gone away.

At the time when Earl Rognvald left Gautland the Gauts held assemblies, and often murmured among themselves about what the Swedish king was intending. They heard that he was wroth with them for having made a friendship with Olaf, King of Norway, rather than quarrel. He also charged with crime those men who had accompanied his daughter Astridr to Norway's king. And some said that they should seek protection of the Norse king and offer him their service; while others were against this, and said that the West Gauts had no strength to maintain a quarrel against the Swedes, "and the Norse king is far from us," they said, "because the main power of his land is far: and this is the first thing we must do, send men to the Swedish king and try to make agreement with him; but if that cannot be done, then take we the other choice of seeking the protection of the Norse king."

So the landowners asked Emund to go on this mission, to which he assented, and went his way with thirty men, and came to East Gautland. There he had many kinsmen and friends, and was well received. He had there some talk with the wisest men about this difficulty, and they were quite agreed in thinking that what the King was doing with them was against use and law. Then Emund went on to Sweden, and there talked with many great men; and there too all were of the same mind. He then held on his way till he came on the evening of a day to Upsala. There they found them good lodging and passed the night. The next day Emund went before the King as he sat in council with many around him. Emund went up to the King, and bowed down before him, and greeted him. The King looked at him, returned his greeting, and asked him what tidings he brought.

Emund answered: "Little tidings are there with us Gauts. But this we deem a novelty: Atti the Silly in Vermaland went in the winter up to the forest with his snowshoes and bow; we call him a mighty hunter. On the fell he got such store of grey fur that he had filled his sledge with as much as he could manage to draw after him. He turned him homeward from the forest; but then he saw a squirrel in the wood, and shot at him and missed. Then was he wroth, and, loosing from him his sledge, he ran after the squirrel. But the squirrel went ever where the wood was thickest, sometimes near the tree roots, sometimes high among the boughs, and passed among the boughs from tree to tree. But when Atti shot at him, the arrow always flew above or below him, while the squirrel never went so that Atti could not see him. So eager was he in this chase that he crept after him for the whole day, but never could he get this squirrel. And when darkness came on, he lay down in the snow, as he was wont, and so passed the night; 'twas drifting weather. Next day Atti went to seek his sledge, but he never found it again; and so he went home. Such are my tidings, sire."

Said the King: "Little tidings these, if there be no more to say."

Emund answered: "Yet further a while ago happened this, which one may call tidings. Gauti Tofason went out with five warships by the river Gaut Elbe; but when he lay by the Eikr Isles, some Danes came there with five large merchant ships. Gauti and his company soon captured four of the merchant ships without losing a man, and took great store of wealth; but the fifth ship escaped out to sea by sailing. Gauti went after that one ship, and at first gained on it; but soon, as the wind freshened, the merchant ship went faster. They had got far out to sea, and Gauti wished to turn back; but a storm came on, and his ship was wrecked on an island, and all the wealth lost and the more part of the men. Meanwhile his comrades had had to stay at the Eikr Isles. Then attacked them fifteen Danish merchant ships, and slew them all, and took all the wealth which they had before gotten. Such was the end of this covetousness."

The King answered: "Great tidings these, and worth telling; but what is thy errand hither?"

Emund answered: "I come, sire, to seek a solution in a difficulty where our law and Upsala law differ."

The King asked: "What is it of which thou wouldst complain?"

Emund answered: "There were two men, nobly born, equal in family, but unequal in possessions and disposition. They quarrelled about lands, and each wrought harm on the other, and he wrought the more who was the more powerful, till their dispute was settled and judged at the general assembly. He who was the more powerful was condemned to pay; but at the first repayment he paid wildgoose for goose, little pig for old swine, and for a mark of gold he put down half a mark of gold, the other half-mark of clay and mould, and yet further threatened with rough treatment the man to whom he was paying this debt. What is thy judgment herein, sire?"

The King answered: "Let him pay in full what was adjudged, and to his King thrice that amount. And if it be not paid within the year, then let him go an outlaw from all his possessions, let half his wealth come into the King's treasury, and half to the man to whom he owed redress."

Emund appealed to all the greatest men there, and to the laws valid at Upsala Thing in witness of this decision. Then he saluted the King and went out. Other men brought their complaints before the King, and he sat long time over men's suits.

But when the King came to table he asked where was lawman Emund.

He was told that he was at home in his lodging.

Then said the King: "Go after him, he shall be my guest to-day."

Just then came in the viands, and afterwards players with harps and fiddles and other music, and then drink was served. The King was very merry, and had many great men as his guests, and thought no more of Emund. He drank for the rest of the day, and slept that night.

But in the morning, when the King waked, then he bethought him of what Emund had talked of the day before. And so soon as he was dressed he had his wise men summoned to him. King Olaf had ever about him twelve of the wisest men; they sate with him over judgments and counselled him in difficulties; and that was no easy task, for while the King liked it ill if judgment was perverted, he yet would not hear any contradiction of himself. When they were met thus in council, the King took the word, and bade Emund be called thither.

But the messenger came back and said: "Sire, Emund the lawman rode away yesterday immediately after he had supped."

Then spake the King: "Tell me this, noble lords, whereto pointed that law question of which Emund asked yesterday?"

They answered: "Sire, thou wilt have understood it, if it meant more than his mere words."

The King said: "By those two nobly-born men of whom he told the story that they disputed, the one more powerful than the other, and each wrought the other harm, he meant me and Olaf Stout."

"It is even so, sire," said they, "as thou sayest."

The King went on: "Judgment there was in our cause at the Upsala

Thing. But what did that mean which he said about the under-payment, wildgoose for goose, little pig for old swine, half clay for gold?"

Arnvid the Blind answered: "Sire," said he, "very unlike are red gold and clay, but more different are king and thrall. Thou didst promise to Olaf Stout thy daughter Ingigerdr, who is of royal birth on both sides, and of Up-Swedish family, the highest in the North, for it derives from the gods themselves. But now King Olaf has gotten to wife Astridr. And though she is a king's child, yet her mother is a bondwoman and a Wendlander."

There were three brothers then in the council; Arnvid the Blind, whose sight was so dim that he could scarce bear arms, but he was very eloquent; the second was Thorvid the Stammerer, who could not speak more than two words together, he was most bold and sincere; the third was called Freyvid the Deaf, he was hard of hearing. These brothers were all powerful men, wealthy, of noble kin, prudent, and all were dear to the King.

Then said King Olaf: "What means that which Emund told of Atti the Silly?"

None answered, but they looked at one another.

Said the King, "Speak now."

Then said Thorvid the Stammerer: "Atti quarrelsome, covetous, ill-willed, silly, foolish."

Then asked the King, "Against whom is aimed this cut?"

Then answered Freyvid the Deaf: "Sire, men will speak more openly, if that may be with thy permission."

Said the King: "Speak now, Freyvid, with permission what thou wilt."

Freyvid then took the word: "Thorvid my brother, who is called the wisest of us, calls the man Atti quarrelsome, silly, and foolish. He calls him so because, ill-content with peace, he hunts eagerly after small things, and yet gets them not, while for their sake he throws away great and good things. I am deaf, but now so many have spoken that I have been able to understand that men both great and small like it ill that thou, sire, keepest not thy word with the King of Norway. And still worse like they this: that thou makest of none effect the judgment of the General Assembly at Upsala. Thou hast no need to fear King of Norway or of Danes, nor anyone else, while the armies of Sweden will follow thee. But if the people of the land turn against thee with one consent, then we thy friends see no counsel that is sure to avail."

The King asked: "Who are the leading men in this counsel to take the land from me?"

Freyvid answered: "All the Swedes wish to have old law and their full right. Look now, sire, how many of thy nobles sit in council here with thee. I think we be here but six whom thou callest thy counsellors; all the others have ridden away, and are gone into the provinces, and are holding meetings with the people of the land; and, to tell thee the truth, the war-arrow is cut, and sent round all the land, and a high court appointed. All we brothers have been asked to take part in this counsel, but not one of us will bear this name and be called traitor to his king, for our fathers were never such."

Then said the King: "What expedient can we find? A great difficulty is upon us: give ye counsel, noble sirs, that I may keep the kingdom and my inheritance from my fathers; I wish not to contend against all the host of Sweden."

Arnvid the Blind answered: "Sire, this seems to me good counsel: that thou ride down to Aros with such as will follow thee, take ship there, and go out to the lake; there appoint a meeting with the people. Behave not with hardness, but offer men law and land right; put down the war-arrow, it will not have gone far round the land in so short a time; send men of thine whom thou canst trust to meet those men who have this business in hand, and try if this tumult can be quieted."

The King said that he would accept this counsel. "I will," said he, "that ye brothers go on this mission, for I trust you best of my men."

Then said Thorvid the Stammerer: "I will remain behind, but let thy son Jacob go; this is needful."

And Freyvid said: "Let us do, sire, even as Thorvid says; he will not leave thee in this peril; but I and Arnvid will go."

So this counsel was followed. King Olaf went to his ships and stood out to the lake, and many men soon joined him there. But the brothers Freyvid and Arnvid rode out to Ullar-acre, taking with them Jacob, the King's son, but his going they kept secret. They soon got to know that there was a gathering and rush to arms, and the country people held meetings both by day and night.

But when Freyvid and his party met their kinsmen and friends they said that they would join their company, and this offer all accepted joyfully.

At once the deliberation was referred to the two brothers, and numbers followed them, yet all were at one in saying that they would

ANDREW LANG AND H. RIDER HAGGARD

no longer have Olaf king over them, and would not endure his breaches of law and his arrogance, for he would hear no man's cause, even though great chiefs told him the truth.

But when Freyvid found the vehemence of the people, then he saw into what danger matters had come, and he held a meeting with the chiefs, and thus spoke before them: "It seems to me that if this great measure is to be taken, to remove Olaf Ericsson from the kingdom, we Up-Swedes ought to have the ruling of it; it has always been so, that what the chiefs of the Up-Swedes have resolved among them, to this the other men of the land have listened. Our fathers needed not to receive advice from the West Gauts about their ruling of the land. Now are we not so degenerate that Emund need teach us counsel; I would have us bind our counsel together, kinsmen and friends."

To this all agreed, and thought it well said. After that the whole multitude of the people turned to join this union of the Up-Swedish chiefs; so then Freyvid and Arnvid became chiefs over the people. But when Emund found this, he guessed how the matter would end. So he went to meet these brothers, and they had a talk together; and Freyvid asked Emund: "What mean ye to do if Olaf Ericsson is killed; what king will ye have?"

Emund answered; "Whosoever suits us best, whether of royal family or not."

Freyvid answered: "We Up-Swedes will not that the kingdom in our days go out of the family who from father to son have long held it, while such good means may be taken to shun that as now can be. King Olaf has two sons, and we will have one of them for king. There is, however, a great difference between them; one is nobly born and Swedish on both sides, the other is a bondwoman's son and half Wendish."

At this decision there was great acclaim, and all would have Jacob for king.

Then said Emund: "You Up-Swedes have power to rule this for the time; but I warn you that hereafter some of those who will not hear now of anything else but that the kingdom of Sweden go in the royal line, will themselves live to consent that the kingdom pass into other families, and that will turn out better."

After this the brothers Freyvid and Arnvid caused Jacob the King's son to be led before the assembly, and there they gave him the title of king, and therewith the Swedes gave him the name Onund, and henceforth he was so called. He was then ten or twelve years old.

Then King Onund took to him guards, and chose chiefs with such force of men about them as seemed needful; and he gave the common people of the land leave to go home. Thereafter messengers passed between the kings, and soon they met and made their agreement. Olaf was to be king over the land while he lived; he was to hold to peace and agreement with the King of Norway, as also with all those men who had been implicated in this counsel. Onund was also to be king, and have so much of the land as father and son might think fit; but was to be bound to follow the landowners if King Olaf did any of those things which they would not tolerate.

After this messengers went to Norway to seek King Olaf with this errand, that he should come with a fleet to Konunga Hella (Kings' Stone) to meet the Swedish king, and that the Swedish king wished that they should there ratify their treaty. King Olaf was still, as before, desirous of peace, and came with his fleet as proposed. The Swedish king also came, and when father-in-law and son-in-law met, they bound them to agreement and peace. Olaf the Swedish king showed him affable and gentle.

Thorstein the Learned says that there was in Hising a portion of land that had sometimes belonged to Norway, sometimes to Gautland. The kings agreed between them that for this possession they would casts lots with dice; he was to have it who should cast the higher throw. The Swedish king threw two sixes, and said that King Olaf need not cast.

He answered, while shaking the dice in his hand: "There are yet two sixes on the dice, and it is but a little thing for God to let them turn up." He cast, and turned up two sixes. Then Olaf the Swedish king cast, and again two sixes. Then cast Olaf, King of Norway, and there was six on one die, but the other split in two, and there were then seven. So he got the portion of land. We have heard no more tidings of that meeting. The kings parted reconciled.

The Man in White

"A little while ago," writes Mademoiselle Aïssé, the Greek captive who was such a charming figure in Paris during the opening years of Louis XV's reign, "a little while ago a strange thing happened here, which caused a great deal of talk. It cannot be more than six weeks since Bessé the surgeon received a note, begging him to come without fail that afternoon at six o'clock to the Rue au Fer, near the Luxembourg Palace. Punctually at the hour named the surgeon arrived on the spot, where he found a man awaiting him. This man conducted the surgeon to a house a few steps further on, and motioning him to enter through the open door, promptly closed it, and remained himself outside. Bessé was surprised to find himself alone, and wondered why he had been brought there; but he had not to wait long, for the housekeeper soon appeared, who informed him that he was expected, and that he was to go up to the first story. The surgeon did as he was told, and opened the door of an anteroom all hung with white. Here he was met by an elegant lackey, dressed also in white, frizzed and powdered, with his white hair tied in a bag wig, carrying two torches in his hand, who requested the bewildered doctor to wipe his shoes. Bessé replied that this was quite unnecessary, as he had only just stepped out of his sedan chair and was not in the least muddy, but the lackey rejoined that everything in the house was so extraordinarily clean that it was impossible to be too careful.

"His shoes being wiped, Bessé was next led into another room, hung with white like the first. A second lackey, in every respect similar to the other, made his appearance; again the doctor was forced to wipe his shoes, and for the third time he was conducted into a room, where carpets, chairs, sofas, and bed were all as white as snow. A tall figure dressed in a white dressing-gown and nightcap, and having its face covered by a white mask, sat by the fire. The moment this ghostly object perceived Bessé, he observed, 'My body is possessed by the devil,' and then was silent. For three-quarters of an hour they remained thus, the white figure occupying himself with incessantly putting on and taking off six pairs of white gloves, which were placed on a white table beside him. The strangeness of the whole affair made Bessé feel very uncomfortable, but when his eyes fell on a variety of firearms in one corner of the room he became so frightened that he was obliged to sit down, lest his legs should give way.

"At last the dead silence grew more than he could bear, and he turned to the white figure and asked what they wanted of him, and begged that his orders might be given him as soon as possible, as his time belonged to the public and he was needed elsewhere. To this the white figure only answered coldly, 'What does that matter, as long as you are well paid?' and again was silent. Another quarter of an hour passed, and then the white figure suddenly pulled one of the white bell-ropes. When the summons was answered by the two white lackeys, the figure desired them to bring some bandages, and commanded Bessé to bleed him, and to take from him five pounds of blood. The surgeon, amazed at the quantity, inquired what doctor had ordered such extensive blood-letting. 'I myself,' replied the white figure. Bessé felt that he was too much upset by all he had gone through to trust himself to bleed in the arm without great risk of injury, so he decided to perform the operation on the foot, which is far less dangerous. Hot water was brought, and the white phantom removed a pair of white thread stockings of wonderful beauty, then another and another, up to six, and took off a slipper of beaver lined with white. The leg and foot thus left bare were the prettiest in the world; and Bessé began to think that the figure before him must be that of a woman. At the second basinful the patient showed signs of fainting, and Bessé wished to loosen the mask, in order to give him more air. This was, however, prevented by the lackeys, who stretched him on the floor, and Bessé bandaged the foot before the patient had recovered from his fainting fit. Directly he came to himself, the white figure ordered his bed to be warmed, and as soon as it was done he lay down in it. The servants left the room, and Bessé, after feeling his pulse, walked over to the fireplace to clean his lancet, thinking all the while of his strange adventure. Suddenly he heard a noise behind him, and, turning his head, he saw reflected in the mirror the white figure coming hopping towards him. His heart sank with terror, but the figure only took five crowns from the chimneypiece, and handed them to him, asking at the same time if he would be satisfied with that payment. Trembling all over, Bessé replied that he was. 'Well, then, be off as fast as you can,' was the rejoinder. Bessé did not need to be told twice, but made the best of his way out. As before the lackeys were awaiting him with lights, and as they walked he noticed that they looked at each other and smiled. At length Bessé, provoked at this behaviour, inquired what they were laughing at. 'Ah, Monsieur,' was their answer, 'what cause have you to complain? Has anyone done you any harm, and have

ANDREW LANG AND H. RIDER HAGGARD

you not been well paid for your services?' So saying they conducted him to his chair, and truly thankful he was to be out of the house. He rapidly made up his mind to keep silence about his adventures, but the following day someone sent to inquire how he was feeling after having bled the Man in White. Bessé saw that it was useless to make a mystery of the affair, and related exactly what had happened, and it soon came to the ears of the King. But who was the Man in White? Echo answers 'Who?'"

The Adventures of "the Bull of Earlstoun"

This is the story of the life of Alexander Gordon, of Earlstoun in Galloway. Earlstoun is a bonny place, sitting above the waterside of the Ken in the fair strath of the Glenkens, in the Stewartry of Kirkcudbright. The grey tower stands ruinous and empty to-day, but once it was a pleasant dwelling, and dear to the hearts of those that had dwelt in it when they were in foreign lands or hiding out on the wild wide moors. It was the time when Charles II wished to compel the most part of the people of Scotland to change their religion and worship as he bade them. Some obeyed the King; but most hated the new order of things, and cleaved in their hearts to their old ways and to their old ministers, who had been put out of their kirks and manses at the coming of the King. Many even set themselves to resist the King in open battle rather than obey him in the matter of their consciences. It was only in this that they were rebellious, for many of them had been active in bringing him again to the throne.

Among those who thus went out to fight were William Gordon and his son Alexander. William Gordon was a grave, courteous, and venerable man, and his estate was one of the best in all the province of Galloway. Like nearly all the lairds in the south and west he was strongly of the Presbyterian party, and resolved to give up life and lands rather than his principles. Now the King was doubtless ill-advised, and his councillors did not take the kindly or the wise way with the people at this time; for a host of wild Highlanders had been turned into the land, who plundered in cotter's hut and laird's hall without much distinction between those that stood for the Covenants and those that held for the King. So in the year 1679 Galloway was very hot and angry, and many were ready to fight the King's forces wherever they could be met with.

So, hearing news of a revolt in the West, William Gordon rode away, with many good riders at his back, to take his place in the ranks of the rebels. His son Alexander, whose story we are to tell, was there before him. The Covenanting army had gained one success in Drumclog, which gave them some hope, but at Bothwell Bridge their forces were utterly broken, largely through their own quarrels, by the Duke of Monmouth and the disciplined troops of the Government.

Alexander Gordon had to flee from the field of Bothwell. He came home to Earlstoun alone, for his father had been met about six miles from the battle-field by a troop of horse, and as he refused to surrender, he was slain there and buried in the parish of Glassford.

Immediately after Bothwell, Alexander Gordon was compelled to go into hiding with a price upon his head. Unlike his father, he was very ready-witted, free with his tongue, even boisterous upon occasion, and of very great bodily strength. These qualities stood him in good stead during the long period of his wandering and when lying in concealment among the hills.

The day after Bothwell he was passing through the town of Hamilton, when he was recognised by an old retainer of the family.

"Save us, Maister Alexander," said the man, who remembered the ancient kindnesses of his family, "do you not know that it is death for you to be found here?"

So saying he made his young master dismount, and carried away all his horseman's gear and his arms, which he hid in a heap of field-manure behind the house. Then he took Earlstoun to his own house, and put upon him a long dress of his wife's. Hardly had he been clean-shaven, and arrayed in a clean white mutch (cap), when the troopers came clattering into the town. They had heard that he and some others of the prominent rebels had passed that way; and they went from door to door, knocking and asking, "Saw ye anything of Sandy Gordon of Earlstoun?"

So going from house to house they came to the door of the ancient Gordon retainer, and Earlstoun had hardly time to run to the corner and begin to rock the cradle with his foot before the soldiers came to ask the same question there. But they passed on without suspicion, only saying one to the other as they went out, "My certes, Billy, but yon was a sturdy hizzie!"

After that there was nothing but the heather and the mountain cave for Alexander Gordon for many a day. He had wealth of adventures, travelling by night, hiding and sleeping by day. Sometimes he would venture to the house of one who sympathised with the Covenanters, only to find that the troopers were already in possession. Sometimes, in utter weariness, he slept so long that when he awoke he would find a party searching for him quite close at hand; then there was nothing for it but to lie close like a hare in a covert till the danger passed by.

Once when he came to his own house of Earlstoun he was only an hour or two there before the soldiers arrived to search for him. His wife had hardly time to stow him in a secret recess behind the ceiling of a room over the kitchen, in which place he abode several days, having his meals passed to him from above, and breathing through a crevice in the wall.

After this misadventure he was sometimes in Galloway and sometimes in Holland for three or four years. He might even have remained in the Low Countries, but his services were so necessary to his party in Scotland that he was repeatedly summoned to come over into Galloway and the West to take up the work of organising resistance to the Government.

During most of this time the Tower of Earlstoun was a barracks of the soldiers, and it was only by watching his opportunity that Alexander Gordon could come home to see his wife, and put his hand upon his bairns' heads as they lay a-row in their cots. Yet come he sometimes did, especially when the soldiers of the garrison were away on duty in the more distant parts of Galloway. Then the wanderer would steal indoors in the gloaming, soft-footed like a thief, into his own house, and sit talking with his wife and an old retainer or two who were fit to be trusted with the secret. Yet while he sat there one was ever on the watch, and at the slightest signs of King's men in the neighbourhood Alexander Gordon rushed out and ran to the great oak tree, which you may see to this day standing in sadly-diminished glory in front of the great house of Earlstoun.

Now it stands alone, all the trees of the forest having been cut away from around it during the subsequent poverty which fell upon the family. A rope ladder lay snugly concealed among the ivy that clad the trunk of the tree. Up this Alexander Gordon climbed. When he arrived at the top he pulled the ladder after him, and found himself upon an ingeniously constructed platform built with a shelter over it from the rain, high among the branchy tops of the great oak. His faithful wife, Jean Hamilton, could make signals to him out of one of the top windows of Earlstoun whether it was safe for him to approach the house, or whether he had better remain hidden among the leaves. If you go now to look for the tree, it is indeed plain and easy to be seen. But though now so shorn and lonely, there is no doubt that two hundred years ago it stood undistinguished among a thousand others that thronged the woodland about the Tower of Earlstoun.

Often, in order to give Alexander Gordon a false sense of security, the garrison would be withdrawn for a week or two, and then in the middle of some mirky night or early in the morning twilight the house would be surrounded and the whole place ransacked in search of its absent master.

On one occasion, the man who came running along the narrow river path from Dairy had hardly time to arouse Gordon before the dragoons were heard clattering down through the wood from the high-road. There was no time to gain the great oak in safety, where he had so often hid in time of need. All Alexander Gordon could do was to put on the rough jerkin of a labouring man, and set to cleaving firewood in the courtyard with the scolding assistance of a maid-servant. When the troopers entered to search for the master of the house, they heard the maid vehemently "flyting" the great hulking lout for his awkwardness, and threatening to "draw a stick across his back" if he did not work to a better tune.

The commander ordered him to drop his axe, and to point out the different rooms and hiding-places about the castle. Alexander Gordon did so with an air of indifference, as if hunting Whigs were much the same to him as cleaving firewood. He did his duty with a stupid unconcern which successfully imposed on the soldiers; and as soon as they allowed him to go, he fell to his wood-chopping with the same stolidity and rustic boorishness that had marked his conduct.

Some of the officers came up to him and questioned him as to his master's hiding-place in the woods. But as to this he gave them no satisfaction.

"My master," he said, "has no hiding-place that I know of. I always find him here when I have occasion to seek for him, and that is all I care about. But I am sure that if he thought you were seeking him he would immediately show himself to you, for that is ever his custom."

This was one of the answers with a double meaning that were so much in the fashion of the time and so characteristic of the people.

On leaving, the commander of the troop said, "Ye are a stupid kindly nowt, man. See that ye get no harm in such a rebel service."

Sometimes, however, searching waxed so hot and close that Gordon had to withdraw himself altogether out of Galloway and seek quieter parts of the country. On one occasion he was speeding up the Water of Æ when he found himself so weary that he was compelled to lie down under a bush of heather and rest before proceeding on his journey. It so chanced that a noted King's man, Dalyell of Glenæ, was riding homewards over the moor. His horse started back in astonishment, having nearly stumbled over the body of a sleeping man. It was Alexander Gordon. Hearing the horse's feet he leaped up, and Dalyell called upon him to surrender. But that was no word to say to a Gordon of Earlstoun. Gordon instantly drew his sword, and, though unmounted, his lightness of foot on the heather and moss more than counterbalanced the advantages of the horseman, and the King's man found himself matched at all points; for the Laird of Earlstoun was in his day a famous sworder.

Soon the Covenanter's sword seemed to wrap itself about Dalyell's blade and sent it twirling high in the air. In a little he found himself lying on the heather at the mercy of the man whom he had attacked. He asked for his life, and Alexander Gordon granted it to him, making him promise by his honour as a gentleman that whenever he had the fortune to approach a conventicle he would retire, if he saw a white flag elevated in a particular manner upon a flagstaff. This seemed but a little condition to weigh against a man's life, and Dalyell agreed.

Now the Cavalier was an exceedingly honourable man and valued his spoken word. So on the occasion of a great conventicle at Mitchelslacks, in the parish of Closeburn, he permitted a great field meeting to disperse, drawing off his party in another direction, because the signal streaming from a staff told him that the man who had spared his life was amongst the company of worshippers.

After this, the white signal was frequently used in the neighbourhood over which Dalyell's jurisdiction extended, and to the great credit of the Cavalier it is recorded that on no single occasion did he violate his plighted word, though he is said to have remarked bitterly that the Whig with whom he fought must have been the devil, "for ever going to and fro in the earth, and walking up and down in it."

But Alexander Gordon was too great a man in the affairs of the Praying Societies to escape altogether. He continually went and came from Holland, and some of the letters that he wrote from that country are still in existence. At last, in 1683, having received many letters and valuable papers for delivery to people in refuge in Holland, he went secretly to Newcastle, and agreed with the master of a ship for his voyage to the Low Countries. But just as the vessel was setting out from the mouth of the Tyne, it was accidentally stopped. Some watchers for fugitives came on board, and Earlstoun and his companion were challenged. Earlstoun, fearing the taking of his papers, threw the box that contained them overboard; but it floated, and was taken along with himself.

Then began a long series of misfortunes for Alexander Gordon. He was five times tried, twice threatened with torture—which he escaped, in the judgment hall itself, by such an exhibition of his great strength as terrified his judges.[1] He simulated madness, foamed at the mouth, and finally tore up the benches in order to attack the judges with the fragments. He was sent first to the castle of Edinburgh and afterwards to the Bass, "for a change of air" as the record quaintly says. Finally, he was despatched to Blackness Castle, where he remained close in hold till the revolution. Not till June 5, 1689, were his prison doors thrown open, but even then Alexander Gordon would not go till he had obtained signed documents from the governor and officials of the prison to the effect that he had never altered any of his opinions in order to gain privilege or release.

Alexander Gordon returned to Earlstoun, and lived there quietly far into the next century, taking his share in local and county business with Grierson of Lag and others who had hunted him for years—which is a strange thing to think on, but one also very characteristic of those times.

On account of his great strength and the power of his voice he was called "the Bull of Earlstoun," and it is said that when he was rebuking his servants, the bellowing of the Bull could plainly be heard in the clachan of Dalry, which is two miles away across hill and stream.

---

1. See the story of "How they held the Bass for King James."

The Story of Grisell Baillie's Sheep's Head

The Lady Grisell Baillie, as she was called after her marriage, was the daughter of a very eminent Covenanter, Sir Patrick Hume of Polwarth. Grisell was born in 1665, and during all the years of her girlhood her father was seldom able to come home to his house of Polwarth, for fear of the officers of the Government seizing him. On one occasion he was taken and cast into prison in Dumbarton Castle for full fifteen months. Grisell was but a little girl at the time, but she had a wisdom and a quaint discretion beyond her years. Often she was entrusted with a letter to carry to him past the guard, and succeeded in the attempt where an elder person would certainly have been suspected and searched.

When her father was set at liberty, it was not many weeks till the soldiers again came seeking him; for new troubles had arisen, and the suspicion of the King was against all men that were not active in his service.

Parties of soldiers were continually searching the house in pursuit of him. But this occasioned no alarm to his family, for they all, with three exceptions, thought him far from home.

Only Sir Patrick's wife, his little daughter Grisell, and a carpenter named James Winter were trusted with the secret. The servants were frequently put to the oath as to when they saw their master; but as they knew nothing, all passed off quite well.

With James Winter's assistance the Lady Polwarth got a bed and bed-clothes carried in the night to the burying-place, a vault under the ground at Polwarth Church, a mile from the house. Here Sir Patrick was concealed a whole month, never venturing out. For all light he had only an open slit at one end, through which nobody could see what was below.

To this lonely place little Grisell went every night by herself at midnight, to carry her father victuals and drink, and stayed with him as long as she could with a chance of returning home before the morning. Here in this dismal habitation did they often laugh heartily at the incidents of the day, for they were both of that cheerful disposition which is a continual feast.

Grisell had ordinarily a terror of the churchyard, especially in the dark, for being but a girl, and having been frightened with nursery stories, she thought to see ghosts behind every tomb. But when she came to help her father, she had such anxious care for him that all fear of ghosts went away from her. She stumbled among the graves every night alone, being only in dread that the stirring of a leaf or the barking of a dog betokened the coming of a party of soldiers to carry away her father to his death. The minister's house was near the church. The first night she went, his dogs kept up such a barking that it put her in the utmost fear of a discovery. The next day the Lady Polwarth sent for the curate, and, on pretext of a mad dog, got him to send away all his dogs. A considerate curate, in sooth!

There was great difficulty in getting victuals to carry to Sir Patrick without the servants, who were not in the secret, suspecting for what purpose they were taken. The only way that it could be done was for Grisell to slip things off her plate into her lap as they sat at dinner.

Many a diverting story is told about this. Sir Patrick above all things was fond of sheep's head. One day while the children were eating their broth, Grisell had conveyed a whole sheep's head into her lap. Her brother Sandy (who was afterwards Lord Marchmont) looked up as soon as he had finished, and cried out with great astonishment, "Mother, will ye look at our Grisell. While we have been supping our broth, she has eaten up the whole sheep's head!"

For indeed she needed to be looked to in these circumstances. This occasioned great merriment when she told her father of it in his hiding-place at night. And he desired that the next time there was sheep's head Sandy should have a double share of it.

His great comfort and constant entertainment while in this dreary abode (for he had no light to read by) was to repeat over and over to himself Buchanan's Latin Psalms. And to his dying day, nearly forty years after, he would give the book to his wife, and ask her to try him at any place to see if he minded his Psalms as well as he had done in the hiding-hole among the bones of his ancestors in Polwarth Kirkyard.

After this, James Winter and the Lady Polwarth made a hole in the ground under a bed that drew out of a recess in the wall. They lifted the boards and took turns at digging out the earth, scratching it with their hands till they were all rough and bleeding, for only so could they prevent a noise being heard. Grisell and her mother helped James Winter to carry the earth in bags and sheets to the garden at the back. He then made a box bed at his own house, large enough for Sir Patrick to lie in, with bed and bed-clothes, and bored holes in the boards for air. But in spite of all this, the difficulty of their position was so great, and the danger so certainly increasing, that it was judged better that Sir Patrick should attempt to escape to Holland.

It was necessary to tell the grieve, John Allen, who was so much astonished to hear that his master had been all the time about the house, that he fainted away. However, he made up willingly enough a story that he was going to Morpeth Fair to sell horses, and Sir Patrick having got forth from a window of the stables, they set out in the dark. Sir Patrick, being absent-minded, let his horse carry him whither it would, and in the morning found himself at Tweedside, far out of his way, at a place not fordable and without his servant.

But this also was turned to good. For after waiting a while he found means to get over to the other side, where with great joy he met his servant. Then the grieve told him that he had never missed him till, looking about, he heard a great galloping of horses, and a party of soldiers who had just searched the house for Sir Patrick, surrounded him and strictly examined him. He looked about everywhere and could not see his master, for he was in much fear, thinking him to be close behind. But in this manner, by his own absent-mindedness, Sir Patrick was preserved, and so got safely first to London and afterwards to Holland.

Thence Sir Patrick sent home for his wife and family. They came to him in a ship, and on the way had an adventure. The captain was a sordid and brutal man, and agreed with them and with several other people to give them a bed on the passage. So when there arose a dispute who would have the bed, the Lady Polwarth said nothing. But a gentleman coming to her said, "Let them be doing. You will see how it will end." So two of the other gentlewomen lay on the bed, the Lady Polwarth with Grisell and a little sister lying on the floor, with a cloak-bag of books she was taking to Sir Patrick for their only pillow.

Then in came the captain, and first ate up all their provisions with a gluttony incredible. Then he said to the women in the bed, "Turn out, turn out!" and laid himself down in place of them. But Providence was upsides with him, for a terrible storm came on, and he had to get up immediately and go out to try to save the ship. And so he got no more sleep that night, which pleased the gentlewomen greatly in spite of all their own fears and pains. They never saw more of him till they landed at the Brill. From that they set out on foot for

Rotterdam with one of the gentlemen that had been kind to them on the crossing to Holland.

It was a cold, wet, dirty night. Grisell's little sister, a girl not well able to walk, soon lost her shoes in the dirt. Whereupon the Lady Polwarth took her upon her back, the gentlemen carrying all their baggage, and Grisell going through the mire at her mother's side.

At Rotterdam they found their eldest brother and Sir Patrick himself waiting to conduct them to Utrecht, where their house was. No sooner were they met again than they forgot everything, and felt nothing but happiness and contentment.

And even after their happy and prosperous return to Scotland they looked back on these years in Holland, when they were so poor, and often knew not whence was to come the day's dinner, as the happiest and most delightful of their lives. Yet the years of Grisell Baillie's after-life were neither few nor evil.

The Conquest of Peru

The Youth of Pizarro

AT THE TIME WHEN THE news of the conquest of Mexico by Cortés, and the report of its marvellous stores of treasure, were inflaming the minds of the men of Spain with an ardent desire for fresh discoveries, there happened to be living in the Spanish colony of Panamá a man named Francisco Pizarro, to whose lot it fell to discover and conquer the great and flourishing empire of Peru. He was a distant kinsman of Hernando Cortés, but had from his childhood been neglected and left to make his living as best he might. He could neither read nor write, and had chiefly been employed as a swineherd near the city of Truxillo, where he was born. But as he grew older and heard the strange and fascinating stories of adventure in the New World which were daily more widely circulated, he took the first opportunity of escaping to Seville, from which port he, with other Spanish adventurers, embarked to seek their fortunes in the West, the town being at this time left almost entirely to the women, so great was the tide of emigration. Thenceforward he lived a stirring life. We hear of him in Hispaniola, and serving as lieutenant in a colonising expedition under Alonzo de Ojeda. After this he was associated with Vasco Nunez de Balboa in establishing a settlement at Darien, and from Balboa he may first have heard rumours of Peru itself, for it was to Balboa that an Indian chief had said concerning some gold which had been collected from the natives: "If this is what you prize so much that you are willing to leave your homes and risk even life itself for it, I can tell you of a land where they eat and drink out of golden vessels, and gold is as common as iron with you." Later, Pizarro was sent to traffic with the natives on the Pacific side of the isthmus for gold and pearls, and presently from the south came Andagoya, bringing accounts of the wealth and grandeur of the countries which lay beyond, and also of the hardships and difficulties endured by the few navigators who had sailed in that direction. Thus the southern expeditions became a common subject of talk among the colonists of Panamá.

Pizarro does not at first seem to have shown any special interest in the matter, nor was he rich enough to do anything without assistance; but there were two people in the colony who were to help him. One of them was a soldier of fortune named Diego Almagro, an older man than

Pizarro, who in his early life had been equally neglected; the other was a Spanish ecclesiastic, Hernando de Luque, a man of great prudence and worldly wisdom, who had, moreover, control of the necessary funds. Between these three, then, a compact was made, most of the money being supplied by De Luque, Pizarro taking command of the expedition, and Almagro undertaking the equipment of the ships. Only about a hundred men could be persuaded to join the explorers, and those but the idle hangers-on in the colony, who were eager to do anything to mend their fortunes. Everything being ready, Pizarro set sail with these in the larger of the two ships, in the month of November 1524, leaving Almagro to follow as soon as the second vessel could be fitted out. With such slender means did Pizarro begin his attack on a great people, and invade the mysterious empire of the Children of the Sun.

The Empire of the Incas

AT THIS TIME THE PERUVIAN Empire stretched along the Pacific from about the second degree north to the thirty-seventh degree of south latitude; its breadth varied, but was nowhere very great. The country was most remarkable, and seemed peculiarly unfitted for cultivation. The great range of mountains ran parallel to the coast, sometimes in a single line, sometimes in two or three, either side by side or running obliquely to each other, broken here and there by the towering peaks of huge volcanoes, white with perpetual snows, and descending towards the coast in jagged cliffs and awful precipices. Between the rocks and the sea lay a narrow strip of sandy soil, where no rain ever fell, and which was insufficiently watered by the few scanty streams that flow down the western side of the Cordilleras. Nevertheless, by the patient industry of the Peruvians, these difficulties had all been overcome; by means of canals and subterranean aqueducts the waste places of the coast were watered and made fertile, the mountain sides were terraced and cultivated, every form of vegetation finding the climate suited to it at a different height, while over the snowy wastes above wandered the herds of llamas, or Peruvian sheep, under the care of their herdsmen. The Valley of Cuzco, the central region of Peru, was the cradle of their civilisation. According to tradition among the Peruvians, there had been a time, long past, when the land was held by many tribes, all plunged in barbarism, who worshipped every object in nature, made war as a pastime, and feasted upon the flesh of their slaughtered captives. The

Sun, the great parent of mankind, pitying their degraded condition, sent two of his children, Manco Capac and Mama Ocllo Huaco, to govern and teach them. They bore with them as they advanced from the neighbourhood of Lake Titicaca a golden wedge, and were directed to take up their abode at the spot where this sacred emblem should sink easily into the ground. This happened in the Valley of Cuzco; the wedge of gold sank into the earth and disappeared for ever, and Manco Capac settled down to teach the men of the land the arts of agriculture, while Mama Ocllo showed the women how to weave and spin. Under these wise and benevolent rulers the community grew and spread, absorbing into itself the neighbouring tribes, and overrunning the whole tableland. The city of Cuzco was founded, and, under the successors of the Children of the Sun, became the capital of a great and flourishing monarchy. In the middle of the fifteenth century the famous Topa Inca Yupanqui led his armies across the terrible desert of Atacama, and, penetrating to the southern region of Chili, made the river Maule the boundary of his dominions, while his son, Huayna Capac, who succeeded him, pushed his conquests northward, and added the powerful kingdom of Quito to the empire of Peru. The city of Cuzco was the royal residence of the Incas, and also the "Holy City," for there stood the great Temple of the Sun, the most magnificent structure in the New World, to which came pilgrims from every corner of the empire.

Cuzco was defended on the north by a high hill, a spur of the Cordilleras, upon which was built a wonderful fortress of stone, with walls, towers, and subterranean galleries, the remains of which exist to this day and amaze the traveller by their size and solidity, some of the stones being thirty-eight feet long by eighteen broad, and six feet thick, and so exactly fitted together that, though no cement was used, it would be impossible to put the blade of a knife between them. As the Peruvians had neither machinery, beasts of burden, nor iron tools, and as the quarry from which these huge blocks were hewn lay forty-five miles from Cuzco, over river and ravine, it is easy to imagine the frightful labour which this building must have cost; indeed, it is said to have employed twenty thousand men for fifty years, and was, after all, but one of the many fortifications established by the Incas throughout their dominions. Their government was absolutely despotic, the sovereign being held so far above his subjects that even the proudest of the nobles only ventured into his presence barefooted, and carrying

ANDREW LANG AND H. RIDER HAGGARD

upon his shoulders a light burden in token of homage. The title of Inca was borne by all the nobility who were related to the king, or who, like himself, claimed descent from the Children of the Sun; but the crown passed from father to son, the heir being the eldest son of the "coya," or queen. From his earliest years he was educated by the "amautas," or wise men of the kingdom, in the ceremonial of their religion, as well as in military matters and all manly exercises, that he might be fitted to reign in his turn.

At the age of sixteen the prince, with the young Inca nobles who had shared his studies, underwent a kind of public examination, their proficiency as warriors being tested by various athletic exercises and by mimic combats which, though fought with blunted weapons, generally resulted in wounds, and sometimes in death. During this trial, which lasted thirty days, the young prince fared no better than his comrades, wearing mean attire, going barefoot, and sleeping upon the ground—a mode of life which was supposed to give him sympathy with the destitute. At the end of that time, the candidates considered worthy of the honours of this barbaric chivalry were presented to the sovereign, who reminded them of the responsibilities of their birth and station, and exhorted them, as Children of the Sun, to imitate the glorious career of their ancestor. He then, as they knelt before him one by one, pierced their ears with a golden bodkin, which they continued to wear until the hole was made large enough to contain the enormous pendants worn by the Incas, which made the Spaniards call them "Orejones." Indeed, as one of the conquerors remarked, "The larger the hole, the more of a gentleman," and the sovereign wore so massive an ornament that the cartilage of his ear was distended by it nearly to the shoulder. After this ceremony the feet of the candidates were dressed in the sandals of the order, and girdles, and garlands of flowers were given them. The head of the prince was then encircled with a tasselled fringe of a yellow colour, which distinguished him as the heir apparent, and he at once received the homage of all the Inca nobility; and then the whole assembly proceeded to the great square of the capital, where with songs, dances, and other festivities the ceremony was brought to an end. After this the prince was deemed worthy to sit in the councils of his father, and to serve under distinguished generals in time of war, and finally himself to carry the rainbow banner of his house upon distant campaigns.

The Inca lived with great pomp and show. His dress was of the finest vicuña wool, richly dyed, and ornamented with gold and jewels. Round his head was a many-coloured turban and a fringe like that worn by the prince, but of a scarlet colour, and placed upright in it were two feathers of a rare and curious bird called the coraquenque, which was found in a desert country among the mountains. It was death to take or destroy one of these birds; they were reserved exclusively to supply the king's headgear. In order to communicate with their people, the Incas were in the habit of making a stately progress through their land once in every few years. The litter in which they travelled was richly decorated with gold and emeralds, and surrounded by a numerous escort. The men who bore it on their shoulders were provided by two cities specially appointed for the purpose, and the service was no enviable one, since a fall was punished by death. Halts were made at the "tambos," or inns regularly kept up by the Government along all the principal roads, and the people assembled all along the line, clearing stones from the road and strewing it with flowers, and vying with one another in carrying the baggage from village to village. Here and there the Inca halted to listen to the grievances of his subjects, or to decide points referred to him by the ordinary tribunals, and these spots were long held in reverence as consecrated by his presence. Everywhere the people flocked to catch a glimpse of their ruler, and to greet him with acclamations and blessings.

The royal palaces were on a magnificent scale, and were scattered over all the provinces of the great empire. The buildings were low, covering a large space, the rooms not communicating with each other, but opening upon a common square. The walls were of stone rough hewn, and the roofs of rushes; but inside all was splendour. Gold, silver, and richly-coloured stuffs abounded, covering the walls, while in niches stood images of animals and plants curiously wrought in the precious metals. Even the commonest household utensils were of gold. The favourite residence of the Incas was the delicious valley of Yucay, about twelve miles from Cuzco; there they loved to retreat to enjoy their exquisite gardens, and luxurious baths replenished with clear water, which flowed through subterranean channels of silver into basins of gold. The gardens were full of flowers and plants, which flourished in this temperate climate of the tropics; but strangest of all were those borders which glowed with various forms of vegetable life, cunningly fashioned in gold and silver. Among these is specially recorded the beautiful Indian corn, its golden grain set off by broad silver leaves, and crowned with a light tassel of silver. But all the wealth displayed by the Inca belonged to himself alone. When he died, or, as they put it, "was called home to the mansions of his father the Sun," his palaces were abandoned, and all his treasures and possessions were suffered to remain as he left them, lest his soul should at any time return to its body, and require again the things it had used before. The body itself was skilfully embalmed and removed to the great Temple of the Sun at Cuzco, where were the bodies of all the former Incas and their queens, ranged in opposite files. Clothed in their accustomed attire, they sat in chairs of gold, their heads bent, their hands crossed upon their breasts, their dusky faces and black, or sometimes silver, hair retaining a perfectly natural look. On certain festivals they were brought out into the great square of Cuzco, invitations were issued in their names to all the nobles' and officers of the Court, and magnificent entertainments were held, when the display of plate, gold, and jewels was such as no other city in the world ever witnessed. The banquets were served by the retainers of the respective houses, and the same forms of courtly etiquette were used as if the living monarch had presided, instead of his mummy. The nobility of Peru consisted of two Orders—the Incas or relatives of the sovereign, and the Curacas, or chiefs of the conquered nations. The former enjoyed many privileges; they wore a peculiar dress, and spoke a peculiar dialect. Most of them lived at Court, sharing the counsels of the king, and dining at his table. They alone were admissible to the great offices of the priesthood, and had the command of armies and the government of distant provinces.

The whole territory of the empire was divided into three parts: one for the Sun, another for the Inca, and the last for the people. The revenue from the lands assigned to the Sun supported the numerous priests, and provided for the maintenance of the temples and their costly ceremonial. The land of the people was parted equally among them, every man when he was married receiving enough to support himself and his wife, together with a house. An additional piece was granted for every child, the portion for a son being double that for a daughter. The division of the soil was renewed every year, and the possession of the tenant increased or diminished according to the number of his family. The country was wholly cultivated by the people. First the lands of the Sun were tilled; then those of the old or sick, the widow and orphan, and soldiers on active service; after this each man was free to attend to his own, though he was still obliged to help any neighbour who might require it. Lastly, they cultivated the land of the Inca. This was done with great ceremony by all the people in a body. At break of day they were called together, and men, women, and children appeared in their gayest apparel as if decked for some festival, and sang as they worked their popular ballads, which told the heroic deeds of the Inca. The flocks of llamas belonged exclusively to the Sun and the Inca, they were most carefully tended and managed, and their number was immense. Under the care of their shepherds they moved to different pastures according to the climate. Every year some were killed as sacrifices at the religious festivals or for the consumption of the Court, and at appointed seasons all were sheared and their wool stored in the public magazines. Thence it was given out to each family, and when the women had spun and woven enough coarse garments to supply their husbands and children they were required to labour for the Inca. Certain officers decided what was to be woven, gave out the requisite material, and saw that the work was faithfully done. In the lower and hotter regions cotton, given out in the same way, took the place of wool. Occupation was found for all, from the child of five years to the oldest woman who could hold a distaff. Idleness was held to be a crime in Peru, and was severely punished, while industry was publicly commended and rewarded. In the same way all the mines in the kingdom belonged to the Inca, and were worked for his benefit by men familiar with the service, and there were special commissioners whose duty it was to know the nature of the country and the capabilities of its inhabitants, so that whatever work was required, it might be given into competent hands, the different employments generally descending from father to son. All over the country stood spacious stone storehouses, divided between the Sun and the Inca, in which were laid up maize, coca, woollen and cotton stuffs, gold, silver, and copper, and beside these were yet others designed to supply the wants of the people in times of dearth. Thus in Peru, though no man who was not an Inca could become rich, all had enough to eat and to wear.

To this day the ruins of temples, palaces, aqueducts, and, above all, the great roads, remain to bear witness to the industry of the Peruvians. Of these roads the most remarkable were two which ran from Quito to Cuzco, diverging again thence in the direction of Chili. One ran through the lowlands by the sea, the other over the great plateau, through galleries cut for leagues from the living rock, over pathless sierras buried in snow. Rivers were crossed by filling up the ravines through which they flowed with solid masses of masonry which remain to this day, though the mountain torrents have in the course of ages worn themselves a passage through, leaving solid arches to span the valleys. Over some of the streams they constructed frail swinging bridges of osiers, which were woven into cables the thickness of a man's body. Several of these laid side by side were secured at either end to huge stone buttresses, and covered with planks. As these bridges were sometimes over two hundred feet long they dipped and oscillated frightfully over the rapidly-flowing stream far below, but the Peruvians crossed them fearlessly, and they are still used by the Spaniards. The wider and smoother rivers were crossed on "balsas," or rafts with sails. The whole length of this road was about two thousand miles, its breadth did not exceed twenty feet, and it was paved with heavy flags of freestone, in parts covered with a cement which time has made harder than stone itself. The construction of the lower road must have presented other difficulties. For the most part the causeway was raised on a high embankment of earth, with a wall of clay on either side. Trees and sweet-smelling shrubs were planted along the margin, and where the soil was so light and sandy as to prevent the road from being continued, huge piles were driven into the ground to mark the way. All along these highways the "tambos," or inns, were erected at a distance of ten or twelve miles from each other, and some of them were on an extensive scale, consisting of a fortress and barracks surrounded by a stone parapet. These were evidently intended as a shelter for the Imperial armies when on the march.

The communication throughout the country was by means of runners, each of whom carried the message entrusted to him with great swiftness for five miles, and then handed it over to another. These runners were specially trained to their work and wore a particular dress; their stations were small buildings erected five miles apart along all the roads. The messages might be verbal, or conveyed by means of the "quipus." A quipu was a cord two feet long, composed of differently coloured threads twisted together, from which were hung a number of smaller threads, also differently coloured and tied in knots. Indeed, the word "quipu" means "a knot." By means of the colours and the various knots the Peruvians expressed ideas—it was their method of writing—but the quipus were chiefly used for arithmetical purposes. In every district officers were stationed who were called "keepers of the quipus"; their duty was to supply the Government with information as to the revenues, births, deaths, and marriages, number of population, and so on. These records—in skeins of many-coloured thread—were inspected at headquarters and carefully preserved, the whole collection constituting what might be call the national archives. In like manner the wise men recorded the history of the empire, and chronicled the great deeds of the reigning Inca or his ancestors. The Peruvians had some acquaintance with geography and astronomy, and showed a decided talent for theatrical exhibitions, but it was in agriculture that they really excelled. The mountains were regularly hewn into stone-faced terraces, varying in width from hundreds of acres at the base to a few feet near the snows. Water was conveyed in stone-built aqueducts for hundreds of miles, from some snow-fed lake in the mountains, fertilising all the dry and sandy places through which it passed. In some of the arid valleys they dug great pits twenty feet deep and more than an acre in extent, and, after carefully preparing the soil, planted grain or vegetables. Their method of ploughing was primitive indeed. Six or eight men were attached by ropes to a strong stake, to which was fastened a horizontal piece of wood upon which the ploughman might set his foot to force the sharp point into the earth as it was dragged along, while women followed after to break up the clods as they were turned.

Much of the wealth of the country consisted in the huge flocks of llamas and alpacas, and the wild huanacos and vicuñas which roamed freely over the frozen ranges of the Cordilleras. Once a year a great hunt took place under the superintendence of the Inca or some of his officers. Fifty or sixty thousand men encircled the part of the country that was to be hunted over, and drove all the wild animals by degrees towards some spacious plain. The beasts of prey they killed, and also the deer, the flesh of the latter being dried in strips and distributed among the people. This preparation, called "charqui," was the only animal food of the lower classes in Peru. The huanacos and vicuñas were only captured and shorn, being afterwards allowed to escape and go back to their haunts among the mountains. No district was hunted over more than once in four years. The Peruvians showed great skill in weaving the vicuña wool into robes for the Inca and carpets and hangings for his palaces. The texture was as delicate as silk, and the brilliancy of the dyes unequalled even in Europe. They also were expert in the beautiful feather-work for which Mexico was famous, but they held it of less account than the Mexicans did. In spite of some chance resemblances in their customs, it seems certain that the Mexicans and Peruvians were unaware of each other's existence. They differed in nothing more utterly than in their treatment of the tribes they conquered. While the Mexicans kept them in subjection by force and cruelty, the Peruvians did everything they possibly could to make the conquered people one with the rest of the nation.

Religion of the Peruvians

IN RELIGION THE PERUVIANS ACKNOWLEDGED one Supreme Being as creator and ruler of the universe, whom they called Pachacamac, or Viracocha. In all the land there was only one temple dedicated to him, and this had existed before the Incas began to rule. They also worshipped many other gods, but the Sun was held far above the rest. In every town and village were temples dedicated to him, and his worship was taught first of all to every conquered tribe. His temple at Cuzco was called "the Place of Gold," and the interior was a wonderful sight. On the western wall was a representation of the Sun-god, a human face surrounded by numberless rays of light. This was engraved upon a huge and massive plate of gold, thickly powdered with emeralds and other precious stones. The beams of the morning sun striking first upon this, and being reflected again upon all the plates and studs of burnished gold with which the walls and ceiling were entirely covered, lighted the whole temple with a more than natural radiance. Even the cornices were of gold, and outside the temple a broad belt of the precious metal was let into the stonework. Adjoining this building were several smaller chapels. One consecrated to the Moon, held next in reverence as the mother of the Incas, was decorated in an exactly similar way, but with silver instead of gold, those of the Stars, the Thunder and Lightning, and the Rainbow were equally beautiful and gorgeous. Every vessel used in the temple services was of gold or silver, and there were beside many figures of animals, and copies of plants and flowers The greatest Sun festival was called "Raymi;" at it a llama was sacrificed, and from the appearance of its body the priest sought to read the future. A fire was then kindled by focussing the sun's rays with a mirror of polished metal upon a quantity of dried cotton, or when the sky was clouded over, by means of friction; but this was considered a bad omen. The sacred flame was entrusted to the care of the Virgins of the Sun, and if by any chance it went out it was considered to bode some great calamity to the nation. The festival ended with a great banquet to all the people, who were regaled upon the flesh of llamas, from the flocks of the Sun, while at the table of the Inca and his nobles were served fine cakes kneaded of maize flour by the Virgins of the Sun. These young maidens were chosen for their beauty from the families of the Curacas and inferior nobles, and brought up in the great convent-like establishments under the care of certain elderly matrons, who instructed them in their religious duties, and taught them to spin and embroider, and weave the vicuña wool for the temple hangings and for the use of the Inca. They were entirely cut off from their own people and from the world at large, only the Inca and the queen having the right to enter those sacred precincts. From them the brides of the Inca were chosen, for the law of the land allowed him to have as many wives as he pleased. They lived in his various palaces throughout the country, and at his death many of them sacrificed themselves willingly that they might accompany him into his new existence. In this wonderful monarchy each successive Inca seems to have been content with the policy of his father, to have carried out his schemes and continued his enterprises, so that the State moved steadily forward, as if under one hand, in its great career of civilisation and conquest.

Pizarro's Expedition

This, then, was the country which Pizarro with a mere handful of followers had set out to discover and subdue. He had sailed at a most unfavourable time of year, for it was the rainy season, and the coast was swept by violent tempests. He steered first for the Puerto de Piñas, a headland which marked the limit of Andagoya's voyage. Passing this, Pizarro sailed up a little river and came to anchor, and then landed with his whole force to explore the country; but after most toilful wanderings in dismal swamps and steaming forests they were forced to return exhausted and half-starved to their vessel, and proceed again on their voyage to the southward. Now they met with a succession of terrific storms, their frail ship leaked, and their stock of food and water was nearly gone, two ears of Indian corn a day being all that could be allowed to each man. In this strait they were glad to turn back and anchor once more a few leagues from their first halting-place. But they soon found that they had gained very little; neither bird nor beast was to be seen in the forest, and they could not live upon the few unwholesome berries which were all the woods afforded. Pizarro felt that to give up at this juncture would be utter ruin. So to pacify his complaining followers he sent an officer back in the ship to the Isle of Pearls, which was only a few leagues from Panamá, to lay in a fresh stock of provisions, while he himself with half the company made a further attempt to explore the country. For some time their efforts were vain; more than twenty men died from unwholesome food and the wretched climate, but at last they spied a distant opening in the woods, and Pizarro with a small party succeeded in reaching the clearing beyond it, where stood a small Indian village. The Spaniards rushed eagerly forward and seized upon such poor stores of food as the huts contained, while the astonished natives fled to the woods; but finding presently that no violence was offered to them they came back, and conversed with Pizarro as well as they could by signs. It was cheering to the adventurers to hear that these Indians also knew of a rich country lying to the southward, and to see that the large ornaments of clumsy workmanship which they wore were of gold. When after six weeks the ship returned, those on board were horrified at the wild and haggard faces of their comrades, so wasted were they by hunger and disease; but they soon revived, and, embarking once more, they joyfully left behind them the dismal scene of so much suffering, which they had named the Port of Famine. After a short run to the southward they again landed, and found another Indian settlement. The inhabitants fled, and the Spaniards secured a good store of maize and other food, and gold ornaments of considerable value; but they retreated to their ship in horror when they discovered human flesh roasting before a fire in one of the huts.

Once more they set sail, and encountered a furious storm, which so shattered their vessel that they were glad to gain the shore at the first possible landing-place. There they found a considerable town, the inhabitants of which were a warlike race who speedily attacked them. After some fighting the Spaniards were victorious, but they had lost two of their number, and many were wounded. It was necessary that the ship should be sent back to Panamá for repairs, but Pizarro did not consider that this place, which they had named Pueblo Quemado, would be a safe resting-place for those who were left behind; so he embarked again for Chicamá, and when he was settled there his treasurer started for Panamá with the gold that had been collected, and instructions to lay before Pedrarias, the governor, a full account of the expedition. Meanwhile Almagro had succeeded in equipping a small caravel, and started with about seventy men. He steered in the track of his comrade, and by a previously concerted signal of notches upon the trees he was able to recognise the places where Pizarro had landed. At Pueblo Quemado the Indians received him ill, though they did not venture beyond their palisades. This enraged Almagro, who stormed and took the place, driving the natives into the woods. He paid dearly for his victory, however, as a wound from a javelin deprived him of the sight of one eye. Pursuing his voyage, he discovered several new places upon the coast, and collected from them a considerable store of gold; but being anxious as to the fate of Pizarro, of whom he had lost all trace for some time, he turned back at the mouth of the San Juan River, and sailed straight to the Isle of Pearls. Here he gained tidings of his friend and proceeded at once to Chicamá, where the two commanders at length met, and each recounted his adventures.

After much consultation over what was next to be done, Pizarro decided to remain where he was while Almagro returned to Panamá for fresh supplies, and so ended the first expedition. But when Almagro reached Panamá he found the Governor anything but inclined to favour him and his schemes, and but for the influence of De Luque there would have been an end to their chance of discovering Peru. Fortunately, however, he was able to settle the difficulties with Pedrarias, who for about 2,500*l.* gave up all claim to any of the treasures they might discover, and ceased to oppose their plans. A memorable contract was then entered into by Father De Luque, Pizarro, and Almagro, by which the two last solemnly bound themselves to pursue the undertaking until it was accomplished, all the lands, gold, jewels, or treasures of any kind that they might secure to be divided between the three, in consideration of the funds which De Luque was to provide for the enterprise. Should they fail altogether, he was to be repaid with every morsel of property they might possess. This being arranged, two vessels were bought, larger and stronger than the ones with which they had started before, and a greater supply of stores put on board, and then a proclamation was made of "an expedition to Peru." But the citizens of Panamá showed no great readiness to join it, which was, perhaps, not surprising, seeing that of those who had volunteered before only three-fourths had returned, and those half-starved. However, in the end about one hundred and sixty men were mustered, with a few horses and a small supply of ammunition, of which there was probably very little to spare in the colony. The two captains, each in his own vessel, sailed once more, and this time having with them an experienced pilot named Ruiz, they stood boldly out to sea, steering direct for the San Juan River. This was reached without misadventure, and from the villages on its banks Pizarro secured a considerable store of gold and one or two natives.

Much encouraged by this success, the two chiefs felt confident that if this rich spoil, so soon acquired, could be exhibited in Panamá it would draw many adventurers to their standard, as a larger number of men was absolutely necessary to cope with the thickening population of the country. Almagro therefore took the treasure and went back for reinforcements. Pizarro landed to seek for a place of encampment, while Ruiz, with the second ship, sailed southward.

Coasting along with fair winds he reached what is now called the Bay of St. Matthew, having seen by the way many densely-populated villages in a well-cultivated land. Here the people showed no signs of fear or hostility, but stood gazing upon the ship of the white men as it floated on the smooth waters of the bay, fancying it to be some mysterious being descended from the skies. Without waiting to undeceive them, Ruiz once more headed for the open sea, and was soon amazed to see what appeared to be a caravel of considerable size, advancing slowly, with one large sail hoisted. The old navigator was convinced that his was the first European vessel that had ever penetrated into these latitudes, and no Indian nation yet discovered was acquainted with the use of sails. But as he drew near he saw it was one of the huge rafts, called "balsas," made of logs and floored with reeds, with a clumsy rudder and movable keel of planks. Coming alongside, Ruiz found several Indians, themselves wearing rich ornaments, who were carrying articles of wrought gold and silver for traffic along the coast. But what attracted his attention even more was the woollen cloth of which their robes were made. It was of fine texture, dyed in brilliant colours, and embroidered with figures of birds and flowers. They also had a pair of balances for weighing the gold and silver—a thing unknown even in Mexico. From these Indians he learned that two of their number came from Tumbez, a Peruvian port further to the south; that their fields were full of large flocks of the animals from which the wool was obtained; and that in the palaces of their king gold and silver were as common as wood. Ruiz only half believed their report, but he took several of them on board to repeat the tale to his commander, and also to learn Castilian, that they might serve as interpreters. Without touching at any other port, Ruiz then sailed southward as far as Punta de Pasado, being the first European who, sailing in this direction, had crossed the equinoctial line, after which he returned to the place where he had left Pizarro.

He did not reach it too soon. The little band had met with nothing but disaster. Instead of being able to reach the open country of which they had heard, they had been lost in dense forests of gigantic tropical vegetation. Hill rose behind hill, barring their progress, alternating with ravines of frightful depth. Monkeys chattered above their heads, hideous snakes and alligators infested the swamps. Many of the Spaniards were miserably killed by them, while others were waylaid by lurking natives, who on one occasion cut off fourteen men whose canoe had unhappily stranded on the bank of a stream. Their provisions gave out, and they could barely sustain life on the few cocoa-nuts or wild potatoes they found. On the shore life was even less tolerable, for the swarms of mosquitoes compelled the wretched wanderers to bury themselves up to their very faces in the sand. Worn-out with suffering, their one wish was to return to Panamá. This was far from being the desire of Pizarro, and luckily for him at this crisis Ruiz returned, and very soon after Almagro sailed into port with a fresh supply of provisions and a band of eighty military adventurers, who had but lately come to Panamá, and were burning to make their fortunes in the New World. The enthusiasm of these new recruits, and the relief of their own immediate miseries, speedily revived the spirits of Pizarro's men, and they eagerly called upon their commander to go forward; but the season of favouring winds was past, and it was only after many days of battling with fearful storms and contrary currents that they reached the Bay of St. Matthew, and anchored opposite the port of Tacamez. This was a large town, swarming with people who wore many ornaments of gold and jewels, for they belonged to the recently annexed province of Quito, and had not yet been forced to reserve all such things for the Inca, as the Peruvians did. Moreover, this part of the country was specially rich in gold, and through it flowed the River of Emeralds, so called from the quarries on its banks, from which quantities of those gems were dug. The Spaniards longed to possess themselves of all these treasures, but the natives were too numerous, and showed no fear of the white men. On the contrary, they were quite ready to attack them; and Pizarro, who had landed with some of his followers in the hope of a conference with the chiefs, found himself surrounded by at least ten thousand men, and would have fared but ill had not one of the cavaliers chanced to fall from his horse. This sudden division into two parts of what they had looked upon as one creature so astonished the Indians that they fell back, and left a way open for the Spaniards to regain their vessels. Here a council of war was held, and once again Almagro proposed to go back for more men while Pizarro waited in some safe spot. But the latter commander had grown rather weary of the part always assigned to him, and replied that it was all very well for Almagro, who passed his time sailing pleasantly to and fro, or living in plenty at Panamá, but that for those who remained behind to starve in a poisonous climate it was quite another matter. Almagro retorted angrily that he was quite willing to be the one to stay if Pizarro declined, and the quarrel would soon have become serious had not Ruiz interposed. Almagro's plan was adopted, and the little island of Gallo, which they had lately passed, was chosen as Pizarro's headquarters.

This decision caused great discontent among the men, who complained that they were being dragged to this obscure spot to die of hunger, and many of them wrote to their friends bewailing their deplorable condition, but Almagro did his best to seize all these letters, and only one escaped him. This was concealed in a ball of cotton sent as a present to the wife of the Governor; it was signed by several of the soldiers, and begged that a ship might be sent to rescue them from this dismal place before they all perished, and it warned others from joining the expedition. This letter fell into the Governor's hands, and caused great dismay in Panamá. Almagro's men looked sufficiently haggard and dejected to make it generally believed that the few ill-fated survivors were being detained against their will by Pizarro, to end their days on his desolate island. The Governor was so enraged at the number of lives which this unsuccessful expedition had cost the colony, that he utterly refused the applications of Almagro and De Luque for further help, and sent off two ships, under a cavalier named Tafur, to bring back every Spaniard from Gallo.

Meanwhile Pizarro and his men were suffering great misery from the inclement weather, for the rainy season had set in, and for lack of proper food, such crabs and shell-fish as they could pick up along the shore being all that they had. Therefore the arrival of Tafur with two well-provisioned ships was greeted with rapture, and the only thought of the soldiers was to embark as soon as possible, and leave for ever that dismal island. But the ships had brought letters from Almagro and De Luque to Pizarro, imploring him to hold fast to his original purpose, and solemnly promising to send him the means for going forward in a short time.

The Choice of Pizarro

FOR PIZARRO A VERY LITTLE hope was enough, but knowing that he could probably influence such of his followers as he cared to retain more by example than by word, he merely announced his own purpose in the briefest way possible. Drawing his sword, he traced a line upon the sand from east to west.

"Friends and comrades," said he, turning to the south, "on this side are toil, hunger, the drenching storm, desertion, and death; on that side ease and pleasure. There lies Peru with its riches, here Panamá and its poverty. Choose each man what best becomes a brave Castilian. For my part I go to the south."

So saying he stepped across the line, followed by Ruiz, Pedro de Candia, and eleven others, and Tafur, after vainly trying to persuade them to return, reluctantly departed, leaving them part of his store of provisions. Ruiz sailed with him to help Almagro and De Luque in their preparations. Not long after Pizarro and his men constructed a raft, and transported themselves to an island which lay further north. It was uninhabited, and being partly covered with wood afforded more shelter. There was also plenty of good water, and pheasants and a species of hare were fairly numerous. The rain fell incessantly, and the Spaniards built rude huts to keep themselves dry, but from the swarms of venomous insects they could find no protection. Pizarro did all he could to keep up the spirits of his men in this dreary place. Morning prayers were duly said, the evening hymn chanted, the Church festivals carefully observed, and, above all, a keen look-out was kept across the ocean for the expected sail; but seven months had passed before one small vessel appeared. The Governor had at last allowed De Luque and Almagro to fit out this ship; but she carried no more men than were needed to work her, and Pizarro was commanded to report himself in Panamá within six months, whatever might be happening.

Taking with him his faithful followers and the natives of Tumbez, Pizarro speedily embarked, and under the guidance of Ruiz sailed to the south for twenty days, and reached at length the Gulf of Guayaquil. Here the voyagers were abreast of some of the grandest heights of the Cordilleras. Far above them in the still air rose the snowy crests of Cotopaxi and Chimborazo, while only a narrow strip of green and fertile land lay between the mountains and the sea. Tumbez proved to be a large town, and the inhabitants received the Spaniards well, supplying them plentifully with fruit and vegetables, game and fish, and sending on board their ship a number of llamas, which Pizarro then saw for the first time. The "little camel," as the Spaniards called it, was an object of much interest to them, and they greatly admired its mixture of wool and hair, from which the beautiful native fabrics were woven. The Indians were much astonished to find two of their own countrymen on board the strange vessel, but through their favourable report of the harmless intentions of the Spaniards, and by their help as interpreters, Pizarro was able to collect much valuable information. At that time there happened to be an Inca noble in Tumbez, distinguished by his rich dress, the huge gold ornaments in his ears, and the deference paid him by the citizens. Pizarro received him on board his ship, showing him everything, and answering his numerous questions as well as he could. He also took the opportunity of asserting the lawful supremacy of the King of Spain over the empire of Peru, and of expounding some of the doctrines of his own religion, to all of which the chief listened in silence. Several parties of the Spaniards landed at different times, and came back with wondrous tales of all they had seen: the temples blazing with silver and gold, and the convent of the Virgins of the Sun, the gardens of which glowed with imitations of fruits and flowers in the same metals. The natives greatly admired one of the Spaniards, a man named Alonso de Molina, who was of fair complexion and wore a long beard. They even invited him to settle among them, promising him a beautiful wife; and on his homeward voyage Pizarro actually left him there, with one or two others, thinking that at some future time it might be useful to him that some of his own men should understand the Indian language. In return he took on board his ship several of the Peruvians, and one of them, named by the Spaniards Felipillo, played an important part in after-events.

Having now learnt all he could, Pizarro pursued his voyage, touching at all the principal points as he coasted along, and being everywhere received by the people with kindness and much curiosity, for the news of the coming of the white men spread rapidly, and all were eager to see the "Children of the Sun," as they began to be called from their fair complexions, their shining armour, and their firearms, which were looked upon as thunderbolts.

Having gone as far south as the port of Santa, and having heard enough to make the existence and position of the empire of Peru an absolute certainty, Pizarro turned and sailed to the northward, landing once or twice by the way, and being hospitably entertained by an Indian princess, and after an absence of more than eighteen months anchored again off Panamá. Great was the joy caused by their arrival, for all supposed them to have perished; yet even now, in spite of all they had discovered, the Governor refused his aid, and the confederates, being by this time without funds, had no alternative but to apply directly to the King of Spain. The mission was entrusted to Pizarro, who set out in the spring of 1528, taking with him some of the natives, two or three llamas, and specimens of the cloth and of the gold and silver ornaments, to attest the truth of his wonderful story.

Pizarro Goes to Spain and Returns

IT WOULD TAKE TOO LONG to tell how Pizarro fared in his native country, but the matter ended in the King's being convinced of the importance of his discoveries, and bestowing many honours and rewards upon him. He was also empowered to conquer and take possession of Peru, and expressly enjoined to preserve the existing regulations for the government and protection of the Indians, and to take with him many priests to convert them. All being settled to Pizarro's satisfaction, he found time to revisit his own town, where, his fortunes having somewhat mended since he turned his back upon it, he found friends and eager followers, and among these his own four half-brothers, Hernando, Gonzalo, and Juan Pizarro, and Francisco de Alcántara. It was not without many difficulties that Francisco Pizarro got together the two hundred and fifty men he had agreed to raise, and escaped from the delays and intrigues of the Spanish Court; but it was done at last, and the adventurers in three vessels started from Seville, and after a prosperous voyage reached Nombre de Dios, and there met De Luque and Almagro. Disagreements speedily arose, for the latter naturally felt aggrieved that Pizarro should have secured for himself such an unfair share of the riches and honours as the King had bestowed on him without putting forward the claims of his comrade, and matters were made worse by the insolent way in which Hernando Pizarro treated the old soldier, whom he looked upon as an obstacle in the path of his brother. Matters got to such a pass that Almagro was actually preparing ships to prosecute the expedition on his own account, but De Luque at last succeeded in reconciling the two commanders— at least for the moment—and the united band started for the third time. Though the number of men in the three ships did not exceed one hundred and eighty, yet they had twenty-seven horses, and were now much better provided with arms and ammunition. Pizarro's intention was to steer for Tumbez, but the wind being contrary he anchored instead in the Bay of St. Matthew, where the troops disembarked and advanced along the coast, while the vessels proceeded in the same direction, keeping as close inshore as possible. When Pizarro and his men reached a town of some importance they rushed in upon it sword in hand, and the inhabitants, without offering any resistance, fled to the woods, leaving the invaders to rifle their dwellings, from which they collected an unexpectedly large store of gold, silver, and emeralds, some of the stones being of great size. Pizarro sent the treasure back to Panamá in the ships, and continued his march, his soldiers suffering terribly in crossing the sandy wastes under the burning sun, which beat upon their iron mail or quilted cotton doublets till they were nearly suffocated. Here, too, they were attacked by a dreadful disease, terrible warts of great size breaking out upon them, of which several died. This plague, which was quite unknown before, attacked the natives also, spreading over the whole country. Everywhere as they advanced the Indians fled before them; the land was poor, and the Spaniards began to grumble and wish to retreat; but at this juncture one of the ships appeared, and the march along the coast was continued. Reaching the Gulf of Guayaquil, Pizarro persuaded the friendly natives of Tumbez to transport himself and his men to the island of Puná, where he encamped for the rainy season; but the islanders resented the presence of their enemies the men of Tumbez, a suspicion of treachery arose, and Pizarro allowed ten or twelve prisoners, men of Puná, to be massacred. Then the whole tribe fell upon the Spaniards and there was a great battle, in which the white men were victorious; but after this their position was a most uncomfortable one, the enemy being ever on the watch to cut off stragglers and destroy provisions, besides making night attacks upon the camp. Fortunately the other two ships came back at this juncture, bringing a hundred volunteers and some more horses, and with them Pizarro felt strong enough to cross to the mainland and resume his march. He had lately learned something of the state of affairs in the country, which he thought he might be able to turn to his own advantage. It seemed that the Inca Huayna Capac, who conquered Quito, had left three sons—Huascar the heir, the son of the Queen, Manco Capac his half-brother, and Atahuallpa, son of the Princess of Quito, who had been married to Huayna Capac after the conquest. To Atahuallpa the Inca at his death left the kingdom of Quito, enjoining him to live at peace with his brother Huascar, who succeeded to the empire of Peru. This happened about seven years before Pizarro reached Puná. For five years the brothers ruled their respective kingdoms without dispute. Huascar was of a gentle and peaceable disposition, but Atahuallpa was warlike, ambitious, and daring, and constantly endeavouring to enlarge his territory. His restless spirit at length excited alarm at Cuzco, and Huascar sent to remonstrate with him, and to require him to render homage for the kingdom of Quito. This at once provoked hostilities. A great battle took place at Ambato, in which Atahuallpa was victorious, and he marched on in the direction of Cuzco, carrying all before him, and only experiencing a slight check from the islanders of Puná. After more desperate encounters, in one of which Huascar was taken prisoner, Atahuallpa possessed himself of Cuzco, and, assuming the diadem of the Incas, received the homage of the whole country.

But his triumph was not to be for long.

We left Pizarro preparing to leave Puná and cross to Tumbez. His surprise when he did so was great, for he found only the ruins of what had been a flourishing town; moreover, some of his men were treacherously attacked by the natives, whom he had supposed to be quite friendly to him. The Spaniards were much disappointed, as they had looked forward confidently to securing the golden treasures of Tumbez of which they had heard so much; nor could Pizarro believe the explanation of this state of affairs given by the Curaca, who was caught lurking in the woods. However, it was his policy to remain friendly with the natives if possible, so no further notice was taken. No true account could be gathered of the fate of the two men who had been left there from the last expedition, though it was evident that both had perished. An Indian gave Pizarro a scroll left by one of them, upon which was written: "Know, whoever you may be that may chance to set foot in this country, that it contains more silver and gold than there is iron in Biscay." But when this was shown to the soldiers they only thought it was a device of their captain to give them fresh hope. Pizarro, seeing that nothing but incessant activity could keep down the rising spirit of discontent, now spent some weeks in exploring the country, and finally assembling all his men at a spot some thirty leagues south of Tumbez, he built there a considerable town, which he named San Miguel. The site afterwards proved to be unhealthy, and was abandoned for another on the banks of the river Piura, where a town still stands. Presently the news reached San Miguel that Atahuallpa was encamped within twelve days' journey, and Pizarro after much consideration resolved to present himself in his camp, trusting doubtless that when he got there circumstances would arise which he could turn to his own advantage.

Pizarro Marches to Meet the Inca

PLACING HIMSELF AT THE HEAD of his troops, he struck boldly into the heart of the country, received everywhere by the natives with confiding hospitality. The Spaniards were careful to give no offence, being aware that their best chance of success lay in conciliating the people by whom they were surrounded. After five days' marching, Pizarro halted in a pleasant valley to rest his company, and finding that some few among them showed discontent and were unwilling to proceed, he called them all together, and told them that they had now reached a crisis which it would require all their courage to meet, and no man should go forward who had any misgivings as to the success of the expedition. He added that the garrison left in San Miguel was by no means as strong as he would like it to be, and that if any of them wished to return there instead of going forward with him they were quite free to do so, and their share in the profits of the expedition should be just the same as that of the men originally left there. Nine of the soldiers availed themselves of this permission to turn back, and having thus got rid of the elements of discontent, which might have become dangerous, Pizarro resumed his march, halting again at Zaran while he sent an officer forward to obtain more certain tidings of the position of Atahuallpa. After eight days the cavalier returned, bringing with him an envoy from the Inca, who bore a present for the Spanish commander, and invited him to visit Atahuallpa's camp among the mountains. Pizarro quite understood that the Inca's object was to learn the strength and condition of the white men, but he hospitably entertained his guest, giving him all the information he demanded by means of the two interpreters, who had by his forethought been taught Castilian, and were now of inestimable service. When the Peruvian departed, Pizarro presented him with a few trifling gifts, and bade him tell Atahuallpa that he would meet him as soon as possible. After sending an account of their proceedings back to San Miguel the adventurers continued their journey towards Caxamalca, and having crossed a deep and rapid river, fell in with some natives, who gave such contrary reports of Atahuallpa's position and intentions that Pizarro sent one of the Indians who accompanied him ostensibly to bear a friendly greeting to the Inca, but really to find out all he could of the state of affairs.

After a further march of three days the little army reached the foot of the huge mountain barrier, and entered upon the labyrinth of passes which were to lead them to Atahuallpa's camp. The difficulties of the way were enough to have appalled the stoutest heart. The path was in many places so steep that the men had to dismount and scramble up as best they could, dragging their horses after them; often some huge crag so overhung the track that they could scarcely creep round the narrow ledge of rock, while a false step would have plunged them into a fearful precipice. In several of the passes huge stone fortresses had been built, and places abounded where a handful of men might have barred the way successfully against an army, but to the relief of the Spaniards they found all quiet and deserted, the only living things visible being an occasional condor or vicuña. Finding that their passage was not to be disputed, Pizarro, who had led the way with one detachment, encamped for the night, sending word back to his brother to bring up the remainder of the force without delay. Another toilful day brought him to the crest of the Cordillera, a bleak tract where the only vegetation was a dry, yellow grass which grew up to the snow-line. Here he was met by one of his Indian messengers, who reported that the path was clear, and an envoy from the Inca was on his way to the Castilian camp. Very soon the Peruvians appeared, bringing a welcome present of llamas and a message from their master, who desired to know when the Spaniards would reach Caxamalca, that he might provide suitably for their reception. The ambassador vaunted the power and the triumphs of Atahuallpa; but Pizarro was not to be outdone, and did not hesitate to declare that the Inca was as much inferior to the King of Spain as the petty chiefs of the country were to the Inca. After another march of two days the Spaniards began the descent of the eastern side of the Cordillera, meeting by the way another and more important envoy, and seven days later the valley of Caxamalca lay before them, the vapour of its hot springs rising in the still air, and the slope of the further hillside white with the tents of the Inca's encampment for a space of several miles—a sight which filled the Spaniards with a dismay they could hardly conceal. Putting on a bold front they marched into the town, which was quite deserted, but seemed large enough to hold ten thousand people, and then Pizarro despatched an embassy consisting of his brother Hernando, another cavalier, and thirty-five horsemen, to the camp of Atahuallpa. The party galloped along the causeway, and, fording a shallow stream, made their way through a guard of Indians to the open courtyard in the midst of which the Inca's pavilion stood. The buildings were covered with a shining plaster, both white and coloured, and there was a spacious stone reservoir in the courtyard, which remains to this day, and is called "The Inca's Bath." The Court was filled with Indian nobles, and Atahuallpa himself sat upon a low stool, distinguished from the rest by the crimson fringe upon his forehead, which he had worn since the defeat of his brother Huascar. Hernando Pizarro rode up to him and, addressing him ceremoniously, informed him by the aid of Felipillo that he came as an ambassador from his brother to acquaint the Inca with the arrival of the white men in Caxamalca, and to explain that they were the subjects of a mighty prince across the waters, who, attracted by the report of his great victories, had come to offer their services, and to impart to him the doctrines of the true faith which they professed, and he brought an invitation from the general to beg Atahuallpa to visit them in their present quarters. To all this the Inca listened with his eyes fixed upon the ground, and answered never a word, but one of the nobles standing by said, "It is well." Hernando Pizarro then respectfully begged the Inca to speak to them himself and inform them of his pleasure, upon which Atahuallpa smiled faintly and replied: "Tell your captain that I am keeping a fast, which will end to-morrow morning; I will then visit him. In the meantime let him occupy the public buildings on the square, and no other, till I come and order what shall be done."

Pizarro and the Inca

ONE OF THE CAVALIERS WHO was mounted upon a fiery steed, seeing that Atahuallpa looked at it with some interest, caused it to rear and curvet, and then dashed out over the plain in a wild gallop, and returning checked it in full career close beside the Inca. But the face of Atahuallpa never for an instant lost its marble composure, though several of his soldiers shrank back in manifest terror as the strange creature passed them; and it is said that they paid dearly for their timidity, as Atahuallpa caused them to be put to death for thus showing fear in the presence of the strangers. Wine was now brought, and offered to the Spaniards in golden goblets of extraordinary size, and then they took their leave and rode gloomily back to Caxamalca. Pizarro alone was not discouraged by the news they brought. He saw that matters had now come to a climax, and determined upon making a bold stroke. To encounter the Inca in the open field was manifestly impossible, but could his person be secured when he entered the city with comparatively few of his followers the rest might be intimidated, and all might yet be well. To this end, therefore, he laid his plans. The building in which the Spaniards were encamped occupied three sides of a square, and consisted of spacious halls opening upon it with wide doors. In these halls the general stationed his men, and there they were to remain under cover till the Inca should have entered the square, when at a given signal, the firing of a gun, they were to rush out uttering their battle-cries, and, putting the Peruvians to the sword, possess themselves of the person of Atahuallpa. After a quiet night and a careful inspection of their arms and equipments, the Spaniards took up their respective positions, but it was late in the day before a great stir was visible in the Peruvian camp. The Inca sent word to Pizarro that he was coming armed, as the Spaniards had come to him. To which the general replied that, come as he might, he would be received as a friend and a brother. At last the procession was seen approaching. First came a large body of attendants, sweeping every particle of rubbish from the road. Then high above the crowd the Inca appeared, carried in a gorgeous litter and surrounded by his nobles, who wore such quantities of golden ornaments that they blazed like the sun. The road was lined with Peruvian troops, who also covered the level meadows as far as the eye could reach. When the company had arrived within half a mile of the city gate Pizarro observed with dismay that they halted, and seemed to be preparing to encamp, and word was brought him that the Inca would enter the city on the following morning. This was far from suiting the general's plans; his men had been under arms since daylight, and to prolong the suspense at this critical moment would he felt be fatal. He returned an answer, therefore, to Atahuallpa, deprecating his change of purpose, and saying that everything was provided for his entertainment and he expected him that night to sup with him. This message turned the Inca from his purpose, his tents were struck again, and the procession re-formed. Only he sent Pizarro word that he should prefer to pass the night at Caxamalca, and so would bring into the town with him only a few unarmed men. It was near sunset when the Peruvians, chanting their triumphant songs, entered the city gate. According to their different ranks their robes were of various colours, some chequered in white and red, some pure white, while the guards and attendants of the Inca were distinguished by their gay blue uniform and the profusion of their ornaments. Atahuallpa sat in an open litter, lined with the brilliantly coloured plumes of tropical birds and studded with burnished plates of gold and silver. His dress was far richer than on the preceding evening; round his neck hung a collar of large and brilliant emeralds, and his short hair was decorated with golden ornaments. He was at this time about thirty years old, and was taller and stronger than most of his countrymen. His head was large, and he might have been called handsome but for his fierce and bloodshot eyes. His bearing was calm and dignified, and he gazed upon the multitudes about him like one accustomed to command. Not a Spaniard was to be seen as the procession, in admirable order, entered the great square of the building that had been assigned to them, and when the place was occupied by some six thousand of his people Atahuallpa halted, and asked, "Where are the strangers?" Upon this Father Valverde, Pizarro's chaplain, came forward Bible in hand, and proceeded to expound to him the doctrines of his faith, declaring finally that the Pope had commissioned the Spanish Emperor to conquer and convert the inhabitants of the western world, and beseeching the Inca to embrace the Christian faith and acknowledge himself a tributary of the Emperor Charles, who would aid and protect him as a loyal vassal. The eyes of Atahuallpa flashed fire as he answered: "I will be no man's tributary; I am greater than any prince upon earth. Your Emperor may be a great prince. I do not doubt it when I see that he has sent his subjects so far across the waters, and I am willing to hold him as a brother. As for the Pope of whom you speak, he must be crazy to talk of giving away countries which do not belong to him. For my faith, I will not change it. Your own God, you say, was put to death by the very men whom he created, but mine"—and here he pointed to the setting sun—'my god still lives in the heavens and looks down upon his children." He then demanded of Valverde by what authority he had said these things. The friar pointed to the book he held. Atahuallpa took it, looked at it for an instant, and then threw it violently down, exclaiming: "Tell your comrades they shall give an account of their doings in my land. I will not go from here till they have made me full satisfaction for all the wrongs they have committed."

The friar thereupon rushed to Pizarro crying: "Do you not see that while we stand here wasting our breath in talking with this dog—full of pride as he is—the fields are filling with Indians? Set on at once; I absolve you."

Pizarro saw that the hour had come. He waved a white scarf, the fatal gun was fired, and from every opening the Spaniards poured into the great square, sword in hand, shouting their old battle-cry, "St. Jago, and at them!" The Indians, unarmed, taken by surprise, stunned by the noise of the artillery, and blinded with smoke, knew not which way to fly. Nobles and soldiers were ruthlessly cut down, or trampled underfoot by the horses, the entrance to the square was choked with the fallen bodies of men, but the desperate struggles of the masses of natives driven together by their fierce assailants actually broke down the wall of clay and stone for a space of a hundred paces, through which the wretched fugitives endeavoured to reach the open country, hotly pursued by the cavalry and struck down in all directions.

The Captivity of the Inca

MEANWHILE, A DESPERATE STRUGGLE WAS going on for the person of the Inca. His nobles surrounded and faithfully strove to defend him; as fast as one was cut down another took his place, and with their dying grasp they clung to the bridles of the cavaliers, trying to force them back. Atahuallpa sat as one stunned in his swaying litter, forced this way and that by the pressure of the throng. The Spaniards grew tired at last of the work of destruction, and, fearing that in the gathering darkness the Inca might after all escape them, they made an attempt to end the fray at once by taking his life. But Pizarro, seeing this, cried out in a mighty voice, "Let no man who values his life strike at the Inca," and, stretching out his arm to shield him, received a wound on the hand from one of his own men—the only wound received by any Spaniard in the action. The strife now became fiercer round the litter, and several of the nobles who bore it having been slain, it was overturned, and the Inca would have come violently to the ground had not Pizarro and some of his men caught him in their arms. A soldier instantly snatched the crimson fringe from his forehead, and the unhappy monarch was taken into the nearest building and carefully guarded. All attempt at resistance now ceased. The news of the Inca's fate spread over town and country, and the only thing which had held them together being gone, each man thought only of his own safety. The Spaniards pursued the fugitives till night fell and the sound of the trumpet recalled them to the square of Caxamalca. That night the Inca supped with Pizarro as he had said, while ten thousand of his faithful followers lay dead about the city.

ANDREW LANG AND H. RIDER HAGGARD

He seemed like one in a dream, not understanding the calamity that had fallen upon him. He even commended the adroit way in which the Spaniards had entrapped him, adding that since the landing of the white men he had been made aware of all their doings, but had felt sure of being easily able to overpower them as soon as he thought fit to do so, and had allowed them to reach Caxamalca unmolested because he desired to see them for himself, and to obtain possession of their arms and horses. This, at least, was the interpretation of what the Inca said given by Felipillo; but he was a malicious youth, who bore Atahuallpa no good will, and the Spaniards were only too ready to believe anything that seemed to justify their cruel deeds. Pizarro replied that the fate of the Inca was the lot that fell to all who resisted the white men, but he bade Atahuallpa take courage, for the Spaniards were a generous race, warring only against those who would not submit themselves. That same night the general reviewed his men, congratulating them upon the success of their stratagem, but warning them to be strictly upon their guard, since they were but a handful of strangers in the heart of a mighty kingdom, encompassed by foes who were deeply attached to their own sovereign. Next morning, the prisoners, of whom there were many in the camp, were employed in burying the dead and removing all traces of the massacre, while a troop of Spaniards was despatched to spoil the camp of Atahuallpa and scatter the remnant of the Peruvian forces. At noon this party returned, bringing the wives and attendants of the Inca, and a rich booty in gold, silver, emeralds, and other treasures, beside droves of llamas.

Pizarro would now have liked to march directly upon the capital, but the distance was great and his force was small. So after sending a message to San Miguel for reinforcements, he set his men to work at rebuilding the walls of Caxamalca, and fitting up a church, in which mass was celebrated daily. Atahuallpa soon discovered that gold was what the Spaniards chiefly coveted, and he determined to try and buy his freedom, for he greatly feared that Huascar might win back his liberty and his kingdom if the news once reached him of his brother's captivity. So he one day promised Pizarro to fill with gold the room in which they stood, not merely covering the floor, but piling it up to a line drawn round the walls as high as he could reach, if he would in return set him free. The general hardly knew how to answer. All he had seen confirmed the rumours of the wealth of the country, and if it could be collected thus by the Inca's order, he might really hope to secure it, whereas if he trusted to being able to seize it for himself the chances were that most of it would disappear for ever, hidden by the natives beyond recovery. At all events he decided it would be safe to agree to Atahuallpa's proposal; when the gold was collected it would be time enough to think about setting the captive at liberty. The room to be filled was seventeen feet broad by twenty-two feet long, and the line upon the wall was drawn nine feet from the ground. A smaller room which adjoined it the Inca offered to fill with silver twice over, and he demanded two months' time to accomplish all this.

As soon as the arrangement was made, Atahuallpa sent couriers to Cuzco and all the other chief places in the kingdom, with orders to strip the royal palaces of their treasures and send them without delay to Caxamalca. Meanwhile he lived in the Spanish quarters, treated with consideration, and allowed to see his subjects freely, but at the same time strictly guarded.

The Inca's Ransom

THE NEWS OF ATAHUALLPA'S CAPTURE and the immense ransom he had offered soon reached the ears of Huascar, who was encouraged by the tidings to make vigorous efforts to regain his own liberty, and sent a message to the Spanish commander saying that he would pay a much larger ransom than that promised by Atahuallpa, who, never having lived in Cuzco, could not know the quantity of treasure there, or where it was stored. This was told to Atahuallpa, who also knew that Pizarro had said that Huascar should be brought to Caxamalca, that he himself might determine which of the two brothers had the better right to the sceptre of the Incas. Furiously jealous, and fearing that the decision would surely be in favour of the more docile Huascar, Atahuallpa ordered secretly that he should be put to death by his guards, and he was accordingly drowned in the river of Andamarca, declaring with his dying breath that the white men would avenge his murder, and that his rival would not long survive him. Week by week the treasure poured in from all quarters of the realm, borne on the shoulders of the Indian porters, and consisting mainly of massive pieces of plate, some of them weighing seventy-five pounds; but as the distances were great, and the progress necessarily slow, the Spaniards became impatient, and believed, or pretended to believe, that the Inca was planning some treachery, and wilfully delaying till he could arrange a general rising of the Peruvians against the white men. This charge the Inca indignantly denied, and to prove his good faith offered to give a safe-conduct to a party of Spaniards, that they might visit Cuzco for themselves and see that the work of collecting the treasure was really going on. Pizarro gladly accepted this offer, and three cavaliers started for the capital. Meanwhile, Hernando Pizarro with a small troop had set out to make sure that the country round was really quiet, and, finding that it was, he continued his march to the town of Pachacamac, to secure the treasures of its famous temple before they could be hidden by its priests. The city was a hundred leagues from Caxamalca, and the way lay across the tableland of the Cordilleras; but after weeks of severe labour the Spaniards reached it, and, breaking into the temple, in spite of the remonstrances of the priests, they dragged forth and destroyed the hideous idol it contained, and secured the greater part of the treasure of gold and jewels, though the priests, having had warning of his approach, had managed to conceal a good deal, some of which the Spaniards afterwards discovered buried in the surrounding land. The people, seeing that their god was unable to defend himself against the wonderful strangers, now came and tendered their homage, and Hernando Pizarro, hearing that one of the Inca's two great generals, a chief named Challcuchima, was lying with a considerable force in the town of Xanxa, resolved to march there and attack him in his own quarters. The road across the mountains was even rougher and more difficult than the one by which he had come, and, to add to his troubles, the shoes of the horses were all worn out, and they suffered severely on the rough and stony ground. Iron there was none, but silver and gold abounded, so Pizarro ordered the Indian smiths to make horseshoes of silver, with which the horses of the troop were shod. On reaching Xanxa the Spaniards found it a large and populous place, and the Indian general with five-and-thirty thousand men was encamped at a distance of a few miles; but, nothing daunted, Hernando Pizarro sent messages to him, and when he at last consented to an interview, informed him that the Inca demanded his presence in Caxamalca. Having been utterly bewildered since the capture of the Inca, and uncertain as to what course to take, Challcuchima obeyed at once, and accompanied by a numerous retinue journeyed back with the Spaniards. He was everywhere received by the natives with the deepest respect, yet he entered the presence of the Inca barefooted and with a burden laid upon his back, and kneeling before his master he kissed his hands and feet, exclaiming, "Would that I had been here! This would not then have happened."

Atahuallpa himself showed no emotion, only coldly bade him welcome: even in his present state of captivity he was immeasurably above the proudest of his vassals. The Spaniards still treated him with all respect, and with his own people he kept up his usual state and ceremony, being attended upon by his wives, while a number of Indian nobles waited always in the antechamber, but never entered his presence unless sent for, and then only with every mark of humility. His dress, which he often changed, was sometimes made of vicuña wool, sometimes of bats' skins, sleek as velvet. Nothing which he had worn could be used by another; when he laid it aside it was burned. To while away the time the Spaniards taught him to play chess, at which he became expert, spending upon it many of the tedious hours of his imprisonment. Soon after the return of Hernando Pizarro the three cavaliers came back from Cuzco. They had travelled six hundred miles in the greatest luxury, carried in litters by the natives, and received everywhere with awe and respect. Their accounts of the wealth of the capital confirmed all that Pizarro had heard, and though they had stayed a week there, they had not seen all. They had seen the royal mummies in their golden chairs, and had left them untouched by the Inca's orders; but they had caused the plates of pure gold to be stripped from the Temple of the Sun—seven hundred of them, compared in size to the lid of a chest ten or twelve inches wide. The cornice was so firmly embedded in the stonework that it defied their efforts to remove it. But they brought with them full two hundred loads of gold, beside much silver, all hastily collected, for the arrogant behaviour of the emissaries had greatly exasperated the people of Cuzco, who were glad to get rid of them as soon as possible. About this time Almagro reached San Miguel, having, after many difficulties, succeeded in collecting a few more adventurers, and heard with amazement of Pizarro's successes and of the change in his fortunes. In spite of the feelings of rivalry and distrust that existed between himself and his old comrade, Pizarro was delighted to hear of his arrival, as the additional troops he brought with him made it possible to go forward with the conquest of the country. So when Almagro reached Caxamalca in the middle of February 1533, he and his men were received with every mark of joy. Only Atahuallpa looked on sadly, seeing the chances of regaining his freedom, or maintaining it if he did regain it, lessened by the increased number of his enemies, and to add to his dejection a comet just then made its appearance in the heavens. As one had been seen shortly before the death of the Inca's father, Huayna Capac, he looked upon it as a warning of evil to come, and a dread of the future took possession of him.

The Spaniards now began to clamour for a division of the gold which had been already collected: several of them were disposed to return home with the share that would fall to them, but by far the greater number only wished to make sure of the spoil and then hurry on to Cuzco, where they believed as much more awaited them. For various reasons Pizarro agreed to their demands; the gold—all but a few particularly beautiful specimens of the Indian goldsmith's work, which were sent to Castile as part of the royal fifth—was melted down into solid bars, and when weighed was found to be worth nearly three and a half millions of pounds sterling. This was divided amongst Pizarro and his men, the followers of Almagro not being considered to be entitled to a share, though a small sum was handed over to them to induce them to give up their claim. The division being completed, there seemed to be no further obstacle to their resuming active operations; but then the question arose what was to become of Atahuallpa, who was loudly demanding his freedom. He had not, indeed, paid the whole of his promised ransom; but an immense amount had been received, and it would have been more, as he urged, but for the impatience of the Spaniards. Pizarro, telling no one of the dark purposes he was brooding over in his own mind, issued a proclamation to the effect that the ransom was considered to be completely paid, but that the safety of the Spaniards required that the Inca should be held captive until they were still further reinforced. Soon rumours began to be spread, probably by Felipillo, who hated the Inca, that an immense army was mustering at Quito, and that thirty thousand Caribs, of whom the Spaniards had a peculiar horror, were on their way to join it. Both Atahuallpa and his general Challcuchima denied all knowledge of any rising, but their protestations of innocence did them little good. The soldiers clamoured against the unhappy Inca, and Pizarro, taking advantage of the temporary absence of some of the cavaliers who would have defended him, ordered him to be brought to instant trial. The evidence of Indian witnesses, as interpreted by Felipillo, sealed his doom, and in spite of the efforts of a few Spaniards he was found guilty by the majority on the charge, among other things, of having assassinated his brother Huascar and raised up insurrection against the Spaniards, and was sentenced to be burnt alive. When Atahuallpa was told of his approaching fate his courage gave way for a moment. "What have I or my children done," he said to Pizarro, "that I should meet such a doom? And from your hands, too!—you who have met with nothing but friendship and kindness from my people, with whom I have shared my treasures, who have received nothing but benefits from my hands." Then in most piteous tones he begged that his life might be spared, offering to answer for the safety of every Spaniard, and promising to pay double the ransom he had already given. But it was all of no avail. He was not, however, burnt to death; for at the last moment, on his consenting to abjure his own religion and be baptized, he was executed in the usual Spanish manner—by strangulation.

A day or two after, the other cavaliers returned, and found Pizarro making a show of great sorrow for what had happened. They reproached and blamed him, saying that there was no truth in the story of treachery—all was quiet, and the people showed nothing but goodwill. Then Pizarro accused his treasurer and Father Valverde of having deceived him in the matter and brought about the catastrophe; and they in their turn exculpated themselves, and upbraided Pizarro as the only one responsible for the deed, and the quarrel was fierce between them. Meanwhile, the death of the Inca, whose power over his people had been so great, caused the breaking-up of all the ancient institutions. The Indians broke out into great excesses; villages were burnt and temples plundered; gold and silver acquired a new importance in their eyes, and were eagerly seized and hidden in caves and forests; the remote provinces threw off their allegiance to the Incas; the great captains at the head of distant armies set up for themselves—one named Ruminavi sought to detach Quito from the Peruvian Empire and assert its independence. Pizarro, still in Caxamalca, looked round for a successor to Atahuallpa, and chose his young brother Toparca, who was crowned with the usual ceremonies; and then the Spaniards set out for Cuzco, taking the new Inca with them, and after a toilful journey and more than one encounter with hostile natives reached Xanxa in safety. Here Pizarro remained for a time, sending one of his captains, named Hernando de Soto, forward with a small body of men to reconnoitre. This cavalier found villages burnt, bridges destroyed, and heavy rocks and trees placed in the path to impede his cavalry, and realised at length that the natives had risen to resistance. As he neared the Sierra of Vilcaconga he heard that a considerable body of Indians lay in wait for him in its dangerous passes; but though his men and horses were weary, he rashly determined to push on and pass it before nightfall if possible. No sooner had they fairly entered the narrow way than he was attacked by a multitude of armed warriors, who seemed to spring from every bush and cavern, and rushed down like a mountain torrent upon the Spaniards as they struggled up the steep and rocky pathway. Men and horses were overthrown, and it was only after a severe struggle that they succeeded in reaching a level spot upon which it was possible to face the enemy. Night fell while the issue of the fight was still uncertain, but fortunately Pizarro, when he heard of the unsettled state of the country, had despatched Almagro to the support of De Soto. He, hearing that there was the chance of a fight, had pushed on hastily, and now advanced under cover of the darkness, sounding his trumpets, which were joyfully answered by the bugles of De Soto.

When morning broke and the Peruvians saw that their white enemies had been mysteriously reinforced in the night, they hastily retreated, leaving the passes open, and the two cavaliers continued their march through the mountains, and took up a secure position in the open country beyond, to await Pizarro. Their losses had not been very great, but they were quite unprepared to meet with any resistance; and as this seemed a well-organised attack, suspicion fell upon Challcuchima, who was accused by Pizarro of conspiring with Quizquiz, the other great general, against the young Inca, and was told that if he did not at once compel the Peruvians to lay down their arms he should be burnt alive. Challcuchima denied the charge, and declared that, captive as he was, he had no power to bring his countrymen to submission. Nevertheless, he was put in irons and strongly guarded. Unfortunately for him, the young Toparca died just at this time, and suspicion at once fell on the hapless general, who, after the mockery of a trial, was burnt to death as soon as Pizarro reached Almagro's camp—his own followers piling up the faggots. Soon after this Pizarro was surprised by a friendly visit from the young brother of Huascar, Manco Capac, and seeing that this prince was likely to be a useful instrument in his hands, Pizarro acknowledged his claim to be the Inca, and, keeping him with him, resumed the march to Cuzco, which they entered on November 15, 1533. The suburbs were thronged with people, who came from far and near to gaze upon the white faces and the shining armour of the "Children of the Sun." The Spaniards rode directly to the great square, and took up their quarters in the palaces of the Incas. They were greatly struck by the beauty and order of the city, and though Pizarro on entering it had issued an order that the dwellings of the inhabitants were not to be plundered or injured, the soldiers soon stripped the palaces and temples of the valuables they contained, even taking the golden ornaments of the royal mummies and rifling the Peruvian graves, which often contained precious treasures. Believing that the natives had buried their wealth, they put some of them to the torture, to induce them to disclose their hiding-places, and by seeking everywhere they occasionally stumbled upon mines of wealth. In one cave near the city the soldiers found a number of vases of pure gold, embossed with figures of animals, serpents, and locusts. Also there were four life-sized figures of llamas, and ten or twelve statues of women, some of gold and some of silver. The magazines were stored with robes of cotton and featherwork, gold sandals and slippers, and dresses composed entirely of beads of gold. The stores of grain and other food the conquerors utterly despised, though the time was to come when they would have been of far greater value to them than all the treasure. On the whole, the riches of the capital did not come up to the expectation of the Spaniards, but they had collected much plunder on the way to it, securing in one place ten bars of solid silver, each twenty feet in length, one foot in breadth, and two or three inches thick.

The natural consequence followed the sudden acquisition of so much wealth. The soldiers, as soon as they had received their share, squandered it recklessly, or lost it over dice or cards. A man who had for his portion one of the great golden images of the Sun taken from the chief temple, lost it in a single night's gaming, whence came the proverb common to this day in Spain, "He plays away the sun before sunrise." Another effect of such a superfluity of gold and silver was the instant rise in the prices of all ordinary things, till gold and silver seemed to be the only things in Cuzco that were not wealth. Yet very few indeed of the Spaniards were wise enough to be contented and return to enjoy their spoils in their native country. After the division of the treasure, Pizarro's first care was to place the Inca Manco upon the throne, and demand for him the recognition of his countrymen. All the coronation ceremonies were duly observed. The people acquiesced readily, and there were the usual feastings and rejoicings, at which the royal mummies were paraded according to custom, decked with such ornaments as remained to them. Pizarro then organised a government for the city of Cuzco after the fashion of his own country, and turned the temples into churches and monasteries. He himself was henceforward styled the Governor. Having heard that Atahuallpa's general Quizquiz was stationed not far from Cuzco with a large force of the men of Quito, Pizarro sent Almagro and the Inca Manco to dislodge him, which they did after some sharp fighting. The general fled to the plains of Quito, where, after holding out gallantly for a long time, he was massacred by his own soldiers, weary of the ineffectual struggle.

About this time, Don Pedro de Alvarado, with five hundred well-equipped men, landed at the Bay of Caraques and marched upon Quito, affecting to believe that it was a separate kingdom, and not part of that conquered by Pizarro. This Alvarado was the celebrated cavalier who had been with Cortés in the conquest of Mexico, and earned from the Aztecs the title of "Tonatiuh," or "Child of the Sun." He had been made Governor of Guatemala, but his avarice being aroused by the reports of Pizarro's conquests, he turned in the direction of Quito a large fleet which he had intended for the Spice Islands. The Governor was much disturbed by the news of his landing, but as matters turned out he need not have been, for Alvarado, having set out to cross the sierra in the direction of Quito, was deserted in the midst of the snowy passes by his Indian guide. His unhappy followers, fresh from the warm climate of Guatemala, were perished with the cold, and still further distressed by suffocating clouds of dust and ashes from the volcano of Cotopaxi. After days of incredible suffering they emerged at last, but leaving behind them at least a fourth of their number, beside two thousand Indians, who had died of cold and hunger. When, after all, he did reach Quito, he found it in the hands of Benalcazah, a cavalier who had been left by Pizarro at San Miguel, and who had deserted his post in order to take possession of Quito, tempted by the reports of the treasure it contained, which, however, he failed to find. Almagro, too, had reached the city before Alvarado got there; moreover, his men had heard so much of the riches of Cuzco that they were inclined to desert him and join Pizarro. On the whole, Alvarado judged it expedient to give up all claim to Quito, and for a sum of money which, though large, did not cover his expenses, to hand over to the Governor his fleet, forces, stores, and munitions. This being settled, he went to Pachacamac to meet Pizarro, who had left his brother Juan in charge of Cuzco, and was inspecting the defences of the coast. There being now no question of rivalry, the two cavaliers met in all courtesy, and Alvarado was hospitably entertained by the Governor, after which he sailed for Guatemala. Peru might now in a manner be considered as conquered; some of the tribes in the interior still held out, but an able officer had been told off to subdue them. Quito and Cuzco had submitted, the army of Atahuallpa had been beaten and dispersed, the Inca was the mere shadow of a king, ruled by the conqueror.

The Governor now turned his attention to building a city which should be the capital of this new colonial empire. Cuzco lay too far inland, San Miguel too far to the north. Pizarro fixed upon a spot near the mouth of a wide river which flowed through the Valley of Rimac, and here soon arose what was then called the "City of the Kings," but is now known as Lima. Meanwhile, Hernando Pizarro returned to Castile with the royal fifth, as the Spanish Emperor's share of the treasure was called; he also took with him all the Spaniards who had had enough of the life of adventure and wished to settle in their native land to enjoy their ill-gotten spoils. Pizarro judged rightly that the sight of the gold would bring him ten recruits for every one who thus returned. And so it was, for when he again sailed for Peru it was at the head of the most numerous and the best-appointed fleet that had yet set out. But as so often happened, disaster pursued him, and only a broken remnant finally reached the Peruvian shore. Quarrels now arose between Almagro and Pizarro, the former claiming to be Governor of Cuzco; and when after many difficulties peace was again made, and Almagro, withdrawing his claim, had led his partisans off to conquer Chili, a new trouble began. The Inca Manco, under pretext of showing Hernando Pizarro a hidden treasure, managed to make his escape; the Peruvians flocked to his banner, and the party of Spaniards under Juan Pizarro who were sent out to recapture him returned to Cuzco weary and wounded after many unsuccessful struggles with the enemy, only to find the city closely surrounded by a mighty host of Indians. They were, however, allowed to enter the capital, and then began a terrible siege which lasted for more than five months. Day and night the Spaniards were harassed by showers of missiles. Sometimes the flights of burning arrows or red-hot stones wrapped in some inflammable substance would cause fearful fires in all quarters of the town at once; three times in one day did the flames attack the very building which sheltered the Spaniards, but fortunately they were extinguished without doing much harm. In vain did the besieged make desperate sallies; the Indians planted stakes to entangle their horses, and took the riders prisoners by means of the lasso, which they used with great skill. To add to their distress the great citadel which dominated the town had fallen into the hands of the enemy, and though after a gallant struggle it was retaken, yet it was at the cost of Juan Pizarro's life. As for the Inca

ANDREW LANG AND H. RIDER HAGGARD

noble who defended it, when he saw that the citadel must fall, he cast away his war-club, and, folding his mantle about him, threw himself headlong from the battlements. Famine now began to be felt sharply, and it added horror to the situation of the besieged when, after they had heard no tidings of their countrymen for months, the blood-stained heads of eight or ten Spaniards were one day rolled into the market place, leading them to believe that the rising of the Indians had been simultaneous all over the country, and that their friends were faring no better than themselves. Things were not, however, quite so desperate as they imagined, for Francisco Pizarro when attacked in the City of the Kings had sallied forth and inflicted such a severe chastisement upon the Peruvians that they afterwards kept their distance from him, contenting themselves with cutting off his communication with the interior. Several detachments of soldiers whom he sent to the relief of his brothers in Cuzco were, however, enticed by the natives into the mountain passes and there slain, as also were some solitary settlers on their own estates.

At last, in the month of August, the Inca drew off his forces, and intrenching himself in Tambo, not far from Cuzco, with a considerable body of men, and posting another force to keep watch upon Cuzco and intercept supplies, he dismissed the remainder to the cultivation of their lands. The Spaniards thereupon made frequent forays, and on one occasion the starving soldiers joyfully secured two thousand Peruvian sheep, which saved them from hunger for a time. Once Pizarro desperately attacked Tambo itself, but was driven off with heavy loss, and hunted back ignominiously into Cuzco; but this was the last triumph of the Inca. Soon afterwards Almagro appeared upon the scene, and sent an embassy to the Inca, with whom he had formerly been friendly. Manco received him well, but his suspicions being aroused by a secret conference between Almagro's men and the Spaniards in Cuzco, he fell suddenly upon the former, and a great battle ensued in which the Peruvians were decidedly beaten and the power of the Inca was broken. He died some few years later, leaving the Spaniards still fighting among themselves for the possession of the country. Almagro after some years of strife and adventure was put to death by Hernando Pizarro when he was nearly seventy years old. His son, a gallant and well-beloved youth, who succeeded him, met the same fate in the same place—the great square of Cuzco—a few years later. Hernando himself suffered a long imprisonment in Spain for the murder of Almagro, with serene courage, and even lived some time after his release, being a hundred years old when he died. Gonzola Pizarro was beheaded in Peru, at the age of forty-two, for rebelling against the authority of the Spanish Emperor. Francisco Pizarro was murdered in his own house in the City of the Kings, in the month of June 1541, by the desperate adherents of the young Almagro, or the "Men of Chili" as they were called, and was buried hastily and secretly by a few faithful servants in an obscure corner of the cathedral. Such was the miserable end of the conqueror of Peru. "There was none even," says an old chronicler, "to cry 'God forgive him!'"

A Note About the Author

Andrew Lang (1844–1912) was a Scottish editor, poet, author, literary critic, and historian. He is best known for his work regarding folklore, mythology, and religion, for which he had an extreme interest in. Lang was a skilled and respected historian, writing in great detail and exploring obscure topics. Lang often combined his studies of history and anthropology with literature, creating works rich with diverse culture. He married Leonora Blanche Alleyne in 1875. With her help, Lang published a prolific amount of work, including his popular series, *Rainbow Fairy Books*.

H. Rider Haggard (1856–1925), also known as Sir Henry Rider Haggard, was an English novelist and scholar. He was educated at Ipswich Grammar School and studied with a private tutor in London. Later, Haggard would travel to South Africa where he worked as a governor's assistant. Upon his return to England, he began writing fiction and nonfiction about his experiences abroad. This led to a successful publishing career which included the novels, *King Solomon's Mines* (1885) and *Allan Quatermain* (1887).

A Note from the Publisher

Spanning many genres, from non-fiction essays to literature classics to children's books and lyric poetry, Mint Edition books showcase the master works of our time in a modern new package. The text is freshly typeset, is clean and easy to read, and features a new note about the author in each volume. Many books also include exclusive new introductory material. Every book boasts a striking new cover, which makes it as appropriate for collecting as it is for gift giving. Mint Edition books are only printed when a reader orders them, so natural resources are not wasted. We're proud that our books are never manufactured in excess and exist only in the exact quantity they need to be read and enjoyed.

Discover more of your favorite classics with Bookfinity™.

- Track your reading with custom book lists.
- Get great book recommendations for your personalized Reader Type.
- Add reviews for your favorite books.
- AND MUCH MORE!

Visit **bookfinity.com** and take the fun Reader Type quiz to get started.

Enjoy our classic and modern companion pairings!

Printed in the USA
CPSIA information can be obtained
at www.ICGtesting.com
JSHW022208140824
68134JS00018B/935